THE ESTUARY PILGRIM

THE ESTUARY PILGRIM

Douglas Skeggs

St. Martin's Press
New York

Library of Congress Cataloging-in-Publication Data

Skeggs, Douglas.
     The estuary pilgrim / Douglas Skeggs.
        p.   cm.
     ISBN 0-312-03827-5
     I. Title.
     PR6069.K34E88   1989
     823'.914—dc20   89-27072
                                                                      CIP

First published in Great Britain by Macmillan London Limited.

First U.S. Edition

10 9 8 7 6 5 4 3 2 1

THE ESTUARY PILGRIM

PROLOGUE

Honfleur, May 1944

Captain Rupert Ashford stood at the window of his cell and watched the preparations for his execution.

It was dawn on May 6th 1944; the belltower of Ste Catherine's had just tolled six. The yard below him was dreary with shadow, the cold morning light forbidding any colour more cheerful than slate-grey.

The Opel truck lumbered across the cobbles, jolting on the uneven surface, its tarpaulin cover flapping and sucking against the frame, and drew to a halt against the far wall The diesel engine fluttered and died. A corporal jumped from the cab and walked back towards the rear end. Banging the wooden side with his hand, he barked out a single order, his voice resonant in the confined space. The tail-flap clanged down and a handful of soldiers shuffled out, the hob-nails of their boots rasping on the stone. Their faces were lean and unshaven, strangely anonymous, with wind-burnt skin and eyes invisible beneath the flange of their steel helmets. From where he was standing, Ashford could see that their uniforms were baggy at the knees and elbows, the leather of their gun belts soft and faded from constant wear; four years of fighting might not have beaten the German Wehrmacht but it had certainly tarnished the spit-and-polish of its turn-out.

At the far side of the yard an officer, wearing the silver epaulettes and single gold pip of an *oberleutnant*, stood waiting with hands on his hips. He watched without interest as the corporal drilled his men into line, forming them up into a single rank.

Ashford knew what lay in store for him.

Two days earlier he had watched the same firing squad execute a group of civilians. Dazed and uncomprehending, their movements stupid with fear, the condemned men had been herded up against the wall, some looking out at the executioners, others facing inwards, apathetic and dejected, their heads hanging, hands thrust deep in their pockets. The ragged volley of gunfire had hardly stirred them; they'd shrugged and stumbled into each other and then, for no apparent reason, their limbs had seemed to grow tired and they'd crumpled to the ground. One of the group, in waistcoat and wing collar, his trousers held in place with bicycle clips, had wandered away towards the gate before his legs had given way beneath him and he'd collapsed face forwards, without putting out his hands to break the fall. As soon as they'd fired the squad had moved forward, hefted the bodies into the back of the lorry and driven away.

The whole episode had lasted less than ten minutes.

Pressing his forehead against the iron bar of the window, Ashford closed his eyes. He felt sick and giddy; a dark swirling wave of nausea lifted and toppled him over, engulfing him in its murky water, threatening to draw him down into the depths of unconsciousness once more. For three days he had been locked in this cell, without sleep or food, and he was faint with exhaustion. Blue-black bruises distorted one side of his face, puffing up the flesh; two ribs were broken and his whole body ached from the relentless beating it had taken.

A major of the Waffen SS had conducted the interrogation. His manner had been quiet and reasonable, he wanted to know the names of Ashford's contacts in the Maquis, the codewords, the targets they had planned. He'd repeated the questions to him over and again until they became an incantation.

Ashford had said nothing. He had his reasons for keeping silent and they gave him the strength to survive. The major had shaken his head sadly at the end of each session, announced himself disappointed by this misguided display of stubbornness and withdrawn. In his place had come Kleber, a butcher from the Gestapo, and the beatings began again, leaving the victim sick and shuddering with pain.

Ashford had no idea how long he could have taken this punishment. Kleber was a professional torturer, violent and sadistic. Unlike his masters, he had no interest in information or confessions, he wanted only to inflict pain. Slowly and deliberately Kleber had gone about his business, sweating with the exertion of each blow, his shaved head glistening like a billiard ball in the dark cell. The only instrument he'd employed in his work was a kitchen pestle, a marble head set on a short wooden handle. It was designed to grind up herbs and spices, but Kleber used it to pulverise the soft tissue of flesh, methodically hitting the extremities of Ashford's body, the fingers and feet, smacking the cold rounded stone into his joints and ligaments.

There was a movement in the yard below. The door from the cookhouse opened and an orderly stepped out into the yard. His sleeves were rolled to the elbow, there was a stained white apron around his waist and he carried a bucket of slops in his hand. Seeing the firing squad he stopped, frozen in the act of emptying the rubbish on to the ground, and stared round over his shoulder. The officer ordered him out of the way, jerking his head towards the door. Curiosity overrode the command, the man lingered for a moment then gave a shrug, up-ended the bucket and vanished back inside.

At the same moment, Ashford heard footsteps in the passage. He clambered down from the window and sat ready on the bed. It didn't do to show he'd been watching.

The bolts were thrown back, the cell door kicked open and two soldiers moved in. They didn't speak or even look at their prisoner as they came towards him. As far as they were concerned he was already dead. Grabbing him roughly by the arms and the scruff of his collar they frog-marched him out into the passage, jolting him off balance so that his feet dragged along the bare wooden boards. Reaching the ground floor his arms were released and he was pushed outside, the two soldiers remaining in the doorway, barring his escape.

Ashford walked a few paces and then paused, not certain what was expected of him.

A terrible silence had settled in the yard.

With a slow, mechanical motion the *oberleutnant* drew his pistol from its holster and held it out from his side, pointed towards the ground. He twitched the short stump of its barrel, signalling the prisoner forwards into the arena.

Slowly and painfully Ashford stumbled towards him, clutching his trousers in one hand. They had removed his belt and the laces from his shoes when he'd first arrived and so he could now walk only with the greatest difficulty,

7

scuffling his feet across the cobbles. His body felt heavy and clumsy, each stride a separate operation. In front of him was the stone wall, its surface pitted from the impact of bullets.

In the middle of the yard he was given the order to halt. The corporal stepped forward, handcuffed his arms behind his back and turned him round to face the firing squad.

They looked very young for executioners, some of them can have been no more than nineteen, but their eyes had the glazed, uncaring expression of men who've witnessed death a hundred times before. One of them, he noticed, was carrying a Russian SVT 40 rifle, a grim souvenir, evidence that he'd been hardened on the Eastern Front.

He too had been young when he'd first enlisted, Ashford reflected, fresh from the schoolroom. When war broke out he'd been on his way up to Cambridge to study law, a promising undergraduate with a glittering future mapped out before him. But it all seemed so long ago now, part of another century. Everything had changed since then: the hopes, the ambitions, even the morals he'd held in such high esteem had all died and rotted away. Two years in the desert, another in occupied France had aged him, brutalising his personality. The glow of youth had been buried beneath the hard shell of the professional soldier.

An order broke through the silence.

The rifles were raised.

Ashford looked up at the sky. The mist was parting, the morning light beginning to melt away the layer of low cloud. The air was fresh and cool and he breathed it deep into his lungs. He could hear the seagulls wheeling and squabbling above the harbour and, far away, above the stink of diesel fumes, gasoline and cookhouse dustbins, he could smell the sea.

The bolts clattered back, the cartridges were inserted into the rifle-breeches and driven home.

Ashford could see the snouts of the barrels as they aimed at him, the insignias on the helmets behind, the raised hand of the corporal beside them.

His trousers slipped. It was to be expected, there was nothing he could do about it; humiliation was part of the performance. He felt them fall until they hung about his knees like an open grain sack.

Lifting his face towards the sky once more, he held it

8

there and then, with a sigh of resignation, his shoulders slumped, his head rolled forward on to his chest.

'I'll talk,' he muttered.

For one sickening moment he thought he'd left it too late.

The *oberleutnant* stared at him in silence. He seemed to be weighing up the situation in his mind, wondering whether it was worth listening or whether it wouldn't be quicker and cleaner to ignore the plea and shoot him where he stood.

Then, with a little sneer of disgust, he put his gun back into the leather holster, turned on his heel and said, 'Take him away.'

'I will speak to General von Eichendorff.'

'That will not be necessary. Whatever information you have can be given to me.'

Ashford lifted his head from his hands. 'Either I speak to the General or I remain silent.'

'It is not for you to dictate terms,' replied the Major sharply. 'The General does not conduct interviews with convicted spies.'

'He will when he discovers what I have to offer.'

The Major hesitated. Folding his hands behind his back he stared down at Ashford in silence. He was a humourless-looking man, thin lipped and sallow, but he was not to be underestimated; he had the agile mind of a chess-player, thinking several moves ahead, sensing a trap long before it came in sight.

His dress was a little more dishevelled than usual, Ashford noticed. The top button of his dove-grey uniform was undone and his hair had been carelessly brushed into place. He had clearly been bundled out of bed in a hurry to receive the prisoner's confession and was now not amused by this last-minute prevarication.

'What is the nature of your information?' he asked softly.

'It concerns the invasion,' replied Ashford, mumbling out the words through cracked lips.

'Of France?'

Ashford closed his eyes for a moment and nodded.

'What of it?'

'I know where it will take place.'

'In that case you may speak freely to me,' replied the Major, dropping his voice to a more conversational level. 'I

9

will convey the information to the General, should it merit his attention.'

'No,' whispered Ashford, leaning back against the wall of the cell and rocking his head from side to side. 'What I have is for the General's ears only.'

'I have already told you that is impossible.'

'In that case I should make it possible, unless you think you can survive the rest of the war on the wages of a private.'

Ashford glanced up at the Major as he spoke; he could see the suspicion in the pale, Prussian eyes and read the thoughts that passed behind them. 'And don't think you can beat the information out of me,' he added, 'because that method has already been tried.'

The Major came to a decision.

Turning to the two soldiers standing to attention behind him he rapped out instructions and left the cell, pausing briefly at the door to say, 'I trust for your sake, Captain, that you are not wasting our time.'

As soon as he was gone the soldiers relaxed, easing the slings of their rifles, their boots crunching and scraping on the dirty floor as they leaned back against the wall, and began talking earnestly under their breath. From time to time they glanced across at Ashford as he sat huddled on the wooden bed. There was no interest in their expression: the fool hadn't saved himself, simply gained a little time. An hour or two, maybe less. The end would be the same. They acknowledged his presence in the cell that morning with the same dispassion that a fisherman feels for his catch as it flaps away the last minutes of its life in the bottom of a rowing boat.

Ashford wasn't concerned with their opinions, his mind was preoccupied with the coming meeting with von Eichendorff. He had no doubt that the General would see him, the bait had already been taken. He looked around the cell as he waited; the walls were scarred with feeble marks that had been scratched into the plaster by its previous owners: ranks of digits measuring the passing of lonely days, four-letter words, obscene drawings. The thick pungent stench of urine, sweat and disinfectant filled his head and underlying this he could detect another, more disagreeable ingredient: the smell of fear.

'On your feet!' ordered the Major, returning to the cell.

10

The decisions were over, he had been given his orders and now was brusque with efficiency.

Ashford was marched downstairs, across the gravelled forecourt and out into the narrow streets of Honfleur. The two guards urged him along, driving him forwards with the butts of their rifles every time he fell out of step.

The whole town was deserted and their footsteps rang loudly on the cobbles, breaking the silence that settles over the last hours of sleep. Mediaeval buildings leaned over them as they walked, their ragged gables closing out the sky. Washing hung out of upper storey windows, shutters hung from ancient hinges, bicycles with tyres of terracotta rubber were propped against half-timbered walls. Only the cats defied the curfew and slunk across their path, low and wary and black as shadows.

General von Eichendorff's headquarters were in the Hôtel de Ville. Two armed sentries stood guard at the top of a graceful staircase. With quick professional movements they frisked Ashford, probing for any hidden weapon on his body, satisfied themselves that he was unarmed, opened the double doors and propelled him inside.

It was a handsome room, well proportioned and superbly furnished. The high windows had been thrown open and the morning sunlight bloomed on the ormolu, rosewood and polished parquet flooring. Above the fireplace was an enormous oil-painting, radiant in a carved gilt frame, while other smaller canvases were arranged around it.

An adjutant, a little bureaucrat in spectacles, looked Ashford over with distaste. He pointed to a chair in the centre of the room. 'Put him over there,' he instructed.

The two guards thrust him down in the chair, pulling out his arms along the rests and strapping them in place with a pair of standard issue military belts, drawing them tight around his wrists.

The adjutant watched with an expression of peeved martyrdom on his face – this interview was not on the agenda for the day, it upset the schedule. As soon as the prisoner was secure he crossed the room, knocked discreetly at an inner door and held it open.

As General von Eichendorff walked into the room Ashford experienced an unwelcome tremor of apprehension. This was the moment he had been anticipating for so long, for which

11

he had survived three days of torture. For one fleeting instant he was back in the wings of the school stage: the rehearsals were over and the curtain about to rise. Through the cloud of black nausea that swamped him, Ashford felt the nerves in the pit of his stomach begin to flutter.

He had seen the General on several occasions before, seated in the back of his camouflaged Mercedes, as he was driven out to inspect coastal defences and troop manoeuvres, but this was the first time he'd had the chance to study the man close at hand.

Von Eichendorff was a slight figure with a statesman's features and silver-grey hair shaved so short that he appeared almost bald. Years of campaigning had tanned his skin and cracked it with fine wrinkles. His manner was calm, even gracious, but there was no mistaking the underlying authority it carried, the unspoken assumption of power. It was in the set of his head, the thrust of his jaw above the collar and the unwavering gaze of the pale sapphire eyes.

He didn't seem to notice Ashford as he came in.

With his hands locked behind his back he crossed the room, acknowledged the guard's salute with a curt nod of his head, and sat down behind the desk. For ten minutes he occupied himself with the morning's business, scanning through the printed sheets that had been laid out ready for his attention. The adjutant hovered at his shoulder all the while, retrieving each document as it was read, indicating where signatures were required and answers needed.

The delay was intentional.

Ashford didn't allow it to unsettle him. For a while he watched the General as he worked and then let his eyes wander up to the huge painting above the mantelpiece. It was rich and warm, saturated in afternoon sunlight. He had no idea who'd painted it but he recognised the subject well enough; it was the harbour outside. Fishing boats with patched sails and fat-bellied hulls bobbed on bright water. The General's love of art treasures was legendary; it was the single streak of sensuality in an otherwise frigid personality.

As he was looking up at the picture Ashford's right eye darkened, the lid fluttered and the colours swam before him. This had happened several times before – Kleber's marble truncheon had damaged the optic nerve. The sight was fading, and Ashford knew that it was only a matter of time before the eye was blinded for ever.

'You are a very tiresome young man, Captain Ashford,' the General said suddenly, without looking up from his desk.

Ashford made no reply; he seemed transfixed by the sunlit painting above him.

'My officers tell me that you have caused them considerable inconvenience in the last few days, but that now you wish to make a confession.'

'I must speak with you,' agreed Ashford, turning to face him. 'But alone. The guards must leave.'

Von Eichendorff considered the request. 'Very well, if it makes you feel more at ease.' He nodded towards the two guards, who at once crashed into a salute and withdrew. The General waited until the door had closed behind them and then, opening the drawer of his desk, he took out a Luger .08 and placed it neatly on the blotter before him. The gesture was theatrical, he permitted himself a thin smile and said, 'Does that satisfy you now, Captain?'

Ashford looked at the adjutant but the General shook his head.

'He stays here.'

The adjutant clucked and tutted his agreement. The very idea that he should leave was outrageous, an insult to his elevated position. Returning to his desk at the far side of the room he began sorting through the sheaves of paperwork, busily arranging them into separate files.

'He won't hear you,' the General continued, 'he has been well trained; he only listens to what I tell him.'

'I'll take your word for it.'

Von Eichendorff leaned back in his seat, meshed his fingers together with the thumbs steepled up against his tunic, and considered Ashford for a moment. 'Major Meuller tells me that you have information on the planned invasion of France.'

'That's what I told him. It's quite untrue. I know absolutely nothing about any plans.'

The General stiffened.

'You don't imagine that agents would be dropped behind enemy lines with that sort of knowledge locked inside their heads, do you?' There was a hint of sarcasm in Ashford's voice. 'And besides, even if I did give you information you wouldn't know whether to believe it or not.'

'I see,' replied the General. 'So what is it that you want?'

For the first time in three days Ashford smiled. The movement split open his swollen lip and a tiny bead of blood appeared, bright as a ladybird, and trickled down the corner of his mouth. 'I've come to tell you that the war is over, General.'

If von Eichendorff was surprised by this reply he didn't allow it to show on his face. Leaning forward he picked up an identity book and showed it to Ashford. 'May I remind you, Captain, that you have not come here, as you put it, of your own free will. You were arrested in the street for carrying forged papers.'

'They were the worst forgery I could find at the time,' Ashford replied simply. 'A child of five, with a potato and a bottle of ink, could have done a better job.'

'I cannot accept that you intended to be arrested.'

'Not only did I intend to be, I went to great lengths to ensure it. Hell, I was even carrying a packet of English cigarettes at the time, which, incidentally, the guard kept for himself.'

Von Eichendorff leafed through the identity papers with quick movements of his fingers and tossed them back on to the desk. Getting to his feet he strolled over to the window and stared out at the harbour. 'You wish me to believe that you were arrested, in the full knowledge that you would be tortured by the Gestapo, simply to contrive a meeting with me this morning?'

Ashford nodded. He was weak and dizzy, his head felt heavy on his shoulders and the movement hurt him.

'It would seem to be an elaborate way of fixing an appointment, Captain.' The General's voice was soft, with practically no trace of accent. 'I am intrigued to know what has prompted such a charade.'

Ashford craned his neck around until he could see him clearly. 'The invasion is coming,' he said with studied emphasis. 'I have no idea where or when, but I do know that there will be no stopping them once they land. The war is over for you, General, it is just a matter of time now. In a few months, a year at the most, you will be on the run like any other common criminal.'

Von Eichendorff turned and studied his prisoner once more. It was impossible to guess what he was thinking at that moment, the muscles of his face never moved and his eyes betrayed nothing.

'And why should that concern you, Captain?' he asked.

'You are a rich man; your paintings alone are said to be one of the most valuable private collections in the world.' As he spoke, Ashford looked up at the vast painting of Honfleur. 'I've heard that even Hermann Goering is jealous of the art treasures you've looted in the course of your campaigns.'

'They were not looted.' An edge came into the General's voice. He returned to the desk and, opening a chased silver box, took out a cigarette. 'Every painting you see on that wall was bought from its original owner. They are mine, I have the receipts to prove it.'

'It will not make the slightest difference. You are still going to lose them,' replied Ashford. 'That is unless I help you.'

Von Eichendorff paused in the act of lighting his cigarette, removed it from his lips and said, 'And why should you wish to do that?'

Ashford smiled and for a moment his eyes blazed, like ice crystals when they are first struck by the morning sun. 'For the money you're going to pay me to hide them,' he replied.

Chapter One

Paris, July 1988

The squad car drew to a halt, the bumper almost touching the ground as it braked. John Napier stepped out of the back seat on to the fan-tailed cobbles and looked up at the building.

It was tall and impassive, a severe Neoclassical façade. The windows were uncurtained, the honey-coloured stone sculpted and brushed with blue shadows. Two sentries in pillbox hats stood on either side of the wrought-iron gates, legs straddled, arms resting on the breech-blocks of their machine pistols, bored and lethargic in the afternoon heat.

Napier looked at the bars on the lower windows, at the tricolour that hung limp as washing above the doorway. He looked at the brass plaque screwed to the porch, the parking reservations neatly painted on the ground and wondered what it was that the French Government wanted with an art historian such as himself.

He had been in Paris for six days and was due to leave that evening. His luggage had been packed and sent clanging down the gilt-framed lift to the hotel foyer while the maid arranged the room for the next arrivals. He had checked the times from the Gare St Lazare and been settling his bill at the reception desk when the call came through.

It had been a woman's voice on the phone, polite and solicitous, the suave tones of a personal assistant arranging a meeting for her superior. She had apologised for the suddenness of her call, asked whether he was enjoying his stay in Paris and inquired whether he could spare an hour of his time. Yes, it was important, she assured him, otherwise they would never have presumed.

The request had touched Napier's curiosity, on a hot afternoon when he had nothing better to do, while he was waiting to catch a train. As far as he knew he hadn't committed any crime, not even run up a parking fine while he was in Paris. He'd asked her why it was so important, what it was that had prompted the call, but this was the wrong question. She didn't know the answer, she was simply relaying a message.

The squad car had arrived moments later. Whoever it was who wanted to see him seemed very sure of himself, confident that Napier was going to comply with the invitation. He'd let them have their way, sat in the back seat and allowed himself to be carried across the city, through the hooting and jostling of the traffic, past shop windows and crowded cafés that spilled out from darkened interiors, past the flash of fountains and the dense aquarium greenness of the trees in the Tuileries Gardens.

The little car had sped up the Faubourg St Honoré, dived into a side street that was narrow and deserted, a private cul-de-sac that didn't invite intruders, and dropped him here in this dusty courtyard, where the sun shimmered on the cobbles and the eyes of the two sentries followed him as he walked.

He could do with a drink, his throat was dry, his suit heavy and clinging to his body. A bead of sweat ran down the cleft of his spine. When this was through he'd find a brasserie, he promised himself, sit out in the street with a glass of beer and watch the world go by.

That was when this was through.

Running up the stone steps of the building he went inside. It was suddenly dark and silent after the brightness of the July sunshine. The distant growl of traffic was extinguished and the coolness of shaded marble embraced him.

Picard stood at the window above.

On the leather-topped desk beside him lay three reports. The first was from the gendarmerie in the village of Criquetot, Normandy. It was five pages long and written in the dry impersonal language favoured by all petty officials. The next was a terse account from the foreman of a demolition site in the same town. Here the sentences were brief and disjointed, almost certainly taken down verbally. The last report was from the commanding officer of a bomb disposal squad, stationed outside Bernay, registering the discovery of a wartime device that had turned out, on closer inspection, to be harmless.

17

Picard had read through each report several times, fusing the different accounts together, visualising the scene they described. He had discovered as much as he could from them, analysed the information they contained. It was not much to go on, just a beginning. The rest he would learn from this Englishman in the pale chalk stripe suit who walked across the courtyard towards the doorway, who ran up the flight of steps as though he owned the place.

Pulling on his jacket, Picard brushed the flecks of dust off his lapel and sat down, rearranging the reports on his desk. There was no hurry. It would take a few minutes for Napier to be signed in at the security desk and then led up the flight of marble stairs into the long gallery with its fluted pilasters and busts of forgotten notables.

His secretary gave a brief knock and came in.

'Dr John Napier,' she announced, holding open the door.

Napier was twenty years younger than he had expected. Slim and neatly dressed, he appeared undisturbed by the formality of his surroundings and moved across the floor with an easy grace. Only his eyes were rapid, glancing around the office, taking in the details, calculating where he had been brought.

'Dr Napier,' Picard murmured, hurrying out to meet him, 'how very good of you to come at such short notice. My name's Picard . . . Charles Picard.' They shook hands and he retreated back behind his desk again. 'Can I get you anything?' he asked, indicating vaguely with one arm. 'Some coffee, maybe?'

Napier shook his head.

'I trust the two officers we sent were not too abrupt in manner.'

'No more than any other press-gang.'

Picard had the decency to wince. 'I assure you that we don't usually use such heavy-handed tactics,' he murmured. 'Unfortunately we had no alternative in this case. We heard that you were about to leave Paris.'

'I was thinking of going up to Normandy for a few days.'

'Research?'

'Seafood.'

The answer was quick but not glib for the walnut-brown eyes narrowed as he spoke, creasing into a smile that was at once engaging.

18

'An excellent reason,' Picard agreed smoothly, leaning back in his chair, studying Napier with interest.

He was in his early thirties with a controlled, well-mannered confidence. There was an air of prosperity about him, of ambition tempered with success. His features were strong and faintly aquiline, dark brown hair brushed back from a high forehead, the set of his mouth carving fine creases into his cheeks.

They said he was an expert, the best in his field. That remained to be seen.

'Has anyone told you why you are here?'

'Not so far.'

'Then let me explain.' Picard spread his fine white hands. 'In the last few days an interesting problem has arisen – one which we feel is more in your field than ours.' He milked a smile of encouragement on to his face. 'And so we were hoping that you might be able to lend us your professional advice.'

'Advice?' replied Napier conversationally. 'What sort of advice do you have in mind?'

It took a few moments for Picard to answer. Steepling two fingers together he pressed them to his lips and stared out of the window, collecting his thoughts in the sunlit street below.

Then, turning back into the room, he said, 'Tell me about *The Estuary Pilgrim*.'

At the mention of this name Napier lifted his eyebrows and an amber light awoke in the pits of his brown eyes.

'*The Estuary Pilgrim*.' His voice had softened, caressing the syllables as he spoke them. 'What do you want to know about it?'

'Everything you have,' replied Picard. 'You are, I believe, an expert on the subject.'

A slight smile curved Napier's lips. 'In that case I'm sure you also know that it's the name of a painting that was destroyed during the war.'

'An important work, would you say?'

'Extremely. It was one of the first major paintings by Monet. Some consider it to be the most significant of his early career.'

'And how was it destroyed?' Picard asked, balancing his chin on the tips of his fingers.

'It was part of the von Eichendorff collection.'

The name meant nothing to Picard.

Napier stood up and walked over to the sash window. 'He was a German General serving on Rommel's staff during the latter stages of the war,' he explained. 'I believe he had something to do with intelligence work in northern France, but he's best remembered today for the massive collection of paintings that he hoarded.'

'You say hoarded, did he buy these pictures or steal them?'

Napier latched a thumb into his waistcoat pocket and thought for a moment. 'I don't know to be honest. There's a difference of opinion on that point. Some claim that the General paid for the paintings, others think he just pinched them.'

'And *The Estuary Pilgrim*, where did that come from?'

'A family in Le Havre. They ran a shipping business on the north coast. As far as I know the painting used to hang in their head office.'

'From where the General removed it.'

'It was the centrepiece of his collection, his most treasured possession.'

'But you say it's been lost?'

Napier nodded. 'In the spring of 1944. Von Eichendorff had his pictures shipped back to Germany by road. The convoy was ambushed about thirty miles inland, the road was mined and the entire collection burned in the attack.'

'Who by, do you think?' Picard asked softly.

'The Resistance. It was well documented at the time, there are several eye-witness accounts of the incident.'

Picard held up his slender hands, framing the next question between them. 'Is it possible that *The Estuary Pilgrim* could have survived this ambush?'

'Certainly it's possible,' replied Napier, 'but not very likely.' He glanced across the desk, suddenly alert. 'Why do you ask?'

A smile of seraphic innocence washed over Picard's face. 'Because we have it downstairs.'

'It was found in Criquetot,' said Picard as he led the way down to the basement. 'It's a small town in Normandy, about five kilometres from where the convoy you were speaking of was ambushed.'

'And where had it been all these years?' Napier asked.

'It was hidden in the roof of a house on the outskirts of town. The canvas was rolled up and sealed into a steel canister. I'll show it to you in a moment.'

He pushed through a pair of swing doors and held them open for Napier. The passageway before them was long and ill-lit. They were below ground level and the classical splendour of the upper floors had given way to vaulted brick. Naked bulbs dangled from their flexes, fire extinguishers were posted at regulation intervals and the walls were painted in the dull yellow of left-over custard.

As they passed through the hallway they were joined by a security guard. Busy and self-important, in a blue serge uniform and peaked hat, he now walked ahead of them, his rubber-soled shoes creaking on the stone floor. He, like the guards outside, carried a gun, Napier noticed, a standard issue Walther. They were evidently expecting a civil war to break out at any minute. The weapon was strapped into a leather holster that rocked comfortably against the man's right buttock as he marched along.

'The painting came to light quite by chance,' Picard continued. He was feeling guilty for having withheld information and was now eager to break the news.

'A group of demolition workers were knocking down some old buildings to make way for a new multi-storey car park,' he explained. 'As far as I can make out, they were swinging their steel ball about without a care in the world, a wall fell down and the canister just slipped out of its hiding place, landed on the ground in a heap of rubble.' He gave a little grin. 'Scared the daylights out of the workmen, of course. They took one look at it, decided it was a bomb and ran for their lives.'

At the bottom of a flight of steps the guard stopped and began counting through the rosary of keys that he had in his pocket. Selecting one, he rattled it into the lock and pushed the door open, directing them inside with a formal flourish of his hand as he did so.

They filed past him into a small room that smelt of damp and trapped air. The floor was uncarpeted, the furniture functional and the atmosphere as cosy as an interrogation cell.

The Estuary Pilgrim was propped against the far wall. It

had no frame, the huge canvas was as bare and flat as the day it had been completed.

Napier's first impression was of brilliant sunlight.

A warm afternoon's sky; intense blues draining away towards the horizon, coral pinks and purple; summer clouds scudding overhead.

Then sparkling water scored with deep shadows; sailing boats; bristling masts; slate-faced buildings; figures; caps flapping in the breeze; seagulls wheeling above.

He gazed at it in silence.

It was so much larger and more magnificent than he'd ever dared to imagine, a painting of hypnotic presence. The colour was rich and vibrant and even in this uncertain light the canvas seemed to glow, filling the room with a radiance of its own. As he ran his eyes over the painting Napier felt a surge of pleasure that spread and warmed, suddenly igniting into excitement in the pit of his stomach.

Behind him Picard fussed about like a nervous housewife, chivvying chairs out of the way and switching on more lights.

'A remarkable painting, Dr Napier,' he ventured after a few moments.

Napier made a small sound in his throat that was neither French nor English in origin.

Encouraged by this rapport Picard walked over and took up position beside him. Brushing the wing of hair from his eyes he stared intently at the canvas. 'I don't know anything about art,' he murmured after a few moments. 'On the whole I don't even know what I like, but I must admit that this is an exception. It's really most . . . impressive.' He paused and gave a quick nod of his head to convince himself that this was the appropriate word and repeated it once more to be certain.

The painting was of the old mediaeval harbour of Honfleur. A flock of fishing boats was moored to the jetty, their rough wooden hulls riding above delicate reflections. The colour in the water was of clouded jade. It reminded Napier of the little scraps of bottle glass you sometimes find on the beach, each sucked smooth and round by the sea, their surface roughened by the grinding of the pebbles but still translucent when held up to the light. It was a flat unbroken expanse of green water, fretted into jigsaw patterns by the shadows of the fishing boats.

22

The day's catch was scattered across the quayside, spilling out of the wicker baskets in a slippery puddle of fish while women gossiped and squabbled around the edge. The silhouettes of ancient buildings framed the painting, their upper floors craning out over the waterfront.

'It's extraordinary,' Picard whispered, thrusting his head forward to see it more closely. 'It's nothing more than a few houses and boats but it seems to be alive, as though it had a personality of its own.'

Napier moved up close to the canvas and reaching out his hand he stroked the rough textures of its crusted paint. He relied on touch as much as sight when he examined a picture, using the soft pads of his fingers to judge the density of pigment, the degree of reworking that had taken place, the sequence of colours that had been applied.

As his fingertips ran across the dark, copper green shadows of the water he sensed the paint suddenly lose body. It grew thin and filmy, became a fine wash of colour. Slightly surprising, not as he'd expected. Then it thickened once more, where the light was striking. He felt the coarseness of heavily scumbled pigment, the dry consistency of repainted layers, and once again his pleasure sparked awake.

In the centre of the picture was a large three-masted clipper. It was leaving port and shaking out full sail in the afternoon light. A steam tug, with smoke pumping from its stack and paddles churning, nudged alongside, manoeuvring it out of the harbour mouth. Napier pointed to the hull of the sailing ship with his finger, indicating its name. For there, carved on the stern and clearly visible on the surface of the picture, were the words *The Estuary Pilgrim*.

'How long has the painting been down here?' he asked after a few moments.

'Since last night,' Picard replied. 'It was sent to a firm of restorers when it first arrived in Paris. They restretched it and then sent it over here.'

'And why do you keep it locked up in this little cubby-hole?'

Picard looked about the room as though seeing it for the first time and said, 'I don't know, to be honest. Security, I imagine.' An expression of mild apology settled on his face. 'The Press haven't heard of it yet – we decided to keep it under our hats, that is until we are quite sure what it is we're dealing with.'

'Has Daniel Wildenstein seen it?'

'Not yet, he's abroad at present,' Picard told him. 'As a matter of fact you are the first person we've shown it to.'

'How flattering.'

'Coincidence actually. The Musée d'Orsay gave us a list of experts on the subject. You are the only one who happened to be in Paris at the moment,' he said, turning and walking across the room. 'It made you the logical choice. We mustn't be seen wasting the tax-payers's money.' He glanced back over his shoulder. 'Take a look at this.'

Lying on a table against the wall was a long metal cylinder. It was as thick as a drainage pipe and encrusted with dirt. A rash of rust spots had broken out along its side, disfiguring the surface and blistering the drab olive-green paintwork. One end was sealed with a steel cap the rim of which had been eaten away to lace. The two spring clips that had originally held it in place had become brittle with age and had broken when the canister was opened. They now hung down on either side of the cap like a pair of uneven earrings.

'This is what the picture was in when it was found,' Picard said. He ran his hand along the length of the cylinder and tiny flecks of paint brushed off beneath his fingers, fluttering down like dandruff. 'Sinister looking contraption isn't it? You can see why it gave the demolition workers such a fright.'

Stencilled along the body of the canister was a series of figures and numerals, only just visible beneath the rust and grime. Picard crouched down and inspected them closely.

'We're getting an expert from the Institute of Military Studies to decipher this lot,' he said, picking away specks of dirt with his thumbnail. 'Some of it seems to be clear enough, though.' He pointed to the letters LaGn printed in heavy black characters near to the opening. 'These presumably stand for "La Roche-Guyon",' he said. 'It was Rommel's headquarters during the latter stages of the war and probably the first stopping place for the painting on its journey back to Germany. God knows what all those numbers are after it.'

'What's this design here?' Napier asked, indicating a stylised motif further along.

'Ah, that's the insignia of the 21st Panzer Division. They were stationed up on the coast,' Picard told him. 'And this CHE underneath could be part of the name "Eichendorff",

24

but that's only a guess, the letters are too badly damaged to be legible.' Picard stood up, brushing the dust off his hands. 'However, I dare say the little boffin from the Institute will be able to read them all like a best-seller.'

Napier looked down at the battered canister, studying its rusted body, while ideas bubbled and broke in the surface of his mind. 'There were twenty or thirty paintings on that convoy,' he said, speaking his thoughts out loud. 'The whole of von Eichendorff's collection. Now if they were to turn up . . .'

'It would be quite a find,' Picard finished for him.

'It certainly would.'

For a few moments there was silence in the room, broken only when Picard glanced at his watch and said, 'How about a drink?'

The guard, who had been sitting reading a newspaper and quietly perspiring in the shadows, jumped to his feet and unlocked the door. They made their way upstairs and out into the sun-drenched courtyard.

'What were the rest of von Eichendorff's pictures like?' Picard asked, nodding to the police sentries at the gate.

'Spectacular,' Napier told him without emotion. He thought of the faded photographs he'd pored over in French archives, the descriptions he'd read, the images he'd conjured in his mind over the years as he studied the General's legendary pictures.

'It was one of the best private collections put together by the Nazis, which is saying something. He had *The Flight into Egypt* by Poussin; several Degas's; Delacroix's *Battle of the Amazons*; a Velázquez portrait and a whole string of Bonnards.'

Picard gave a little whistle.

'But that is just the beginning,' Napier continued as they walked out into the dazzle and activity of the Faubourg St Honoré. 'Most of his pictures were landscapes. He liked to collect paintings of the district where he was living, which is why *The Estuary Pilgrim* was the centrepiece of the collection. Not only was it the best picture he'd come across, it had also been painted in Honfleur – right on his doorstep.'

Crossing the road into a side street they sat down at a tin table outside a café. Picard summoned the waiter, ordered drinks and then sat back, stretching out his legs on the pavement. Away from the protocol of his office he seemed to relax, becoming lighter, more boyish in manner.

'Well, what do you think of our discovery?' he asked.

Napier gave a laugh and spread his hands. 'Hard to say at present – I need a little time to get over the initial shock.'

'Was it as you expected?'

'I never expected to see it at all.'

'I mean in technical terms.'

Napier rested his arm along the back of his chair and thought for a moment. He visualised the painting once more, summoned its colour, its great patterned structure into his mind, feeling the texture of the paint beneath the pads of his fingertips.

'Not entirely,' he said. 'The paintwork in the shadows of the picture is slightly thinner than I would have expected.'

'Does that surprise you?'

'Not really,' replied Napier. 'Monet was only twenty-seven when he painted *The Estuary Pilgrim*. His style was still variable, the technique changes slightly from one picture to the next at that period. What surprises me is that the painting exists at all, as far as I know there has never been any suggestion of it surviving the attack.'

'Ah, now there you're wrong.' Picard sat forwards and raised a finger. 'About six months ago the curator of a museum in Honfleur put forward a theory that the picture might still exist. He wrote an article about it in the local press which I must admit I haven't been able to read yet. He's sending a copy down to me, I'll show it to you when it turns up.'

'It should be interesting to see what he has to say.'

The waiter arrived, gliding his tray above the sea of heads and bringing it down to rest on the edge of the table. He unloaded a glass of ice-cold lager and a cup of black coffee, slipped the tariff under one corner of the ashtray, scooped a tip into his apron and was gone again.

Napier pulled the glass towards him and took a sip of lager. It was cool and sweet and made up of more frozen gases than Haley's Comet. 'The real question now,' he said, brushing the froth off his upper lip, 'is who owns *The Estuary Pilgrim*?'

'Ah,' said Picard, taking his spoon from the coffee and waggling it across the table, 'now that's a good point. It's anybody's guess at present.'

'Who are the contenders?'

He thought for a moment. 'The prime candidate is Lebas, the grandson of the original owner in Le Havre. But there is a distinct possibility that von Eichendorff's family could have rights to it.'

'I thought the Germans lost all claim to their treasures after the war.'

'Not necessarily. The General's relations do have a case, tenuous I grant you, but technically feasible nonetheless.' Picard drank some of his treacle-black coffee and settled the cup on its saucer once more. 'It all rests on whether von Eichendorff bought the painting from the Lebas family or just helped himself to it. I was hoping you might know the answer to that.'

Napier shook his head.

'Pity,' he said. 'It would have made life easier.'

'And what if no one can establish a legal claim?'

The question seemed to unsettle Picard. Looking away to the street, he fixed his attention on the distant traffic and his voice dropped to a murmur. 'Well in that case the painting would naturally revert to the French Government.'

'Which is why your shady little department is taking such a keen interest in its welfare.'

'Possibly,' he admitted, 'but then we're not running a charity. Added to which we need to know the answer. When the news of this discovery hits the Press there will be claims crawling out of the woodwork. Every opportunist, chiseller and con-artist is going to make a bid for it.'

Napier ran his finger down the side of his glass, drawing lines in the condensation. 'One thing that is for sure,' he said, 'whoever does turn out to be the lucky owner has just become extremely rich.'

Picard nodded. The idea of so much stray wealth with no permanent address to it seemed to sadden him. 'Will you put a few of these facts down in writing for us?' he asked, swirling the black grit of his coffee dregs about in the cup.

'What facts are those?'

Picard shrugged. 'The history of the picture, the condition of the paint, those technical points you were talking about just now – anything that comes to mind really. I'm going to draft out a press release in the next few days, it would help a great deal if I had your professional opinion to call on.' He stood up and held out his hand. 'We'll pay you, of course,' he murmured with a slight twinkle.

'I'd hate to waste your tax-payers's money.'

'I daresay they can afford it,' he replied as they shook hands. 'Besides, I doubt if you'll be able to retire on the proceeds.'

After Picard had gone, Napier finished his lager in peace. It was only four o'clock and he considered going over to the Bibliotèque Nationale before it closed.

He liked the solitude of the library, the dusty silence of strangers reading together.

Napier was a planet with both a dark and a light side to his personality. He was the third of five brothers who had tumbled through childhood like a pack of terriers: playing and fighting, resolving their differences in games and feuds and shifting alliances. Their home, a large rambling manor house in the West Country, had been filled with noise from morning to night and the only quiet that Napier had known as a boy was in the privacy of his mind. He had learned to remove himself, to withdraw into the sanctuary of his imagination, when he wanted to be alone. 'John's dreaming again,' his brothers would tease when they found him gazing into space, but they had come to respect these occasional spells of silence and had the good grace to leave him in peace.

At Oxford Napier had rowed for his college, belonged to numerous dining societies, danced at Commem Balls, flirted on punts and been gated for climbing the clock tower, like most other undergraduates who find themselves on the threshold of manhood with time on their hands, but the periods of solitude remained. His manner was gentle and invited intimacy, he listened well and people, particularly women, tended to confide in him. He was conventional in dress and modest in lifestyle but the one remarkable feature of his personality to emerge during these years was that he loved paintings – all paintings. Napier would spend hours in museums and galleries, standing before the old masters. But he was equally happy studying amateur watercolours in a provincial exhibition, commercial paintings on the railings of Green Park or chalk drawings on the pavement. He preferred great paintings to minor but there was no picture, however insignificant, that didn't hold his interest.

To John Napier paintings were mystery and excitement, part of the private world of his imagination. But now the idea of returning to the library held no attraction for him. He was too absorbed by what he'd seen in the last hour to be able to concentrate on anything else.

Leaving the café he walked down the Rue Royale, picking his way through the current of summer tourists, and crossed over into the Tuileries Gardens.

In the far distance the hazy outline of the Louvre wavered in the rising heat and the air was filled with the fragrance of parched earth and baking bread.

He paused by the edge of an ornamental pond and watched the light winking and flashing off the ripples. In the centre a bronze fountain splashed and played in the warm air, the plume of its water drifting out in a veil that caught the sunlight and shattered it into prismatic rainbows. Small children raced around the perimeter, shouting excitedly to each other as they retrieved and relaunched the yachts that tacked about its surface. As he looked on, the light became the colour in his eye, the boats and water turned to paint and the image of *The Estuary Pilgrim* burst into his head once more.

The sight of the great painting in the gloomy vault had disturbed memories that had lain dormant in Napier's mind for years.

Honfleur had been an important place in his life.

The first time he was there had been with Jane Fairfax, a girl as sleek as a seal, with a ribbon of shining brown hair that reached to her waist and skin tanned from the French sun. They had stopped in the town for a night on their way back to England at the end of one summer vacation. The next day they'd had a long and lazy lunch together in a restaurant on the waterfront. She had found a postcard with an old photograph of *The Estuary Pilgrim* and they had whiled away the afternoon sitting on the quayside, their heads together, poring over the little picture.

That winter Napier had written about the painting, trying to work the sunlight, the boats, the wine and the contented dreaming conversation of the afternoon into his words. As he wrote the ideas grew and blossomed, further paintings were introduced into the text and the description of *The Estuary Pilgrim* became one chapter in a book on Monet. In the following year, rather to his surprise, it was published and established

29

his reputation as an art historian. The critics announced it was too personal a style of writing to be successful, Napier's Oxford colleagues thought it lacked academic weight but the book sold. A paperback edition came out and then another, it was translated into eight languages and made into a television documentary.

In Napier's opinion it was not the best of all the books he had written subsequently but nevertheless he still loved it as his firstborn.

'God, that was over ten years ago,' he reflected. He hadn't thought of that day in Honfleur since he and Jane had parted but now, as he gazed out across the gardens, the memory welled up in him, warm and urgent, spilling over into a loneliness that he couldn't explain.

Chapter Two

Before leaving Paris, Napier spent three days with the picture. Locked in the little basement room, with only the guard for company, he examined the canvas in detail until he came to know every brushstroke, each mark and configuration of paint by heart.

He wasn't entirely sure what was expected of him, but while he was down there he wrote a carefully worded report on the picture, outlining the techniques, the materials and pigments that had been used in its creation.

A series of X-rays had been taken of the canvas, smoky images that exposed the bone structure beneath the surface of the painting, and from these Napier was able to detect each stage of its construction: the initial drawing of the composition, the building up of solid layers of paint and the various alterations and additions that had taken place as the picture had developed.

The guard sat beside him as he worked, squat as a mushroom, reading a newspaper that he brought in each morning secreted somewhere inside his uniform. In all the time they were together he never once spoke or showed the slightest interest in the proceedings, but whenever Napier touched the canvas he solemnly lowered his paper, watched him for a few moments and then sank back out of sight again, satisfied that no premeditated act of vandalism was taking place.

Three days after Napier returned to London *The Estuary Pilgrim* hit the headlines.

The painting's wartime record, its destruction by the Resistance and dramatic resurrection on a demolition site made juicy reading and newspapers all over the world carried the story.

Speculation as to who owned the painting ran riot and all the old and well-thumbed puns to do with Monet and money were dragged out of retirement and blazed across the front pages of the tabloids.

For a few days the town of Criquetot was famous. The workman who'd first spotted the container in the rubble appeared on television; the chief of police described how he'd called in the bomb disposal squad, knowing from the start that it was harmless; the local curate told the Press that the find was a miracle and took the opportunity to launch an appeal for the church spire.

Napier first read of the discovery in the *Evening Standard*. He was surprised, and not entirely displeased, to find his own name mentioned in the article. Billed as a leading authority on French art, he was quoted as calling *The Estuary Pilgrim* a landmark in 19th-century painting, a remark that he had no recollection of making at the time.

Picard kept in touch. He wrote to Napier on several occasions thanking him for his help and keeping him abreast of the news on his side of the Channel. Enclosed in one of his letters were a couple of pages from a society magazine covering *The Estuary Pilgrim*'s opening night at the Grand Palais. There were a series of little pictures of museum curators, celebrities and critics, all rigid in black tie and boiled shirts, posing before the canvas. They were blurred, unflattering photos on the whole: faces bleached, smiles frozen in place and eyes glazed. Picard himself appeared in one of them, talking to a magnificent girl in a strapless dress, her blonde hair tumbling down on to bare shoulders. She was looking round at that moment, as though someone had called her name, while Picard stood before her, nervous and self-conscious, a champagne glass in one hand and his eyes glued to her cleavage. Napier studied the picture closely; it wasn't clear what the girl's role was, whether she was connected to the art world in some way or just part of the decoration for the evening. He glanced down at her name but it meant nothing to him. The incident had evidently impressed itself on Picard's memory, however, for alongside the photo he'd added a large exclamation mark in red ink.

Later that summer *The Estuary Pilgrim* came to London.

The legal rights to the painting were still in dispute but the French authorities had allowed it to go on tour in the meantime.

Napier left his flat to attend the private view on a fresh evening in early September. It had been raining all that day and the air was now sharp and fragrant, scrubbed clean by the downpour. He hailed a taxi in Piccadilly and, as it barged its way between the streams of traffic, he looked out at the drooping park. The sky was parting and a timid evening light glistened on the pavements and wet grass. Branches stood out firm and black against the mist of damp foliage and the green material of empty deck-chairs flashed like emeralds.

Leaving the cab in Trafalgar Square he crossed the road, scattering pigeons as he went, and ran up the steps of the National Gallery. Napier didn't particularly like these formal occasions but he had to admit that he was excited by the prospect of seeing *The Estuary Pilgrim* once more. He'd thought about the painting often in the past few weeks: the glow of its colour, the crust of thick paint, the image of sea and sunlight had returned to him over and again, relentless and insistent, filling his mind like a tune that wouldn't go away.

The room was crowded by the time Napier arrived.

An efficient-looking girl in evening dress and spectacles took his invitation at the door, tore off the corner and dropped it into a silver ice-bucket along with the others. Napier collected a glass of champagne in return and moved forward on to the tightly packed floor. All around him were faces he recognised, some that he didn't and several that he should have. Bond Street dealers, bored and haughty, affecting a professional disinterest in the proceedings. Gallery staff, *The Times* saleroom correspondent and research historians from the Warburg Institute. Christie's and Sotheby's fielding a full team of directors. The Arts Minister was there, he noticed, smiling and bobbing and talking with enthusiasm.

Nodding to acquaintances, deflecting passing comments and greetings, Napier gently pushed his way through the patterns of conversation towards *The Estuary Pilgrim*.

The painting hung on the far wall and dominated the room, clearing a space on the floor before it. Standing sentry on either side was a bouquet of flowers. A gilt frame had been made for the canvas, increasing its size and presence. Napier took a sip of dry bubbles and ran his eyes across the picture, taking in the familiar details.

'Delicious looking fish on the quayside . . .' he heard a voice behind him murmur.

'I appreciate we're talking about light,' said another, 'but are we talking about light as a concept or as a physical presence . . .?'

'I heard it was found on a rubbish tip . . .'

Napier absorbed himself in the painting, while fragments of conversation collided and burst about his head.

'I'm a convert to fish, you know, hardly ever eat anything else . . .'

' . . . Well, what other ways are there of talking about light . . .?'

' . . . I used to think it was terribly dull and Fridayish, but it's just not true anymore. There's a marvellous little restaurant in Pimlico . . .'

Napier's name was suddenly fired at him from short range. He glanced round to see Tristan Wentworth bearing down on him, smiling beguilingly and extending a brittle hand in greeting.

'John,' he repeated, drawing out the name as though it were made of elastic, 'how good to see you here. This is exciting – are we going to have to revise our opinions of Monet? I think we are; I shall certainly do so.'

Napier shook the porcelain hand and attempted to staunch the flow of words with a reply but Wentworth was not through, there were more questions he needed to answer. 'Were you very excited when you first saw it? I thought you would be; I'd have been thrilled; what a discovery.'

As they were speaking a handsome woman with auburn hair and earrings of solid geometry drew alongside.

'Darling,' she growled at Napier, breathing cigarette smoke out through her nostrils. 'How very clever of you to come up with this new treat for us.'

'As a matter of fact, Margot, and as you very well know, all this has practically nothing to do with me,' Napier told her. 'I just checked the painting over for the French authorities.'

'But what needed checking?' she inquired. Reaching up and draping one arm around Napier's neck she kissed his cheek and the scrap-yard of her jewellery jangled about his ears. Margot Latchman was a journalist; every morning she poisoned a column of the *Daily Express* with her social diary. Very little escaped her attention, she was a fund of gossip and rumour and no opening night was complete without her. 'The whole canvas exudes Monet,' she continued, indicating the canvas with her cigarette. 'The brushwork says Monet, the colour says Monet . . .'

'Well that may be true . . .' said Napier.

'Even the subject says Monet.'

'Not forgetting the signature.'

'Yes,' she agreed, 'that too.' A cloud passed over her face, as though a recent bereavement in the family had come to mind. 'But I find that rather less convincing.' She turned slightly and indicated the man who stood poised behind her. 'You know Rodney, don't you?'

Napier did know Rodney. He ran a gallery in Cork Street that handled modern art in its most virulent form. Conceptualism, Minimalism and sculpture made from recycled central heating systems.

Rodney, who had been waiting in the wings, now came in on cue. 'I'm absolutely furious with you, John,' he announced, pausing to allow the words to sink in before rushing on. 'You go to Paris for a holiday and come back the hero of the colour supplements; it's really too upsetting.'

'It was purely coincidence,' Napier murmured. 'I thought at the time that they were trying to arrest me.'

'You realise that I don't like the painting, of course,' Rodney added, well pleased by the sound of his opinions. 'I find Monet thoroughly overrated.'

Napier could well see that compared to a canvas lightly splattered with yoghurt-coloured distemper or a piece of sculpture fashioned from broken down Hoovers and cannibalised kitchen utensils, *The Estuary Pilgrim* was something of a disappointment.

Margot dismissed him. 'Oh Rodney, do shut up,' she breathed, 'you can be a testicle at times.'

'I was only making a point.'

'Well don't,' she told him. 'Just stick to making money, it's more becoming.'

'I must be off,' said Tristan Wentworth suddenly. 'I have a date elsewhere.' He thrust out his hand and allowed Napier to shake it once more. 'John,' he drawled, 'so good to see you here. I have a picture I'd love you to take a look at; I think you'll find it very exciting, I certainly do . . . Would you care to drop round to the gallery one day? We could have a spot of lunch together, catch up on the news . . . or tea?'

Tristan was a difficult man to answer. He left only the

occasional blank space in his conversation and it was rarely long enough to type in a reply. Napier attempted to say that he was rather pressed for time but missed his chance.

'Next week would suit me best,' Tristan continued. 'I have a terrible cold brewing but it'll be over by then. I'll give you a ring. Why don't we say Thursday? Lemsip and biscuits round at my place about four? See you then.'

He vanished into the crowd, leaving a vacuum in his place.

'There's a curious little man over there who seems to know you,' said Margot Latchman, who had taken the time to study the faces around her. 'He's been watching you like a hawk ever since he came in.'

Napier followed the direction of her gaze.

He was an unprepossessing individual standing by himself in one corner. His suit had been bought by instalment: the trousers were older than the jacket and had become shiny from constant wear. There was no glass in his hand and he seemed rather to be waiting for someone.

As their eyes met across the room he smiled at Napier and gave a little bobbing bow.

'Ghastly little man,' observed Margot. 'He looks like the editor of some dreary Left-wing newspaper. Do you recognise him, John?'

'Never seen him before in my life,' said Napier, turning back to her.

'Well he certainly seems to know you.'

'Everyone knows who John is,' said Rodney petulantly.

'On the contrary,' corrected Margot. 'They know what he is, not who he is.'

The fine difference was enough to silence Rodney once more. He stopped a passing waiter and encouraged him to fill his glass.

Taking Napier by the arm, Margot leaned in close to him. 'John darling,' she said confidentially, 'between you and me . . .'

'And your five million sensation-starved readers.'

'Them too,' she agreed. Inclining her head towards the canvas that loomed above them she continued, 'But what I wanted to ask you is, who owns this painting?'

Napier shrugged. 'How should I know?'

'Hasn't your mysterious little French friend told you anything?'

'Picard?' said Napier. 'No, the only thing he told me was that the case was going to court.'

'Did he give odds on the outcome?'

'He hasn't even posted the full list of runners yet.'

Margot looked him over thoughtfully, drew in a lungful of cigarette smoke and exhausted it down her nose in a manner that might have excited St George.

'Who do you think will get it?' she asked.

'I would have thought the heirs of the original owner have the best chance.'

'Maurice Lebas, you mean?'

'You know him?'

Margot pivoted around on her heel, scanning the room. 'He's here tonight,' she said, 'or at least he was.' With a little jerk of recognition she pinpointed him. 'There he is, over by the door.' She glanced up at Napier. 'Do you want to meet him?'

'Why not?'

'Because he's a surly bastard, that's why not,' she told him.

'I thought that's how you liked them, Margot.'

She dropped her lashes, flashing blue eyeshadow at him. 'We'd better hurry,' she said, 'I think he's on his way out.'

Trailing scent and sienna hair, the lavender muslin of her dress floating out in her wake, Margot led the way across the room. With a burst of speed at the last moment she intercepted a couple as they were heading out of the door.

'Maurice,' she said, offering the man the flat of her hand and barring his path as she did so, 'how nice to see you here. Margot Latchman – we met at Cannes last year.'

Lebas bowed stiffly from the waist. 'Of course, madame,' he said with pea-soup vowels. He clearly didn't recognise her and made no attempt to disguise the fact.

'I so wanted you to meet Dr Napier before you left,' Margot continued smoothly, extracting her hand and using it to draw Napier into view.

Lebas looked him over with small bullet-hole eyes. He was a short, powerfully built man, dressed in a blue blazer and livid red tie. His face was thick set and plebeian, the salt and pepper hair cut down to bristle.

'Should I know you?' he asked.

'Why of course,' his wife fluttered at him. 'This is Dr

Napier, *chéri*. We have him to thank for authenticating the picture. You read about it in the news.'

'Ah, yes,' said Lebas, a gleam of interest coming into his eyes, 'and you were well paid for your services I believe, Dr Napier.'

'I was paid,' Napier agreed, 'although I wouldn't necessarily say well.'

'By the French Government.'

'Presumably.'

Lebas's head nodded on the solid base of its neck. 'And are you also going to support their claim to owning my picture?' he asked softly.

'But we're not sure if it is yours yet, Maurice,' his wife interceded, a nervous little smile flittering about her face. 'That is until the court has made its decision.'

An expression of disbelief mobilised Lebas's features. Raising his arm he pointed the stub of a finger towards the painting. 'That picture was bought by my family,' he said flatly. 'It was stolen and has now been recovered.' He turned to Napier, dropping his arm and rolling on the balls of his feet like a boxer. 'That painting is mine, Dr Napier, I own it. It is ridiculous for anyone to contest the claim. Tell that to your friends in the Faubourg St Honoré next time you see them.'

'I'm certain you're right,' said Napier soothingly.

Lebas seemed to collect himself; the intensity washed out of his eyes. He glanced down at the gold watch that lay bedded in the dense black hairs of his wrist. 'Will you excuse us,' he said, 'we are already late for an appointment.' Taking his wife by the arm he propelled her towards the doorway.

Margot waited until they had left the room.

'One of life's natural gentlemen, wouldn't you say?'

'He certainly comes straight to the point.'

'I did warn you,' she reminded him. 'I must be going too. Why don't we have lunch sometime?'

'I'd like that.'

She reached up, brushing his cheek with a kiss, and then drawing back she ran her hand down his shirt front. 'I think you've put on weight,' she said. 'It's rather becoming; are you in love?'

'I don't think so.'

'Well you should be,' she told him. 'If you don't find

38

yourself a woman soon you'll become cantankerous and eccentric like all the other art historians I can think of. Besides, you owe it to your breed; you must be the only red-blooded heterosexual here tonight.'

'What about Rodney?'

'He's one or the other,' she replied, waving her long-nailed fingers at him in parting. 'But never both at the same time.'

Napier turned and strolled back across the floor. It was after nine and the room was beginning to clear. The last strands of the party were lingering on while waiters shuffled between them, emptying ashtrays and collecting up the glasses that littered the tables and mantelpiece. An atmosphere of dishevelled elegance had invaded the place.

Standing in front of *The Estuary Pilgrim* was a narrow-shouldered, faintly familiar figure. It was the man Margot had observed watching him earlier that evening. He appeared to be engrossed by what he saw. His feet were planted together, his arms hung at his sides and he stood, like a shabby sentry, staring up at the canvas, a dark silhouette against the radiance of sea and sunlight.

As Napier passed the man turned, as though he'd been waiting for his moment, and gazed at him with pale eyes.

'Dr Napier?' he asked quietly.

'That's right.'

The man blinked and a small smile budded on to his lips. 'I was hoping I might run into you.'

'How's that?' Napier asked, pausing by the carved woodwork of the gilt frame.

'I was admiring the painting,' he continued, looking up at it once more. 'It's really most remarkable.'

'I'm glad you like it.'

'Yes indeed,' he murmured. 'You do realise that it's a fake.'

As he spoke these words, the little man lowered the pale searchlight of his eyes from the canvas and directed them at Napier.

'What makes you say that?'

'Because it's the truth.'

'Can you prove it?'

Again the smile pouted his lips. 'But of course, Dr Napier, I wouldn't be here this evening if I couldn't.'

It might have been the implication of what he was saying,

or the expression of curdled benevolence on his face, but as Napier looked at him he felt his skin crawl. The man had spent too long in the shade, his flesh was soft and white and his mouth as red as a poisonous berry. 'And what is this proof that you have?'

He appeared to be offended by this remark. 'Come, come, Dr Napier,' he said, with a note of reproach in his voice, 'this is hardly the place to talk of such things. Shall we discuss the matter elsewhere?' He held out his hand as he spoke and gestured towards the door.

Napier hesitated. The refusal was ready on his lips, curt and final. It would only take a word to brush this man aside, to extricate himself from the situation as politely as possible and walk away. But he was curious to know what he had to offer. Something had led him to come here and gate-crash the private view. Something had encouraged him to stand against the wall, to watch with his pale drained eyes and wait his chance. He wanted to know what this might be.

'It'll be worth your while, Dr Napier. That I can promise you.'

The room was almost empty, the time had come to leave. Napier had nothing arranged, nowhere else he had to go and his curiosity was pricking him. What did he have to lose?

Draining his glass, he put it down carefully on the table behind and said, 'Very well.'

They left the National Gallery together, walking down the lava flow of marble steps and out on to the porch. Darkness was drawing in and between the massive trunks of the Corinthian columns was spread the blue-black shadow of the city. Shop windows, neon signs and street lights glistened in the twilight, illuminating the bronze flanks of the lions and the traffic that surged around the Square.

Napier's companion didn't pause to admire the view but turning to his right he led the way down on to the pavement. He was several inches shorter than Napier but he was careful not to fall behind him and strode along with great determination, keeping exactly in step and turning up his toes as he walked. He made no attempt to speak as they made their way up into the small backstreets behind the gallery but from time to time he turned his head and smiled.

Napier couldn't escape the uneasy sensation that the whole performance was planned; that the direction they were taking, the words that the man had used in front of the painting and even the expressions he'd put on his face had all been rehearsed beforehand.

Reaching a wine bar near the Haymarket the man stopped and looked in through the plate-glass window.

'This should serve our purpose,' he said, and pushing in through the door he made his way to a table at the far end of the room. He slid himself along the bench until his back was against the wall and folded his hands on his lap. 'Perhaps you would do the honours, Dr Napier,' he murmured, nodding his head towards the bar.

It was on the tip of Napier's tongue to tell him to go and boil his head but he checked himself. Aggravating the little fellow wasn't going to help matters; better to follow the script for the time being and do as he was told.

'The Châteauneuf-du-Pape is quite acceptable here, so I'm told,' he added.

'Is it?' said Napier. 'Very well . . . I'm sorry, I didn't catch your name.'

'Barnabas; you may call me Barnabas.'

It was clearly a pseudonym.

'Barnabas?' repeated Napier. 'Barnabas who?'

He was not to be drawn on the point however. 'I think that is sufficient for now,' he said primly.

The bar was a solid wooden contraption, stained to the colour of smoke-blackened oak and lit from within like a fishtank. Napier went round to the far side and picking up a wine list he briefly scanned the contents. From where he was standing, through the screen of figures who jostled around him, he had a clear view of Barnabas.

He was sitting at the table staring out into space, absorbed in his own thoughts, calm and composed. The performance was evidently coming off as rehearsed.

It was impossible to judge Barnabas's age: his hair was thin and beginning to recede but the face beneath was not that of an old man. It was round and pasty, the flesh slightly flabby, the expression sensual. It was a weak face, an indulgent face – the face of a rogue vicar.

'Can I get you anything, sir?' asked the barman.

Napier turned round a few degrees and without taking his eyes off Barnabas said, 'Give me a bottle of house red will you. Two glasses.'

The barman reached down below the counter, hoisted out a bottle and tearing off the metal seal he thrust it into the bar-pull and pumped out the cork. Reaching above he unlatched a pair of glasses and set them on the bar alongside. Napier paid and gathering them together into one hand he returned to the table.

'Now,' he said, taking a seat opposite Barnabas and filling the glasses. 'If I understood you right, you are able to prove that *The Estuary Pilgrim* is a fake.'

Barnabas took a pull at the wine and wiping his lips on the back of his hand said, 'That's right.'

'How?'

'Ah, don't get me wrong,' he said, emptying the glass and putting it down beside the bottle. 'I'm not an art historian like yourself, Dr Napier. I know nothing about the different periods and styles of painting, but I do have evidence, irrefutable evidence I might say, that the picture you've discovered is not all that it seems to be.'

'Do you have this evidence with you?' asked Napier.

'Not with me,' he replied, taking up the bottle and refilling his glass.

'Are you going to give me some idea of what it is?'

Barnabas took a mouthful of house red and, with the wine still wet on his lips, said, 'I was wondering how much it would be worth to you, Dr Napier.'

'You want me to pay for it?'

He turned his pale sheep's eyes on to Napier and nodded slowly. 'After all, it's your reputation that's at stake,' he murmured. 'If I can prove that your picture is a fake it's going to make you look rather foolish, isn't it?'

Napier shook his head in disbelief. 'It wouldn't do me much good, I grant you, but it wouldn't do much damage either.' He leaned back and spread his hands along the table-top. 'You've picked the wrong man, Barnabas. I'm interested to see what you have, for purely academic reasons, but I'm not going to pay for it.'

'I see,' he replied evenly. The rejection didn't seem to perturb him and he sat staring at Napier with unblinking eyes.

'If it's money you want you should approach the owner; he's the one with something to lose.'

'I thought of that,' Barnabas agreed. 'Unfortunately no one seems to know who owns the painting.'

'Start at the top of the list,' said Napier with a touch of irony in his voice. 'Try your luck with Maurice Lebas; see how he takes to being blackmailed.'

Barnabas took the remark seriously. 'That would be a most unsatisfactory solution,' he replied. 'I imagine he'd react very violently to the suggestion. Lebas is an influential man, Dr Napier, he's quite capable of having my evidence suppressed or, worse still, destroyed.'

'And you along with it, no doubt,' Napier added.

'My thoughts exactly,' replied Barnabas. He looked away into the shadows and his voice dropped to a sigh. 'But if, on the other hand, you were to approach him . . .'

There was a moment of complete silence.

Napier examined his companion with rather more interest. You had to admire his cheek. He had worked the whole scheme out, carefully plotting each stage of the conversation, coaxing him forward to the right conclusion.

'So what you're suggesting . . .'

'What I'm suggesting is a partnership,' said Barnabas, suddenly leaning forward so that the table-top lamp lit his face from below, creating unnatural shadows on his face. 'That painting is worth millions, as you very well know, Dr Napier. What I have in my possession will reduce its value to nothing, an ingenious fake – a curiosity worth no more than the price of its frame.'

'And you think the owner, whoever he turns out to be, will pay to keep you quiet?'

'If the threat is real enough, yes,' replied Barnabas. 'And that's where you fit into the equation. I have the evidence but not the influence to make it stick. You, on the other hand, have the reputation as an art expert; people listen to you. If you were to announce that the painting was a fake they'd pay attention.'

'So you want me to act as your front?'

'If you like to call it that.'

'And if I don't, you'll take your information elsewhere thereby ruining my budding career?'

'If necessary.'

'Aren't you overlooking one thing?' asked Napier. 'If you've managed to find this evidence there's a good chance someone else might also come across it.'

'It's most unlikely,' replied Barnabas and the little smirk of

43

complacency returned to his mouth. 'Really most unlikely. I was led to it through the most improbable chain of events; the chances of someone else following the same sequence are minute. I'm not a gambling man, Dr Napier, but I'd say the odds of that happening are a million to one against.'

He reached out for the wine bottle but Napier moved more quickly, snatching it away from his outstretched hand.

'How long have you been festering on this one, Barnabas?' he asked softly, holding the wine out of his reach.

'I don't follow you.'

'Is there a bedsit somewhere in Earl's Court where you sit and hatch your nasty little schemes,' he continued, 'or do they come naturally?'

The words must have been closer to the truth than Napier expected for as he spoke Barnabas's whole body seemed to stiffen, his eyes glittered in the darkness.

'Don't mock me, Dr Napier,' he said with sudden intensity, 'that would be most unwise.'

'I'm not mocking you,' replied Napier amiably, 'I'm just suggesting that your safety valve has jammed.'

'It has not. I've thought this through with great care; nothing has been left to chance.'

The man was a crank; the thought of so much wealth locked into a single work of art had scrambled his wits. Napier couldn't help laughing at him. 'Nothing left to chance, Barnabas?' he echoed. 'You don't even know who you're try-ing to blackmail yet.'

'Who owns the painting is quite immaterial at present,' Barnabas spat back at him.

'What if it turns out to be the French Government?'

'That, I admit, would be unfortunate but it's a risk we're going to have to take.'

'We?' repeated Napier. 'I'm not part of this tacky little fund-raising venture of yours.'

'You think it won't work?'

'I think it will give you ten years banged up in Wormwood Scrubs; time enough to learn the basic principles of macramé and reflect on a more practical way of earning a living.'

Barnabas had lost the initiative and he knew it. With an almost physical effort of will he fought to bring his temper under control. 'Of course I had to expect this reaction at first,' he said, taking deep breaths. 'It's only natural I suppose. You'll change your mind when you see what it is I've discovered.'

'Don't bank on it, Barnabas.'

'I suggest therefore that we call a temporary halt to the proceedings while you consider my proposal.' Pulling himself to his feet he prepared to leave. He had regained his composure as quickly as he'd lost it and now beamed down at Napier. 'In the meantime I shall fetch the evidence . . .'

'If it exists.'

'Oh, it exists all right,' said Barnabas. 'I must confess that it will take me a little time to lay my hands on it, however. Shall we say a week? I'll return in a week and this time I'll prove to you that the painting is a fake.' He sketched a quick bow and turning about he pushed his way through the crowd to the door and was gone.

Napier poured himself the remains of the bottle. Leaning back with a groan of relaxation, he raised the glass to his lips and let the wine run across his tongue, savouring the warm flavour on his palate.

After a few minutes he stood up and went out into the night.

The street was empty. He glanced at his watch; it was not yet ten, the whole interview had lasted under an hour. He strolled along Pall Mall and would have put the incident out of his mind had Barnabas not been murdered three days later.

Chapter Three

Barnabas was found floating in the harbour at Honfleur.

The morning tide had carried his body in beneath the moored boats where it lay face down amongst the seaweed and flotsam, patiently nudging against the wooden sides of a trawler. The dark mackintosh that he had been wearing at the time of his death held him low in the water so that his outspread limbs scarcely broke the surface. The grey-green water licked over his shoulders and his hair was fanned out around his head, opening and closing in the swell like the fronds of a sea anemone.

It was a cold, damp morning and the body went unnoticed until after nine o'clock when a yachtsman, tying up his dinghy while he waited for the lock-gates to open, spotted it in the water and raised the alarm. The police were summoned, a crowd assembled on the quayside and watched in horrified excitement as a boat-hook was hitched into the collar and the corpse was dragged ashore with water streaming from the sodden clothing. His skin was white and pulpy from the salt, his eyes open and opaque like two sugared almonds.

The post-mortem revealed that Barnabas had been drifting in the sea for over six hours before he was discovered. His lungs were flooded and his body already beginning to bloat on the trapped gases. It was not the sea that had killed him, however, he had already been dead for some time when he was pitched into the harbour. Barnabas had died from a knife wound in the back.

'Death would have been almost instantaneous,' the police pathologist announced, stripping back the white covering and spreading it neatly across Barnabas's legs. 'The blade entered the body between the seventh and eighth rib, close to the spinal column, puncturing the pleural membrane and severing the aorta as it passed.'

'Any sign of a struggle?'

'None. There's some slight bruising along the left leg but it's not relevant to the cause of death.' The pathologist lifted one of Barnabas's arms, spreading out the fingers on the palm of his hand. The nails were long and stained to the clouded yellow of beeswax. 'They haven't been damaged at all,' he told Chief Inspector Chaumière. 'If there had been any sort of a fight you'd expect at least one of them to be broken.' He dropped the arm again and it fell back into place slowly, like a piece of half-thawed meat. The flesh was hard and white and retained the indentations where the pathologist had handled it as though it were made of cold lard.

Chaumière looked down at the body with a mixture of pity and revulsion. Barnabas lay on the aluminium trolley with his eyes closed and his head propped up on a wooden block. The chest had been opened from the pelvis to the base of the throat and the ribcage parted like the belly of a gutted fish. The major organs had been removed and lay to one side, their individual weights chalked up on a blackboard that hung from the wall.

In all the years he'd been in the police force Chaumière had never become accustomed to the mortuary. The stench of formaldehyde, the grim humour of the mortuary assistants, the slap of living flesh on dead turned his stomach.

'Can you give any idea of when he died?' he asked.

The pathologist spread his hands along the trolley, as though it were a shop counter, and gave a nod. 'Possibly,' he said. 'Of course he's been in the water too long to be able to assess anything from his body temperature, but the contents of his stomach have hardly deteriorated. I'd say he'd eaten a meal no more than an hour before he was killed. You can estimate the time of death from that.'

'You can't say exactly when he last ate?'

The pathologist shook his head. 'No, but I can tell you what he had for dinner,' he replied, giving the Inspector a wintery smile. 'It might help you track down the restaurant.'

Chaumière stared at him in horror.

'I'm only joking,' he continued pleasantly. 'But you might find this helpful.' He dug his spider-thin arms under the body and locked them together in a half-Nelson. The mortuary assistant, who had been leaning against the wall, took the legs and together they rolled Barnabas over until he lay face downwards on the aluminium slab.

47

The knife wound was no larger than a button hole in his back. The salt water had swollen the skin, puffing the flesh up into two purple lips.

'He was stabbed from below,' the pathologist explained, prodding his finger into the aperture at an acute angle to simulate the blade.

It took a few moments for Chaumière to grasp the implication of this. 'You mean he was killed by a child?' he asked incredulously.

The idea seemed to amuse the pathologist; he gave a little chuckle. 'What a vivid imagination you have, Inspector,' he murmured. 'No, what I meant was that he was bending over at the time of his death. The killer stabbed him from behind while he was leaning forwards.'

'Was he sitting or standing?'

'I'd say standing.'

Chaumière took his word for it. The man was almost invariably right on these matters; his sense of humour might leave something to be desired but he knew his business well enough. Chaumière watched as the body was thrown over on to its back once more and the limbs arranged alongside. He noticed that beneath his green surgical apron the pathologist was wearing a pair of fiercely checked trousers; he'd probably been on his way out to play golf when he was called to the mortuary. It reminded Chaumière that he was due at lunch with his brother-in-law at twelve-thirty. He glanced up at the clock set in the white-tiled wall; there was no chance of making it on time. His wife would be boiling herself into a fury by now. Never, in all their married life, had she been able to accept the demands of his work, especially when they interfered with the ritual of weekends. The thought of the impending storm drew an involuntary sigh from the Inspector and he framed his mouth around a four-letter word.

The pathologist took it as a rebuke. 'I'm afraid that's all I can give you at present,' he said, peeling off the cellophane gloves.

'I'm sorry,' replied Chaumière. 'It's not that, I was thinking of something else.' He turned to the police sergeant who stood ashen white and rocking on the balls of his feet by the door. 'What do we have on him?' he asked.

The sergeant tore his eyes off the body and swallowed a couple of times in quick succession as he grappled with the question. Chaumière waited patiently while he fumbled with the button of his breast pocket, extracted his notebook and leafed through the pages.

'Charles Barnabas,' he read out. 'He was English, lived in London, presently staying at the Hôtel Delaroche.'

The pathologist threw up his hands. 'Poor man,' he cried, looking down at Barnabas's composed face and shaking his head sadly. 'If he hadn't been murdered he would have died of food poisoning.'

Chaumière ignored him. 'Go on,' he grunted to the sergeant.

'He arrived in Honfleur on Thursday evening, having booked ahead by phone, and was due to leave on the Le Havre–Southampton ferry this morning.'

'Any reason why he was in Honfleur?'

The sergeant shook his head, the answer wasn't written in his book. 'Not that I know of,' he replied, 'but he has been here before – earlier this year he spent four days in the same hotel.'

'Personal belongings?'

'They're upstairs.'

Chaumière glanced around the white sterilised room and went out. Running his hands through the wiry curls of his hair to rid it of the smell of the mortuary, he followed the sergeant to an office on the first floor.

The damp clothing that Barnabas had been wearing was bundled up in a large polythene bag which was now misted with condensation. The contents of his pockets had been transferred into a cardboard box. Chaumière turned them out on to the desk and began sorting through, arranging them into patterns. They were pathetic, useless possessions on the whole: a handful of coins, of both English and French currency, a disposable lighter, several ballpoint pens, a packet of indigestion tablets and a wallet of imitation leather. The only object to catch his attention was a medal.

It was a German Iron Cross, second class.

Chaumière examined it closely, turning it around in the palm of his hand, and then glanced up, a question framed on his face.

'He was a research historian,' the sergeant told him before being asked. 'Specialised in the period of the Second World War.'

Thoughtfully, Chaumière rubbed the enamel surface of the medal with the pad of his thumb and then tossed it back on the desk-top and picked up the wallet. It was cold and clammy like seaweed and peeled open with a lisp of wet leather. There were several bank notes inside, along with the usual collection of receipts, credit cards, laundry slips, business cards and bus passes. One by one Chaumière extracted them and laid them out before him. The bill from a restaurant in Honfleur he set to one side as he did with the stub of a ticket from the Boudin Museum. Written on a sheet of paper that had been torn from a notebook was an address in Shepherd Market, London. The words were smudged from the water but still legible.

'Dr John Napier,' Chaumière read, picking out each letter in turn. Handing the scrap of paper over to the sergeant he said, 'Get on to Scotland Yard, ask them to check it out.'

As Barnabas's body was being dragged from the cold water of Honfleur harbour, Jacqui Fontenay was walking past on her way to work. She saw the crowd pressing around the quayside and felt the current of static electricity that magnetised them.

A police van was parked by the harbour wall, its blue light revolving above their heads, and in the distance the siren of an approaching ambulance was wailing. She paused and asked the man nearest her what was going on but he was too absorbed by the spectacle to reply. At that moment the crowd stirred and gave a gasp, a sudden combined intake of breath that rose above them like a sigh of satisfaction.

Through the jostling figures Jacqui caught a brief glimpse of the dead body as it was rolled on to the shore and lay huddled on the quay in a puddle of water that darkened the dry stone as it spread. The sight of the pathetic bundle of clothing and the excited audience around it sickened her. She turned her head away and hurried on, banishing the memory from her mind.

Skirting the church and the separate stump of the bell-tower, whose clock was laboriously chiming out the first quarter of the hour, she walked down into the Place Hamelin. A group of workmen were sitting outside the café on the corner of the square, tasting the first Calvados of the morning. They grumbled out their appreciation of Jacqui's legs as she passed, grinning and gesturing towards her with outspread hands. She flashed a smile back at them over her shoulder and the burst of cat-calls and lewd suggestions that it provoked followed her up the street.

The Musée Eugène Boudin was closed when she arrived. A handful of early visitors stood around in the forecourt, shuffling their feet in the gravel, waiting for nine-thirty. Seeing her approach, the elderly doorman unlocked one of the glass doors and held it open wide enough for her to slip inside.

Jacqui was the assistant curator of the museum. She was twenty-six and proud of her position, although it hardly taxed her capabilities and left her with a good deal of spare time on her hands. Murmuring good morning to the doorman, and to the lady in the ticket booth who was busy counting out small change for the float, she went upstairs.

The main gallery was deserted and still dark, the gilt-framed paintings blackening the walls like oak panelling. She reviewed each of them as she passed: scenes of Honfleur harbour filled with amber light; fishing boats laying out their nets, heeling and tossing on tortoise-shell seas; views of the Seine estuary with the wind whipping across the water.

Jacqui knew them all, recognised each one like an old acquaintance. She had loved paintings for as long as she could remember, ever since she'd looked at the colour reproductions in her father's books as a child, ever since she'd been on a school outing to the Jeu de Paume and bought a reproduction of *The Bridge at Bougival*. Pictures fascinated her, touched her imagination, filled her with sunlit moods and memories.

Going to her office she began sorting through the day's mail. Amongst the requests for copyright, bills and circulars was a postcard from a member of the museum staff on holiday in Greece, a picture of rocks and ringing blue sea with a short message on the other side. She smiled as she read it and pinned the card on the notice board. Catching her reflection in the mirror, she tossed her head and combed back the shining mane of tawny hair with her fingers.

She had left work early the day before; her guardian had been giving a reception and she'd been needed over at his house to act as hostess. It was a role she often assumed, a part she was expected to play for him. Jacqui was his ambassador as much as his ward.

51

This had been quite an occasion, dinner served in a marquee on the lawn, a small band playing in the background. It had gone on longer than she'd expected. By the time she had turned down an invitation to go on to a nightclub in Trouville, avoided the clumsy passes of an art dealer, driven herself back to Honfleur and crawled into bed, it had been almost three in the morning.

Fortunately this lack of sleep didn't appear to show; her eyes were clear, skin warm in the morning light but there was a dull pain in her temples. She had drunk more than she intended as she listened to anecdotes and gossip, offered introductions, laughed at the right moments, smiling all the while until her jaw ached. She pulled a face in the mirror at the memory and having made herself a cup of coffee she sat down.

There was a knock on the door.

'You wanted to see me?' It was the janitor – long brown overcoat, hands thrust into the pockets, his voice wary.

Jacqui looked up from the desk.

'Yes Jules. You've remembered that the photographers are coming this morning to take pictures of the gallery?'

He blew out his lower lip and shook his head, this was the first he'd heard of it.

'Photographers?' he repeated. 'I don't know anything about no photographers.'

Jacqui smiled with her calm grey eyes. She'd talked to him only the day before, explained what was needed, but Jules often chose to forget what he'd been told.

'It's for the new brochure,' she reminded him. 'You were going to move the drawings cabinet back against the wall to give them room to set up their cameras.'

'The drawings cabinet? That weighs a ton.'

'I'm sure you can manage somehow.'

He sucked in thin cheeks and shook his head once again. The door opened behind him and Chantal arrived. Short spiky hair and heavily made-up eyes, a pink T-shirt stretched tight over a heaving bosom. She was bursting to speak but seeing Jules she contained herself.

'Have you heard the news?' she panted as soon as he'd gone.

Jacqui glanced up at the clock but Chantal ignored the reprimand and hurried on, flushed and excited.

'A man's been murdered, they've just found his body in the harbour.'

'I know,' replied Jacqui.

'But I saw him.'

Getting to her feet Jacqui went over to the filing cabinet and opened the drawer, holding it in place against her hips.

'So did I, but that doesn't mean—'

'You don't understand,' Chantal cut in, the words frothing out of her under the force of enthusiasm. 'I recognised him.'

Jacqui turned around.

'He was here.'

'Are you sure?'

'Didn't you read my message?' Exasperation in her voice now. She pointed to the desk where a patch of yellow paper was stuck to one leaf of the rubber plant.

Jacqui peeled it off and read the scrawled handwriting. A man calling himself Barnabas had called. The note said he'd be returning first thing in the morning.

'When was this?' she asked.

'Just after you'd left,' Chantal explained, delighted to have finally secured Jacqui's full attention. 'He came in here and demanded to see you.'

'Did he mention me by name?'

She nodded, her eyes shining with the intrigue.

'He said he needed to speak to you about the article – the one you wrote in the newspapers.'

Chapter Four

Detective Sergeant Baker didn't stand on ceremony.

'Charles Oliver Barnabas,' he said, holding up his warrant card in the passageway. 'He was an acquaintance of yours, I believe.'

Napier turned the name over in his mind. 'Not that I know of,' he replied.

Baker tucked his card back into his jacket pocket and, producing a small black and white photograph, handed it across to him.

'Oh, Barnabas,' said Napier, grasping the name as he recognised the picture.

'That's what I said, sir.'

'I'm sorry Sergeant, I thought that was his Christian name,' replied Napier, holding the door of his flat open for him. 'Actually, I didn't think it was a name at all.'

Baker digested this information.

He was a quiet, soft-spoken man, with the pleasant authority of a schoolmaster. His hair was thick and unruly, his collar unstarched and the suit that he wore appeared to have been pressed under the mattress.

'I see,' he said, clasping his hands behind his back and looking around Napier's flat with interest, subconsciously assessing income and lifestyle from a habit born out of long experience. 'So I take it that you didn't know the gentleman that well?'

'I only met him once in my life,' replied Napier, sitting down by the open window. He gestured towards the sofa but Baker preferred to stand.

'Only your name and address were found in his wallet at the time of his death,' Baker continued.

Napier looked up sharply. 'He's dead?'

'Murdered, to be more precise.'

The Sergeant observed Napier's reaction. It often taught

him all he needed to know: the slight flush of complicity, the affected disinterest of the guilty, but Napier didn't fall into either of these categories. He seemed surprised but unaffected by the news.

Baker pulled out a notebook and flicked open its cover, pressing his chin into the loose flesh of his neck as he consulted the contents. 'Charles Oliver Barnabas: freelance historian, presently working for Agamemnon Books,' he read. 'He died from a single knife wound in the back and his body was later discovered floating in the harbour of Honfleur. The French police have estimated that he was killed around ten-thirty on the evening of 6th September.' He shut the book again and tucked it away. 'That's the night before last.'

'And you found my name on the body?'

'That's correct, sir. We were wondering if you could clarify how it came to be there.'

Napier stood up and buried his hands deep into his pockets, thinking back to the shadowed room – the jostling figures, the low lights glowing on cellar walls, the smell of stale cigarette smoke in the air and Barnabas watching him across the table, his eyes hard-focused and malignant, the crushed raspberry of his mouth set into its complacent smile.

In a few sentences he outlined the conversation they'd had in the wine bar and the carefully planned proposition that Barnabas had put to him.

Baker listened in silence.

'This painting you mention,' he said when Napier was through, 'what is it exactly?'

Crossing over to the Regency desk Napier drew out a folder. In it was a large coloured photograph of *The Estuary Pilgrim* that Picard had sent him earlier that summer. Baker sat down and examined it thoughtfully, holding the print in solid spatulate fingers.

'Haven't I seen this before?' he asked eventually.

'It's been in the news recently.'

'And Mr Barnabas suggested that it might be a fake.'

'That's right.'

'Is it?' he asked bluntly.

Napier smiled at him; he had been waiting for the question. 'It could be.'

Baker looked up in surprise; it was not the answer he'd expected.

'The possibility has been there ever since the painting was discovered,' Napier continued.

'But I thought you'd proved it was genuine?'

'So did I,' Napier replied. 'But with every painting there is a grey area, a margin of doubt.'

'And that's increased since you heard of Mr Barnabas's death?'

'It does rather strengthen his claim.'

Baker accepted the remark. 'But why do you say that it was always a possibility?'

Getting to his feet, Napier went over to the open window and stared down through the wrought-iron scrolls of the balcony into the street below, his mind racing back to the stuffy basement room in Paris and his first impression of the painting, the sudden shock of its colour in the gloom. He remembered reaching out to touch the canvas, the texture of the paint beneath his fingers, the unexpected translucence of the shadows . . .

He pulled his attention back into the present.

'Let me explain something,' he said, turning into the room and facing the Sergeant. 'It's very hard to fake a painting. Every stage of the technique must be reproduced with meticulous care. The paint must be laid on to the canvas in an identical style to that of the artist you are trying to imitate. When that is done, the surface of the picture must be made to crack and the pigments encouraged to deteriorate, as though the painting were several centuries old.'

'But that can all be done, I imagine.'

'Oh yes,' Napier agreed, 'and has been on several notable occasions. With small additions of some siccative, iron sulphate for example, the pigment can be made to oxidise, then a modicum of cunning with the gas cooker will dry out the paint and help it to crack. But what is much harder is fabricating the provenance of the picture.'

The word was lost on Baker.

'Every picture has a history,' Napier explained. 'They are mentioned in letters and documents; there are records of them at exhibitions and in private collections. This is much harder to forge than the painting itself and usually proves to be the stumbling block for anyone who tries. Most fakes are exposed because they don't have a past – a painting turns up out of the blue but no one has ever heard of it; there is no description of it in the artist's studio; it's never appeared in an inventory or catalogue. It's immediately suspicious.'

'None of which applies to this painting,' said Baker, prodding the photograph of *The Estuary Pilgrim* with his forefinger, 'because its history is already well known.'

'That's right,' Napier agreed. 'Anyone forging *The Estuary Pilgrim* would have no problem with the painting's past, it's documented in a dozen books, including my own. He hasn't even got to worry about the composition of the painting as there are several good black and white photographs to copy.'

A gleam of understanding came into Baker's eye. 'Which makes it an ideal subject for a fake.'

'Practically irresistible, I would have thought.'

'And the French authorities knew this?'

'Certainly, why do you think they were so keen to have it checked out before releasing the news to the press?'

'But couldn't it just be tested in some way?'

'It was,' replied Napier. 'A scrap of paint was carbon-dated and then the canvas analysed with reflectology but the results were hardly conclusive. The trouble is that the picture is only just over a century old and that, in terms of oil-paint, is not even middle-aged. Besides, all those laboratory tests can be deceived; the chemical processes can be anticipated and persuaded to come up with whatever result you want.'

'So what convinced you that it was the real thing?'

'The X-rays,' Napier told him. Jumping to his feet he returned to the desk and picking up the folder he pulled out a sheaf of photographs. These he spread out on the flat surface of the coffee table, assembling them into a rectangle.

Baker sat down on the sofa, spreading his legs wide and resting his elbows on his knees as he studied the composite picture. At first he could see nothing. The photos didn't appear to have been developed properly, they were a smudge of grey without form or shape, clouded in places with black shadows. Fine tendrils of white coiled across the dark surface like trails of cigarette smoke. Gradually, as his eyes adjusted to the subtle tones, he discovered recognisable details, then whole areas and finally a ghostly image of *The Estuary Pilgrim* appeared before him.

Napier knelt down beside the table.

'Oil-paintings react to X-rays in much the same way as

57

our own bodies,' he said, adjusting the set of the pictures with his fingertips. 'Some pigments block the rays, others let them through. The solid white paint is made of lead and this absorbs the rays, rather like a bone, leaving a pale mark on the surface of the picture. The thicker the paint, the whiter it appears to be.'

'So what we're looking at here is really a skeleton of a painting,' said Baker.

'Exactly,' agreed Napier. 'The X-ray has stripped away the surface of the picture and exposed what's going on beneath.' He pointed to the dark silhouette of the quayside. 'Here, for example, there used to be two figures leaning on the parapet. They are quite clear in the X-ray but if you look at the finished picture you'll see they've been painted over. This boat beside them must have been added later, however, because you can still see the horizon of the sea cutting through its sails.'

For the next ten minutes Napier worked his way across the picture, revealing further inconsistencies and alterations, showing how the design of the painting had changed and evolved as work progressed.

Baker had to admit that he was fascinated.

As he followed Napier's directions the dull vapour of the X-ray came alive before his eyes: experiments, new ideas, changes of heart swam up out of the indistinct haze of grey. He began to sense the ingenuity of the artist at work; the frustration, the determination and labour that had gone into the great painting. He'd never realised how much thought and preparation went into a picture. The end result looked so effortless.

'Now if this painting were a copy,' Napier said eventually, sitting back on his heels, 'there wouldn't be any of these alterations. The artist would have traced the finished design straight on to the canvas and never thought about it again.'

Baker nodded thoughtfully. 'So what you're saying is that if it is a fake it's a very good one.'

'Certainly the best I've ever seen.'

An idea came to the policeman. 'You're really a detective, aren't you sir. You examine the clues, assemble the facts and from them you reconstruct the crime.'

'In a way,' Napier agreed.

'And in this case all the evidence suggests that the painting is genuine.'

'That's right,' said Napier. He gazed down at the X-rays and then smiled at Baker, 'And yet I have the strangest feeling that it's not.'

'Not?' Baker echoed. 'I don't follow . . .'

'In formal terms this picture is perfect in every sense, I can't fault it at all but it's not right.' Once again Napier's mind was back in the basement room with its damp odours and clinging atmosphere, his fingers were running across the tooth of the canvas, feeling it, sensing the texture. 'The paint is thinner than it should be. It doesn't have the density of Monet's brushwork, the solidity and determination. It's fine and slightly translucent.' His voice lightened and drifted as he looked away into the distance. 'As though it were not a painting but an illustration of a painting . . .'

'It's no good,' he said, 'it'll have to go.'

'What's the problem?' Jacqui asked.

The photographer turned and stared at her. 'It's the glass on that picture, dearie. The lights are reflecting off the surface.'

'Oh, I see.'

'It's playing havoc with my light readings.'

'In that case I'll have it moved out of the way.' She turned to Jules who was lounging against the wall. It was the fourth time that they had rearranged the pictures in the gallery, the fourth time that the photographer had buried his head beneath the black hood, squinted at the view and emerged again, his tongue clicking, face pinched into an expression of disapproval, demanding new alterations. He was a man in adversity, working under strain.

Jacqui didn't let his agitation infect her. She did as he asked, carried out his instructions but her thoughts were elsewhere. They were of a dead body in the harbour, of a white corpse rolled out on to the quayside, the water soaking into dry stone.

She asked Jules to remove the painting with its flashing glass and found another to hang in its place; the photographer, in his suede jacket and open collar, pivoting and fretting as he watched the change, brittle with impatience.

'How's that?' she asked.

'Better.'

Jacqui's smile was disarming as she excused herself. 'I'll

leave you to get on with your work then. Call me if you need anything further.'

She walked away across the gleaming floor, her cool summer dress moulding around the flow of her body. Pictures on either side of her, gilt frames around fragments of sea and landscape. Jacqui looked at the paintings, at the visitors who stopped to peer at them, but in her mind she saw a man floating in the water, a man called Barnabas who had come to the museum asking to see her and left a message sticking to the leaf of her rubber plant.

Her high-heels tapped on the wooden boards, the sunshine was warm on the flimsy material of her dress. Behind her the voice of the photographer was shrill with authority as he went about his business.

She paused in the passageway between the two main galleries. Set on the wall was a tall exhibition board. It carried an enlarged black and white photograph with printed captions arranged around the perimeter, bold letters on a white ground.

The photograph was of General von Eichendorff's apartments in the Hôtel de Ville. An elegant room, impeccably furnished, two stewards standing to attention by the door and a junior officer sitting at the second, smaller desk. Field telephones and ordered paperwork, bronze table lamps and silver-capped inkstands. An atmosphere of high command.

On the wall above the carved fireplace was the famous collection of paintings. The photo included all twenty-five of the framed canvases and the definition of the plate was so sharp that the details of each one were perfectly clear to the naked eye.

Jacqui inspected the exhibition board thoughtfully. This was where it had started. This was the photograph that had led her to write the article, the photograph that had prompted her to suggest that *The Estuary Pilgrim* might still exist.

She had found it in the museum archives, chanced upon it one day while she was looking through some old catalogues. In Jacqui's opinion the picture was of considerable local interest. She'd showed it to the museum curator and, with his agreement, had it enlarged and set up in the gallery. She wrote the captions, describing the history of each painting, what it represented and where it had come from. Beneath the picture she added a short biography of von Eichendorff, explaining the way in which the famous collection had been put together and how it was destroyed on the morning of 16th May 1944. Further pictures of the General and his staff completed the effect.

Jacqui had put a good deal of thought and care into the layout of the board and the result pleased her.

A few weeks after it was put on view, an art dealer from Geneva had presented himself at her office. He was polite and scrupulously dressed, with a rose-bud in the lapel of his double-breasted suit and spectacles hanging from a gold chain. Bowing stiffly from the waist, he presented Jacqui with his card.

Madame had been deceived, he announced, after first showering her with a confetti of little compliments. The view of *La Ferme Saint Siméon* by Alexander Dubourg, that he had just seen in the photograph upstairs, was not destroyed during the war, as was being suggested. He had it in his gallery back in Switzerland.

Jacqui asked him if he was sure. Could it not be another version of the same subject? The dealer held up a well-manicured hand and stilled her. Madame must forgive him, but that was impossible. There were several subjects on which he was not sure of his facts, but on paintings . . . No, he never made mistakes . . . She must take his word for it. He had a photographic memory, he assured her, and tapped the side of his silver-haired head to show her where he kept it.

He was right.

From Geneva he sent her the catalogue of his summer collection. In it was a colour reproduction of the Dubourg. Jacqui compared it to the painting in her photograph. The two were identical. She was interested; her instincts were aroused. Going to the public records office in Le Havre, she applied to see all documents relating to General von Eichendorff in the period 1943/4. To her surprise this consisted of a thick file of letters, official orders, telegrams and other miscellaneous information. Most of it wasn't relevant to her researches but amongst the sheaf of papers she found a memorandum from von Eichendorff to his aide, dated 9th May 1944, ordering that twenty-five paintings be taken down from his apartments and packaged ready for shipment. Beneath this, written in his own handwriting, was a list of the paintings in question.

It included the little landscape by Alexander Dubourg.

She had a copy made of the document, and various others that caught her attention, and returned to Honfleur. From there she wrote to the town hall at La Roche-Guyon, the D-Day museum at Arromanches and the National Archives in the Hôtel Soubise, Paris. Gradually, during the course of the summer, she built up a dossier on von Eichendorff's collection, but nothing in it could explain why a single painting, that had left Honfleur on the ill-fated convoy, had survived the attack and was now alive and well and living in Geneva.

On a warm Sunday afternoon she drove out to the country and walked along the road between Gaillon and Criquetot until she found the exact site of the ambush. It was on a dusty stretch high above the Seine valley. The road was cut into the ragged slope of the hillside and the metalled surface was scattered with small avalanches of chalk.

Climbing on to a large rock she sat down, hugging her knees as she looked out at the view. It was a beautiful day, fresh and breezy, with newly laundered clouds tumbling through a summer sky. Below her, the river curved away into the distance, winking back the sunlight, and she could make out the long vertebrae of barges patiently working their way upstream.

It was here that fifteen men had died, here that the picture had been burned, but it was warm and peaceful and if the ghosts of the past still haunted the place she didn't sense them that day.

A local farmer, passing on a tractor, helped her to find the information she needed. He was too young to remember much about the war himself but his uncle had been in the Resistance. Taking Jacqui to a café in the nearby village he summoned the older generation of his relations and explained what it was she wanted. They sat her down at a table in the square, with the church before her and the shade of the pollarded trees cool on her skin. Others soon wanted to join in the debate; this striking girl with her curious mission and long legs was an interesting diversion from the dull routine of Sunday afternoon. Chairs were drawn up around the table, cigarettes rolled, glasses of Calvados ordered and the inquiry became a major council meeting.

The uncle said he knew of the ambush . . . Hadn't old Pierre Chazal been part of it? . . . No, he was dead now, but his cousin would know who else had been there that day.

The cousin was sent for, more drinks were ordered in the meantime and memories of the war brought out of retirement. Jacqui was shown a battered cigarette lighter. An American GI had given it to him on Liberation Day, the owner told her proudly as he tucked it back in his pocket. That was nothing, said another, Yvette Marchon was given a baby that day, and what's more she was paid to accept it. Toothless gums grinned, tanned leather faces creased into wrinkles and a cackle of laughter ran round the table. The patron came out to see what the excitement was. They told him to leave the bottle and go away.

The cousin arrived from his afternoon siesta. Yes, he remembered the day of the attack... No, most of them were gone now. But there was Père Bouvier, he'd been part of that group.

That's right, agreed the uncle, and he was living with his grand-daughter over at Epreville; they'd had a Christmas card from the family only last year.

The following weekend Jacqui visited the old man at his home.

Paul Bouvier had been put out in the garden for the morning. He was over ninety and as fragile as china. With a childlike expression of curiosity on his face he sat in the shade of an apple tree, neither asleep nor awake but hovering on the threshold of both. At times he seemed to be dozing: the tufts of his eyebrows dropped and the shoulders slumped, but then the large, crab-like hands would twitch, his head give a slight upwards jerk and he was back in the present once more.

The grand-daughter led Jacqui across the lawn to him. She treated the old man with a brusque affection; as far as she was concerned he was part of the household chores, another problem in her life. She plumped up the cushions behind his back, retrieved the packet of cigarettes that had fallen to the ground and put it on his lap. With that she left them together.

The old man's memory was vague. He spoke of the war with a quiet sadness, holding Jacqui's hand as he talked.

'There were reprisals,' he said. 'Always there were reprisals. We didn't think of them then, the fighting was all that mattered. We told ourselves that we were helping to win the war, that there were bound to be casualties ... but I think of them now. Nothing else is important any longer, you see.'

He looked at her with eyes that had grown gentle with age. 'All the rest is forgotten, now . . . It's all for nothing. Do you have a boyfriend?' he asked suddenly, and then smiled when Jacqui shook her head, embarrassed by the question. 'You should,' he said, 'you're so lovely . . . golden like summer.' The words seemed to stir the surface of his memory. 'It was summer then,' he said, 'at Criquetot.'

Jacqui leaned forwards, her voice soft as the coming of evening. 'Do you remember it?'

The old man nodded, gazing back into the past. 'Yes,' he murmured, 'I remember – it was the Maquis, not us. They'd ambushed a convoy on the high road above the valley. It was a terrible sight: lorries overturned and burning, dead men lying on the roadside.' He shook his head in wonder. 'You shouldn't think of these things, better to let them be forgotten.'

'Was everything in the convoy burnt?' Jacqui prompted gently.

'No, the charges had gone off late.' The frame of the image was steady in his mind now and he spoke with greater confidence. 'The two front lorries were ahead of the explosion. The Maquis had killed the drivers but the vehicles were undamaged.'

'Did anyone look inside them?'

'Of course,' he replied with a little shrug of his shoulders. 'We always took what we could find. It wasn't much in this case, just wooden crates and some old sticks of furniture. There were several boxes of papers, I remember, and two or three metal canisters.'

Jacqui's heart leapt. 'Canisters?'

'Large round tubes.'

'Do you know what was in them?' she asked.

'I've no idea. The Chazal brothers took them off, they thought they must be some new weapon, a mortar maybe.' He smiled to himself. 'One of them was enormous, as large as a telegraph pole. It needed both of them just to pull the thing out of the lorry.'

'Where did they take it?'

The old man shook his head once more; he was growing tired, his memory drifted and lost its focus. He didn't know what became of the canisters, he mumbled, looking down at his hands. The eyelids fluttered; past and present merged once more. He never saw them again . . . It was a long time ago . . . They were taken away.

Getting to her feet Jacqui leaned over and kissed his white stubbled cheek. She thanked him for his patience, promised to see him again soon and left him dozing in the shade.

Over the next two days she wrote an article for the *Normande Soir*. In it she laid out her researches. She described the paintings hanging in the General's apartment and how he had ordered them to be taken back to Germany. She described the ambush on the high road above Criquetot and the late detonation of the mines, how two lorries had escaped the fire that gutted the rest of the convoy and been looted by the Resistance fighters. In conclusion, she suggested that the large canister, that Paul Bouvier had seen carried away after the attack, contained the rolled up canvas of *The Estuary Pilgrim*.

Six months later, when the painting was discovered on a demolition site nearby, her theory was proved correct and Jacqui became a minor celebrity. Her article was reprinted in several papers around the world, extracts from it appeared in *The Burlington Magazine* and *Apollo*. The Ministre de la Culture invited her to the picture's opening night at the Grand Palais. She was interviewed by a couple of society magazines and, to her intense private satisfaction, her face appeared on the cover of *Elle*.

And now this man Charles Barnabas had come to her office wanting to talk of her article and his death preyed on her mind. But there was nothing to connect the two, no reason to assume a link between his visit and his death and as Jacqui walked back across the gallery, back to the impatience of the photographer and the sound of his voice raised in exasperation, she dismissed the doubts that had gathered in her mind.

'What was he like?'

'Who Barnabas?'

Margot Latchman nodded.

'The word that springs to mind is venomous,' Napier told her.

'I am glad,' she murmured, breathing out a trail of cigarette smoke that matched her blue eyes. 'It's so tiresome when people turn out to be nicer than you'd expected. They should have the good grace to remain ugly and unpleasant and not try to improve with acquaintance; it's really too hard to cope with.' Reaching out her hand she drew a flower from the decoration on the table; it was a single Canterbury bell with a head of wedding ribbon whiteness, and her eyes smiled beguilingly above it as she touched it to her nose.

Lunch at Green's was drawing to a close: the bustle had left the room, tables had been cleared and relaid with fresh damask and the afternoon light was bowling in through the plate-glass window.

Margot had hardly eaten. Pleading a diet, she had ordered six oysters and then toyed with a salad of frilly green lettuce. Nevertheless she'd helped to sink a bottle of champagne, followed it with a glass of brandy and as the meal progressed her conversation had grown drowsy with gossip and flirtation.

'Who do you think killed him?' she asked, slipping the flower back into its vase.

Napier shrugged.

'Maurice Lebas?' she inquired softly, reducing the name to a purr in her throat.

'He certainly wouldn't welcome any suggestion that the picture was a fake, but I can't believe he'd resort to murder.'

'Well someone did, duckie. Your friend Barnabas didn't just reverse into that knife by mistake.'

'Well that's true, but Lebas doesn't even know whether he owns the picture yet.'

'He certainly thinks he does, which comes to much the same thing.' Margot hunched her shoulders and stuck out her lower lip. ' "That picture belongs to me, Dr Napier," ' she mimicked. ' "It is ridiculous for anyone to contest it" – Christ, he was like a hen who's had its first egg stolen.'

'What do you know about him?'

Margot's eyes hooded. 'You want me to divulge trade secrets?' she murmured.

'Of course.'

She thought for a moment. 'Unfortunately I don't know anything particularly revealing,' she confessed. 'He's not on my pitch.' Reaching forward she stubbed out her cigarette and the gold bracelets jangled around her wrist. 'Besides, it's all very dull and industrial.'

'Not your brand of dirt.'

'Not really,' she agreed dryly. 'About twenty years ago Lebas inherited the family shipping business in Le Havre: freight liners, grubby little tugs, that sort of thing.' She spread her hands in horror at the thought of this legacy of grease and rust. 'It wasn't making the level of profit that he had in mind so he expanded into the construction business and now builds supermarkets, concrete car parks and motorways all over northern France. It's quite an empire he's set up for himself.'

'Is he influential?'

'Enormously.'

'So if Barnabas had proved to be a thorn in his side you think that he would have had no difficulty in having him removed?'

Margot looked him over with cool appraising eyes. 'None.'

'Where is he at present.'

'He's still here in London, holed up in the Ritz along with his private army of chauffeurs and bodyguards.'

Napier shook his head. 'I just can't believe it, Margot. Lebas might look like the classroom bully but hardly like a murderer.'

The fine pencilled eyebrows were raised. 'Appearances can be deceptive, John,' she growled and pointed across the restaurant. 'Take him for example.'

Her painted finger was aimed towards an alcove in the far corner of the room. Beneath the discreetly lit print by 'Spy' sat a man in his early fifties, sleekly dressed in a lightweight suit. His chair was drawn back from the table, his legs were crossed and there was an even inch of ash on the tip of his cigar. Across the table was an attractive girl, drinking Perrier water, who listened to him speak with rapt attention.

'What would you say he was?'

'He looks like a commodity broker,' Napier replied, turning back to face Margot, 'but I've no doubt that you're going to tell me that he's a white slave trader.'

'Close,' she acknowledged. 'Enrique de la Pena. He's a dealer in illegal arms, working out of South America. Also reputed to traffic in drugs and anything else that catches his fancy, but you'd never guess it to look at him.' She smiled seductively. 'It's the same with Lebas; I don't think you can judge him by appearances. He had the power and the motive to kill Barnabas; I'd say he did it.'

'But then you always see the best in people, don't you, Margot.'

'Don't be cheeky, darling.' She leaned back and stretched one arm along the back of her chair. As usual she was dressed in pale lavender, the colour of morning mist, and the flimsy material of the frock clung to her like woodsmoke. Napier had no idea how old she was; as with oriental porcelain it was impossible to date Margot accurately to within twenty years. She could be thirty-five and slightly ravaged by experience or a well-preserved fifty.

'Do you mind if I use this story?' she asked.

'You're not going to suggest that Lebas murdered Barnabas, are you?'

Her eyes widened. 'Heavens no,' she cried indignantly. 'I'm going to suggest that he faked the painting, planted it on that building site and then had Barnabas killed when he tried to blackmail him.'

'You do, Margot, and we'll all end up with a knife in our back.'

'I won't go so far as to accuse him of it,' she drawled, her eyes lazy with speculation. 'I'll just plant some innuendoes in the readers' minds and see what they grow into.'

'You realise that you've absolutely no evidence.'

'I know,' she agreed, 'but there is a delicious aroma of foul-play about this story that isn't to be missed. That's what I love about you, John, you're always involved with the most unsavoury characters.' She glanced across at him. 'Any objections?'

'None,' replied Napier. 'I was going to pay for lunch but if you're going to risk our necks I'll leave it to you; you can charge it up to expenses.'

'In that case I'll have another drink,' she said, turning and catching the waiter's attention. 'One should always be tight at three o'clock, it's such a pointless hour of the day.' She looked back at Napier. 'You'd better have a glass of water if you're feeling faint.'

Napier didn't rise to the bait.

He waited until the balloon of Cognac had arrived before asking, 'Have you heard of Agamemnon Books?'

'Should I have?'

'Not necessarily. I just wondered, since Barnabas was working for them when he went over to France.'

Margot said, 'Ah,' and lifted the brandy to her lips, her
eyes suddenly magnified in the lens of the glass. 'Yes,' she
said, 'I've come across Agamemnon. They're a packaging
company up near Covent Garden, specialise in those big,
glossy books you see at cut-price on railway stations: *The
Anorexic Cookbook*, *How to Enjoy Life with a Broken Back* –
that kind of thing. I reviewed a biography of Bonnie Prince
Charlie for them last year.'

'Any good?'

'Dozens of illustrations; dreadful text.' She pulled a face.
'Ethnic metaphors, split infinitives, transitive verbs sponsored
by London Transport, you know the type.'

'Yes,' said Napier sadly, 'I think I do.'

Margot finished her Cognac and they went out into the
sedate congestion of Duke Street. Spotting a taxi pulling
out of the Cavendish Hotel she flagged it down and left in a
flutter of lavender skirts and parting kisses, promising to see
him soon.

Napier walked up into Piccadilly and looked into the
window of Hatchards. Then, on impulse, he headed on
towards Covent Garden.

It took him some time to find Agamemnon Books.

The publishing house was situated on a landing between the
second and third floor of a tall brick building in Long Acre.
The only indication of its existence in the street was a brass
plaque screwed to the doorpost beneath an entryphone.

The editor was solicitous. He introduced himself as James
Wilmott and answered Napier's questions with a quiet reserve.

'Charles Barnabas,' he said, 'yes, of course. He worked
for us on several occasions.'

'Doing what, exactly?'

'Picture research on the whole.'

As he spoke he led Napier back into a small private office. It
was lined with bookshelves that landslided in towards a central
desk piled high with letters, bills and unread documents. A
small casement window looked down over the untidy clutter
of backyards and a coffee percolator perched on the sill, surrounded by mugs and cartons of milk.

Wilmott waved Napier towards a chair and began rummaging through the shelves above his head.

'We were very sorry to hear about Mr Barnabas's accident,' he said over his shoulder. 'A terrible business.'

Napier made small sounds of agreement. 'What was he working on at the time?' he asked.

'He was collecting pictures for a new book we're doing on the D-Day invasion,' Wilmott replied in a distracted voice. 'I was trying to find it but it seems to have evaporated.' He returned to his desk and began shuffling through the heaps of paper, taking care not to disturb the delicate equilibrium of each pyramid. 'Ah, here it is,' he announced, drawing out a large book from its hiding place and handing it across to Napier.

The cover showed a stylised map of the northern coast of France. The area of land was black, marked with a swastika and divided the page diagonally. Large arrows, formed from a combination of the Stars and Stripes and the Union Jack, thrust in from the English Channel. The design was a simple and graphic image of the D-Day invasion.

Napier opened the book but the pages were blank.

'That's just a dummy we ran up for the Frankfurt Book Fair,' Wilmott told him, sitting down behind the ramparts of correspondence.

'But aren't there a hundred books on this subject already?'

'Oh yes,' Wilmott agreed, 'but there's always room for another, that's the beauty of the subject. It must have one or two new documentary pictures to distinguish it from the others, of course, but apart from that the market is inexhaustible.'

'And that's what Barnabas was doing for you?'

Wilmott nodded. 'He was going through the public records in Normandy, looking for any previously unpublished photographs we could use as illustrations.'

'I see,' said Napier, laying the book back on the desk. 'Why did he choose Honfleur in particular?'

'I've no idea,' replied Wilmott. Swivelling round in his chair he pulled out a file from the shelf behind him. 'I hadn't actually seen him since he went over to France earlier this year. He was not the most forthcoming of men, never came in here, for example, unless he had to. But I think he must have been on to something – he rang in July asking me to check a name for him.' Wilmott thumbed his way through the file and extracted a scrap of paper. 'He wanted information on a

German officer serving in Normandy during the latter stages of the war.'

'What name?'

'Schwartz – Dietrich Schwartz.' He passed the note over to Napier.

'Did you find anything?'

Wilmott nodded. 'We have a rather useful contact in Berlin who does some freelance work for us.' He picked up a flimsy telex sheet. 'Dietrich Schwartz signed into the German Wehrmacht in 1937, rose to the rank of major in the 21st Panzer Division and was, for a short time, the adjutant to General von Eichendorff.'

Napier looked at him in wonder. 'Does it say what became of him?' he asked softly.

Wilmott returned to the sheet. 'Yes. Schwartz was shot for desertion in May 1944. He's buried in Honfleur.'

Chapter Five

Edward Roland Spooner didn't have an appointment.

The oversight distressed him. It was inefficient and un-businesslike and what was worse it introduced an element of chance into the otherwise ordered routine of his day. And so it was with an air of fatalism that he pushed the doorbell of Napier's flat.

As he'd expected, there was no reply.

He waited for exactly one minute and then tried once more. Again nothing.

Spooner didn't allow this failure to interfere with his plans. Rising on to the tips of his toes he swivelled around and scanned the terrain of the street through his spectacles. The café on the corner of Shepherd Market had tables laid out on the pavement. Skimming across the road he selected one with a commanding view of Napier's front door and sat down, settling his briefcase on the ground beside him. He then ordered a pot of tea and a slice of fruit cake. The proprietor brought the first and flatly denied the existence of the other.

As soon as the tea was finished he planted the tip of his umbrella between his feet, folded his hands across the curved bamboo of the handle and waited. No one noticed him sitting at the table. Spooner was not a man to catch the eye. In his black coat, striped trousers and bowler hat he was like a thousand other office-bound employees who file on to the tube each morning on their way up to the City. The one striking feature was his solemnity. It was a solid, palpable presence, as real as the glass case around the exposed works of a bell clock.

Some of the junior executives in the firm made fun of this gravity. They mimicked his slow, deliberate speech, encouraged the secretaries to titter at him behind his back, referred to him as 'the undertaker'. Spooner ignored their clumsy humour, never allowed it to interfere with his work.

He was good at his job and that was all he cared about. Where others failed he got results. In his bare furnished office high on the twenty-first floor of the silver-sheathed building, surrounded by computer consoles and the ranks of filing cabinets, with his back to the large plate windows that looked over the smoky silhouette of Tower Bridge, he worked his way through the close-printed figures of account books, statements and insurance claims. Searching for inconsistencies, for weak links and flaws in dating, for explanations that didn't ring true.

The petty claims on property and household possessions didn't concern Spooner, these he passed on to the appropriate departments. It was the rare cases that interested him – the taxation frauds, the embezzlement of corporate funds, the computer swindles. It was in the labyrinthine coils of City finance that he tracked his prey – the manipulators, the high fliers – through the columns of computer read-outs, the ambiguities of the system, the grey areas of the law.

Spooner had a nose for fraud. Just as some men can scent danger or the presence of rain in the air, he could scent deceit, the intent to defraud, in the forms before him. It was a talent, a gift he had been born with. When his colleagues asked for the secret he would avert his eyes, look down at his feet and tell them, 'Printed reports are like the faces on a train, most of them you forget immediately they've gone. They make no impression, leave no mark. But occasionally one stands out from the others. You remember it, for no particularly good reason. It stays with you, nags at your mind. That's where I begin.'

His investigations were meticulous and often painstakingly slow. The fastidious mind that insisted that pencils and notepads were arranged in geometric patterns on the desktop, that obliged him to order the same lunch every day and sit in one particular compartment of the commuter train to Woking each evening, enabled Spooner to strip down a financial report with the skill of a craftsman. To test each statement, examine each figure and entry without ever tiring or losing interest and then to go back and begin all over again if he hadn't discovered the error, the weakness he was searching for, to put his finger on the mistake he needed to break the case.

Spooner enjoyed his work. It gave him a satisfaction that no entertainment or vice could compete with and consequently his career was his life, his single consuming passion.

After an hour, sitting stiff as a tailor's dummy outside the café, Spooner's patience was rewarded. A taxi drew up against the building opposite and Napier stepped out on to the pavement.

Spooner recognised him immediately. John Napier was something of a celebrity. He appeared on television, in documentaries and chat-shows, talking about the arts in his soft, educated voice.

Jumping to his feet he hurried across the road, paused as Napier was unlocking the door and gave a little cough to register his presence.

'Dr Napier?' he queried, and as the other turned he pivoted on the balls of his feet, thrust out his hand and said, 'Spooner.'

Napier glanced across the street. 'You've been waiting for me?'

'Only a few minutes,' he lied in the interests of good manners. 'I was hoping to have a word with you.'

Napier led the way upstairs, waited until Spooner had taken a seat, removed his hat and straightened the creases of his trousers before asking, 'And how can I help you?'

'The Monet on loan to the National Gallery,' replied Spooner, coming straight to the point. 'I believe that you suggested to the police that it might be a fake.'

'I told them that they shouldn't rule out the possibility.'

'And then in the morning papers I discovered this article.' He clicked open his briefcase and drew out a page from the *Daily Express*. Margot Latchman's column was outlined in red ink. 'You've read it no doubt?'

Napier nodded.

'It accuses Lebas of killing Charles Barnabas.'

'It doesn't actually accuse him of it,' Napier replied, with a vague sense of loyalty. 'It just happens to place his name nearest to the accusation.'

Spooner looked less than convinced. 'Is there any truth in it, do you think?'

'There may be, but then it's never wise to believe everything you read in the papers,' Napier told him. 'You must remember

74

that Margot's a creative journalist: what she doesn't know she creates.'

'She's created quite a scandal in this case.'

'I'm certain she intended to.'

'Of course, only one issue of any importance emerges from the whole affair,' Spooner continued, slipping the article back into his briefcase, 'and that is whether *The Estuary Pilgrim* is a fake or not. The rest is mere speculation.'

'Why should all this concern you?' Napier asked.

'I represent Wallace-Jones,' Spooner replied primly. 'We're a firm of accountancy consultants, financial loss-adjusters you might say.'

'For Lloyds?'

'Amongst others.'

'Who are already anticipating the massive scale of the insurance claim if the painting turns out to be a fake.'

Spooner inclined his head a few degrees to indicate that this deduction was a near-miss. 'Something like that,' he allowed. 'Let me explain the situation to you.' He wriggled on his seat, crossed one leg over the other and arranged his hands neatly on his lap. Napier noticed that his movements were quick and precise as those of a small rodent. 'In the last two years a number of potential forgeries have come to our attention,' he continued. 'They have all been well researched and impeccably constructed, anticipating all the tests to which they might be subjected; in fact they're so good that we have no firm evidence that they are forgeries in the first place.'

'How very frustrating for you. And now you're scared that *The Estuary Pilgrim* might turn out to be the latest in this line of latter-day masterpieces.'

'Quite so,' Spooner agreed. 'In which case it is considerably more ambitious than anything we've seen before. The other pictures that were brought to us were valued between ten and a hundred thousand dollars. *The Estuary Pilgrim* is presently insured for ten million while it's here in London, and Sotheby's have already suggested this estimate should be raised.'

'You think your forger is becoming more confident?'

Spooner nodded and behind his composed, serious expression Napier detected a twinkle of excitement. 'More confident and more ingenious, Dr Napier,' he announced. 'But this time we have a lead on him.'

75

'You mean Barnabas?'

'Charles Barnabas,' he repeated in reverence. 'He was convinced *The Estuary Pilgrim* was a fake and died, it seems, trying to prove it. The interesting thing is, Dr Napier, that Mr Barnabas was not an art historian. He knew nothing about paintings and yet he was so sure of his facts that he was prepared to blackmail you over it.'

'How does that help your investigation?'

Spooner leaned forward and his voice lowered with the close proximity. 'Charles Barnabas was only in Honfleur for a few days, but in that short space of time he must have heard something, or seen something, that proved beyond question that *The Estuary Pilgrim* was a forgery.' The ghost of a smile flitted across his face. 'I would have thought that our next course of action was clear.'

Napier looked at Spooner in astonishment. He could see exactly where the little man was leading him. 'You're not suggesting that I go over to Honfleur to search for it, are you?'

'That's precisely what I'm suggesting,' replied Spooner. 'Naturally I'll come with you.'

Napier thought back to his brief meeting with Barnabas, trying to draw the thread of their conversation up from his memory. 'As far as I can remember, Barnabas said that the chances of anyone else finding his evidence were a million to one against.'

'He found it in Honfleur, that much is clear,' said Spooner quietly. 'We know which hotel he was staying in at the time, what he was doing there, even some of the restaurants he visited. I'd say that improves the odds.'

Napier had to admit he was intrigued. 'So you think that if we went over to France and reconstructed Barnabas's movements we might stumble across the same information?'

'It's a long shot, I grant you, but I feel it's worth a try.'

'Aren't you forgetting what happened to Barnabas when he tried?' asked Napier. 'I don't mind going over to Honfleur for the weekend but I've no particular desire to end up floating in the harbour.'

'That's why we must go together,' replied Spooner solemnly.

Napier held his gaze for a moment. 'It sounds like a hair-brained scheme to me,' he said eventually.

'But you'll consider it?'

Napier nodded.

Immediately Spooner was on his feet and holding out his hand. 'Good,' he murmured. Opening his briefcase he flicked out a card and handed it to him. 'Here's my number,' he announced. 'Give me a ring when you've reached a decision.'

Jacqui Fontenay also read Margot's article.

Holding the little cutting in both hands, her elbows resting on the desk-top, she went through it in silence.

'Where did you find this?' she asked Chief Inspector Chaumière when she had finished.

'It was printed in an English newspaper this morning,' he replied.

'How very observant of you to have noticed it.'

Chaumière waved the compliment aside. 'I didn't,' he admitted with a shy smile. 'Scotland Yard rang me and suggested I look out for it.'

Jacqui dropped the slip of paper on to the desk and sat back brushing the thick wave of hair from her eyes. Her white shirt opened slightly with the movement and Chaumière caught sight of a locket gleaming in the darkness of her cleavage.

He had often seen Jacqui around Honfleur but never had reason to speak to her before. She was a handsome girl, well groomed and expensively dressed, but what impressed him most that afternoon was the elegance of her bearing. There was a quality of stillness about her that made Chaumière feel clumsy and dull by comparison.

Jacqui seemed to sense his discomfort and smiled at him with her clear agate eyes.

'What do you make of it?' he asked, nodding towards the article.

'I think the heading is more interesting than the contents,' she replied. 'It comes from a gossip column, Inspector. The lady who wrote this is not interested in the painting, she's just stirring up a bit of scandal to sell newspapers.'

'Yes, but what if there is some foundation to her allegations?'

'You're not going to take it seriously?'

Chaumière shrugged slowly and luxuriantly. 'If the painting turns out to be a fake . . .'

'It's not.'

'What makes you so sure?'

Jacqui ran her fingers along the column of text. 'This whole article is hearsay. It's based on the evidence of one art historian,' she said. 'And you'll notice that he's not even mentioned by name.'

'It's the chap who authenticated it in the first place.'

Jacqui's eyes clouded. 'John Napier?'

'You know him?'

'I've read one of his books,' she murmured with a frown.

The name lingered with her after Chaumière had left, tugging at her mind, distracting her from the day's business.

That evening, on returning to her apartment, she pulled out a heavy volume on Monet, cradling it in her arms. She flipped open the cover and there on the front page, beneath the title, was the name John Napier.

This was the first art book she'd ever owned and still the most treasured of her collection. Her parents, keen to encourage Jacqui's awakening sensuality in the arts, had given it to her on her sixteenth birthday and she'd studied it fervently, examining the pictures, absorbing the text with teenage intensity. Now she felt only disappointment that this book, that she had admired so much and referred to so often, could have been written by the same person who was involved in some shabby publicity stunt.

Taking it over to the table, Jacqui began reading through the author's biography on the flyleaf. It didn't tell her much, just an outline of Napier's academic training, an indication of his background. There was no photograph, nothing to help visualise the man.

On the opposite page was an inscription from her parents, words that she had taken for granted at the time but which were so precious to her now. Smoothing down the page she touched the dried ink, feeling the faint ridge of lettering beneath her fingers, as though this minute contact would bring the memory of them closer.

Hearing her return, Pacquetta had put down her work and come to the kitchen door, wiping her broad red hands on a dishcloth.

'The police were looking for you,' she said gruffly.

'I know,' said Jacqui, 'they found me.' She glanced up to see Pacquetta staring at her suspiciously. 'It's all right,' she added, 'I'm not going to prison.'

Pacquetta gave a grunt of acknowledgement and tossed the cloth down on the work-top. 'Are you going out tonight?' she asked, but Jacqui was immersed in the book and didn't reply.

She repeated the question.

'I might go riding later on,' Jacqui mumbled.

'How much later on?'

'Please Kettie, don't bother me, I'm trying to read.'

Walking across the room, Pacquetta peered over Jacqui's shoulder at the opened book. 'If you ask me you spend too much time reading, my girl,' she said darkly. 'You should be going out, meeting people, not sitting in here reading books.'

'I've been out every night for the last two weeks,' Jacqui reminded her but Pacquetta ignored the statistic.

'Reading is all very well. I'm certain it makes you all very clever but it won't find you a husband,' she announced triumphantly.

Jacqui smiled and closing the book she returned it to the shelf. Pacquetta's ambitions for her were predictable and pleasantly uncomplicated.

She was the one constant in Jacqui's life. Solid, dependable and warm-hearted. Good-natured and unimaginative. Slow to take offence and suspicious of change but always there when she was needed.

Pacquetta had arrived when she was just over a year old, too young to remember. She had been her nanny throughout childhood, scolding and encouraging her, rough and affectionate at the same time. After the death of her parents, Jacqui had returned to Honfleur and Pacquetta had followed. She had never questioned this decision and Pacquetta had never offered an explanation. It was a tacit agreement, a pact between them.

Leaning over, Jacqui kissed her lightly on the forehead. 'What nonsense you talk sometimes,' she said, walking away towards the bedroom, unbuttoning her shirt as she went. Stripping off her clothes, she showered and then wrapped herself in a dressing gown of rough white towelling that reached down to her ankles.

'Did the Inspector come here himself?' she asked, sitting down at the dressing table.

'No further than the door,' Pacquetta replied. 'I wasn't having him inside.'

Jacqui inclined her head as she fitted a pearl on to one ear. 'I thought he was rather sweet,' she said. 'All the time he was talking to me he kept fiddling with his tie and blushing like a nervous schoolboy.'

Pacquetta came over and stood behind her. Taking a hairbrush she ran it through Jacqui's hair, drawing her head back like a bow. It was a ritual, a gesture that had lingered from childhood. Slowly and methodically she worked, until the golden mane was polished and glowing and crackling with electricity.

'What did he want of you?' she asked after a few minutes.

'He showed me a newspaper article – about the man who was found in the harbour.'

Pacquetta hesitated, the brush poised in her hand. 'Don't get involved in that business, my love,' she said quietly.

'Why not?' Jacqui asked, twisting round on the stool.

'Best to leave those things to the police.'

'What makes you say that, Kettie?'

'No reason in particular.'

'Have you heard something?'

'Just rumours.'

Jacqui turned back to the mirror and looked up at Pacquetta's reflection. She smiled wickedly. 'You're always hearing rumours. I think you start them up yourself,' she said, but the eyes that met hers in the glass were dark and troubled.

They were waiting for him when he returned to his flat.

Napier put his key to the lock but the door was already open and swung back on its hinges. At first he thought he'd been burgled but the furniture was undisturbed. The curtains were drawn, the room was dark and a man leaned against the fireplace.

There was a lazy confidence in the way he stood with his head cocked to one side and his hands buried in the pockets of his denim jacket.

'How did you get in here?' Napier asked inconsequentially, and as he spoke the door closed. Glancing around he saw another figure, taller and younger, take up position behind him.

'You've been interfering with matters that don't concern you,' said the first of the intruders.

'But they do concern you, is that it?' replied Napier, realising at the same moment that the remark was unnecessarily provocative.

The man smiled briefly at this return, his small eyes disappearing into soft pouches. 'Leave it alone,' he ordered.

'You're referring to *The Estuary Pilgrim*, I take it.'

The intruder didn't seem to like this specific reference. Levering himself away from the mantelpiece he stood with legs straddled and jacket parted, his belly pressing out against a white T-shirt. 'The property you mention doesn't belong to you.'

'You've been sent here by Maurice Lebas.'

The statement was ignored.

'You will forget about it, Dr Napier,' he said. 'This is just a warning, of course, but I recommend you take it.'

'And if I don't?'

The signal was imperceptible, a slight movement of the head.

The younger of the two picked up a bronze statuette from the desk and brought it down on the back of Napier's neck.

The blow came without warning. Napier was given no time to react. All he saw was a flicker of movement behind him and then the room burst open before his eyes, the shadows exploded into light and he fell forwards without feeling the ground that came up to hit him.

When he came round the two intruders had left.

For a few moments he lay quite still. There was no pain, only a pleasant sensation of floating.

Slowly and peacefully he bubbled up towards consciousness. Opening his eyes he looked up at the shadowed ceiling. It was a pool of warm darkness. Gradually the details focused and became recognisable, realisation flooded back to him and with it came the pain, a sharp insistent ache that throbbed in his head like a heartbeat. His body gave a groan; he rolled over and then sat up, nursing the back of his neck with his hand.

Getting to his feet he stumbled into the bathroom and put his head under the tap. The shock of the cold water cleared his mind and the conversation with the two intruders returned to him piece by piece, each sequence in reverse like a film being wound back on the spool.

He looked up at the mirror and as he stared at his reflection he felt a sudden surge of anger. It spread through his veins like an electric charge, tensing his muscles, sweeping aside all other considerations. Taking a towel he went next door and sat down at his desk. He picked up the card on his blotter and dialled the number, drying his hair as he did so. There was a click at the other end and the line came alive. Napier quoted an extension number and waited for the connection to be made.

'Wallace-Jones,' said a cautious voice. 'Can I help you?'

'Is that Mr Spooner?'

'Speaking.'

'Pack your toothbrush, Spooner, we're going to France.'

Chapter Six

The Hôtel Delaroche was a large family house that had fallen on hard times. It stood on the crest of the hill above Honfleur at the point where the town dissolved into orchards and wooded lanes. The gates were rusted open but the high stone wall that enclosed the grounds lent the place a forbidding air of privacy.

Napier and Spooner arrived by taxi.

They had taken the night ferry over from Southampton and then completed the journey by train, stopping at every station along the line. Napier had wanted to take his car but Spooner wouldn't hear of it. 'Barnabas travelled to Honfleur on public transport,' he had reminded him, 'and we must do the same.'

The taxi crunched to a halt in front of the hotel entrance. Napier climbed out and, leaving Spooner to pay the driver, he walked up the flight of steps. There was nothing to indicate that this was a hotel, no sign above the porch or credit cards advertised on the glass panels of the door.

The hall was empty. It was high ceilinged and silent. An ornate staircase tumbled around two sides of the room and flowed out into a floor of worn marble. The walls were painted with pale decorations that had faded in the sunlight and the air was heavy with the sweet musk of decayed stone.

In the shadows of the staircase was a young man. He was formally dressed in a black bow tie and low-cut waistcoat that framed his white shirt. Poised and balanced, he stood with one hand on his hip like a figure from a drawing by Erte. A cigarette was held vertically between two fingers and the thin blade of its smoke sped upwards to cut fine trails against the darkness.

Napier paused in the doorway and looked across at him.

'Am I right in thinking this is the Hôtel Delaroche?' he asked, his voice breaking the stillness of the room.

The young man nodded and relaxing his pose he walked towards him, gliding across the floor in black-slippered feet.

As he came into the light his face was transformed. It aged by half a century and with a little shock of surprise Napier realised that he was looking not at a young man but at a woman.

'I'm Eugenie Delaroche,' she said, as if to confirm this observation.

It was the short bobbed hair and round olive eyes as much as the clothing that had deceived him into thinking she was a boy. She must have been seventy; her skin was translucent with age and scored with fine wrinkles and yet as she drew close Napier still found her curiously ambiguous: neither male nor female, old nor young.

'Have you booked?' she inquired, going round behind the reception desk.

Napier gave his name and she checked it in the ledger. At that moment Spooner appeared in the doorway, a suitcase in one hand and his briefcase in the other. He stared at Eugenie in wonder but kept his thoughts to himself.

'Ah yes,' she breathed, taking down a key and walking away towards the staircase. 'If you come with me I'll show you to your room. Leave your luggage, Albert will bring it up in a moment.'

They followed her up the staircase to the first floor.

'Did you have a good journey?' she asked, turning down into a broad but dimly lit passage.

'As good as can be expected,' Napier replied.

'It was terrible,' corrected Spooner.

Eugenie Delaroche accepted this contradiction as a fair assessment of the situation. Unlocking a door she threw it open and walked inside. The room was large and sparsely furnished with a chest of drawers and double bed. A clean, washed light fell in through the French windows and sparkled on the brass fittings, waxed floor and white porcelain.

Spooner looked about himself suspiciously. 'And where is the other room?' he wanted to know.

Eugenie gave a quick shrug and asked, 'Do you not sleep together?' The question was factual, there was no veiled innuendo, she might have been asking whether they took tea in the morning.

Spooner opened his mouth to reply but his grasp of the French language failed him in the breach.

'Not unless it's a rule of the hotel,' Napier filled in for him.

'Ah, then one of you can have the room opposite,' she replied and went off to fetch the key.

Spooner sat down on the bed and clutched his briefcase on his lap. 'I thought that was a bit much,' he hissed, nodding towards the door.

'She must have misunderstood your letter.'

'Yes, but if she . . .' The words died on Spooner's lips, he stared across the room and gave a little groan.

Napier turned and followed the direction of his gaze. Hanging on the wall behind him was a painting of a nude girl. Neat and small-breasted, with short clipped hair, she lay sprawled across a rumpled bed while the drooping fronds of an aspidistra licked over her body. It was unmistakably Eugenie.

'Do you like it?' she asked.

They both started at the sound of her voice.

Eugenie had returned, silent as a moth, while they were looking at the picture and now stood in the doorway. She came over and studied it critically. 'It was painted a long time ago,' she said, tilting her head to one side, 'but I think there's still a certain resemblance, don't you agree?'

Spooner, relieved to be cast in the role of a connoisseur, nodded seriously.

Turning around she held out a second key to Napier. 'The door is unlocked, I'll have the bed made up in a moment.'

The room that he had been allocated was smaller but otherwise identical to Spooner's. Napier opened the French windows, that shuddered as they parted, and stepped out on to the balcony. The old mediaeval town of Honfleur lay below him, the soft brown-tiled roofs piled one on top of the other like slabs of turf from a garden lawn. He could make out the tight cluster of buildings around the old Bassin, the long wooden roof of Ste Catherine's and the sharp stiletto blade of its spire. Beyond it the estuary stretched away into the distance, the mirror of its water flashing back heliographic messages in the sunlight.

A maid came in and busied herself about the room behind him.

'How long are you staying?' she asked.

'I'm not sure,' replied Napier, turning around and leaning back on the wrought-iron balcony. 'A few days, maybe a week.'

'Only you'll have to move out of here if Monsieur Delaroche returns,' she continued, thumping the bolster into position with her arms. 'This is his dressing room.'

The woman was old and bent as a dead insect but as she spoke she looked up at Napier with an expression of unblemished innocence. For a moment she stared at him, her eyes as blue-green as deep water, and then a smile cracked her face and she returned to her work.

Eugenie appeared in the doorway. 'Are you finished in here, Madeleine?' she asked.

The old woman nodded. 'All finished, all done,' she croaked and picking up the laundry she paddled out of the room.

Eugenie watched her go. There can have been little difference in their ages and yet she had spoken to her as if to a small child.

'I gather that this is someone's dressing room,' Napier said.

'Is that what she told you?'

'She said it belonged to your husband.'

Eugenie smiled sadly. 'Madeleine gets a little confused at times,' she said, throwing down the towels she had been carrying and joining him on the balcony. 'My husband has been dead for many years.'

'I'm sorry . . .'

Eugenie shook her head and stared out over the estuary. 'It was not important,' she murmured. 'A marriage of convenience I believe it is called.' For a few moments she stood motionless, her gaze fixed on the distant horizon where the docks of Le Havre basked in the heat, and then turning around she spread her hands along the rusted iron railing and said, 'I hear you know Honfleur well.'

'I've been here several times before,' Napier admitted.

'So what was it that brought you to this hotel?' Her manner, as with everything she said, was forthright; it was not an answer she was wanting so much as an explanation.

'We were hoping to learn something about the death of Charles Barnabas,' Napier replied.

Eugenie tilted back her head. 'Ah,' she purred on an intake of breath, 'I thought as much.'

'It's not the curator you want,' said Chantal, 'it's his assistant, Jacqui Fontenay.'

'Oh, I see – very well.'

'If you wait here I'll see if I can find her.'

Spooner murmured his thanks and did as he was told. He looked around himself, examining the general layout of the museum and then, going over to one wall, he began to inspect the paintings in detail. Bending forward he quizzed each canvas through steel-rimmed spectacles, making small noises of approval and interest in his throat, then stepping back a pace he reassessed it at a distance.

Like so many occasional art-lovers, Spooner was convinced that the appreciation of paintings was simply a question of finding the correct range.

'It's odd,' he observed after a few minutes. 'This place calls itself the Boudin Museum but as far as I can see there are no pictures by him.'

'No, that's right,' said Napier who was wandering restlessly about the room. 'It was named after Boudin because he was born here but it doesn't actually own much of his major work. It's got everyone else who ever painted in Honfleur on the other hand.' He tapped the name placard of a picture with the back of his finger.

The screw was loose and to his horror it fell out of the wall on to the ground.

He bent down to pick it up.

As he reached out he heard the click of approaching footsteps and a pair of smart Italian shoes appeared beside his hand.

He glanced up to see Jacqui towering above him.

Very slowly Napier straightened up and sketching the outline of a bow he presented her with the little placard. 'I believe this is yours,' he murmured.

Jacqui accepted it gravely, swept him with her cool grey eyes and turned away to Spooner.

'I'm sorry to keep you waiting,' she said when he'd completed the introductions. 'I've been held up in a meeting all afternoon.'

Spooner at once assured her that it was no problem.

'Shall we go up to my office, it's easier to talk there.' She led the way across the floor, politely answering the questions that Spooner put to her, inclining her head towards him and occasionally turning to indicate something of interest as they passed. She walked with an easy, open stride, Napier noticed. Her legs were shapely, the calves well rounded by her high-heels, and the hem of her pleated skirt amplified the casual sway of her hips.

'Have you seen this?' she asked, pausing before a framed canvas no larger than an envelope. It was a view of Honfleur harbour on a blustery day; ships reefing in their sails, figures on the jetty leaning into the wind, the sea boiling amongst the wooden piles – mute greys and greens shattered into tiny flickering brushstrokes. 'It's our most recent acquisition.'

'Charming,' diagnosed Spooner, giving the little picture his close-quarters inspection. 'And who is the artist?'

'It's by Jongkind,' she told him and then turning around she added, 'that is unless Dr Napier wants to tell us that it's a fake.'

There was no humour in this remark. Her expression as she looked at him was challenging, the chin was held high, hair swept back in a shining wave and in the depths of her eyes he detected a glint of hostility.

'You saw the article?'

'Yes,' Jacqui acknowledged, moving on down the gallery. 'The police showed it to me.'

Her office was small and flooded with afternoon light. The desk was arranged neatly with letters stacked in a wire tray, pens and pencils bristling from a pottery mug and an anglepoise lamp craning down over the blotter. Notices and posters of recent exhibitions were pinned to the wall. Chantal sat behind an electric typewriter busily making alterations to a letter with correcting fluid.

'Is it true you think there is a connection between *The Estuary Pilgrim* and that poor man who was found in the harbour the other day?' Jacqui asked, opening the window.

'I think it's a coincidence that should be looked into.'

'Which is why you're here in Honfleur.'

'More or less.'

She turned and faced him. 'I don't understand you, Dr Napier. Two months ago you assured the world that this painting was genuine, now on the flimsiest piece of evidence you want to change your mind. Why is that?'

Napier spread his hands. He knew that she wasn't going to like what he was about to say. 'I find the discovery of the picture a little too convenient for my liking.'

'What is convenient about it?'

'It appeared exactly where it was expected.'

Jacqui frowned. 'And you'd rather it turned up somewhere unexpected?'

'Maybe.'

Jacqui sat down, smoothing her skirt under her. 'Did you read the report I wrote in the papers?'

Napier nodded.

'Were you not convinced?'

'Certainly, but . . .' His voice trailed off.

Jacqui looked at him with her fierce grey eyes. 'But?' she prompted.

'By suggesting that the painting still existed and broadcasting where it was lost, I'm wondering whether you didn't inadvertently create the opportunity for a fake.'

Napier's voice was soft, almost apologetic, but to Jacqui his words were like a slap in the face. She flushed, the colour rising to her cheeks, and in the warm rush of blood she felt a burst of anger.

'But you have no proof of this,' she flashed.

'I'm hoping to find it while I'm here in Honfleur.'

'You sound as if you want it to be a fake.'

'On the contrary,' replied Napier shaking his head, 'I'd much prefer it to be the real thing; I've written about that picture so often— '

'So I believe,' Jacqui cut in. 'Unfortunately I've never read one of your books.'

The lie came out before she'd even realised it. She could think of no reason for it other than she wanted to snub him. He was very sure of himself, this Englishman, confident of his opinions.

Nevertheless Jacqui was startled by the violence of her own reaction. It was quite uncharacteristic. Her voice sounded shrill and rather churlish in her ears and she was ashamed to hear it. But John Napier was so different from how she'd imagined: younger and more assertive, used to getting his own way – particularly with women.

89

Lowering her head she stole a glance at him from behind the curtain of her hair. Certainly he had charm, his smile was gentle and his eyes had a pleasant way of crinkling when he talked, but she had known men with more.

Spooner was looking at her expectantly and she realised that he'd asked her a question.

'I'm sorry,' she said, collecting herself, 'I didn't catch that.'

Spooner mustered his schoolboy French once more. 'I was wondering whether we could look over the information you put together: the notes and documents you refer to in your article.'

Jacqui smiled. 'Of course,' she said, forcing herself to relax. She liked this little man, he was so very formal and worried as an owl. 'The file is at home at present but I could bring it in tomorrow.'

'That would be most kind of you.'

He stood up to leave.

Jacqui accompanied them downstairs. 'I'll see you in the morning then,' she said, giving Napier her hand in parting.

They studied each other briefly in the instant of contact.

'We are staying at the Hôtel Delaroche, should you wish to alter the arrangement,' Spooner informed her.

A glint of amusement passed across her face and she raised her eyebrows.

'It doesn't seem to be a very well-known establishment,' he added.

'No,' she agreed, 'but it has quite a reputation none-theless.'

Returning to her office Jacqui found Chantal eager for a post-mortem.

'Are you going to let them look at those files?' she asked, savouring the encounter she'd just witnessed.

Jacqui stood at the window, her thoughts drifting out into the labyrinth of the streets below.

Chantal tried again. 'Do you think there was anything in what he said?'

Looking around over her shoulder Jacqui asked, 'Have you posted that letter?'

'Not yet.'

'What have you been doing for the last hour?'

'I was listening to what those two men had to say.'

'You mean you haven't finished it?'

'Well I wasn't able to type while you were talking, was I?' she said defensively.

Jacqui stamped her foot. 'Oh God, you are hopeless sometimes.'

Chantal watched her over the rim of the typewriter and smiled sweetly to herself. 'He did get under our skin, didn't he,' she thought as she began to type. 'It's good to know that someone can, *chérie*.'

Napier was disgusted with himself.

Line by line he went over the confrontation with Jacqui and however he looked at it he found himself at fault.

His whole manner had been aggressive.

The discovery of the painting was important to her, that was all too evident from the way she had leapt to its defence. Christ, it was hardly surprising. She must have put a great deal of time and imagination into her research and now, in a few tactless words, he had threatened to belittle the achievement.

He took a sip of lager and put the glass back on its mat, watching the sudden upward rush of bubbles that followed the movement, and promised himself he'd be more considerate when he saw her in the morning.

At the thought of this appointment with Jacqui a worm of excitement moved and wriggled down into Napier's belly. He wanted to see her again, to repair the damage of their first meeting, to get closer to her.

He tore his mind away from the speculation and looked up.

The café around him was crowded and as busy as a bee-hive. Bright yellow umbrellas puddled the tables with shadow and beyond them the harbour shimmered in the sunshine. A band was playing on the quayside, a saxophone and an accordian, accompanied by a dented tuba that pumped out fat notes to the milling crowds.

In front of them a juggler was working his pitch, fanning small coloured balls into the air. Napier leaned back in his chair and locking his fingers behind his head he studied the man through half-closed eyes.

He was a diminutive figure dressed in bright red breeches and the long flat shoes of a clown. A crumpled top-hat was perched on the back of his upturned head and all the time he performed he harangued the circle of admiring spectators

91

who'd gathered around him. Shouting obscenities, dancing and grimacing, grinning at the shock waves of laughter, pleased with his own ingenuity.

At that moment Spooner appeared, picking his way through the crowd, briefcase in hand, murmuring small apologies as he passed.

Catching sight of him, in his black jacket and striped trousers, the juggler dropped his act, the balls falling back into his hand with the speed and accuracy of rabbits returning to their holes.

'Excuse me, monsieur' he cried, lifting his hat and placing it over his heart. 'I hadn't realised there was a funeral today.'

The audience tittered.

It took a few moments for Spooner to appreciate that he was the butt of this humour. He glanced about himself, grasped the situation, ignored it and hurried on.

The juggler stepped out into his path and bowed. The top-hat rolled down his arm and landed upended in his hand.

He held it out expectantly.

Spooner had no alternative but to take out a coin and drop it in. The juggler thanked him, tapped him on the arm and with a quick, caressing movement of his palm removed Spooner's watch.

'Merci, monsieur,' he murmured, dropping his upper body into another low bow. 'And do you have the time by any chance?'

Instinctively Spooner felt in his waistcoat pocket and stood frozen as he realised what had happened. The crowd stirred and gave a murmur of appreciation as the juggler lifted the watch from Spooner's collar and held it up, dangling and turning on its gold chain, for everyone to see.

'Pardon, monsieur,' he grinned as he handed it back. 'I wasn't intending to steal it, you understand.'

Spooner nodded magnanimously.

'It was your wallet I was wanting.' The juggler drew the wallet from behind his back and coyly fanned himself with it.

A burst of applause sprang from the crowd.

'I assumed that a man with two watches wouldn't be needing so much money.'

Again the watch was dangling enticingly from the juggler's hand.

With unruffled dignity Spooner took back his possessions and retreated into the safety of the café amidst a renewed burst of laughter and clapping.

The juggler passed his hat around the tables and grinned with sharp teeth as he heard the coins clinking into place.

'Incorrigible young man,' Spooner puffed, sitting down beside Napier and flicking open the cap of his watch to check that all was in order.

Napier put on a straight face and nodded his agreement. The sight of Spooner being unburdened of his valuables had quite restored his spirits.

'Would you like a drink?' he asked, turning around and catching the waiter's attention.

Spooner was a strict sun-over-the-yard-arm drinker but he allowed himself the indulgence of a cup of coffee, stirred in some sugar and drank it thoughtfully.

'How did you get on with the police?' Napier asked.

'Well enough. I had a long talk with their Chief Inspector Chaumière; he was most accommodating but I don't think we're going to get much help from him.'

'Why's that?'

'He doesn't believe there is any connection between the painting and the murder.'

'Did you tell him about my meeting with Barnabas?'

Spooner nodded. 'He feels that it was an interesting coincidence but purely circumstantial.'

'He may be right, of course.' Napier's mind drifted back to the memory of tawny gold hair and eyes as cool as the dawn sky. 'In which case we can make our apologies and all go home.'

'Not yet,' replied Spooner, picking up the briefcase and unlocking the clips. There was a glint in his eye that only came at moments of repressed enthusiasm. 'While I was there I picked up Barnabas's personal effects, as I'd been instructed to do.' He drew out a small paper bag and placed it on the table, glancing across to the juggler at the same time. 'There was nothing in his pockets of any great interest except this.' Dipping his hand into the bag he took out the German Iron Cross and handed it to Napier.

The medal had been treated roughly over the years. The black enamelled surface was faintly clouded and the blade of its edges was blunt and serrated with small nicks.

'Look at the back,' Spooner instructed.

Napier turned it around in his palm. Engraved on the flat steel of the reverse surface was the name: D. Schwartz.

Spooner took off his glasses, cleaned them on his handkerchief and then reaching forward he tapped the Iron Cross with one lens. 'This says we stay.'

They left the café and walked along the quayside, following the line of rope-worn bollards. The water below them was rainbowed with motor oil and the lazy ripples blinked back the sun.

As they reached the Lieutenance, the old customs-house of Honfleur, Napier paused, took two steps to the left and pointed towards the outer harbour. 'What's that remind you of?' he asked.

Spooner consulted the view for a moment, repeated the question to himself, and then the answer dawned on him. 'Why, it's the setting of *The Estuary Pilgrim*.'

'Almost unchanged from the day it was painted.'

Spooner checked the scene, comparing it to his mental image of the painting, and his face registered an emotion approaching excitement. 'It's extraordinary,' he announced. 'The jetty, this building here, the stone steps . . . even that lighthouse in the distance – it's just like the picture.' Stepping back he looked down at the cobbles at his feet. 'And to think that Monet stood right here while he was working.' He glanced up at Napier, coughed and looked away again, suddenly embarrassed by this outburst.

'It was not only Monet who stood here,' Napier replied. 'Your forger would have also.'

'How do you know that?'

'Stands to reason.' He swept his hand through the air in a vague gesture that included the whole town. 'Anyone forging *The Estuary Pilgrim* would be bound to come here to check his facts, make sure he'd got all his colours right before starting work.'

'I take your point.'

They walked on beneath the overhanging poop of the Lieutenance. Seagulls swooped and tumbled in the sky, filling the air with their desolate calling. A light breeze struck them as they rounded the front; it was fresh and cool and reeked of salt and oozing mud.

★ ★ ★

94

They parted on the steps of the hotel.

Napier leaned on the balcony for a few minutes and looked down at the overgrown gardens. Standing against the far wall was a stone statue. He walked over to it, following a narrow pathway that had been mowed in the long grass.

It was a little wood nymph, set high on a pedestal, the stonework green with lichen. Behind it, arranged against the brick wall, was a garden seat. Napier sat down and stretched his arms along the warm blistered paintwork. The sky above him was skimmed with high cloud and beginning to lose its intensity as evening approached.

He let his eyes close and the sunlight gilded his lashes with unfocused orbs.

A voice broke into his daydream.

'Do I disturb you?'

Napier looked up with a start. Eugenie Delaroche was standing before him, a dark silhouette against the brightness. He pulled his feet beneath himself to stand up but she held up one hand.

'Don't move,' she ordered and stepping forward she sat down, perching on the edge of the seat beside him. 'It's pleasant here, isn't it?' she said, gazing up at the little stone figure in its cocoon of high grass. 'I often come here in the evening. Statues are so peaceful; they lead such private and mysterious lives.'

Napier was about to reply to this quaint observation when she turned her round eyes on him and said, 'I hear you're an art historian, Dr Napier.'

'That's right.'

'Come,' she said, holding out her hand, 'I've something to show you.'

The gesture was at once inviting and intimate, as though they were friends of old.

Skirting the overgrown lawns, she led the way towards a dovecot that stood in the corner of the garden. It was short and round, with a slate dunce-hat for a roof. Eugenie climbed the flight of steps that curled around its outer wall and went inside.

The circular room was unfurnished, the floor laid with rough boards. Slumped against the wall was a dishevelled figure in baggy blue trousers and a vest. A bottle of wine was wedged in the cleft of his legs and his hands rested on its neck.

Seeing them come in he started and lumbered to his feet.

Eugenie paused in the doorway. 'Haven't you something better to be doing with your time?' she asked impatiently.

He grunted a reply to himself and pulled on his jacket, stuffed the bottle into one pocket and left, rolling his wet pug-dog eyes at Napier as he passed.

'That's Albert,' Eugenie said after he'd gone. 'He mows the lawns around here.'

Napier watched the man shamble down the steps and then, ducking through the doorway, he looked about himself.

The place was some sort of artist's studio. Several easels stood by the window. A kitchen table was littered with palettes, plastic bottles of turpentine and a paint box bursting with rolled up tubes of colour. Small, brightly coloured canvases, at various stages of completion, were propped against the table legs.

Eugenie picked one up and handed it to Napier. It was a view of the harbour, built from dabs of fat paint, the outlines of the buildings wobbly with artistic licence. She took it back and replaced it with another and then a third.

'What do you think?'

'They seem to be cheerful little characters.'

'They're crap,' she told him, but she said it on an up-note as though it were a compliment.

'Who painted them?'

'Bernard Totier, he's staying at the hotel at the moment. I give one or two artists a free room for the summer in exchange for some of their pictures.'

'What's the point if you don't like what they paint?'

Eugenie turned and looked at him. 'Because the tourists like them and that's what matters,' she said dryly. 'I sell them to the galleries around the harbour and, believe me, they earn more than I could ever get for a hotel room.'

Napier put the pictures back on the floor and walked over to the window. The air was warm and pungent. He breathed it in as he looked out at the house: it was the smell of seed boxes and raffia, woodworm and drying apples and bricks crumbling with age.

'I'm told that this hasn't been a hotel for long.'

'That's true.'

'Was it a private house before?'

'No, it was a brothel.'

The abruptness of her answer made him turn.

Eugenie stood in the centre of the room, her hands thrust deep into her pockets. There was a sadness about her, Napier had noticed, a sense of withdrawn melancholy. It was as though she was immensely tired; a small boy who has stayed up later in life than he intended.

She smiled. 'Do I shock you?'

'I don't think so,' replied Napier. 'A little surprised maybe.'

'That I ran a brothel?'

'That you speak about it so openly.'

'Ah,' she said, 'once you've run an establishment like mine for a few years you lose the fear of admitting it.'

'So what made you change it into a hotel?'

'That was decided for me,' she replied. 'There were complaints to the council and it was closed down.'

'For what reason?'

Eugenie came over to the window and leaning against the sill she stared out through the dusty panes. 'They said I was a collaborator.'

'You ran it during the war?' Napier asked, his voice soft now that she stood so close.

'It made no difference to me who came here,' she replied. 'You can only collaborate with armies, soldiers in uniform, but these were just men like any others. They paid to be allowed to take their uniforms off for a few minutes, so who was I to object?'

'Were they aggressive?'

Eugenie shook her head. 'Not really, most of them were just lonely and missing their homes and families. Some came here to forget wives and girlfriends, others to remember them. Towards the end . . .' she paused and frowned, 'I don't really know what they wanted.'

Napier looked at her in wonder. 'It's strange,' he murmured, 'I always imagined that soldiers would be somehow more assertive than civilians.'

'They weren't saints, if that's what you mean.' She gave a little snort. 'I can tell you, we were beating the German army long before the Allies.'

'And after the war you were branded as a collaborator.'

She nodded, tracing lines in the dust of the window with her finger. 'They signed a petition and then took everything I owned: furniture, paintings, even the curtains off the walls.'

Her words came in a sudden rush. 'God, they were like vultures, picking and thieving. I was left with nothing but the carcass of a house, an empty space that could never be filled again.'

As she spoke Eugenie turned to Napier and in the depths of her eyes he saw a hatred that had festered there for forty years. It flowed from her, vital and tangible, a dark malignant presence that filled the room.

Napier walked to the centre of the floor. 'Did a German officer called Schwartz ever come here?' he asked, twisting around to face her. 'Dietrich Schwartz?'

'Maybe,' she replied with a shrug. 'I don't remember their names.'

Taking a silver cigarette box from her jacket she offered it to Napier. He shook his head.

'How did you find out about all this?' she asked, tapping a cigarette on the lid of the box before lighting it.

'It was a remark I heard in the museum.'

She smiled, breaking the spell she'd cast on the room. 'You've been talking to the Fontenay girl?'

'You know her?'

Eugenie nodded. 'I knew her father slightly, before they moved away to Rouen.'

'You put that in the past tense.'

'He was killed in a car crash about ten years ago, along with her mother.'

'I hadn't realised . . .'

'She's been living with a guardian until recently.' She studied Napier critically. 'You're rather taken with her, I see.'

'She's a striking girl,' Napier replied cautiously.

'Yes, she is,' Eugenie acknowledged, and then raising one eyebrow she added, 'Ah, the money I could have made from that one.' She pondered this waste of natural resources for a few moments. 'The aloof ones were always the most popular, you know.'

Napier looked down at the ground and shovelled the dust with the point of his toe.

'Black lace underwear, a peaked Gestapo hat on the back of her head and they'd have been queuing all the way back to the harbour.'

He smiled shyly.

'Ah, I see I have shocked you at last, Dr Napier,' she crooned, drawing in close and looking up at him with her dark eyes. 'Come we must go, it's almost dinner time.'

They walked back to the house in silence. On the steps Eugenie suddenly stopped and turning to Napier she said, 'I was lying back there, you realise?'

'Lying?'

'I knew Dietrich Schwartz.'

Napier waited for her to continue.

'He was nothing – a little postman – forever scuttling about after his seniors.'

'Do you know what he was doing here in Honfleur?'

Eugenie shook her short-cropped head. 'The only thing I remember about Schwartz was that he had the most extraordinary taste in women . . .' She narrowed her eyes at the memory and was on the point of expanding when Madeleine appeared in the doorway, mumbling and crowing and in need of instructions.

Eugenie's thoughts returned to the present, she murmured an apology at the interruption and went inside.

Chapter Seven

Jacqui was talking on the phone when Napier arrived at her office. Standing with her back to the door she was gazing out of the window as she spoke, the receiver buried in the depths of her hair, its flex snaking down around her body. She had dressed with more than usual care that morning in a light grey dress, simple but well tailored to show off her figure to its best advantage, and black stockings with a fine seam at the back that dived down into high heels.

She looked chic and invulnerable.

Hearing Napier come in she twisted around and reaching out her arm she pointed towards a chair. He obeyed the command and sat down, glancing around at the little office, taking in the small personal details: a handbag hanging from the back of a chair, a bundle of keys on the desk-top, a spiky pink shell that acted as a paperweight for the day's post. A bright morning light gilded the room and the air carried the first suggestion of autumn.

Jacqui was speaking with considerable animation, her voice was low and intent and expressions flickered across her face in response to the conversation at the other end of the line. One ankle was crossed over the other and her hips rested against the windowsill. Her free hand she held in the air, the palm upwards as though she was balancing an invisible plate, and with this she made rapid gestures, emphasising her words as she talked.

The conversation came to an end, she put the phone down and walked round behind the desk.

'Good morning, Dr Napier,' she said, sitting down and studying him gravely. 'I'm sorry to keep you waiting.'

Napier assured her it was no problem.

'I see you haven't brought your little friend with you today.'

'He's in the Hôtel de Ville, going through the archives.'

At this Jacqui raised her eyebrows. 'That should keep him busy for a few weeks.'

'He likes paperwork.'

The door opened and the upper part of Chantal's body came in view.

'Could you bring Dr Napier some coffee,' Jacqui told this section of her assistant.

Seeing who the visitor was Chantal introduced the rest of herself into the room. 'Black or white?' she asked, standing provocatively on one leg.

Napier told her he liked it white and she vanished again.

'I've brought in the documents you wanted to see,' Jacqui continued as soon as she was gone. Leaning over she opened a drawer and pulled out a loose-leaf file which she handed across to Napier.

He laid it on the desk and flicked through the pages. There were fifty or more photocopied documents arranged in chronological order. They were terse paragraphs of instructions on the whole, dated and signed with hastily scrawled signatures. Many of the sheets were embossed with the stylised spreadeagle of the Third Reich.

Alongside each document was a neatly typed translation.

Napier was impressed; it was a business-like piece of research. 'Did you make these translations yourself?'

Jacqui nodded.

'You must speak very good German.'

'I studied Modern Languages at university,' she replied, politely declining the offered compliment.

'I'm astonished that you managed to find so much information,' he added, judging the thickness of the file in his hand. 'The Germans normally destroyed their official papers.'

'These have no military significance. I doubt if they were considered to be dangerous.' She leaned across the desk and began turning the pages of the file, tilting her head to read the words upside down. 'Let me show you some of the more interesting items. This first section . . .'

Chantal burst into the room without knocking, a cup of coffee in her hand. She put it down on the desk in front of Napier.

He murmured his thanks.

She hovered for a moment, gathered from Jacqui's frown that she was not invited to stay and flounced out again.

Napier watched the tight black skirt tacking out of the room and then turning back to the desk said, 'I'm sorry, you were saying . . .?'

Jacqui's grey eyes held his for a moment and then returned to the open file.

'This first section', she repeated, 'is made up of various letters and orders that I discovered in the public records office. Most of them are from General von Eichendorff's headquarters here in Honfleur.'

Napier leaned forwards, just touching the aura of her scent, and examined the pages she held open for him.

One by one she turned them, indicating relevant sentences with the tip of a pencil. 'Some of the references are rather vague,' she told him, 'but in one or two cases the pictures are mentioned by name.' She leafed through the file until she reached one letter in particular.

It was written in ink.

Jacqui's pencil skimmed down the page and paused on the title of a minor painting in the collection.

'Is this the General's own handwriting?'

'Presumably.'

Napier stared down at the firm italic script and the illegible signature beneath and for a moment the past seemed to crowd in around him.

'Then in this second part,' Jacqui continued, 'I've added some eye-witness accounts of the ambush.'

She turned the file towards her and began flicking through the pages with quick, sure movements of her hands.

Napier lifted his eyes from the desk and stole a glance at her as she worked, admiring the finely sculptured planes of her cheeks and nose. Her hair was polished and radiant in the morning sun, casting warm lights on honey-coloured skin.

' . . . Of course I had to write it all down afterwards,' she was saying.

He watched the movement of her lips and the downward curve of her eyelashes as she scanned the documents before her.

She was warm and desirable and yet somehow untouchable.

As Napier looked at her he was filled with a strong but uncomfortable sensation of possession; it was as though she belonged to someone. She was evidently not married, the only ring that she wore was a simple gold band engraved with a family crest, but at the same time her bearing and her cool reserved elegance managed to convey that she was not available.

She reminded him of some precious object in a glass case, to be seen and admired but not handled by the public.

'But I think it is an accurate account of the meeting,' she continued, glancing up at him.

Quickly Napier dropped his attention back on to the desk and tried to pick up the thread of the conversation.

'Didn't I hear that you'd talked to some Resistance fighter?'

'Yes,' she replied dryly, 'that's what I've just been telling you about.'

'I'm sorry . . . I must have misunderstood you.'

It was a gaff, a dead giveaway. The grey eyes appraised him once more, drawing the thoughts from his mind.

'Then I'll try to speak more clearly,' she murmured.

For the next half-hour she went over the rest of the documents, explaining each one in turn. At the end she had added a number of newspaper articles, irregular shaped clippings, covering the discovery of the painting earlier that year.

'I'd no idea it received such publicity,' Napier said, thumbing through them thoughtfully.

'Oh yes,' said Jacqui, 'and there'll be a great deal more if it turns out to be a fake.'

'Do you think so?'

'Certainly,' she replied. 'But then isn't that what you want?'

The glint of hostility was there once more, a sharp drawn blade in her voice. Jacqui sat back in her chair and for a moment their eyes met across the desk.

It was maddening, frustrating. Whatever he did or said she misunderstood. She seemed determined to see the worst in him, to mistake his motives.

'I don't think that's necessarily true,' he said carefully.

'What then?'

'I just want to be sure before I commit myself.'

Jacqui leaned forward. 'But why do you refuse to accept the evidence of your own eyes?' she asked patiently. 'Everything I've shown you today, everything you discovered in your own researches proves the picture is genuine. So why do you insist it's a fake?'

'I don't know,' replied Napier, his voice dropping to a

103

murmur as though he was talking to himself. 'I really don't know.'

Jacqui waited, her head cocked to one side.

Napier gathered his thoughts. He wanted her to understand the situation, to see it from his point of view. 'When I was first shown the painting I thought something was wrong,' he began, 'but the more I tried to discover what it was the less certain I became. It was rather like repeating your own name to yourself over and again until it no longer makes any sense.' He shrugged his shoulders and smiled. 'Now I just want to be sure of what it is I'm dealing with.'

The smile was infectious, disarming, but Jacqui made no response. She sat looking at him in silence, letting his words run on.

'The only tangible piece of information that we have found is a single name – Dietrich Schwartz.'

'The General's adjutant?'

Napier nodded. 'Wherever we go that name seems to crop up.'

'In what way?'

In a few words Napier described the meeting he'd had with Barnabas's publisher and the discovery of the Iron Cross on his body. 'Even Eugenie Delaroche admitted she knew Schwartz,' he added.

'She told you that?'

'Yesterday evening. And I'm fairly certain she knows more than she's telling.'

For the first time he had Jacqui's interest.

Standing up she walked over to the window and looked down at the street for a few moments, lost in thought. Then turning around and leaning back on the sill she said, 'But this doesn't make sense, Dr Napier. Schwartz is a name from the past, he died over forty years ago.'

'And *The Estuary Pilgrim*, if it is a fake, would have been made in the last few months.'

'Exactly.'

The smile returned to Napier's eyes. 'The two don't seem to fit together, do they?' he agreed, pressing home his advantage. 'But that's why we need to know more about Dietrich Schwartz.'

Jacqui's manner thawed a few degrees. 'You think this is important?'

'I'm certain that he's the key to this whole affair.' Picking up the file Napier leafed through the pages. 'Look at these documents; nearly every one is either to him, or from him, or signed by him in the General's absence.'

She drummed her fingernails on the sill, coming to a decision in her mind.

'I may know someone who can help you,' she said, pushing herself away from the wall and facing Napier. 'He's an expert in the history of this district, especially the war years.'

'Could I meet him?'

'I'll see what I can do.'

Napier left a few minutes later with an assurance from Jacqui that she would be in touch as soon as she'd rung her friend.

That evening, when he and Spooner returned from dinner, they were stopped in the hall by Eugenie Delaroche.

'There's a message for you, Dr Napier,' she announced, materialising out of the shadows on silent slippered feet. 'The Fontenay girl rang while you were out to say that you're invited to lunch tomorrow.'

Napier took the note that Eugenie held out to him. 'Did she say how I was going to get there?'

'She's going to pick you up around midday.'

The shed was a simple wooden lean-to. It lay in the crook of the garden wall, half-buried in undergrowth. The tiled roof had been patched with successive generations of corrugated iron and the chimney stack had crumbled down. Logs were stacked against the wall along with garden tools and a broken knife-grinding wheel.

There was a movement inside.

Napier walked over and stood in the entrance, his eyes adjusting to the darkness. He had been giving the hotel grounds a thorough tour of inspection. Immediately after breakfast Spooner had scuttled back to the Hôtel de Ville, eager to pursue his investigations amongst the archives, and so Napier had been left to his own devices for the morning.

Standing in the gloomy interior was a dishevelled figure whom he recognised as Albert. He was bending over the cylinder-block of an engine, his arms black with oil. A bottle of wine stood on the work-bench amidst the debris of spanners and machinery.

105

He looked up as Napier came in and gave a grunt of recognition.

'That's a Lister diesel, isn't it?' Napier asked, drawing closer and inspecting the ancient engine.

Albert gave a repeat performance of his grunt.

'Good engines, I believe.'

This statement was followed by a sound that Napier took to be affirmative.

'I see it's water-cooled,' he pressed on. 'Does it belong to a boat?'

Albert straightened his back and regarded Napier through slack-rimmed eyes with rather more interest. He was an unkempt looking individual with unshaven jowls and a black moustache that sprouted from the base of wide flared nostrils.

'Yes,' he agreed. 'My boat.' He put the bottle to his mouth and took a long pull at the wine. Replacing it on the bench he wiped the back of his hand over his wet lip, which still hung open after the neck of the bottle had been withdrawn.

'What seems to be the problem?'

'The bitch won't go,' Albert replied succinctly. 'I take her out on the estuary, she stops, she starts, she stops again.'

'How very uncomfortable for you.'

'She makes me sick.'

Napier wasn't sure whether this was Albert's opinion of the boat or the effect it had on him.

'It's the fuel pipe,' Albert assured him, diving his hand down into the opened cylinder. 'It's all shitted up with mud.'

'What sort of boat is it?' Napier asked.

Albert looked at him in disbelief. 'It's a fishing boat,' he replied and then taking out his hand he jabbed a thick thumb into his vest. 'I'm a fisherman.'

'Ah,' said Napier, 'I'm sorry, I didn't know that.'

Albert looked around the shadowed interior, searching for further proof of his profession. 'My father was a fisherman . . .' he said earnestly. 'My brother was a fisherman . . .' He paused, reflected for a moment, and then stretching his eyes he added, 'My grandfather was a fisherman . . .'

'Runs in the family does it?' Napier cut in before Albert could recite his entire family tree.

He nodded seriously. 'I have the sea in my blood.'

Added to the alcohol already swimming through his veins this gave Albert a considerable liquid content, but Napier kept this observation to himself.

'I thought you were the gardener here.'

'I do a little gardening,' he allowed. 'This place needs a man to look after it, but that's only part-time.'

'How long have you worked at the hotel?'

Albert made calculations. 'About fifteen years.'

'You must have been in Eugenie's service longer than anyone.'

'I have,' he agreed, 'except old Madeleine. She's been here forever.'

'Not during the war surely?'

Albert nodded and took another pull at the bottle, the wine running down his chin like blood from a punch in the mouth. 'Even then,' he grunted.

'Really,' Napier murmured. 'I must have a word with her about it.'

'You won't get anything.'

'Why's that?'

'She's screwy in the head.' He revolved one finger by his ear to clarify the condition and then leaning forward and dropping his voice to a conspiratorial level he added, 'You heard about the hotel during the war?'

Napier nodded solemnly.

Reaching out Albert rested one hand on his shoulder. 'You heard, eh?' he repeated and sticking his tongue into his lower lip he spread his mouth in a lewd grin.

The grin became a chuckle, he drew Napier in close and offered him the bottle.

Napier declined the invitation. 'It was a dressing station for the Red Cross, wasn't it?'

Albert nodded and the smile widened. The answer reached his brain and it faded again. He frowned, made a little noise of discontent and consoled himself with the wine.

There was a sound outside.

A daffodil-yellow Citroën had pulled in through the gates. It bounced up the drive and parked in front of the house. Jacqui jumped out, checked her hair in the wing mirror and ran up the steps. Catching sight of Napier she paused by the open doors and came out again.

107

'You got my message?' she asked, walking across the gravel and shaking his hand.

'I did.'

Jacqui went back to the car and opened the door on the driver's side. 'Are you ready to go?' she asked, turning to Napier.

'Of course.' He slipped into the passenger seat beside her.

'What were you doing in that garden shed?' she wanted to know as they drove out into the street.

'I was discussing the future of the fishing industry.'

She shot him a sideways glance, decided he meant what he said and turned her attention back to the road.

Taking the coastal route they headed out of town.

Jacqui drove hard and skilfully, frequently changing gear as they climbed the headland above Honfleur. There was practically no traffic that day and the little car buzzed along, swaying round the corners like a yacht heeling in the wind.

For some time they drove in silence. The Seine estuary was spread beneath them, vast and still and hazy in the midday heat. Napier gazed out of the window and watched the breeze swarming on the surface of the water, acutely conscious of the girl's perfume and the proximity of her body in the confined space of the car.

As they were coming down into a village Jacqui turned to him and said, 'I think I should explain where we are going.' She slowed the Citroën as she spoke, indicated to the left, and swung in through a pair of high wrought-iron gates.

'The man you are about to meet is my guardian,' she told him as they made their way up a long gravel drive vaulted with beech trees.

Before them lay a magnificent château, its ornate, sculptured façade rising above terraces and formal gardens. The stonework was warm and mellow with age, the high mansard-roof pierced with dormer-windows and sheathed in tiles of a soft green-grey tone.

'He seems to do pretty well for himself,' Napier murmured as he looked out at the swathe of parkland that opened around them. 'Did you say he was a historian?'

'No, he's an art dealer.'

'He must be a very successful one.'

'Yes, he is,' she said lightly. 'I think you'll find him interesting.'

108

Skirting around an ornamental pond, thick with clustered lilies, they parked in the shade of the front wall and climbed out.

Jacqui's guardian had seen them arrive and now stood on the terrace waiting to greet them. He was a tall handsome figure, in a silver-grey suit and silk cravat, looking down from his superior height.

Jacqui ran up the steps towards him and reaching up on tiptoes she kissed him on both cheeks.

He accepted this display of affection with good grace and then standing back he inspected her critically, gave a nod of approval and turning to Napier he held out his hand.

'Welcome to my house, Dr Napier,' he said in unflawed English. 'My name is Rupert Ashford.'

Chapter Eight

Ashford's smile as they shook hands was warm and welcoming. 'I'm so glad you were able to come at such short notice.'

'It was good of you to invite me.'

'Can you stay long?' he asked, turning to Jacqui who had watched this exchange closely.

'For a little while,' she told him as they walked back towards the house. She spoke in English to compliment him, her accent just roughening the edge of her consonants. 'There's no great rush, but I must be back at the museum by three.'

'Ah, well that gives us two hours,' he said, taking her arm and drawing closer to her with the gesture. 'I've asked Louis to serve lunch in the dining room but I thought we'd have drinks on the terrace beforehand, if that suits you.'

'It sounds very nice.'

'We must make the most of the summer while it lasts,' he continued suavely. 'I was going to ask in some other guests to entertain Dr Napier, but then I decided it would be cosier with just the three of us.'

'I think so,' Jacqui agreed.

'And in that way we can talk more easily,' he added, turning to Napier, including him in the conversation.

Ashford's whole manner was gracious, almost deferential. He seemed eager to please. The smile of welcome had never left his face but, as he looked at him now, Napier couldn't help noticing that the expression in his eyes was curiously dull and lifeless.

'There's so much I would like to discuss with you,' he was saying as he ushered them through the tall glass-panelled door. 'It's not every day I have such an eminent visitor all to myself.'

The hallway they had walked into was majestic in its scale

110

and simplicity. A carved staircase rose up around two walls, curving round to a high gallery. There was no furniture, the floor was uncarpeted and polished boards mirrored the daylight.

Ashford led the way across this gleaming expanse of wood and out through French windows to a terrace on the far side of the house.

Standing on a table by the wall was an ice bucket and a silver tray with three fluted glasses, each one containing a measure of some dark, toffee-coloured spirit in the point of its base. 'Can I give you a little champagne?' he asked, drawing the bottle from its container and checking the label before stripping away the wire cage. 'Or would you like something stronger?'

'Champagne would be fine.'

The cork came out in Ashford's hand with a dry, gaseous report and he filled the first glass as the bubbles seethed up the neck.

'It's a cocktail,' he explained, handing it to Napier. 'One of Louis's specialities: champagne mixed with an orange Armagnac. He makes it himself.'

'It's good,' Napier remarked, tasting the faint, lingering sweetness of the spirit on his tongue.

Ashford glanced up at Jacqui. 'Would you like some, my dear?'

She accepted the glass with a quick smile of thanks and taking it across the terrace she leaned against the stone parapet and gazed down at the gardens.

Ashford watched her thoughtfully for a moment and then, turning back to Napier, said, 'It was fortunate that our paths crossed here in Normandy. I've been up in Paris for the last few days, catching up on recent events. There's so much on at present – tell me, what did you make of the new Cezanne exhibition?'

'I can't say I've seen it.'

Ashford paused and raised his eyebrows. 'Really?' he murmured, his voice suddenly soft. 'You surprise me, Dr Napier. I'd have thought you'd have been the first to visit it.' He studied him with his flat, unfocused stare and it was only then, with a little shock of awareness, that Napier appreciated the cause of this expression.

Ashford was blind in one eye.

The socket contained a glass replica, identical in shape and colour to the other, but quite unable to move.

'I haven't been in Paris since August,' Napier told him, using the words to cover the moment of hesitation that had followed his discovery.

'Of course you haven't,' Ashford smiled, and brushing his forehead with two fingers he laughed at his own stupidity. 'I'm forgetting what a busy man you are. I have so much time on my hands these days that I assume everyone else has the same.'

'Do you go up to Paris often?'

'I try to get there once or twice a month,' he confided. 'Living here in the country has its advantages, but there is the inevitable danger of vegetating.'

Napier looked down at the classical serenity of the gardens, the lawns inlaid with a marquetry of rose beds and box hedges leading away to a perspective of trees and ornamental lakes.

'If you have to vegetate I can't imagine a better place to do it,' he observed.

Ashford was delighted with the compliment. 'That's true of course,' he agreed. 'I always try to remember what a privilege it is to live in surroundings such as these.'

A stocky figure dressed in a black suit appeared in the doorway at that moment to announce that lunch was ready.

'I must show you round the house before you leave, Dr Napier,' Ashford commented as they crossed the hall.

'I should like that.'

'It's not the most important château in Normandy but I think it has a few points that will merit your attention.'

They came into the dining room of panelled oak, the wall dominated by a cavernous stone fireplace. Three places had been laid on a table that could have seated fifty.

'The house was built in the early 18th century by the Duc de Montreuil,' Ashford continued, touching the back of Jacqui's chair as she sat down before taking his own place at the head of the table. 'A remarkable man in many ways, Dr Napier, remembered today as the author of a few minor essays but better known in his own time as a successful and energetic womaniser. It's said he kept both a wife and a mistress here for twenty years without either of them ever discovering the existence of the other.'

'How very convenient for all concerned.'

112

'Not that I can believe it,' he added. 'There's not a floor in the place that doesn't creak and since the house only boasted one serviceable privy in those days I must confess that I find the whole story slightly improbable.'

Lunch arrived swiftly and silently in porcelain dishes. A light mousse of salmon was brought in and presented for Ashford's approval before being taken round. It was moulded to the shape of a fish, the scales ingeniously reconstucted from slices of translucent cucumber and the eye added with a single stuffed olive. Crisp slices of toast, wrapped in a linen napkin, were put on the table along with wafers of butter that had been curled like wood-shavings.

Ashford talked easily and fluently all the while, describing the owners and visitors and alterations that had taken place to the house over the years.

'Napoleon stayed here,' he was saying as the first course drew to a close and the plates were removed. 'They held a banquet in his honour, here in this very room, but unfortunately the food was cold and he refused to come again until the kitchens had been knocked down and moved closer to the dining-hall.'

As he was talking he turned and looked at Jacqui. She seemed to fascinate him. Throughout the meal the full force of his conversation had been directed at Napier but over and again his attention had wandered back to her and while he was speaking he'd watched the changing expressions of her face, every movement of her hands as she ate.

'I'm sorry, my dear,' he murmured with an apologetic smile, 'this must be very boring for you.'

'Not at all, Rupert.'

'You've heard it all a thousand times before.'

'I like to hear you talk of the house.'

Napier had noticed that Jacqui had said very little since their arrival. She'd listened attentively, smiling when it was expected, but she seemed subdued in Ashford's presence, very different from the self-assured girl he'd met in the museum.

Leaning forward, Ashford stroked her arm with a quick caressing gesture of his hand. 'What are you doing this coming Saturday?' he asked.

Jacqui paused and thought for a moment. 'Oh, I'm having lunch with the Descamps.'

Ashford sat back in his chair and his voice dropped a tone. 'I'd rather you were here that day,' he replied.

'I promised to go—'

'I feel this is more important,' he interrupted politely. 'I have a business acquaintance coming to stay for the weekend. I'll need you here to entertain him.'

'But it's Gabrielle's birthday.'

Ashford made no movement but imperceptibly his manner hardened. He held her gaze with his unblinking stare.

For a moment Napier thought she was going to resist. Her eyes widened and she opened her lips in protest but then she checked herself, the fight went out of her, and looking down at her plate she said, 'Of course, Rupert.'

He spread his hands. 'I mean, if you think it's essential . . .'

'No,' she replied quickly. 'I can ring and explain.'

Ashford's smile returned. It was a small victory but it seemed to please him. Getting to his feet he walked over to the sideboard and picking up a bottle of wine that stood ready, he filled Jacqui's glass. He leaned over her as he did so, murmuring a few words under his breath, and then straightening up he stroked her hair with the same caressing movement of his hand.

Once again Napier was filled with the disturbing sensation of possession. It was quite clear that this brief charade had been staged for his benefit. Ashford had asserted his authority intentionally. He wanted Napier to understand that Jacqui was his. She belonged to him, part of his property, as much as the great house he owned and all the history he had inherited with it.

He pretended not to notice. 'How long have you been living here?' he asked innocently.

'Almost fifteen years now,' Ashford replied. 'I'm a comparative newcomer to the district – as the locals are constantly reminding me. They don't accept you into the community until at least three generations have been buried in the village graveyard. I can't say I blame them, but still,' he paused and gave a small self-deprecatory laugh, 'I find it mildly irritating when I get letters addressed to "the present occupant" from the council.'

Napier smiled. It probably drove him insane with anger, he thought to himself, but repressed the desire to say so and instead asked, 'How did you come to buy it? I can't imagine

114

that houses like this appear on the market every day.'

'No,' Ashford agreed. 'But there I was fortunate. I managed to acquire it from a bankrupt millionaire. He'd made a fortune on the Le Havre cotton exchange back in the twenties and then spent the next thirty years methodically losing it again. The house was in a terrible state when I took it over but, nevertheless, this had its compensations.' He walked around the table and filled Napier's glass as he spoke. 'The contents of the cellars came with the place. This wine we're drinking today, for example, was laid down some years before the war.'

'Quite a bargain.'

'I'm sure you'll recognise it.'

'I don't think I will unfortunately,' Napier replied.

'It's not hard to identify.'

'I'm afraid I know very little about wine.'

'Taste it,' Ashford ordered pleasantly. He stood behind the chair as he spoke, holding the bottle out of sight. Napier glanced across the table to Jacqui but she avoided his eye and with a little start he realised that he was being put on trial.

There was no alternative but to play along.

Putting the glass to his lips he tested the flavour; it was as rich and warm as new-mown hay but refused to reveal its identity. He visualised the bottle and guessed, 'It's a claret.'

'Certainly it's claret,' Ashford agreed, returning to his seat. He filled his glass and syphoned a little wine across his tongue, looking up at the ceiling as he considered the evidence of his palate. 'The question is which claret?'

Napier shrugged; the game was becoming tiresome. 'I've no idea,' he replied.

There was silence in the room.

'As I said, I know nothing about wine.'

The smile was suddenly condescending. 'You disappoint me, Dr Napier. I'd have thought a man of your taste would have taken an interest in wine.'

'I enjoy drinking it, nothing more.'

'Do you not consider it to be an art form?'

'Not really.'

The dull eyes studied him.

Napier was on the point of making some more cutting comment but Ashford sensed it coming; his manner changed. 'And why should you?' he cried, the warmth flooding back

115

into his voice. 'You're an expert on paintings, not a wine merchant. Besides, we're wasting time.' He sat back in his chair and spread his arms along the rest so that the hands hung limp. 'Jacqui tells me you're looking for information on the German occupation of Honfleur.'

'That's right,' Napier agreed, adjusting to this sudden shift in the conversation.

'There was a name.' He touched his forehead to indicate that it was gone and turned to Jacqui for help.

'Schwartz,' she reminded him. 'Dietrich Schwartz.'

'Ah, yes indeed; the General's adjutant.'

'Does the name mean anything to you?'

Ashford raised the wine glass to his lips and pondered for a moment, gazing back down the corridor of years. 'I can't say it does,' he replied. 'One tends to look at the man not his shadow. I must have seen Schwartz in the wake of the General but I must admit I can't put a face to the name.'

Napier grabbed the remark. 'You saw von Eichendorff?'

'Oh yes,' he said lightly, 'on several occasions, everyone in Honfleur did. The General kept a high profile in the district. I had the impression that he rather liked to be seen in public, it was part of his image you might say. At the same time I can't claim that I ever had more than a fleeting glimpse of him as he was driven past in his staff car, surrounded by a swarm of bodyguards. He was very conscious of security – not an easy man to approach socially.' This expression seemed to amuse him and looking up at the glass chandelier he smiled quietly to himself.

'I'm sorry,' Napier murmured in wonder. 'I hadn't realised you were in Honfleur during the war.'

'Oh yes, for well over a year . . .'

'Rupert was a member of the SOE,' Jacqui put in, a touch of pride in her voice.

'Not that they called it that in those days,' Ashford added. '"Agents" was the name they preferred then – or "spies", depending on which side you were on.'

'So you worked with the Resistance?'

'In an advisory capacity. We were trying to coordinate all the separate groups in the district, encourage them to act together rather than as a bunch of independent hooligans.'

Napier was intrigued, this image of Ashford's past added a little depth to his character. An idea came to him. 'You didn't have anything to do with the bombing of the convoy at Criquetot, did you?'

Ashford gave a short laugh. 'I was waiting for you to ask that,' he replied, getting to his feet and strolling over to the window. 'It was the first question Jacqui put to me.' He looked out at the gravelled forecourt of the house and the afternoon light explored the firm sculpture of his features. He was a handsome man and his face, although lined and slightly pouched with age, remained boyish and it was easy to picture him in his early twenties.

Napier waited expectantly.

'No,' Ashford said eventually, turning round from the window. 'Criquetot is a long way south of here, it was well away from my sphere of influence. Added to which I was hiding from the Gestapo at that time. I'd recently escaped from one of their jails and far from attracting attention, I was doing my best to avoid it.' The memory twitched a smile on to his lips and he changed the subject. 'I've heard also that you think *The Estuary Pilgrim* is a fake.'

'It's a possibility,' Napier replied, glancing across the table at Jacqui as he spoke. She studiously avoided the contact and turning his attention back to Ashford he asked, 'What do you think?'

'I've no idea,' he replied quickly. 'I only saw it at a distance in the Grand Palais. There was a barrier, two security guards and an atmosphere as thick as semolina separating us. What could I see through that?'

'Not much I imagine,' Napier agreed.

'All I do know is that you'll have a great deal of trouble convincing anyone of your opinion.'

'Why do you say that?'

Ashford moved forward until he stood behind Jacqui's chair once more. 'I imagine that pictures are rather like English criminals,' he said touching his hands on to her shoulders. 'They're innocent until proved guilty. When you say *The Estuary Pilgrim* is genuine the public will take your word for it, but if you suggest it's a fake you'll need to prove it.' He stroked her hair thoughtfully and then raising his eyes to Napier asked, 'Where are you going to find that proof?'

It occured to Napier to tell him of Barnabas, and the evidence he claimed to have found in Honfleur, but the chain of events suddenly seemed weak and rather improbable

117

and so he allowed Ashford to score his point and said, 'I've no idea.'

'That's what I feared,' he continued calmly. 'Not that I disagree with you, in fact I rather hope you're right. There hasn't been a decent scandal in the art world for over twenty years.' Walking over to the wall, he touched a bell that was set in the panel. Immediately the two silent figures who had served lunch appeared and began clearing away the remains.

At Ashford's suggestion they went next door to a small study, lined with leatherbound books. Jacqui began pouring out the coffee that stood ready on a side table.

'Who's behind all this do you think?' Ashford asked, stirring his cup with a diminutive silver spoon.

'I'm not sure.'

'If there's a crime there must be a culprit,' he pressed, sipping the scalding coffee and slitting his eyes at the temperature.

'In that case I would suggest Maurice Lebas.'

Ashford raised his eyebrows at this. 'Really?' he murmured. 'And why him in particular?'

'He has both the means and the motive.'

'Well that's certainly true . . .'

'Added to which he has already tried to warn me off the case.'

'In person?'

'No,' replied Napier. 'He got a couple of his heavies to do the job for him.'

'Did he, by God?' Ashford settled his coffee cup on its saucer and studied him speculatively. 'Not that it surprises me,' he said. 'Maurice has the manners of a guttersnipe. He inherited a fortune from his father and made another for himself but he's still a docker at heart.'

'You know him?'

'Slightly.'

'I hear he's quite a presence in the district.'

'Oh yes,' Ashford replied, placing his cup on the table behind him and turning to face Napier once more, 'quite a presence. I shouldn't stand in his way, if that's what you're thinking, Dr Napier. He'd make a formidable opponent.'

Louis appeared between them at that moment. He was a short, compact man, with a balding head set on a thick neck, more like a bouncer at a nightclub than a butler. His jacket was off and his shirt sleeves rolled back from meaty white arms. He held a silver tray in his hands.

'A glass of dessert wine, Dr Napier?' Ashford inquired.

Napier took the offered glass and touched it to his lips. It was sweet and sticky as a crystallised fruit.

'Ah, now this I do know,' he said after a moment's thought.

'Is that so?'

Napier reached out and placing the glass on the marble mantelpiece he inspected the wine closely.

'Beaumes de Venise,' he diagnosed.

'It is indeed.'

Napier put his face closer to the glass and examined it once more. 'And the year is almost certainly . . . 1965.'

Ashford paused, his expression wary. 'Right again, Dr Napier,' he said softly and then raising his arm he made a little gesture of mock reverence. 'For a man who knows nothing about wine you seem to be remarkably well informed.'

Napier was modest. 'I'm not at all.'

'I can't believe you were guessing.'

'No, it was simply a question of position.'

The inference was lost on Ashford.

'By putting the glass on the mantelpiece and looking at it from this angle,' Napier explained politely, pointing across the room, 'I can see the reflection of the label in the mirror.'

Ashford's head snapped round.

He glanced across the study to where the opened bottle stood on the sideboard and then back at the mirror above the mantelpiece, grasping the simplicity of the trick that had been played on him.

Napier's tone was courteous. 'Art historians don't have much in the way of taste,' he continued, 'but they do have very good eyes.'

There was a moment of complete silence in the room.

Ashford turned and faced him.

The false eye retained its benevolent stare, the other had grown small and hard, fixed in its intensity. The colour had drained from the pale crystal of its iris and now blazed at him in fury.

For a split second it burned with a fierce white anger and then, as quickly as a light bulb blowing, it was gone again.

The single eye warmed, the pupil dilating to match the other, and a glint of humour broke the stillness of his face.

'What a very amusing young man you are, Dr Napier,' he murmured. 'I must remember that in future.' He turned to Jacqui who stood watching them, her wine glass cradled in both hands and her lips slightly parted. 'Which reminds me, my dear, there is something I want you to see.'

'I think we should be going soon,' she replied hastily, glancing down at her watch. 'It's already two-fifteen.'

'This'll only take a moment,' Ashford assured her, opening the door in readiness.

Jacqui obeyed him and left the room. As she passed Napier she shot him a quick look; it was sharp and quizzical, like an unexpected question, but he was unable to grasp its meaning.

Ashford took them out on to the terrace and over to a low brick building that jutted out from the side of the house. The tall lunette windows that pierced the walls from floor to ceiling suggested that this was an orangery but as soon as they were inside Napier discovered that it had been converted. It was now an orchid house.

The plants were rowed up in tiers all around them and the flowers, with their hard waxy petals, floated above the foliage on stems as delicate as insect legs.

The atmosphere in the place was warm and fetid and wrapped about them like a wet towel as they stepped through the doorway. Moisture trickled down the windows cutting trails in the condensation, leaves dripped and drooped in the damp air.

'Growing orchids is the art of deception, Dr Napier,' Ashford announced, closing the door behind them. 'They are extremely sensitive creatures that only survive in their natural habitat. Unlike our own race, they have no ability to adapt to their environment.'

As he spoke Ashford led them through a series of small glass chambers each hotter and more humid than the last. 'In these rooms I recreate the exact conditions of the orchid's native country and so deceive them into believing they are still at home in the rain forests of South America, the Thai jungle or the hills of Kashmir.'

Napier followed Ashford through the dense luxuriance of the hothouse. Jacqui walked ahead of him, her hands held up

120

in a gesture of surrender, carefully picking her way between the wet plants that reached out like beggars's arms to touch her as she passed.

'Now these I had brought to me from Malaysia,' Ashford continued, indicating some drooping growths that hung from the roof in wooden baskets. 'It's practically impossible to have orchids exported from eastern countries nowadays, the whole subject is tied up in red tape. Fortunately I know the French ambassador in Bangkok and he has the decency to send me the occasional specimen in the diplomatic bag.'

'That can't do the dispatches any good,' Napier observed.

'I imagine they don't all travel together in the same briefcase.' He studied the condition of the plants critically, turning the fleshy leaves in his hands.

Jacqui wrinkled her nose at them. 'They're very ugly, Rupert.'

'They need this thick coat of fibre to protect them from the heat, my dear,' he explained, and then turning to Napier he added, 'Jacqui doesn't share my enthusiasm for orchids, she finds them too exotic for her taste and so I'm usually left to admire them alone.'

'They're such sad little flowers,' she said defensively. 'They don't have any scent.'

'That's part of their beauty,' Ashford replied. 'They make no attempt to seduce us.'

'I think they're ugly and primitive.'

'But they're also extremely rare, my dear. Did you know that in any European garden there are only a handful of different species? The flowers you see there in summer are all descended from a few simple prototypes. In the orchid kingdom, on the other hand, there are over seventeen thousand different species on record and God knows how many that haven't been discovered yet.' The idea seemed to give him infinite pleasure and his voice dropped away to a sigh as he caressed the trailing leaves above him. 'Each time you crossbreed two species you produce a completely new orchid – as unique as a Ming vase or a drawing by Raphael.'

'Does that necessarily make it beautiful?' Napier inquired.

'It makes it valuable, Dr Napier, which is much the same thing.'

He let this pass. 'Why are they hanging from the roof?'

'Ah, well these prefer to live in trees.'

'You mean they're parasites?'

Ashford wasn't allowing the description. 'Not really, Dr Napier,' he reproved, 'they don't feed off the tree or damage it in any way. In fact their needs are very simple.' He pointed to a short length of stick hanging from the ceiling. 'What do you think that is?'

'I'd say it was a dead twig.'

'You might think so,' Ashford agreed. 'But it may surprise you to know that it's a living orchid. *Rangaeris Ameniensis*. It just happens to keep its roots in the air rather than the ground. They draw the moisture from the humidity of the atmosphere. Far from being a parasite, it's probably the most independent creature in existence.'

Napier looked up at this free spirit in wonder.

'But what I wanted to show you was this,' Ashford continued. Moving further along he picked up a flower-pot packed with damp soil and handed it to Jacqui in reverence.

'What is it, Rupert?' she asked, turning the empty pot in her hands.

'*Rhizanthella Gardneri*, the invisible orchid. It grows under the ground.'

Jacqui looked at him wide-eyed. 'Are you being serious?'

'Completely,' he replied. 'Not only is it growing in there, it's also flowering at this very moment.'

'How do you know it is?'

'The flower emits small sounds as it grows.'

Burying the pot in her hair Jacqui pressed it to her ear and listened expectantly. 'I can't hear anything,' she said after a moment.

'You have to be patient,' Ashford told her, taking the pot out of her hands.

'But what's the point of having a flower if it's hidden?' she asked. 'You can't see it.'

'You don't have to see it,' he replied quietly, touching the surface of the soil with the tips of his fingers. 'Just knowing it is there is enough.'

His eyes flicked up and met Napier's. For an instant they remained there and then dropped to the invisible plant in his hands. 'Come, we must go,' he said, returning the pot to its place, 'or you'll be late back to the museum, my dear.'

They went out into the fresh air and autumn sunshine.

Jacqui ran back indoors to pick up her bag, leaving Napier alone with Ashford.

'I hear you're an art dealer,' Napier said as they walked around to the front of the house.

'Does that surprise you?'

'In a way.'

Ashford paused and his raised eyebrows invited him to explain.

'I didn't see a single painting in the house.'

'Ah, that's because you didn't look in the right places,' he remarked, moving on again. 'As it happens I have a great number of pictures but they're all upstairs. You must come again, Dr Napier, I'll show them to you.'

'That would be most interesting.'

Ashford leaned against the stone balustrade and appraised him thoughtfully. 'Why not Saturday,' he said after a few moments. 'I have a few guests coming in for drinks around five.'

'That would suit me very well,' Napier replied. 'I shall look forward to it.'

'Good, I'll have Louis pick you up from your hotel.' He nodded down to where the Citroën stood in the drive. 'And then I'm sure Jacqui can take you back in her little casserole.'

'It's not a casserole,' she cried reproachfully, coming across the terrace to join them. 'It's a very smart car.'

'I've offered to buy her something more dashing,' Ashford continued, 'but she won't hear of it.'

'I like it just the way it is,' she said lightly and reaching up she kissed him on both cheeks, thanked him for lunch and then turning to Napier added, 'We must hurry now.'

They drove in silence.

Jacqui concentrated on the road in front of her, focusing her thoughts on the ribbon of tarmac that sped under the bonnet.

She'd never seen Rupert behave like that before. He was often competitive, overbearing at times, but he wasn't usually so touchy. He'd been on edge from the moment they'd arrived, as though repressing some secret animosity. When Napier had read the label of the wine bottle in the mirror she'd thought he might have hit him.

123

Admittedly Rupert had deserved that. He'd been needling Napier with his knowledge of wine all through lunch.

Still, she hadn't expected Napier to fight back in that way. It was quite a revelation. He was more resilient than he looked. Beneath that easy-going English manner of his he was surprisingly tough. She changed gear as they breasted the hill above Honfleur and stole a glance at him out of the corner of her eye.

Napier was gazing out through the open window at the estuary below them, absorbed in thoughts of his own. His mood had changed. On the way over he had been watching her closely. She'd felt his eyes brush over her from time to time, admiring her as she drove, but now he seemed withdrawn, more remote than before.

'You didn't like him,' she said flatly.

He turned and looked at her in surprise. 'Was it that obvious?' he asked.

'Painfully.'

'I'm sorry, I didn't mean to be rude.' His eyes assumed their usual slightly mocking smile. 'At the same time I think it's fair to say that he didn't particularly like me either.'

'That's not necessarily true,' Jacqui told him. 'It's just Rupert's way.'

'He likes to play games with people, but he doesn't like it when one is played back on him, you mean?'

He was right of course, but the sharp tip of his remark pricked Jacqui's sense of loyalty and she retorted, 'He's achieved a great deal in the course of his life.'

'So it would seem,' Napier agreed, returning to the view from the window. 'How did he lose his eye?' he asked as the car bounced into the outskirts of Honfleur.

'It was during the war,' she replied. 'He was tortured by the Gestapo.'

'Here in Honfleur?'

'I think so,' she said, placing her words with care as she threaded the little car through the narrow streets, 'but I must admit I don't know exactly how it happened – he doesn't like to speak of it.'

'But he managed to escape?'

Jacqui nodded.

'I'm amazed,' replied Napier. 'He must have been one of the very few who did.'

124

'As far as I know he started a fire in the building where he was held and then climbed over the roof while the guards were trying to put it out.'

'Ingenious fellow.'

'He's treated with great respect in the district, especially by the older generation,' she told him. 'They still think of him as a war hero.'

They reached the gates of the hotel.

Jacqui parked the car in the street outside and jumped out to say goodbye.

'I'm sorry you didn't learn more about your German lieutenant,' she said, resting her arms on the open door.

'It's not important,' Napier murmured. 'I learned plenty of other things today.'

There was a slight shyness in his voice and Jacqui sensed that he was on the point of offering an invitation. She waited for it to come but made no attempt to help him.

'Will I see you again?' he asked.

'I'm sure you will, this is a small town.'

'Maybe we could have dinner one night?'

'Yes,' she replied lightly. 'That would be nice.'

Napier shrugged and gave a laugh at his own reticence. 'How about this evening?'

'I can't unfortunately.'

'Tomorrow then?'

She shook her head. 'It's very short notice, I'm afraid I'm rather busy this week.'

The refusal was polite but firm and she saw the disappointment flash in his eyes.

At the same time Jacqui felt a twinge of conscience. She'd known she was going to turn him down even before he'd made the suggestion, although she couldn't explain quite why she should want to do so. As it happened it was quite untrue; she had nothing else to do that evening, the words had just slipped out automatically.

She frowned. This was the second time she'd snubbed him for no apparent reason. He must find her very rude.

Napier saw her expression darken. 'I'm sorry,' he said quickly, 'I didn't mean to pressurise you . . .'

She tossed her head. 'It's not that.'

'It's just that I'm only here for a few days . . .'

'I know,' she said.

'It doesn't give me much time.'

'Didn't I hear Rupert invite you on Saturday?'

'Yes he did . . .'

She held out her arm and said, 'In that case I'll see you there.'

They shook hands. Napier murmured a few words in parting and then turned to go.

Jacqui hesitated.

She had a sudden desire to stop him, to talk to him about Rupert and his house and all its possessions – to tell him something of her own thoughts. She glanced back over her shoulder but Napier was already walking away towards the hotel. She opened her mouth to call after him but it was too late.

The moment passed.

Long after the daffodil-yellow car had disappeared down the drive Ashford remained on the terrace, staring at the spot where it had vanished out of his sight.

He lit a cigarette and smoked it down to the butt, deep in thought, letting the ash bend and drop to the ground under its own weight.

Louis stood a respectful distance behind him.

He knew this mood well and made no move to interrupt but waited with hands on hips for his cue.

Ashford turned his head. 'He's dangerous, Louis,' he said in a distant voice, as though talking to himself. 'Did you know that?'

Louis accepted the question in silence.

'As long as that man's here in Normandy he's dangerous.' He flicked the cigarette end into the flower bed and looking up at the sky asked, 'What do you know about him?'

'Only scraps at present.'

'Such as?'

'He's been in Honfleur for three days.'

'Staying with Eugenie Delaroche?'

Louis nodded.

'Why her?'

'I don't know. I could find out.'

'How about his companion, what's he up to?'

'He's been going through the archives.'

Ashford gave a little grunt of amusement. 'Good luck to

him. He won't find much in there.' He turned his attention back to Napier. 'How did he come to meet Jacqui?'

'He went to see her at the museum.'

'That damned article of hers, I suppose. She hasn't shown any interest in him has she?'

'Not that I've heard of.'

'Good,' Ashford breathed to himself in the quiet, soothing voice that a doctor assumes to calm his patient. 'We don't want the silly girl getting any ideas into her head.'

'Apart from today she hasn't seen him outside the museum.'

Ashford turned to confront him.

'I want him watched, Louis,' he ordered. 'Whatever he does, wherever he goes, I want to hear of it – do you understand me?'

Louis gave a single quick nod of his head.

'And have a car sent round to his hotel on Saturday afternoon,' he added, strolling back towards the house. 'I think we should keep an eye on Dr Napier.'

Chapter Nine

The brush pressed into the wet paint on the palette, mixed flake-white with a speck of cadmium yellow and returned to the painting.

Here it paused.

The artist glanced up at the harbour and back at the unfinished picture, screwing up his eyes against the light. Sucking in his cheeks he touched the brush on to the canvas with a quick movement of his arm. The bristles curved and spread with the pressure and the paint came off in a thick, juicy stroke.

Pale yellow against the dark green water.

He stood back and assessed the effect, holding his head on one side. Reaching forward again he picked out a smaller brush. With this he made slight improvements to the form, flicked in the vertical of a mast and added a purple-blue shadow beneath.

Miraculously the pale yellow brushstroke became sunlight on the side of a yacht.

'I say, that was rather clever,' said Spooner, who was watching over the artist's shoulder.

He turned to Napier for corroboration.

Napier nodded but made no reply. He was standing with his hands buried deep in his pockets, an expression of rapt concentration on his face.

They had spent over an hour on the quayside, going from one easel to the next, watching the different artists at work. There was over a dozen of them that day, all strung out around the harbour busily painting the same scene.

Spooner was impressed by the ritual.

He had expected Napier to dismiss the paintings as cheap and commercial but it was quite the opposite. He seemed fascinated by them. Each one in turn had something that held his attention, something that interested him. But whether he actually liked them was impossible to tell.

'They're as cunning as monkeys,' he said when Spooner put this question to him. 'They catch an effect of light as quickly as we catch cold but none of them could have faked *The Estuary Pilgrim*, if that's what you're thinking.'

'No?'

Napier shook his head. 'Unfortunately not. The technical problems would be far beyond the scope of this lot.'

'Pity.'

They moved back and leaned against the harbour wall. A breath of wind gusted down the quayside, ruffling the awning of the nearby café.

Spooner gave a shiver and glanced round over his shoulder.

The tide was out and fishing boats lay stranded in the mud, the painted hulls resting on their plump bilges. They looked forlorn and abandoned.

Perched on the hatch of one boat, his feet set against the sharp incline of the deck was a lone figure. He was staring out at the empty expanse of mud, a cigarette dangling from his lips.

Napier leaned over the parapet and called down to him, 'How's the engine running?'

The man peered round suspiciously, decided his ears had deceived him and returned to his contemplations.

Napier tried again.

This time the fisherman calculated the trajectory of the sound and looked up. Giving a grunt of understanding he lumbered to his feet and began to climb the iron ladder.

'It's going pretty good,' he said as his head appeared over the harbour wall beside them.

'You're not going out then?'

'I can't,' he replied, 'the boat's stuck on the mud.' Crossing his thick forearms the man settled his weight on the parapet, his belly pressing comfortably against the stone wall like a ship's fender.

'This is Albert,' Napier explained.

Spooner bobbed his head in introduction. 'It seems rather a waste of resources,' he remarked conversationally. 'Couldn't the channel be dredged in some way?'

'It is,' Albert replied. 'Every bloody year they have a go at digging it out but it doesn't make a bugger of difference. There's mud now and there always will be. The whole damned town's floating on mud.'

'It's not going to sink is it?'

Albert shook his head. 'The harbour will just silt up one day and that'll be the end of it.'

Spooner stared across the water and tried to picture this gloomy prophecy.

A flash of colour on the far shore caught his attention. Walking down the quayside opposite them was the slim figure of a girl. The thick mane of golden hair and the graceful movements of her body were unmistakable, even at this distance. It was that young lioness from the museum, Jacqui Fontenay.

What a tactless moment for her to appear.

Spooner glanced at Napier out of the corner of his eye to see if he had noticed her.

He had.

Napier was watching her intently. His mood darkened as though a shadow had passed over him.

Spooner turned back to the harbour.

He had no idea what had passed between those two. There must have been some sort of disagreement. Ever since Napier had returned from lunch at her guardian's house he had been unusually silent. He hadn't wanted to discuss the occasion and managed to change the subject whenever Jacqui's name was mentioned.

There was a bleak, haunted look in Napier's eyes as he looked at her now.

Spooner felt faintly inadequate.

He would have liked to have smoothed over the moment, made light of it with some understanding remark, but he didn't know what to say. The trouble was he was not a man of experience, never would be. Women were an alien territory to him. He found them unpredictable and rather daunting at the best of times, while a strong-willed madam like this one was positively frightening.

Jacqui had paused by a waterside café and was scanning the tables. She seemed hesitant, uncertain, as though searching for someone she might not recognise. A figure at a far table had half-lifted himself from his seat and now beckoned towards her. Jacqui pushed through the café towards him, there was a brief greeting and they sat down together.

Napier was suddenly alert.

'You don't have any binoculars, do you?' he asked Albert.

He nodded. Pushing himself away from the harbour wall he clambered down on to his boat, rummaged about in the little deck cabin and emerged with a brass telescope. 'This any good?' he asked.

'Perfect.'

Napier directed the telescope in towards the café. He held it there for a moment and then allowed himself a growl of satisfaction.

'Good legs, eh?' Albert asked, his face melting down into a grin.

Napier ignored him and handed the telescope over to Spooner. 'Take a look,' he ordered.

'What at?'

'The man she's talking with.'

Gingerly Spooner set the telescope against his eye. The image was blurred and dark on one side like the onset of an eclipse. He twisted the head and it shrank into focus.

Jacqui was sitting with her back to them, her elbows set on the café table. She leaned back at that moment, giving Spooner a clear view of her companion.

He must have been thirty years older than Jacqui. His head was held low, as though he were speaking confidentially and he was gesticulating freely with one hand.

Spooner steadied the telescope. He was able to make out the man's features but still didn't recognise them. Turning to Napier he asked, 'You know him?'

'Certainly,' he replied. 'It's Maurice Lebas.'

Luc Gabot lit a cigarette.

He turned slightly as he did so, as though shielding the flame from the wind, and glanced up over his cupped hands.

The Englishman hadn't moved.

He was still there, leaning against the harbour wall talking with his two friends. One of them had taken the telescope from him and was now peering across the water.

What were they looking at, for Christ's sakes?

Luc returned the lighter to his pocket and strolled on down the quayside, keeping in with the throng of tourists.

A large crowd had gathered around one of the artists' easels. Luc pressed in amongst them and stared at the unfinished painting. It was the third time he'd seen it. If the Englishman didn't shift in the next few minutes he would have to find new

131

cover. He couldn't go on looking at these damned pictures all morning.

It might arouse suspicion.

There was a row of shops further along the harbour. Luc examined them carefully. They would be a good vantage point to watch from and he could kill time looking in the windows. But to reach them would mean walking right past the Englishman. He assessed the possibilities in his mind.

It was worth the risk.

Extracting himself from the crowd he sauntered down the quayside towards the three men.

As he approached them, the large untidy-looking fisherman detached himself from the group and clambered down on to the deck of his boat. The other two leaned over the wall and watched him go.

Luc grasped the chance. It was the ideal moment to pass.

He walked on a little faster.

They were very close to him now, just a few yards away. As he drew level he could hear their voices talking together.

The Englishman suddenly turned.

Luc's heart gave a thump. Just keep going, he told himself, pretend you don't know he's there.

The Englishman was looking straight at him.

Whatever you do don't catch his eye.

Luc looked up at the sky and whistled casually to himself. He forced himself to slow down, reduce his pace to an amble.

The Englishman's attention brushed over him and away to the harbour.

The danger had passed.

Luc relaxed. He allowed himself to walk on a shade faster. He was on the home stretch now and gaining ground with every stride. Reaching the shops, he buried himself behind a rack of postcards and was hidden from sight.

It was so easy.

He'd walked within a few inches of the Englishman without him having an inkling of who he was.

Luc smiled to himself as he thumbed through the postcards. He liked this work. It required guts and initiative and he had plenty of both. Better than that damned job he'd had in the docks, better than breaking his ass all day long unloading ship containers.

He glanced back along the quayside.

Ah, at last. The Englishman had moved. He had left the harbour wall and was strolling down the quayside with the older of his two companions.

Luc waited until he had estimated their precise direction and then, slipping out from the safety of the shop entrance, he followed on behind.

Chapter Ten

The trees were beginning to turn, Jacqui noticed as she
drew in off the road and accelerated up the drive to the
château. Gusts of autumn wind tugged and fretted at the
branches above the car and the first leaves were beginning
to fall. They drifted across the avenue like the last-minute
figures who dart across a racetrack before the start.

She parked in her usual place below the terrace and jumped
out, glancing at her watch. It was twelve-forty. She'd spent the
morning shopping and lost track of the time, setting off from
Honfleur later than she'd intended.

The hallway was deserted.

Jacqui guessed that Rupert would be in the upper gallery.
It was the largest and most formal of the rooms in the château
and he preferred to use it whenever he was entertaining anything more than a handful of guests.

She ran up the stairs.

The double doors at the head stood open and a murmur
of voices filtered out on to the landing. Jacqui touched her
waist and hair in a quick instinctive gesture, checking her
appearance. She'd put on a black cocktail dress for the
occasion, light and flimsy, cut high enough above the knee
to draw attention to her legs without putting them on public
exhibition.

Brushing a smile on to her face she went in.

There was a dozen or more guests in the room. They
stood grouped around the fireplace halfway down the long
gallery.

Jacqui walked towards them with a firm, determined stride,
announcing her presence with the sharp click of her heels.
She had an unnatural fear of going unnoticed in a crowd of
strangers, of being left on one side.

As she drew close Ashford broke off his conversation
and turned towards her, questioning her late arrival with a

slight lift of his brow. She kissed him quickly and, without apologising, turned to the couple nearest her.

They were a quiet, urbane pair – the husband pink and slightly flushed as though his collar was too tight, the wife thinner and more assertive, evidently the spokesman of the two.

Jacqui couldn't place them. As usual she'd been carefully briefed on the guest list by Rupert beforehand but these two didn't seem to fit any of his descriptions.

'Of course Deauville isn't fashionable at this time of the year,' the woman was saying, 'but it's nice to get away from the city from time to time.'

She had them now. They were clients of Rupert's: a property dealer and his wife who were staying on the coast for the winter.

'But still it's very beautiful here in the autumn,' Jacqui replied, searching for their names in her mind. A tall figure drew close and hovered at her shoulder. She turned slightly, allowing him into the circle.

'Jacqui,' he murmured, stooping and kissing her on both cheeks. 'How very good to see you again.'

'And you, Antoine.'

'You're looking ravishing as usual,' he drawled, 'the sea air obviously does you good.'

The compliment was studied, mechanical, but she thanked him with her light laugh. 'Have you met?' she asked, turning back to the couple beside her. 'This is Claude and Rose-Marie Delfargue.'

They stepped forward and shook hands, delighted to have been recognised in this way.

Louis appeared at her elbow with a tray of drinks.

She took a glass and touched it to her lips. It was rich and delicious; a Bellini, her favourite cocktail. She took the moment to turn to the group next to her, engaging them with her dazzling smile, drawing them into the conversation around her.

Within a few minutes Jacqui was the centre of attention.

She was playing a part. It was all she ever seemed to be doing nowadays, she realised, but it didn't really matter. Rupert wanted her to behave this way; it was why he needed her.

135

He seemed pleased by her performance. Coming and standing behind her, he ran his hand down her back until it rested on her hip. She turned and looked up at him.

'Come my dear,' he said softly. 'You must meet our guest of honour.'

With a slight pressure from his fingers he propelled her through the crowd towards a figure in a cream-white suit who lounged against the marble fireplace. Jacqui could tell by the slightly self-conscious pose he affected that he was waiting for her.

His eyes explored her as she approached.

'This is Enrique de la Pena,' Ashford announced as he presented her, 'an old and dear friend of mine.'

Enrique took her offered hand in both of his, holding the palm and the wrist as though he were checking the value of her ring. 'It's a pleasure to meet you.'

'Enrique and I used to do business together.'

She knew exactly who he was. Rupert had given her a detailed account of him on the phone the night before, repeating the relevant points until she had them off by heart.

'I don't believe you've met before,' he added.

'No,' Enrique assured him, 'I would have remembered.'

'Are you able to stay long?' Jacqui asked politely.

His eyes frisked over her. 'Alas no,' he replied. 'I'm just passing through. I have to be in the South next week on business.' He gave a little bow. 'Had I known who my hostess was to be I might have contrived to stay a little longer.'

Jacqui accepted the remark with a flash of her eyes and tried to withdraw her hand from his grasp but he held it firmly. Raising it to his lips he kissed it slowly and deliberately before returning it to her.

He wore too much gold Jacqui noticed. His cufflinks were as large as walnuts, there were rings on three of his fingers and a thick gold watch on his wrist whose strap dug into the flesh.

'I was showing Enrique one of my drawings,' Ashford put in, indicating a small framed pastel that stood on an easel by the wall.

'Oh, you've brought out the little Degas,' Jacqui cried, turning her attention to the picture. 'I'm so glad, it's my favourite. Do you like paintings?' she asked Enrique.

136

'Of course,' he replied without looking at it. 'I admire anything of beauty.'

The innuendo was intentional and laboured.

Jacqui deflected it with a change of subject. 'You've been to the château before, I believe.'

'About four years ago.'

'Ah, that would explain why I wasn't here,' she said brightly. 'I must have been away at university at the time.'

She wondered which country he came from. The name sounded Spanish but he could well be South American. Argentinian maybe, or Brazilian? It was impossible to tell from his accent. His skin was sallow and slightly unhealthy-looking, his expression sensual. She could feel his eyes searching under her clothes, touching her as she spoke. Her instinct was to flinch away but she overcame it and stood before him relaxed and confident.

'Do you live here now?' he asked.

'No, I have an apartment in Honfleur.'

He inclined his head a degree. 'I must pay you a visit. It's such a picturesque little town.'

'You know it?'

'Vaguely,' he replied. 'I remember it as a place of indifferent art galleries and rather better restaurants.'

'I'm not certain that's entirely fair.'

Ashford gave a little laugh. 'You two obviously have a great deal to talk about,' he cut in. 'I've put you together at lunch so you can discuss it all then.'

His manner was genial but he seemed more preoccupied than usual. On the way downstairs he drew Jacqui aside for a moment.

'Dr Napier,' he began in a low voice. 'I invited him this evening for a drink but not to lunch beforehand. Was that a mistake?'

Jacqui was surprised by the question. 'I don't think it matters either way, does it, Rupert?'

'You don't mind?'

She shook her head. 'Of course not.'

'I thought you might have wanted him here.'

'I hardly know him, Rupert.'

He seemed faintly relieved by this answer. 'Have you seen him at all recently?'

'Not since we were here last. Why do you ask?'

'He seemed very interested in you, I thought maybe there was something between you.'

Jacqui smiled. 'He means nothing to me,' she said gently. 'It was just business.'

Crossing the room she took her place at the far end of the table. Enrique sat down on her right but he didn't seem inclined to speak at first. Instead he ate industriously, frequently mopping his lips with the white damask napkin.

Jacqui turned her attention to the elderly gentleman on her left and listened appreciatively as he explained the changes of agriculture that had taken place in the district since the war. He was polite and well meaning but his conversation was inclined to ramble and after a few minutes she found her concentration beginning to slip.

She was puzzled by Rupert's questions. It seemed strange that he should bother to invite Napier in the first place. The tension between the two men had been so pronounced that she would have expected him to have avoided a second meeting.

And why did he want to know whether she'd seen him again?

She gave a start and almost spilled her wine. Under cover of the table Enrique's hand had found its way on to her thigh. Abruptly she crossed her legs and returned to the subject of agriculture.

At that moment Rose-Marie Delfargue butted into the monologue. Craning down the table she said, 'Aren't you the clever girl who discovered that painting the other day?'

'I didn't discover it,' Jacqui replied modestly. 'I happened to come across some information just before it was discovered.'

'Still,' she pursued stolidly, 'it was all very exciting. I read about it in the papers.'

Enrique's hand returned. This time it was more insistent, gliding beneath her thigh and pushing up under her dress. Jacqui turned and shot him a look that should have shrivelled him in his seat but he merely took it as a cue to join in the discussion.

'I have heard a rumour that it's a fake,' he remarked, raising his knife with his free hand and waving it in the air like a conductor's baton.

'Really?' breathed Rose-Marie, her mind alerting to the scent of scandal. 'Is that true?'

'An English art historian has suggested it's a fake,' Jacqui acknowledged quickly, brushing Enrique's hand away. 'But I don't think he has much evidence.'

'Then why has he said it?'

'I don't really know but you can ask him yourself. He's coming over here later this afternoon.'

Rose-Marie Delfargue turned to her neighbours and began telegraphing the news up the table.

'Are you something to do with the art world?' Jacqui asked, sitting back and looking at Enrique.

'Not directly.'

'But you've been involved with Rupert's business?'

'Only in financial terms.'

Jacqui realised that she knew very little about Rupert's affairs. He owned galleries in London and New York as well as most of the major capitals of Europe but she had no idea of how they were operated. 'Are you some sort of merchant banker?' she asked.

Enrique's eyes veiled. 'More like an investment broker.'

'And you provided the financial backing for his galleries?'

'In the early years.'

He seemed disinclined to say more. Jacqui pressed him but he wasn't going to be drawn on the subject again.

As soon as lunch was over Ashford took his guests out into the garden. The wind had dropped, the grass was damp and the rich, fertile scent of the earth hung in the air.

Jacqui loved this time of year. The stillness of the light, the slight sense of sadness as summer slipped into autumn was so peaceful. It reminded her of bonfires, roasted chestnuts and childhood walks with Pacquetta.

After half an hour, as Rupert was taking them into the orchid house, she made excuses and ran up to her room. She no longer lived at the château but she kept a few clothes there for occasions such as these.

Taking off her dress and hanging it on the back of a chair, she changed into her riding clothes. She tied back her hair and inspected the overall effect in a full length mirror, twisting round to inspect the view from behind. Carrying her riding boots in one hand she padded downstairs on white-stockinged feet.

Enrique was waiting for her on the landing.

'Ah,' he exclaimed, 'I see you're going riding.' His eyes ran

139

down over her tight white breeches in satisfaction. 'I thought girls lost interest in horses when they were sixteen.'

It was on the tip of her tongue to tell him that she thought men stopped making such remarks at much the same age but she bit it back. Instead she asked, 'Are you not interested to see the orchids?'

'I decided I'd leave that pleasure to the others and take the time to finish my coffee in peace.'

Jacqui tried to pass him but he barred the way.

'You're just the person I need at this moment,' he said, taking her by the arm and drawing her into the gallery. 'I was admiring this little picture of Rupert's but I know so little about art.'

He positioned her in front of the Degas and studied it with interest.

'Is it a watercolour?' he asked.

'No, a pastel.'

'Ah, now how can you tell that so easily?'

'Pastels are like coloured chalks,' she explained obligingly, 'they're much drier looking than watercolour.'

Enrique was standing very close to her.

He leaned towards the painting as she spoke and examined the surface, absorbed by what she was telling him.

Jacqui stiffened.

His hand slipped around her waist.

She stood quite still and stared at the little pastel. It was of a young girl brushing her hair in a mirror. She was seated at a dressing table, the bodice of her dress was open and her bare breasts just visible in the cleavage.

He studied it critically.

Jacqui had a sudden desire to snatch the picture away from him, to hide the girl's nakedness from his eyes.

He straightened up. As he did so his hand glided off Jacqui's waist and on to the smooth surface of her bottom.

She twisted away with a little smile of reproval.

'Why not?' he asked under his breath.

'I'd rather you didn't.'

He shrugged. 'As you like.'

Standing back he looked at her thoughtfully. His voice became business-like. 'I'm travelling down to the South of France later this week,' he told her. 'I'll be there for a month, maybe more. Why don't you join me?'

'I don't think that would be a very good idea, would
it?'

'Why not?'

'I hardly know you.'

The reply seemed to amuse him, as though it betrayed
some hidden naïvety on her part. He drew in close again.

'I don't think that need worry us,' he murmured. 'There
must be things a girl like you needs – things that require
money and influence. There is a great deal I could offer you.'
The smile was confident. 'I'm certain we can come to some
arrangement.'

'I'm not sure I would like that,' she replied quietly.

Enrique glanced around at the elegant rococo gallery.
'You say that, but don't you already have—'

'No,' she said sharply, 'I don't.'

'But surely . . .'

'It's not what you think.'

'What then?'

His voice was low and urgent now, his lips so close that
she could feel his breath on her face. He ran his arms around
her shoulders, down the curve of her back, drawing her into
himself. The sweet scent of pomade wafted from his body.
She tried to pull away but he held her, his hands clinging to
her like wet leaves.

A wave of anger welled up in her.

Putting her forearms against his shirt front she pushed
him away. For a moment they struggled together and then
Enrique's grip broke and he stepped back.

They faced each other warily.

Enrique straightened his tie. 'I'm sorry,' he said with heavy
sarcasm. 'It seems we have misunderstood each other.'

Jacqui looked down at the ground. 'Yes,' she said quickly,
'I think so.'

'I had naturally assumed . . .'

'I'd rather you hadn't.'

He stared at her, his expression sullen. 'Maybe when you've
had time to consider my proposal.'

'I don't think so.'

'Had I realised you were so cold-natured I would have . . .'

'Just go please.'

He looked as though he was about to speak, checked
himself, and turning on his heels he left the room.

141

As soon as he was gone Jacqui smiled ruefully to herself and let out a sigh of relief.

It wasn't the first time that a man had jumped on her and it probably wouldn't be the last. But why did it always have to be the odious ones who tried their luck?

Quickly she began to repair the damage. Fastening a button that had come undone in the struggle she tucked in her shirt and turned to leave.

She gave a jump. Someone was standing behind her.

It was Ashford.

He had come in through the far door and now stood in the centre of the floor watching her.

'Oh,' she cried, 'I didn't see you there.'

He walked towards her.

'What are you doing?' he asked as he drew close.

She made light of the affair. 'I was just trying to dampen your friend's enthusiasm.'

'Did you have to behave like that?'

Jacqui looked at him in surprise. 'I'm sorry,' she said slowly, 'I didn't intend it to happen.'

She had somehow assumed that Rupert would take her side over this, possibly even apologise for Enrique's behaviour, but she saw now that she was mistaken.

Ashford was white with anger.

'I asked you here today to entertain my guests,' he snapped, 'not insult them.'

'Is it my fault if he made a pass at me?'

Ashford waved this aside. 'It's just his way of showing appreciation.'

'Appreciation?' she echoed. She was becoming angry herself now. 'Is that what you call it?'

'Appreciation, excitement, lust – what does it matter what it's called?'

'It matters a great deal to me.'

Ashford's voice became silky. 'I don't expect much of you, my dear. I've given you a home to live in, a career and anything else you wanted. I don't ask for love or even gratitude from you in return, but you could at least be civil to my friends when I want it.'

Jacqui gaped at him. 'You're not suggesting that I . . .' Her voice trailed away.

Surely he couldn't mean that?

'Quite how you conduct yourself is your affair, my dear, but I feel you could be a shade more accommodating.'

My God, it was exactly what he did mean.

She rounded on him. 'You want me to provide room service for your friends, is that it?'

Ashford ignored the remark.

'Is that it?' she repeated. She could feel her anger seething up inside her, hot and dangerous.

'I didn't say so.'

'I'm one of the perks of the house now, am I? The complimentary tart for the weekend.'

'Of course not.'

'Well, what then?'

'I just ask you to be a little more accessible, that's all.'

'Who the hell do you think I am?' she cried, the words rising on the crest of her temper.

Ashford paused. The suggestion of a smile touched his lips. 'I don't know,' he replied softly. 'Sometimes I ask myself the same question.'

There was a frozen silence.

'What do you mean by that?' Jacqui asked.

'These high-blown morals of yours – these fine sentiments. Where do they all come from?'

She stared at him, her eyes round and startled.

'I mean, they can't be inherited.'

Her anger evaporated.

Ashford smiled again.

She felt a sudden clutch of panic in her stomach. 'What are you trying to say?' she asked quickly.

'I was thinking of your mother, if you must know.'

'What of her.'

Ashford looked at her thoughtfully, calculating his reply. He was in control now, master of the situation. 'Your mother was a remarkable woman in many ways,' he said eventually. 'Talented and intelligent – beautiful like yourself, my dear – but hardly renowned for her virtue.'

Jacqui gave a little cry and fell back a pace as though she'd been hit in the face.

Ashford stepped forwards. Reaching out he put his hand into her shirt and grasped the locket that hung around her neck.

He gave a quick pull.

143

The fine gold chain stretched and snapped.

He held it in the palm of his hand. Putting his thumbnail into the joint he prised open the lid.

Inside were two tiny photographs; portraits of a man and a woman.

Ashford studied them for a moment and then shut it again.

'This sentimental attachment to your parents' memory is all very charming, my dear,' he said softly, 'but in the circumstances I find it faintly ridiculous.'

He threw the locket aside in disgust. It tinkled down on to the polished wooden floor and skittered away against the wall.

Without another word he went out.

Jacqui stood quite still.

She listened to his feet retreating downstairs.

Her body trembled. She was breathing heavily. Dark and ugly thoughts swirled through her mind. Putting one hand to her neck she touched the red weal where the gold chain had cut into her skin.

Gradually she collected her wits and looked about herself.

The locket lay further down the room. She walked over and picking it up she held it tightly in her clenched fist.

The panic that had gripped her died away and in its place there rose a new emotion.

It was fierce and raw but as yet it had no name.

Luc Gabot read the newspaper without taking in a word.

He turned the page, stealing a glance over the top as he did so.

The Englishman was still there, sitting in the next-door café drinking coffee.

Luc returned to his reading.

He was becoming slightly bored by this assignment. The trouble was that the Englishman never did anything. In the last three days he had wandered about the town with no apparent purpose, talking to waiters and shopkeepers and parking wardens around the harbour. It was as though he was searching for something but didn't know where to begin.

There was one spot on the quayside that seemed to interest him in particular. He frequently stopped there and stood gazing out at the harbour in a sort of trance.

Luc had no idea who this John Napier was or why he

needed to be followed and he hadn't bothered to ask. He never did.

It was better not to know.

Nevertheless, he'd stick to divorce work in future. That was far more exciting.

Turning to one side, he cleared his throat and spat on the ground.

There was a flutter of movement in the café.

Napier was getting up to go. Luc watched as he counted through his small change, left a few coins on the table and sauntered out on to the quayside.

Without looking round he headed off towards the town.

Luc waited until he was some distance away before leaving his seat and slipping into his wake.

Taking a short cut through the market square Napier returned to his hotel.

Luc hovered in the street outside.

A large blue convertible was parked in the driveway. Napier had paused and was talking to the driver. The door was opened and he climbed in, stretching out his arms along the fawn leather seat as he sat back.

Luc glanced rapidly up and down the street.

There was a telephone booth on the corner. He went over to it and picked up the receiver, turning his back to the hotel entrance.

The car pulled out of the gates, turned downhill and purred away into the distance, its twin exhausts dribbling vapour.

Luc hung up the phone and stepping out into the road he watched it go. He sat down on the grass verge and lit a cigarette. He could relax for a while.

He didn't have orders to follow Napier away from Honfleur.

Jacqui spurred the horse to a gallop.

Leaning forwards she urged him on, pushing him to his limit. The wind roared in her ears, snatching the breath from her mouth. The wiry hairs of the mane whipped at her face and clods of earth spun up from the drumming hooves. She could feel the powerful muscles of the animal bunching and stretching beneath her. Moulding herself to the rhythm, she let the energy of his body flow into hers until horse and rider became one and they flew across the open heath together.

145

Her one thought was to escape, to get as far away from the château as possible. Rupert's words thrummed in her ears as she rode. She saw his pale face before her, furious in its intent. Heard his voice, felt the bite of the chain in her skin as he wrenched the locket from her neck. But for the time being the resentment, the fierce uncontrolled emotion that had swept through her in the gallery, was lost in the beat of the galloping hooves, the excitement of the moment. The strength and speed of the horse possessed her, filling her with a wild exaltation that allowed for no other sensation.

As they reached the high ground above the estuary she stood back in the stirrups and reined him in. The horse snorted and tossed his head, breaking stride as he slowed to a walk. Jacqui reached down and stroked the thick neck, murmuring a few words of praise in his ear. She was flushed and breathless from the ride, her face still tingling from the rush of wind.

Sitting back in the saddle she dropped the reins, letting the horse take its own path. The racing of her heart steadied; thoughts became coherent once more.

Rupert used her, this she knew.

She was an instrument, a necessary component of his private kingdom. He had practically said as much to her earlier that year. They had been to the opera, as they often did when they were in Paris together. At the end of the performance, as they were leaving the lavishly carved and gilded foyer, evening dresses, jewellery and fur coats sweeping around them, Rupert had turned to her and said, 'You are looking very beautiful tonight, my dear.' She had smiled, slipping her arm through his, pleased by this unexpected compliment. 'I like that in you,' he'd continued, 'it amuses me to see the envy on other men's faces.' And then sensing her stiffen he'd added, 'Desire is a weakness, my dear, did you not know that? It makes men vulnerable, makes them malleable.'

The bluntness of this observation, the quiet satisfaction it seemed to give him, had shocked her, the words lingering in her mind long afterwards. But it hadn't surprised her. She understood that Rupert had no interest in her personally, only in the effect she had on others. He needed her to fascinate his friends, to charm his rivals. She was his agent, his ambassador. She served a purpose.

And for this he despised her.

His remarks just now in the gallery had been deliberate, sharp and cruel. He had invoked the name of her mother to scare her, to prey on the fears that haunted her mind. Speaking out of spite more than anger, twisting the situation around to his advantage, using it as a weapon to inflict pain.

There were times when she thought he enjoyed hurting her.

'Well I'm not going to let him,' she said fiercely. 'I don't care what he does to me, I'll ignore it. He can't hurt me unless I let him.'

Turning around in the saddle she looked back at the château. It lay about a mile away, the carved stone façade half-clouded in autumn trees. The early evening light warmed the seal-grey rooftops, misting the shadows with bluish vapours.

It was a beautiful building, majestic and serene, graced with the privacy of extreme wealth.

How had Rupert made his money? she wondered. The house alone must be worth a fortune. She knew several art dealers in Paris. They were well off, some of them could even be considered rich, but nothing compared to Rupert. As far as she knew his money wasn't inherited. It couldn't be. She'd often heard him boast that he'd made everything he owned.

Thoughtfully she stroked the palms of her hands down over her thighs. It was strange, until Enrique's arrival she had never really thought about Rupert's wealth. It had just been there, one side of his personality. There had been no reason to question it.

But then there was a great deal that she didn't understand, that she needed to learn.

The horse ambled forwards, following the narrow thread of a path in the chalk. Jacqui's eyes rested on the distant horizon as she thought back over her conversation with Enrique at lunch. She recalled how his eyes had veiled, how his voice had dropped when she asked him of Rupert's business, evading the questions she put to him.

But then the clammy warmth of his hand sliding down over her body returned to her, she felt his breath on her face, the clutch of his arms. Reason enflamed into emotion once more. Arching her back she shook her head, her breath hissing between clenched teeth. 'Not like that!' she cried to herself. 'It shouldn't be like that!'

A rabbit suddenly darted across the path in front of them.

147

The horse shied. With a quick buck of his head he jumped and danced away to one side on stiff legs.

Jacqui was taken by surprise.

The sudden jolt threw her forwards over the horse's neck. She tried to save herself, grasped at the mane but missed. With a yelp she left the saddle and plunged downwards, landed on the edge of the pathway. The ground was steep and fell away beneath her. Jacqui tumbled down over the damp grass and came to rest against a clump of gorse bushes in an undignified heap of legs and arms.

Her head swam and cleared.

Slowly she rolled herself over on to her back. The breeze was fresh and cool on her skin, the salt tang of the open sea brushed over her. For some minutes she lay staring up at the sky while her thoughts settled like dust in her mind.

It was no good, she must go back to the château. It had been her intention to leave, to collect her clothes and drive back to Honfleur, but she saw now that was not the solution. Running away from Rupert wasn't going to help. She must play the part that had been written for her, return to his house and wait her chance. If she was ever going to break free, Rupert must be confronted. She must face up to him. Only then could she escape, only then could she sever the invisible cords that tied her to him.

Now that her mind was made up, she felt calmer. The decision gave her strength once more. Getting to her feet she slapped the dirt and grass off her breeches. Her horse stood on the path above her, innocently nibbling at the grass. She scrambled up the hillside towards him and picking up the reins she stroked his forelock.

'Thought you'd knock some sense into me, did you?' she murmured reproachfully. Putting one foot into the stirrup she swung herself up into the saddle, glancing at her watch as she did so.

It was almost five, Rupert's guests would have arrived by now. He'd be expecting her, growing impatient at her absence.

Turning the horse around she cantered back down the hillside. Taking a short cut through the park she reached the driveway. She gathered in his head and trotted him up the avenue of trees.

As she approached the château she noticed a figure standing

on the front steps. The slim build, the neat tailored jacket were unmistakable.

It was John Napier.

Jacqui paused. She'd forgotten that he'd been invited that evening but now at the sight of him she felt a sudden spark, a gleam of interest that, had she been less preoccupied with her own thoughts, would have surprised her.

The horse slowed to a walk.

Napier saw her hesitate.

Running back down the steps he crossed the gravel drive towards her.

Jacqui reined in her horse and waited for him to approach, the leather of the horse's tack creaking comfortably.

She sat well, he noticed, her back straight, her heels down in the stirrups.

'How did you get here?' she asked after they had come close enough to exchange cautious greetings.

'A car came to pick me up at the hotel,' he replied. 'A Rolls – blue, with an open top.'

Jacqui nodded and said, 'Ah yes.'

'At least that's what I assume it was. It felt more like a private hovercraft.'

Napier took hold of the bridle, cupping the horse's velvet muzzle in his other hand and glanced up at Jacqui thinking, not for the first time in his life, how sexy some women could look in their riding clothes.

Her hair was tucked away out of sight in her hat. The upper buttons of her white shirt were open and the collar spread wide across her shoulders. Her sleeves were rolled back from brown forearms and her tall black boots were polished like the barrels of a shotgun.

'I didn't know you had a horse.'

'I don't,' she replied quickly. 'This is one of Rupert's. I just exercise him at weekends.'

For a moment Jacqui looked down at him from her superior height and then, kicking her toes from the stirrups, she swung one leg over the horse's neck and vaulted to the ground beside him.

There was a fresh green stain on her shoulder, he noticed, and another on her hip.

'You came off?'

'Yes,' she said primly.

'Any particular reason, apart from a natural desire to return to Mother Earth?'

She shot him a glance out of the corner of her eye. 'A rabbit startled him.'

She led the horse around to the stables, the hooves suddenly loud and hollow on the cobbled surface of the yard, and put him into one of the loose-boxes.

Napier leaned on the stable door and watched as she busied herself about the place.

'How are you getting on with your investigations?' she asked, unstrapping the buckle of the girth.

'Not very well, to be honest.'

She ducked her head under the horse's neck and looked at him. 'Are you going to give up?'

'Not yet.'

She emerged into the light, carrying the saddle over her arm.

'Would you like me to take that?' he asked.

'It's quite all right, I'm used to it.' She went into the tack-room, bearing the weight on her hip as though it were a child. Napier followed her to the entrance. It was dark inside and rich with the heavy fragrances of hay and oiled leather. Polished brass gleamed in the crack of light from the opened door.

Jacqui settled the saddle on its rack and reaching up on tiptoe she hung the bridle in place. She came out, closing the door behind her. Taking off her hat she shook her head and the golden avalanche of hair fell about her shoulders.

'So you still think something will turn up?' she asked.

'Somebody does.'

'How do you mean?'

'I have a strong suspicion that I'm being followed.'

Jacqui paused and swung round on him. 'What makes you say that?'

'I've seen one face too often for coincidence.'

She glanced round at the deserted yard, peacefully settling in the evening sunshine. 'Do you see him here?'

'No.'

She looked at him speculatively for a moment. 'Maybe you're imagining things.'

'I don't think so.'

150

She rested her hands on her hips and the wings of her eyebrows arched at him.

Napier sighed inwardly. She was the most frustrating girl he'd ever met. Nothing he said or did ever managed to convince her.

It would be easier to take it if he didn't find her so attractive – if he could find some flaw in her. But standing there in the sunlight, her skin still glowing from her ride, she looked strong and healthy and infinitely desirable.

He wanted to reach out, to take hold of her in his arms.

Jacqui seemed to sense his thoughts for, turning on her heel, she stalked away towards the château.

'I must go and change now,' she said as they came round into the front driveway. 'I'll see you later.' She paused on the foot of the steps and added, 'You'll find the others round on the terrace.'

A large group was assembled at the rear of the house. They were smartly dressed and talking noisily, moving amongst each other in the slow ritualised dance of cocktail parties.

Waiters pressed between them, bearing trays and bottles of champagne scarved in white napkins.

Napier's arrival didn't pass unnoticed.

As soon as he appeared a woman fluttered over to him. Was he the art historian who was causing all the fuss about the picture? she wanted to know.

He admitted he was.

Others followed in her wake, eager to join in the discussion. Napier took a glass and fended off the attack as best he could.

'I mean, either it is a fake or it isn't,' the woman pointed out.

'I think that's right,' he agreed.

'But you're not going to tell us which, I suppose.' She stopped a passing waiter and helped herself to a little roll of smoked salmon.

'I wish I could.'

'I do hope it is fake,' put in another, 'one gets so tired of seeing the real thing all the time.'

Napier steered his way through their opinions. After fifteen minutes Ashford came over, wreathed in smiles, his hand extended. 'Will you excuse us?' he asked politely. 'I'd like to borrow Dr Napier for a moment.'

He took him through the opened windows into the sudden silence of the hallway.

'Last time you were here I seem to remember you wanted to see my pictures.'

'That's right, but don't let me distract you from your guests.'

'They won't miss me,' he remarked. 'One of the advantages of a house this size is that you can get away from people when you want without being noticed.'

He led the way upstairs into the gallery.

It was a graceful room, long and light, with delicately ornate panels leading up to a painted ceiling. As with the rest of the house it was barely furnished.

Ashford paused by one of the windows and looked down at the crowded terrace.

Jacqui had just arrived. She was standing directly below him, talking to a handful of the guests. At that moment she laughed, her head back, her eyes sparkling.

Ashford watched her intently.

'A beautiful creature, Dr Napier,' he said eventually, 'as I'm sure you'd be the first to admit.'

He glanced around at him.

His expression had changed, Napier noticed, it was suddenly hard and somehow predatory.

'Certainly,' he replied evenly.

Ashford turned his attention back to the terrace. 'She reminds me so much of her parents. She has the best of both of them: her mother's figure and her father's wits.' Again he looked at Napier, his single eye cold beside the replica. 'A fortunate combination – had it been the other way round we might all be a shade less interested in her.'

'You knew her parents well, did you?' Napier inquired politely.

Ashford suddenly laughed, as though the suggestion was faintly absurd. 'I wouldn't put it that strongly. I knew her mother, but that's hardly the same thing.'

It was a curious remark. All the more so since it was contrived, a carefully manufactured innuendo. Napier made no response but took the opportunity to ask, 'How did you come to be appointed as her guardian?'

Ashford studied him for a moment, weighing the question.

'You don't mind me asking?'

'No, not at all,' he assured him quickly. 'As a matter

of fact it was my own idea. Jacqui's parents had made no provision for the eventuality – people never seem to expect catastrophes to strike in their own lives, do they? And so when they died there was no one to take their place. And so I offered my services to the family. They appreciated that it was the obvious solution. Jacqui was at school in Rouen and I had recently moved to Normandy. I was fortunate enough to have considerable wealth and a secure home to give her. Added to which, I was not without influence in the district. There were strings that could be pulled for her benefit.'

'And so they accepted your offer.'

'Naturally, it solved a problem for them. Besides, I think they saw a certain justice in the appointment.' Before he could be asked to explain this last remark he moved away from the window.

'But come, Dr Napier, we didn't come up here to discuss past history. I have more interesting candidates for your attention.'

Napier followed him across the floor. Set in the far wall of the gallery was a door, superbly crafted into the panelling, the joints scarcely discernible from a distance.

Ashford took a key from his pocket and unlocked it.

It led through to a smaller room, carpeted and dimly lit. The walls on every side were lined with polished racks.

Ashford gestured towards them and said, 'My paintings.'

Napier looked around in wonder. There must have been five hundred pictures stored in there, maybe more.

Flicking on overhead lights Ashford went over to the nearest rack and drew one out at random. It was a Dutch seascape with becalmed ships on metallic water, limp sails beneath a sun-washed sky.

'You recognise it I'm sure.'

'Van de Velde.'

'It is indeed, Dr Napier. I acquired it in New York in the early sixties.'

'It's a beautiful piece.'

'And worth twenty times what I paid for it at the time.' He slipped it back into its place and pulled out a little Rubens sketch: fine brown washes floated on to a wooden panel.

'But of course your taste is for the 19th century, isn't it?' He crossed over to the racks opposite. Taking out a canvas he showed it to Napier. It was a still–life by Manet, a single rose in a cut–glass vase.

Napier studied it in reverence. The paintwork was exquisite: darting lights dashed ·over warm shadows, the yellow of the rose petals singing out from a ground of lavender grey.

Ashford took it back and handed him a Constable in its place and then a tiny portrait of a girl by Renoir. The sequence was seemingly endless. Ashford's collection was a treasure house, and for almost an hour Napier was lost in it.

'Why do you keep them locked up in here,' he asked at one point, 'if that's not a rude question.'

Ashford spread his hands. 'Paintings are nothing to do with interior decoration, Dr Napier. They should never be hung in a room to suit the colour of the wallpaper.'

'But that's no reason to hide them away completely.' ·

'That's true,' Ashford agreed. He leaned back against the painting racks and folded his arms.

Napier waited for him to continue.

'I don't display them around the house simply because I don't like to be ostentatious about my possessions,' he said after a few moments.

It wasn't the true reason. Ashford had no such reticence, there had to be a more tangible reason, something more practical.

Ashford smiled. 'You don't believe me, Dr Napier?'

'I imagine there's rather more to it than that.'

He nodded thoughtfully. 'You may be right.' Pushing himself into a standing position he walked over to the single window. 'Let me explain. At the end of the war I was given the unenviable task of returning stolen art treasures to their rightful owners in the district. The Germans had systematically looted from every house in northern France. It wasn't just major works. They had taken practically everything they could find with a gold frame around it.'

He paused and stared back through the years.

'They were rather like squirrels, Dr Napier. Some of the paintings had been sent back to Germany, others were sealed up in mineshafts and old railway tunnels or dropped to the bottom of lakes. There were thousands of works of art secreted away in France, all stored up safe, ready for the war to end.'

154

He brushed his hand to one side. 'I need hardly tell you the job of finding them all, identifying their owners and returning them was considerable.

'The tragedy was that in most cases the owners didn't want them back. They were broke, you see. Most of the great families around here had lost everything they had ever owned in the war. What they needed was money not art treasures.

'There was one elderly couple I came across over by Pont-l'Évêque. They were living in a single room of their house, the rest had been destroyed in the Allied advance up the Seine. I brought them a painting, a Tiepolo panel that had once hung in the ceiling of their hall.

'They were cooking their supper when I came in and didn't even bother to look at it.'

He smiled sadly at the memory. 'You can't blame them. What use was it to them? A worthless picture that had been painted for a room that no longer existed.'

'Couldn't they have sold it?' Napier asked.

'Who to? It was 1946, there was no art market. They'd have been lucky to have got the price of the canvas for it.'

He gave a shrug. 'Of course, I did the best I could in the circumstances. Fortunately I had recently come into a small inheritance and was able to buy one or two of these pieces. I didn't want to take advantage of the situation but it was almost impossible not to. People were begging me to take their possessions. Before I knew it I had become a picture dealer.' He gave a little nod of his head to indicate the serried ranks of pictures. 'The rest followed from there.'

'You mean you built everything from those first sales?'

'The art market boomed after the war, as you know Dr Napier. Property and antiques were the best investment going and I was lucky to be involved in both.

'Make no mistake, I'd paid a good price for my pictures at the time but it bore no resemblance to the value they reached a few years later. Increases of a thousand, two thousand per cent were commonplace. It was almost embarrassing how much money I made on the market.' He turned, his voice suddenly light. 'Which is why I don't display my collection all over the house nowadays. To some families around here the sight of them would be like salt in the wound.'

155

Following this disclosure Ashford seemed suddenly self-conscious and there was a moment's hush in the room.

A thought bubbled up to the surface of Napier's mind. 'Did you buy anything from Eugenie Delaroche?'

The question startled Ashford. He looked round sharply. 'What makes you ask that?'

'No reason,' Napier replied quietly. 'I just wondered.'

Ashford studied him.

'Yes,' he said, 'I bought her paintings.'

'And were they worth anything?'

'Not much.' He took a cigarette from his silver case and lit it, drawing in a lungful of smoke. His manner relaxed again. 'Poor Eugenie,' he murmured, the smoke pouring out with the words. 'She'd fallen on hard times.'

'I hear she was accused of collaboration.'

He nodded. 'It didn't take much to earn that distinction in those days. I bought one or two trinkets from her. At the time I thought I was doing her a good turn but, looking back at it now, I think she resented the intrusion.' He smoked pensively, gazing away into the distance. 'I still try to help her out on occasion. That hotel of hers is hardly a commercial success as you've probably noticed. I buy a few pictures off her when I can – vulgar little things on the whole. I've no idea what she expects me to do with them.'

He turned and looked up at Napier. 'How did you know all this?'

'It was just a guess,' he replied. 'I noticed that some of the wallpaper in the hotel had dark rectangular patches on it. I assumed they had been caused by paintings. Since there's nothing of that scale in the house today I took it that they had been sold. I calculated when from the age of the paper.'

'An ingenious piece of detective work,' Ashford said, touching the cigarette to his lips and studying him through the screen of smoke. 'I was forgetting what a very observant young man you are, Dr Napier.' He paused and then added, 'I do hope this talent of yours doesn't get you into trouble one day.'

They were interrupted by the sharp click of heels.

Napier looked out through the door to see Jacqui approaching down the length of the gallery. She was walking across the polished floor with her long, open stride. As she passed through the shaft of light from each window in turn the shadow of her body was silhouetted against the flimsy material of her dress.

She paused in the doorway.

'You're not leaving already are you?' Ashford asked, going across to her.

'I have to.'

'But I've hardly seen you today, my dear.'

She gave a little shrug, as if to say it was not her fault. There was a tension between the two of them, Napier noticed, an unmistakable wariness. Jacqui's eyes smouldered as she waited. Ashford reached out to touch her but she glided away from his hand and turning to Napier said, 'If you want a lift you must come now.'

'You were showing him your pictures?' Enrique was disturbed at the prospect. Taking a silver swivel-stick from his lapel pocket he revolved it in his champagne, replaced it and drank half the glass in a single mouthful. 'Was that wise?' he asked.

'Not wise but necessary.'

'How's that?'

'Dr Napier wants to know more about me,' replied Ashford. 'I felt it was better to feed his curiosity rather than starve it.'

'He doesn't suspect anything?'

'No, why should he?'

They strolled across the lawn, leaving the few guests who lingered on the terrace behind them. The sun had gone down and a slight chill had invaded the air.

'Do you think he will manage to discredit *The Estuary Pilgrim?*' Enrique inquired.

'Oh yes, I'm sure he will.'

'You seem very certain.'

'No fake is perfect,' Ashford replied. 'There's bound to be a flaw somewhere. Now that his suspicion is aroused I'd say it was only a matter of time before he finds it.'

'That doesn't worry you?'

'There's still no way he can link my name to the painting.'

'Can't he?' Enrique drained his glass and tossed the dregs on to the grass. 'I would have thought he has come dangerously close to doing so already.'

'Yes,' said Ashford dryly. 'Well, should that situation arise I would have to dispense with him.'

157

'Isn't that rather risky?'

'Not necessarily,' Ashford replied. 'We've been given a slight advantage. Napier is convinced that *The Estuary Pilgrim* has been forged by Maurice Lebas.'

'Who's he?'

'The legal heir to the painting. He's a businessman in Le Havre – runs a shipping line of some sort. I've met him a couple of times socially. He's an aggressive, pushy sort not above tailoring the law to his requirements. I wouldn't be in the least surprised if he's not on the police files already.' Ashford smiled. 'He fits the part perfectly.'

Enrique nodded. 'So if anything were to happen to Dr Napier you think the finger would point at this Maurice Lebas.'

'Almost certainly.'

'And would it stay there?'

'I should think so. Lebas was stupid enough to threaten Napier the other day. He sent a couple of gorillas around to his flat.'

'How very convenient,' Enrique observed. 'And the girl?'

Again the smile touched Ashford's lips. 'You can leave Jacqui to me,' he murmured. 'I'll take care of her.'

'Do you have time for a drink?'

Jacqui slowed the car and nosed it between a group of people who stood in the street, using the moment's distraction to come to a decision.

'Yes,' she said lightly. 'I think so.'

She parked by the Hôtel Cheval Blanc and jumped out. It was dark now and the lights of the harbour glittered on the slick of water. She collected her handbag from the back seat and reaching into the glove compartment took out a little bunch of foliage.

'What's that?' Napier asked.

'Parsley. I picked it in the garden. It never seems to grow properly in my window box.'

'You live near here, do you?'

'Not far.' She thought he was fishing for her address and replied quickly.

Napier looked across at the moored boats stirring in the darkness. It hadn't been what he meant.

He felt suddenly tired and dispirited. They had hardly

158

said a word on the way back. Jacqui had been curt and preoccupied as she drove. The anger he had sensed when Ashford had spoken to her had remained, darkening her mood. He had tried to draw her out but she had resisted, clasping her thoughts to herself.

They sat down outside a café on the waterfront. She put the bunch of parsley on the table and, stroking her bare upper arms, gave a shiver.

'Are you cold?'

'A little.'

'We could go inside if you prefer.'

'No, I'll be all right.'

The waiter brushed past, pausing with a jerk of his head to take their order. Jacqui asked for white wine and then sat back, crossing her legs.

There was an awkward silence.

Napier glanced round at the other tables.

'Who are you looking for?' she asked, catching the movement.

'No one in particular.'

But she had read his thoughts. 'You still think someone might be following you?'

'It crossed my mind.'

She brushed the possibility aside. 'I can't think who'd want to.'

'Can't you?' he echoed. 'I'm surprised.' His voice was sharper than he intended.

She frowned. 'Why do you say that?'

Napier shook his head. It was a stupid remark to have made. He tried to change the subject but she wasn't letting go of it.

'Why should I know who's following you?' she demanded.

'It's not important.'

'Yes it is,' she replied hotly.

Napier drew in his breath. He didn't want to be sucked into an argument with her but he was haunted by a suspicion that compelled him to go on. 'I saw you talking with Lebas the other day.'

Jacqui was suddenly very still.

'Is there anything wrong with that?' she asked carefully.

'It seemed a strange person for you to be meeting.'

'There was nothing strange about it. He rang me at the

159

museum and said he wanted to talk to me so I arranged to have a drink with him after work one day.'

'And I suppose you discussed *The Estuary Pilgrim*.'

'Well of course we did.'

Napier shrugged. 'That's what I thought.'

'I see,' she said with sudden force, 'you're the only one who's allowed to mention it, are you? We all have to sit and wait while the great Dr Napier comes to his decision? No one else's opinion matters I suppose.'

'You've never met him before?'

She shook her head. 'No, never.'

Napier was miserable. He wanted to stop himself but he couldn't. The frustration and disappointment of the last few days welled up in him, forcing the accusation from his lips. 'He didn't come to you about six months ago and ask you to help him discover a fake painting?'

'No!' she cried. 'He did not. And if he had I wouldn't have agreed. Who do you take me for?' Her voice was shaking with shock and anger. She stared across the table at Napier. He was suddenly dangerous and very frightening. 'Lebas just wanted to know what you had discovered while you were here in Honfleur and asked me to keep him informed in future.'

'You mean he wanted you to spy on me?'

'It wasn't spying.'

'But presumably he offered to pay you for your services.'

'Yes,' she shouted at him, 'if you must know he did.'

'And I suppose you refused.'

'Of course I refused him. I don't accept bribes, not from him or anyone else.'

'Don't you?' asked Napier, sitting back and looking away to the harbour. 'Not even from Ashford?'

There was a sudden deathly hush.

The metal chair toppled back and clattered to the ground.

Jacqui had jumped to her feet, and now stood above him, her eyes blazing in fury.

'How dare you say that to me!'

She gave her head a violent shake and the harbour lights caught and shattered in the gold of her hair.

'What do you know about anything?' she cried. 'You come here with your stupid schemes and theories and expect everyone to stop what they're doing and listen to you. Well I won't do it any more!'

Her voice broke on the impact of her words.

Napier suddenly realised that she was very close to tears. The colour had drained from her cheeks. Her eyes were round with hurt and rage.

'I'm sick of all this talk of fake paintings and German soldiers and people following you,' she shouted, catching her breath. 'It's all in your imagination. Go away and prove it. Find some real evidence, for God's sake, and don't come back to me until you have it.'

She turned and pushed her way out of the café, knocking into the other tables in her haste. A few yards down the quayside she stopped and rummaged in her handbag. Running back she slammed a hundred franc note down on to the table.

'That's for the drink,' she sobbed. 'Just so you don't think you've managed to bribe me as well.'

She vanished into the darkness. Napier watched her go, striding away on long legs.

Silence had settled on the café. All around him faces gaped.

Slowly his mind froze with realisation. How could he have been so stupid, so unnecessarily aggressive?

He cursed himself.

What had started the argument in the first place? And why hadn't he had the sense to stop it before it got out of hand?

The waiter was standing at his shoulder, a tray in his hand. He set the two glasses down on the table and slipped the tariff beneath the ashtray.

Mechanically Napier took out his wallet and handed him a note.

The waiter shrugged. 'Do you have anything else?'

He looked up at him without understanding. 'What's that?' The note was for a thousand francs. 'Oh, I'm sorry.' He took it back and searched for something smaller but it was all he had. There were no coins in his pocket either. With a sigh of resignation he picked up the note that Jacqui had left and passed it to him.

The waiter spilled change into the ashtray, nodded towards the overturned chair and gave a wink.

Napier ignored him. Taking the glass of Cognac he drained it in one and stood up to leave.

Lying discarded on the table was the little bunch of parsley. He picked it up and walked out into the night.

As soon as she was out of sight Jacqui broke into a run and didn't stop until she reached the door of her apartment.

She fumbled through her keys and dropped them on the landing floor. She swore under her breath and groped in the darkness. Hasty, impatient in her movements. Finding them again she unlocked the door and let herself in.

The room was dark. Only the small casement window cast silvery lights on the wall.

Throwing her bag down on a chair she began to pace the floor, too restless to sit. Muttering to herself, occasionally pausing to stamp her foot, she raged at her mental image of Napier. The pent-up fury that had been generated by Enrique and Ashford merged together, became a single passion that she directed at him.

How dare he accuse her in that way, she demanded. Who the hell did he think he was?

The angry black thoughts coursed through her mind wild and fierce and unchecked. She felt hot and flushed. Her mouth was dry. Going into the kitchen she took some water from the fridge and drank it straight from the bottle. She put it back in the rack and slammed the door shut.

It swung open again.

In a fit of temper she lashed out at it with her foot. There was a hollow report and a clatter of glass from inside.

She swung round, took one pace and gave a gasp as the pain registered. Kicking off her sandal she clutched at her foot.

'Goddammit!' she hissed through clenched teeth.

Hopping through into the front room she threw herself down on to the sofa and nursed her bruised toes.

The occupation began to calm her. Hugging her leg to her chest, she rested her cheek on the knee. Slowly and methodically she went back over the argument, picturing the scene to herself, her eyes still burning with resentment.

When Pacquetta came in fifteen minutes later she found her in this same position.

'What are you doing sitting there in the dark?' she asked, going into the kitchen and unloading her basket.

Jacqui didn't answer.

'I thought you were going out this evening,' she continued

162

comfortably, padding about the room switching on lights and drawing the curtains.

She paused in front of the sofa.

'What's got into you then?'

'Go away Kettie,' Jacqui replied without looking up. 'I'll talk to you tomorrow.'

'You should take that dress off, my girl. You'll crumple it if you sit like that.'

'I don't care, just leave me alone.'

Pacquetta rested beefy fists on her hips and looked down at Jacqui suspiciously. 'What's eating you?'

'I don't want to talk about it.'

'Is it Rupert Ashford?'

Jacqui concentrated on her bruised toes.

A slight smile of understanding touched Pacquetta's eyes. 'I see,' she said. 'It's that Englishman, is it?'

'He's so arrogant,' Jacqui retorted hotly.

'I thought as much.'

'He thinks he can just come into my life and push me about as he chooses – well he can't!'

Pacquetta gave a grunt. 'And of course you've been all sweetness and light in return, haven't you, my love.'

Jacqui stared down at the floor. 'No,' she said miserably, 'I've been beastly to him. Ever since I met him I've been cold and difficult and argumentative.'

Her lower lip trembled.

She frowned, trying to control herself.

Her shoulders suddenly jerked, a little choking sob escaped her and putting her head into her hands she burst into tears. The anger she'd bottled inside her was gone, dissolved away in the warm release of emotion, and in its place came a terrible sense of loneliness. Napier's accusations were loud in her ears. She heard the contempt in his voice, felt the cut of his words and his rejection ached in her like a wound.

Pacquetta's manner had softened. Drawing close she wrapped solid arms around her. With a quick movement Jacqui slipped to her knees, grasping the older woman round the waist, and buried her face from sight.

Stroking the golden head Pacquetta rocked her gently, making soft crowing noises in the back of her throat.

'It's all right, my love,' she murmured.

'No it's not all right,' Jacqui said fiercely, turning to one side. 'I've been a calculating bitch.'

'Oh là,' she responded, half scolding and half laughing at the same time, 'you mustn't say such things.'

Jacqui sat back on her heels and looked up at her. The confusion was in her voice and in her eyes.

'I didn't mean to be nasty to him, Kettie.'

'I know, my love.'

'I just wanted him to notice me . . . not take me for granted.'

Pacquetta laid her hand on the upturned cheek, wiping away the tears with a blunt thumb, and shook her head in wonder.

'It's all got muddled up, Kettie.' The realisation was firm in her mind. 'It's not him I'm cross with – it just came out that way.'

'Don't fret yourself, my love,' she whispered. 'He'll be back.'

Chapter Eleven

'Ashford's a bastard,' said Eugenie.

Her voice was slow and matter-of-fact but she pronounced the words with care, lending them an unexpected ferocity.

She stood with her back to the fireplace, her elbows resting on the mantelpiece. As usual she was dressed in black, her slight figure scarcely filling the suit. There was a silk handkerchief in her lapel pocket and mother-of-pearl buttons on her waistcoat.

Pushing herself upright she moved across the shadowed study and opened the doors of a walnut cabinet.

'Would it offend your English sensibilities to have a drink at this time of the morning?' she inquired, taking out a bottle of brandy and two glasses.

'I daresay I could stretch a point,' Napier replied.

He lay sprawled in a high-backed velvet chair, his hands folded against his chest. They had been talking together for almost an hour now, letting the conversation follow its natural course in the warmth of the little room.

Eugenie pushed the cork from the bottle with her thumb and splashed brandy into the glasses.

She handed one across to him. 'Did he tell you how it was he came to buy my pictures?' she asked, walking back to the fireplace.

'Only vaguely. He said he'd been in charge of returning stolen art treasures.'

'And I suppose he gave you that sad story about how he bought paintings out of charity? All those poor people pressing their family heirlooms on him in return for the few francs he had to offer?'

'Is it not true?'

'Of course not,' she replied contemptuously, setting the

glass on the mantelpiece and looking at him with her intense round eyes. 'Ashford's never helped anyone in his whole miserable life. He bought my pictures, it's true – but he might as well have stolen them.'

Napier sipped at the brandy, feeling the spirit scorch down into his stomach, and waited for her to go on.

'It was the first summer after the end of the war,' she continued. 'We had just finished lunch and I was upstairs in my room. Ashford walked into the hall demanding to speak with me immediately.'

She narrowed her eyes at the memory.

'He can't have been more than twenty-six at the time – blond, good-looking in a gaunt way. He had a patch over one eye, I remember, which gave him a roguish expression that he seemed keen to cultivate.

'I'd never met him before but I knew his name, of course. We all did in those days. Rupert Ashford, the hero of the Resistance. The man who had been taken by the Gestapo and escaped after they'd tortured him for six days. He was very polite, and efficient in a clipped manner.

'"I have some pictures, madame," he said to me. "I believe they could belong to you."

'He took me outside. There was a car parked in the drive, one of those military jeeps with a covered back. Inside were five or six paintings and various other bits and pieces.

'"Are these your property?" he asked.

'They were mine all right. I recognised them immediately, they were all pictures that had belonged to my husband's family. You can imagine how pleased I was, I'd never expected to see them again. I thanked him and asked whether I could take them inside but he said that would have to wait for the time being.

'"Can you prove you own them?" he asked.

'I told him I couldn't prove it further than that I recognised them.

'He shook his head. Unfortunately that wasn't good enough. He'd have to take them back to headquarters.

'I asked him when I would get them back.

'He shrugged and said he couldn't tell. "I'm afraid that without some sort of positive proof I might not be able to release them to you."

'I couldn't believe my ears.

166

'"Of course you could simplify matters by selling them to me," he said.'

Eugenie gave a snort as she spoke. Picking up her glass she drank some brandy and stared out of the half-closed shutters.

'Well, I could see his game – either I sold him the paintings or he took them away and denied they'd ever come to light.

'I told him he was out of his mind. I wasn't going to be blackmailed like that.

'So he left.

'The next day he was back again. This time he had a warrant with him. It gave him permission to strip the house of its possessions.

'"You're a collaborator," he told me. "We have to impound your vauables pending an investigation into your wartime activities."

'There was no escape. I asked him if we couldn't come to some agreement.

'"Sell me your pictures, all of them," he replied, "and I'll tear up this warrant."'

Eugenie stood quite still, gazing out at the overgrown gardens.

'And was that the end of it?' Napier asked quietly.

She shook her head. 'I sold him the pictures he wanted. He paid a few hundred francs and made me sign a paper disclaiming all legal rights to them.' Her voice trembled. 'The next day the police arrived and stripped the house down to the plaster.'

She spoke with sudden passion, spitting out the words as though they were bitter in her mouth.

Once again her hatred filled the room. It was alive and dangerous. Napier could sense it in the darkness as he might have sensed the presence of a wild animal.

Eugenie had turned and was now looking towards him but her eyes were glazed and unseeing, still locked on this image of the past.

'The worst of it was that he enjoyed it,' she continued on a calmer note. 'He came here after the police had left to check that they had done the job properly. I think it gave him some primitive satisfaction to see the house in ruins.'

She gazed across the room. Through the opened door

167

the kitchens were just visible at the end of the passage. Old Madeleine was bending over the cast-iron range, busily frying garlic with bacon to flavour the oil, and the rich aroma of her cooking reached out to them.

'He told me that you still sell him pictures,' Napier put into the silence.

'Ah yes,' she replied, 'he buys the odd piece. It helps to salve his conscience. Mind you, he doesn't like doing it. He detests the sight of them – particularly the erotic ones.'

Napier stared at her in amazement. 'You sell him erotic pictures?'

She drained her glass. Picking up the brandy bottle she offered it to Napier but he shook his head.

'Just the occasional nude,' she replied, her eyes suddenly malicious. 'All pink and sugary – very nasty. He burns them the moment my back is turned. They offend him, you see. And anything that offends Rupert Ashford has to be destroyed.'

'I'm certain I've seen him before, but I can't for the life of me think where.'

'Describe him to me,' Spooner suggested.

Napier looked down through the bare trees at the surface of the water, summoning the image of the man into his mind. They were sitting on a bench, high above the estuary, eating their lunch together.

'He's tall, swarthy and rather overweight. I'd say he's South American, certainly Latin. His eyes are brown but soft around the edges, like melted chocolate, and his skin has a slight sheen to it, as though he's been kept wrapped in an oily rag all his life.'

Spooner listened with the keenest interest. 'And you say his name was Enrique?'

Napier nodded. 'I didn't catch the rest. Unfortunately I only saw him for a few minutes, just as we were leaving. But from the way Ashford introduced him I had the impression he was some sort of business associate of his.'

'Can you remember how you came to see him before?' Spooner pressed. 'Was it through your work, for example?'

'I don't think so.'

Spooner chewed on a piece of cheese and pondered. 'But you're sure you saw him in London, not here in France?'

'It was certainly in London,' Napier replied. 'I can see his face but I can't picture the setting.'

He pummelled at his memory but with no result. Giving a shake of his head he gave up the struggle.

'It'll come to me in a while,' he said, checking the time. 'I must go now, there's someone I have to meet. I'll see you this evening.'

Luc Gabot saw them part.

Turning around he immersed himself in the view, cupping his hands around his eyes to shield them from the light.

Napier walked down the hill towards him.

Luc waited until he had passed by before dropping his hands and stepping out into the road.

As soon as Napier reached the outskirts of the town he dived off into a side street. He was walking faster than usual and kept glancing down at his watch as he hurried along as though he was late for an appointment.

Luc followed a discreet distance behind, keeping in contact without getting too close.

It would never do to spook him at this stage.

Napier threaded his way through the small half-timbered streets, past opened doors and parked cars, occasionally glancing up at the first-floor windows. He seemed to be looking for something in particular.

Luc quickened his pace. This was more like it.

Reaching an alleyway Napier paused, glancing quickly up and down the street, and vanished out of sight.

Luc took out a guide book and opened it at random. Assuming the distracted expression of a sightseer, absorbed in the mediaeval architecture around him, he sauntered past the entrance to the alley.

It led into a small courtyard. A poky little square, enclosed on all four sides and unwarmed by the sunlight.

The place was deserted. Napier had disappeared.

Luc paused and examined it more carefully. Was it a dead-end? No, unfortunately there was an exit down one side.

That's where Napier had gone.

He'd have to follow. It was a bit of a risk but he had no alternative. Pocketing the book he sidled down into the courtyard.

169

Immediately he discovered there was not one way out but two. Damn it!

He glanced up both alleys, thin ribbons of light threaded between the timbered buildings. There was no sign of Napier in either.

Where the hell had he got to?

Of course. He had been checking the first-floor windows as he went along.

Luc looked up. One of the buildings that loomed over him appeared to be inhabited, there was a light burning in an upstairs room. Could Napier have got up there? Possibly, there was an entrance further along.

Luc went over to it.

The door was open. He touched the knob and it swung back on its hinges, silent and inviting. Craning forward he peered inside.

Suddenly Napier was there beside him.

Luc gave a little cry and jumped back but there was no time to get out of the way. Napier had already reacted. Taking a step forward he struck Luc in the throat. It was a short stabbing blow, too quick to avoid. It knocked the breath from his windpipe, jolting back his head.

In the same movement Napier grabbed him by the collar and pulled him inside. Twisting him about he forced him up against the wall.

'I thought it was time we introduced ourselves,' he said conversationally.

Luc's brain was swimming from the blow. 'I don't know what you're talking about,' he spluttered.

'You've been following me for the last three days.'

'Not me, you've got the wrong man.' He gave a sudden jerk and tried to break free but Napier held him. He was much stronger than he looked.

'Who are you?' he asked.

Luc's brain whirled. Don't give him your real name, he told himself. Think of another. 'Lecomte,' he said. 'Pierre Lecomte.'

'Try again,' replied Napier, and with a quick thrust of his arm he cracked Luc's head against the stone wall.

Light exploded before his eyes. The shadowed room seemed to heave before him, his knees sagged.

'Luc Gabot,' he cried.

170

'Who sent you?'

'I don't know.'

Napier pushed one hand into Luc's collar until the knuckles pressed painfully against his bruised throat. 'Don't lie to me, Luc.'

'It's the truth.'

The grip tightened on his collar. He couldn't breathe. 'I never met him,' he gasped. 'I was given instructions on the phone.'

Napier turned his hand, twisting the knot of the tie like a tourniquet. The knuckles drove into the cartilage. Luc gave a strangled cry and tried to speak but the words choked in his mouth. A trickle of saliva ran down his chin.

Napier loosened his grip enough to let him talk.

'I was just told to follow you,' Luc mouthed weakly.

'Why?'

'They didn't say.'

Again the fist twisted into Luc's throat. The blood pounded in his temples, his sight dimmed.

Oh Christ, the bastard was going to throttle him.

'It's the truth, I swear it,' he screamed.

Napier still held him.

'Let me go, I've told you everything I know.'

'The next time you get a call I suggest you explain to them you've changed your mind,' he said. 'Tell them that you've decided not to work for Maurice Lebas any longer. Is that clear?'

Napier's voice was pleasant, almost sociable. Where the hell did he think he was? At some frigging soirée?

Luc nodded as best he could.

Suddenly the pressure was off his throat. He leaned against the wall gasping for breath.

Napier had stepped back a pace and was now looking at him thoughtfully. Without warning he gave a kick.

Luc's legs were knocked from under him. He fell heavily on the ground and rolled over in the dust. For a few moments he lay still, his eyes closed.

When he opened them Napier had gone.

Slowly Luc sat up and looked around himself. Loosening his tie he pulled it from his collar and threw it to one side.

Nursing his throat in his hand he thought back over Napier's words.

He'd get even with the bastard, that was a promise.

The idea pleased him.

Reaching into his pocket Luc took out a knife and flicked open the blade. It was thin and sharp as a needle. Why hadn't he used it on Napier just now? Because he wasn't given the chance, that's why not.

He wouldn't make that mistake again. Next time he'd be ready.

Luc's head was clearing, his breathing had returned to normal. Getting to his feet he went outside and walked back towards the harbour.

His mission was quite simple. He knew exactly what he had to do. Only one thing still puzzled him.

What had this got to do with Maurice Lebas?

Chapter Twelve

The fishing boat chugged along at a steady six knots.

Slowly and patiently it made its way across the estuary, the broad hull shouldering through flint-grey water.

Napier leaned against the forward deck-winch and watched the sea shovelling up against the wooden bows, foaming white as it lifted and tumbled aside. The smaller drops were thrown out far ahead where they pricked the surface of the oncoming water before being swept back in again.

He found it strangely peaceful on the estuary. The breeze ruffled his hair and his face was damp from the spray that wisped over the sides. He could taste the salt on his lips.

Easing his position against the winch he looked up.

It was a dull overcast day, the sky herring-boned with low cloud. The sun had broken through in places and flashed on the water. Seagulls swooped above the pale green shadows.

A mile ahead of them lay Le Havre.

Napier could see it gradually materialising from the headland as they approached: the ranks of high-rise buildings, the innumerable cranes and gantries that marked the docks. Petroleum reservoirs were clustered along the shoreline and the tall stacks of the oil refineries spat their burning gases into the air, flaming up against the sky like giant altar candles.

Napier studied the town thoughtfully, his mind leaping forward to the meeting that awaited him on arrival.

Maurice Lebas had rung him the night before.

He had stated his name and, without any further discussion, had suggested they should meet and talk. There was new information on the painting, he'd explained, and he wished Napier to see it straight away. Giving a time and a place for the appointment he had then hung up.

His voice had been polite but the implication behind it had been clear. He was issuing an order rather than an invitation.

Napier had accepted with good grace.

He wasn't looking forward to the occasion but at the same time he felt that a second meeting with Lebas was now long overdue.

Rousing himself he walked back along the untidy deck, his legs braced against the roll of the hull.

Spooner was sitting perched on a locker beneath the wheel-house. He had his hands plunged deep into his over-coat pockets and his briefcase clamped between his feet.

He looked cold and miserable.

It had been his idea to cross the estuary on Albert's boat. Napier was going to hire a car and drive around to Le Havre but Spooner had felt that this was an unnecessary expense. 'It would be much cheaper by boat,' he'd pointed out, 'and probably quicker in the long run.'

He now appeared to be regretting this hasty decision. White-faced, he was staring out at the empty expanse of water.

'It's not the sea that's upsetting me,' he hissed when Napier asked how he was feeling, 'it's the smell of this revolting boat.' He gave a vague wave of his hand to indicate the piles of cordage, the rusting apparatus and the fish-scaled decking.

'Go up into the bows, the air's fresher there.'

'No thank you,' he replied, looking disapprovingly at Napier's wet hair. 'I'd rather be sea-sick than drowned.'

Albert clambered down from the wheel-house and came round to join them. He was in rare good spirits. There were three steaming mugs of coffee in his hands.

'My God,' he said, looking Spooner over. 'You look pretty sick.'

'It's the sea,' Spooner replied politely. 'It's a little choppy today.'

Albert thrust a mug into his hand. 'Drink this,' he ordered, 'it'll settle your stomach.'

Before Spooner had a chance to taste it, Albert had reached into his pocket, drawn out a half-bottle of whisky and slopped a generous measure into each cup.

'For the cold,' he explained, taking a pull straight from the bottle for additional insurance. Tucking it back in his pocket he picked up his cup and clinked it with the other two.

'Cheers,' he said in an attempt at English.

174

Napier took a mouthful of the coffee. The spirit burst inside him, spreading out into his veins. He heard Spooner choke and say good heavens.

'Too strong?' Albert asked.

'Not at all,' Spooner replied stoutly. 'Just a little hot.'

The whisky seemed to have done him good. Twin spots of colour appeared in his cheeks. He looked at Albert and then round at the wheel-house.

'Who's driving this thing?' he asked.

Albert grinned with delight and spread his hands. 'No one.'

'Is that sensible?'

'I lash the wheel and she drives herself,' Albert replied. He saw the doubt lingering in Spooner's eyes and laughed hugely. Reaching up he slapped the woodwork of the wheel-house with one hand. 'Don't worry, monsieur, this one knows the way to Le Havre. She should do, she's been there a thousand times before.'

Spooner glanced back at the wake they were leaving across the estuary.

'It's a question of navigation,' Albert continued, 'and navigation, as my grandfather used to say, is simply the art of running aground in the right place.'

'So much for the gentle art of seamanship,' Spooner said under his breath.

Albert patted him on the shoulder, hustling him to his feet. Opening the locker where Spooner had been sitting he took out a reel of green fishing line. Attached to the end were a series of large barbed hooks and a section of lead piping which served as a sinker.

He unrolled a few yards on to the deck and searched about until he came across a sardine in the scuppers. This he began cutting into sections with a knife, fastening each piece in turn on to the bare hooks.

Spooner watched with queasy eyes.

When he was done, Albert walked over to the stern and splashed the weight overboard, letting the line run out in his hands.

Napier joined him there. 'What do you hope to catch?'

'Anything that's feeling hungry.'

He gazed out at the pale scar of their wake. 'And how long before we reach Le Havre?'

175

Albert looked up at the sky and then round at the approaching shoreline. 'About half an hour,' he said with a shrug.

The engine thumped on, exhausting a fine trail of cinnamon-coloured smoke that drifted out of the stack and settled on the slick of water behind them.

'Napier has gone over to Le Havre to see Lebas.'

Ashford reached into the damp foliage of an orchid and snipped out a dead shoot with a pair of scissors.

'I thought he might,' he observed, standing back to inspect the plant.

'He crossed the estuary by boat.'

Ashford turned and looked at him. 'What boat is that, Louis?'

'It belongs to a fisherman in Honfleur. He does a few odd-jobs for Eugenie Delaroche.'

'How do you know all this?' Ashford inquired. 'I thought your man had lost Napier.'

'I have a contact in Honfleur,' Louis replied. 'A juggler; he keeps me informed of what takes place in the harbour. According to him, Napier left for Le Havre just after two. The crossing took them almost two hours. The boat's presently moored in the roadstead outside the Commercial Dock.'

'Was he the only passenger?'

'No, that friend of his was with him also. He's gone to the Public Records Office.'

'So is anyone left onboard?'

'Just the owner.'

'And when do they intend to return?'

'Later this afternoon, I believe.'

Ashford paused and considered for a moment. 'Delay them,' he said, turning his attention back to the orchid. 'I don't care how you do it, Louis, but make sure that that boat doesn't leave until nightfall.'

The meeting with Lebas was short.

Napier took a cab from the Commercial Dock to the address he'd been given over the phone. It was a large modern block of offices just off the Rue Victor Hugo. From an information board in the front hall Napier discovered that this was the centre of the Lebas empire. Twenty or more separate companies were listed there under his name.

A receptionist took him up to the fifth floor by lift and ushered him through into a private office. It was large and well lit. Two of the walls were plate-glass, the others covered in graphs and crowded pin-boards. Computer consoles crammed the workspace. There was no concession to decoration, the furniture on the white carpet was sparse and strictly functional.

Overall the place created an impression of hard, uncompromising business efficiency.

In the centre of the floor was an architect's model of some industrial development. Three men stood around the Perspex case.

The shorter of them was Lebas.

The moment Napier arrived he straightened up and came over to meet him. He walked with the quick, crouched movements of a wrestler. His jacket was off and his sleeves rolled back from thick forearms.

'I'm glad you could make it,' he said shortly, shaking hands. 'I hear you've been in Honfleur for over a week now.'

'Something like that,' Napier agreed.

'And to very little effect.'

Napier inclined his head. 'We've discovered one or two interesting facts.'

'But nothing that helps to substantiate your theory, Dr Napier, according to that haughty girl in the museum.'

'Unfortunately that's true.'

Lebas gave a grunt of acknowledgement. Going over to his desk he picked up a sheaf of papers and handed them to Napier. 'What you haven't seen yet is this.'

Napier glanced at the topmost sheet. It appeared to be a legal document of some sort.

'It's the court decision on *The Estuary Pilgrim*,' he explained. 'They've upheld my claim to the picture.'

'Congratulations,' Napier replied pleasantly.

'It now belongs to me,' Lebas continued, 'and as the legal owner I'm asking you to drop the case. Forget *The Estuary Pilgrim* and go back to England.' He looked at Napier with his pebble-hard eyes. 'Otherwise I can't be held responsible for your safety.'

The threat was simple and unveiled.

Lebas gave a brief nod of dismissal and returned to the discussion around the display model.

177

The interview was evidently over.

Napier made his way downstairs again and out into the street. As he was walking across the shallow forecourt in front of the building he heard his name called.

He turned to see a woman hurrying after him.

'You probably won't remember me,' she said as she caught up. 'Nadine Lebas – we met in London this summer.'

'Of course,' Napier replied.

'You've been talking with my husband.' She sounded faintly apologetic.

'Briefly.'

She nodded in understanding. 'Do you have some time to spare?' she asked. 'There's something I'd like to show you.'

A cream-white Mercedes was parked by the curb. Nadine Lebas ran around to the driver's side and unlocked the door.

Napier climbed in beside her.

Skirting around the Bassin Vauban she directed the car inland on the main road to Tancarville. As they drove along she made a little small-talk, asking him where he was staying and how long he intended to remain in France. She must be in her early fifties, Napier calculated, an attractive woman, small and slightly brittle. But he noticed that she was flustered, as though acting without orders.

Leaving the town they followed the shore of the estuary. It was a bleak, desolate landscape, ragged chalk cliffs rising on one side of the road and the empty expanse of the open sea on the other. After two or three miles Nadine turned off on to a smaller side road. It was narrow and badly rutted. The car jolted along until they came to the edge of the water.

'I think this is the right place,' she said, switching off the engine. 'I've only been here once before.'

Napier got out and looked about himself.

There was nothing to see.

The estuary was stretched out before them, vast and motionless. The water had carved the mud flats into tiny grass-topped islands. Sea birds picked about the network of black creeks and one or two sailing dinghies lay on their sides. Further down the shore was a derelict shed.

Apart from that the place was deserted.

Nadine Lebas seemed relieved. 'Yes,' she said, 'this is

it.' She pointed across the lonely wasteland to where some blackened timbers reared up out of the mud.

'There.'

'What is it?' Napier asked.

'It's *The Estuary Pilgrim*.'

With a little thump of understanding he realised why he'd been brought here, what it was that Nadine Lebas wanted him to see.

'At least,' she corrected, 'it's all that remains of it.'

Napier walked a little closer and gazed at the frame of the ship in wonder.

It was the mud that had preserved it this long. The lower parts, that lay bedded in the estuary, were almost intact. The rest had been washed away by the sea.

He could make out the line of the keel, stretching away towards the edge of the water, and the stump of the bow-post. The sharp black bones of its ribs were stuck out on either side, like the carcass of some enormous sea creature.

'*The Estuary Pilgrim* belonged to my husband's family,' Nadine said, coming to stand beside him. 'It was the first ship they owned. The start of their fortunes.'

'Which is why they bought the painting?'

She nodded. 'And why my husband wants it back.' She moved away down the shore, her small, neatly dressed figure quite incongruous in the setting. Napier watched her closely. She was twisting one ring on her finger and seemed to be struggling to find a way of expressing what was pressing on her mind.

'The painting is very important to Maurice,' she said after a few moments. 'It's not the money. He really wants it. You must understand that to him it's a symbol of what his family has achieved. He'd never sell it.' She made a small helpless gesture. 'I know that he can be brusque at times, even bullying, but he would never have forged that picture, Dr Napier. A forgery would have no value to him.'

When Napier returned to the docks he found Spooner waiting for him.

He was sitting on an iron bollard, his briefcase clasped on his lap. Bad news was printed across his face.

'We've lost Albert,' he announced.

'What do you mean we've lost him?'

'I came back here about half an hour ago and he was gone,' Spooner replied grimly. 'Since then I've searched the quayside but there's no sign of him. I didn't want to go further until you arrived.'

Napier muttered a curse to himself and looked round the sprawling limbs of the docks. Why couldn't the man stay on the boat as he'd promised? He could be anywhere by now.

'We must search the cafés,' he said. 'My guess is that he'll have pushed off for a drink.'

'My thoughts exactly,' Spooner agreed.

They walked down the jetty to the road. There was a brasserie on the corner, its name stamped in gold letters on a faded red awning.

Inside it was noisy and crowded, the atmosphere thick with cigarette smoke. Several customers were leaning against the bar, others crowded around the tables in the window. The glass panes were misted with condensation and a pin-ball machine was clanging away in one corner.

Napier glanced around the room but there wasn't a face he recognised. He pushed his way to the counter.

'I'm looking for a man called Albert,' he called to the barman, who was busy polishing glasses.

'Albert who?'

'I don't know his other name.'

The barman thrust out his lower lip and gave a shrug.

This wasn't going to be easy. 'He owns the boat that's moored up over there,' Napier explained, pointing outside.

The barman looked where he was directed but the jetty was almost invisible through the clouded window. 'Can't say I know him,' he said, holding the glass to the light, putting it down and taking up another.

They went out into the street and tried the next café.

'We could just forget about Albert and hire a taxi,' Spooner suggested when they had drawn a blank.

Napier considered the idea. 'No, I think we'd better find him,' he said. 'He'll only go and drown himself if we leave him to cross the estuary alone.'

They turned up towards the cathedral.

In the fifth café they struck lucky. One of the customers stopped them, just as they were about to leave. 'You looking for Albert Fichet?' he asked.

'Have you seen him?'

'He was here about an hour ago,' he replied. 'Had a couple of friends with him.'

'You don't know where they went by any chance?'

'Can't say.' He turned and consulted with his companions. 'You might try in the Brasserie Astoire in the square.'

It took over an hour to track Albert down.

He had worked his way around the town, going from one café to the next. When they finally discovered him he was slumped in the corner of a small brasserie near the Digue Nord. There was a glass of brandy in his hand and he was glowing with goodwill.

'Ah doctor,' he cried as they came in, 'you've come to join us.'

The two friends he had discovered were seated either side of him, quiet, hard-eyed men who studied the new arrivals with interest.

Albert had risen to his feet in greeting. He reached out at Napier, misjudged the distance and tottered against the metal table.

Napier caught him by the arm. The two friends stood up and melted away into the crowd.

'Okay Albert, we're off now,' Napier told him.

'Just one more before we go.'

'I think you've had enough for the time being.'

They hauled Albert out into the street. He staggered in the fresh air and leaned against a lamppost. 'Where now?' he asked Spooner, who was trying to prise him free.

'Back to the boat,' he replied testily.

'Ah,' said Albert, throwing one arm around his shoulders. 'Time to go home, eh?'

'It most certainly is.'

'Home,' Albert agreed, 'that's the place,' and leaning over he planted a wet kiss on Spooner's cheek.

'Oh really . . .'

'You're so very kind to me.'

Slowly and laboriously they manoeuvred him down to the harbour. It was dark now and the lights glimmered on the water. The tide was falling and the boat had settled below the level of the quay. Albert clambered down the iron ladder, jumped the last few rungs and fell on to the deck, rolling away against the gunwale.

Napier grasped him beneath the armpits and pulled him

up into a sitting position. Face pale and waxy, breath coming in short gasps. His body was clammy and there was a sour smell of sweat and alcohol on him.

Going over to the wheel-house Napier searched in the dark until he found a small Primus stove and kettle. He boiled the water and made a mug of black coffee.

'I'm not drinking that muck,' Albert announced, rolling his head.

Napier thrust the mug into his lips and began to pour the coffee down his throat.

There was a splutter and liquid dribbled down Albert's chin. 'All right, all right,' he said, quelling Napier with one hand. He took the mug, drank the rest of the coffee and shuddered.

Napier filled it again. The coffee appeared to be taking effect. On the third cup Albert's eyes focused, his wits returned from exile.

'Can you get this contraption going now?' Napier asked.

'Of course,' he replied sulkily. Walking down the deck he relieved himself noisily over the stern before clambering up into the wheel-house. He pressed the electric starter. The engine kicked over and died with an asthmatic wheeze.

'Bitch,' Albert muttered to himself.

Opening the hatch he groped about the cylinder head and tried again. This time the engine caught and fired. Albert nursed the revolutions until it was running smoothly and then lumbering up to the bows he cast off the mooring and flopped the heavy rope down on to the deck. Putting one leg over the side he pushed the hull away from the shore and returned to the wheel-house.

For a man who was only half conscious Albert had remarkable control over the little boat. Swinging it in a tight circle he threw the engine into reverse and whirled the wheel about in the opposite direction. The screw churned in the water, the stern juddered and the boat pirouetted around on its axis.

He opened the throttle, the cylindrical cover rose and danced on the exhaust, and they thrust forwards.

Leaving the sanctuary of the port they rounded the semaphore and headed out to sea, the boat lifting and pitching as it hit the swell.

Night closed in around them.

'Can you see where you're going?' Napier asked from the door of the deck cabin.

Albert grunted and jerked his head to where the distant shoreline was prickled with lights. He was hanging over the wheel breathing heavily, his face pressed against the glass screen.

In the glow of the navigation lights Napier noticed the half-bottle of whisky conveniently placed by his right elbow. He confiscated it and stepping down on to the deck he walked forwards. Spray licked and spat at his face as the boat butted into unseen waves.

Spooner had taken his place on the locker cover.

For half an hour they sailed along in a silence that was broken only by the steady heartbeat of the engine and the lisp of the sea flowing by the hull. Napier leaned against a steel halyard and stared out into the darkness.

'How did you get on with Lebas?' Spooner inquired after a while. 'I quite forgot to ask you in all this excitement.'

'He wants me to go back to England,' Napier replied. 'The court has ruled in his favour. He now owns *The Estuary Pilgrim*.'

'Predictable I suppose.'

Napier had paused and was looking out over the bows.

'Are you going to give up?' Spooner asked.

'I might do . . .' His voice trailed off.

'What's the matter?'

'I thought I heard something,' replied Napier in a distracted voice. He listened hard but it was gone. Turning back to Spooner he was about to go on when it came again.

Was it his imagination? No, it was there: minute but tangible.

Spooner scrambled to his feet. He'd heard it also.

It was a slight rumbling off the starboard bow. As they listened it grew, becoming firmer and more insistent.

Albert had stepped down on to the deck and was peering out into the darkness.

The sound clarified. It was a rhythm now, deep and resonant and unmistakable.

The beat of a ship's engine.

Napier felt icy fingers clutch in his belly. He stared out over the bows, searching for the sound. At that moment an area of the darkness deepened, solidified, taking on form and bulk.

The noise was loud now – very close. Eyes straining to penetrate the gloom, to pinpoint the direction.

Suddenly it was on them. A great black mass rearing up out of the night, rushing down on them.

'Oh God, it's going to hit us!' Spooner shouted.

Napier stood frozen to the deck.

It was a tugboat, barging through the sea towards them. Rapid and menacing, materialising out of the darkness. He could see the angry white bow-wave, the low hull, the outline of wheel-house and stack. Dimly he was aware of Spooner's voice still shouting and Albert beside him frantically waving his arms.

He tried to move but his limbs had turned to lard.

The steel prow grew, black and malignant, filling his vision, towering up above him.

Sea and engine thundered in his ears.

As if drawn by some hidden force, the little fishing boat bucked to one side. The hull dropped for an instant and was sucked inwards. With a sudden violent lurch it lifted, sea boiling beneath, as the tug crashed into its side.

The deck was hurled over and the hull burst on the steel bows, cracking into two like a broken egg. Napier felt himself falling backwards. The boat was toppling over him. Water was pounding in on every side. The air was full of the screams of voices and tearing wood.

Something struck him on the shoulder. Pain and shock suddenly registered, galvanising him into life. Kicking his legs, he threw himself away from the shattered deck.

For a moment there was nothing, he was floating in darkness. And then the sea came up from an unexpected angle to hit him. It was cold and black, grasping his body, sucking him downwards. A terrible high-pitched singing filled his ears. It bored into his head, sharp and painful, like the whine of a circular saw. He felt himself turning, his legs and arms flailing.

Light and darkness collided before his eyes.

He struggled frantically against the cold enveloping water. His lungs began to tug for air but he had no idea where to find the surface. A sudden blow from behind stunned him, his mouth opened and the sea filled his lungs.

He choked it out, gasped for air and felt only more water. His energy was beginning to sap, the movements of his body becoming weaker. The painful noise had dulled in his ears, he felt himself spinning over and over in the darkness and a pleasant sensation of dreaming crept over him.

The struggling grew feeble.

At that moment his body broke the surface.

A wave caught him, rolling him over on to his back. He coughed out water, his lungs retching and clearing. It felt like an hour since he had hit the water but it could only have been a matter of seconds. The tugboat was still there, its squat hull sliding away into the night.

A moment later it was gone, swallowed into the dark as quickly as it had come, and he was alone. He breathed in air, drawing it deep into his lungs. Immediately he choked and more water came up.

There was a foul, unclean taste in his mouth.

Gradually other sensations came to him. He became aware of the sea slapping around his body and felt himself rising and falling on the waves. Kicking against the cold that was numbing his limbs he began to swim. He didn't know in what direction he was going. It wasn't important, the activity was good, invigorating. The knowledge of being alive was all that mattered.

Ahead of him was some solid object.

He could see it rolling sluggishly on the water, its outline dull in the night, hardly visible, nothing more that an interruption in the steady rise and fall of the swell. Redoubling his efforts he worked his way through the sea.

It was a large piece of wreckage, shattered planks moulded to a frame, part of the boat's hull.

He met it in the trough of a wave and grasped out wildly, his fingers scrabbling for a handhold. The woodwork was splintered and rough, scratching at his hands. He found a smoother surface further up and held it firmly. With a heave he pulled his chest and shoulders up out of the water. The wreckage shifted and toppled with his weight, he threw one leg over the edge, correcting the balance. As he did so he felt something moving in the dark beside him, something living.

Instinctively he reacted, pushing it away, struggling for the rights to this makeshift raft when a voice said, 'John?'

Napier paused in astonishment. He reached out a hand and touched wet clothing.

It was Spooner.

He was clinging to the other side of the wreckage. Napier could see the pale moon of his face in the dark.

'How did you get here?' he cried out.

The question sounded absurd. As he spoke he felt himself beginning to laugh, his body shaking with cold and fatigue. Spooner was doing the same and for a few moments they laughed helplessly, gripping hold of each other, burning out the adrenalin that flowed in their veins. The sea slapped about them, the salt was acrid in their throats and eyes.

'And Albert?' he asked when he'd caught his breath.

'I've got him here,' Spooner called back. 'But he isn't moving.'

'Is he breathing?'

'I can't tell.'

Albert was lying in the water, his head just resting on the edge of the raft. His eyes were closed and his mouth hung open.

Napier worked his way around the wreckage, fumbling across sharp wooden shards, until he was beside Albert. He grasped him by the scruff of the neck. Spooner did the same, and between them they pulled him up on to the wooden decking.

Albert groaned at the interference. He stirred, moved one arm and, rolling over on to his side, he was sick into the sea.

'Well that's one question answered,' Napier observed, slipping back into the water.

The darkness pressed around them. It was growing colder. There was no wind but Napier could feel the current tugging at his feet.

'What do we do now?' Spooner asked.

'Hang on and hope for the best.'

Slowly the raft drifted out to sea, lifting and toppling on the crest of each wave.

Jacqui stepped out into the street.

The others had come to the door and stood framed in the glow of the passage. They were old friends, warm and affectionate, pleased to have seen her.

She kissed them all goodnight, turned and waved as she went, thanking them for dinner and promising to see them again soon.

As she walked down the street she heard her name called.

It was Jules, one of the other guests. He was running after her.

She turned and waited for him to catch up.

'You're not going home yet, are you, Jacqui?' he asked as he reached her. 'It's only just past eleven.'

She smiled. 'I have an early start tomorrow.'

'But still, there's time for a drink,' he said. 'We could go back to my place. I live pretty close.'

Jacqui shook her head gently. He was very sweet but she wanted to be by herself.

'Just for a few minutes,' he pressed.

She kissed him on both cheeks. 'Another time, Jules,' she said. 'Come round to the museum after work one day.'

When he was gone she went down to the Quai St Étienne and walked along the harbour. At the entrance to a café she paused and looked inside. It was bright and cheerful. One or two heads turned and studied her. She turned up the collar of her coat, hiding herself from their curiosity, and walked on to the next café.

She wasn't looking for him, she told herself, just passing by. What could be more natural?

But there was no one there she recognised.

Reaching the Lieutenance she paused, undecided. Her apartment lay on the far side of the harbour. Turning away from it she hurried up to the Place Ste Catherine.

It wasn't true, she reprimanded herself. She was looking for him. There was no point in deceiving herself any longer. She was hoping to come across him by mistake, to bump into him on neutral territory.

But there was no sign of him in the square either.

Where could he be, she wondered? He always ate out in the evenings. He'd told her so himself.

She walked back down the street towards her home. Could he have gone back to England? It was possible. But he wouldn't have left without saying goodbye, would he?

She unlocked the front door and let herself in.

Why not? She'd given him no reason to stay in Honfleur.

Spooner was losing his grip on the raft. His fingers were numb with cold. They had lost all feeling. One by one they let go and he slipped back in the water.

Napier grabbed him by the arm. 'Hang on,' he said, 'I don't think this is the ideal moment to go off swimming by yourself.'

Spooner nodded faintly and managed a smile.

He was growing weaker by the minute. Napier could feel him shivering through the sodden material of his coat. He considered trying to get him up on to the deck of the raft beside Albert but there simply wasn't room for two. It would upset the whole thing.

They had been adrift for over an hour now. Napier looked around the darkness and felt the first flutter of despair in the pit of his stomach. They were still in the estuary. He could see the distant lights on either shore but quite where they were and how far they had drifted he didn't know.

A piece of weed touched his foot, he kicked it away.

Spooner stirred himself. 'I felt something,' he gasped.

'So did I,' replied Napier.

It came again, butting against him. With a sudden wild surge of hope he reached out with his foot and touched a substance more solid than weed. It was firm and continuous.

'My God,' he shouted, 'it's land.'

Desperately he dug his toes into the soil trying to hold it as it passed. The surface gradually rose beneath him then fell away again. He kicked out wildly, searching to find it once more. The next instant it was back, pressing up beneath them.

The raft suddenly jolted and came to a halt. The current lost its grip on the wreckage and broke over the surface.

They were aground.

Water pouring from their clothes, arms and legs sprawling with the impact, rolling over with cries of surprise and relief. Napier staggered to his feet, his limbs scarcely answering the commands of his mind, and half walking, half crawling he dragged the raft away from the water.

Spooner followed and tumbling down beside him he lay stretched out on his back. 'Where are we, for goodness sakes?' he panted.

'I don't know, on some sort of sandbank by the feel of it.'

Pitch blackness all around, winking lights from the far shore, the rough texture of the ground beneath his feet and hands. For several minutes Napier lay still, savouring the delicious sensation of being on dry ground. Then clambering up he began to inspect their new home.

Groping for the water's edge in the dark he worked his way around the perimeter of the sandbank. It was almost twenty feet long, he discovered, and humped like the back of a whale. The soil was firm and gritty to the touch. By the time he returned to the others he found that the area of the island had increased. The tide was falling and the raft was now beached five yards further up the shore than it had been.

Spooner was sitting huddled on the ground. His teeth were chattering with cold and he was shivering in long, convulsive spasms.

'You must move about,' Napier ordered. 'Get your circulation going.'

Pulling him to his feet he marched him up the hip of the sandbank, dragging him forwards step by step.

'You're not going to make me sing, are you?' he asked as he stumbled along, 'like they do in the war films.'

'I'll make you morris-dance if you don't keep up,' Napier replied.

There was a solid weight bumping against his hip. He felt it through the material, recognised it and reaching in his pocket he pulled out the whisky bottle. Miraculously the glass hadn't broken, it was intact and still half full. 'Here drink some of this,' he said, handing it to Spooner.

'Do you think we should?' he asked. 'Alcohol only produces an illusion of warmth, you know.'

'The illusion would be a fine thing at present.'

Spooner agreed and unscrewing the cap he took a long pull at the neck before giving it back to Napier.

The whisky went down fierce and hot, igniting in his veins. Napier gritted his teeth at the after-burn.

'Good, isn't it?' Spooner observed, drinking some more. He looked around himself. 'Where did this place come from?'

'God knows. Something to do with the tide, I suppose.'

'It's a miracle that we hit it.'

'"Good navigation",' Napier quoted, '"is the art of running aground in the right place."'

They moved on, hugging themselves against the cold that

seeped in through their wet clothing. After a few minutes Spooner paused and voiced the question that was on both their minds.

'It was an accident, wasn't it, John?'

'That we were delayed in Le Havre until nightfall and then mowed down by a boat that wasn't carrying navigation lights?' Napier inquired. 'It's just possible, I suppose.'

Spooner nodded to himself. 'That's what I thought,' he said. 'Who do you think did it then? Maurice Lebas?'

'It looks that way, doesn't it,' Napier replied, 'but I'm not sure.' He stared across at the distant lights, seeing the skeleton of *The Estuary Pilgrim* lying stranded in the mud, Nadine Lebas's concerned expression as she tried to explain herself to him. 'To be honest I'm not sure about anything at present.'

They were interrupted by a groan from the raft.

Albert had recovered consciousness. Slowly he uncoiled himself, tipped his legs on to the ground and sat up.

'How are you feeling?' Napier asked, peering at him in the darkness.

Putting one hand around his neck, Albert craned his head back and rolled his eyes in two complete orbits of the socket. A sudden eruption from inside blew out his cheeks and a moment later he belched loudly.

Napier took this for some sort of answer.

'Where the bloody hell are we?' Albert asked petulantly, gazing around.

'On a sandbank,' Spooner told him.

Albert repeated the words to himself. Bending down he shovelled up a handful of the soil and lifted it to his nose.

'Sand?' he said flatly. 'This isn't sand. It's that damned mud again.'

Chapter Thirteen

The dawn rose in silence.

At first the changes were imperceptible. The night seemed to lose something of its density. It became translucent. Sky and land gradually separated and they could make out the dark headland of the Cap la Hève rising above the lights of Le Havre. The cell of darkness that had enclosed them for the last few hours drew away and then evaporated. Coral pinks touched the horizon, the pearl-grey of the sky melted into a delicate enamel blue. The light spread upwards like a stain, filaments of cloud caught the coming sun and glowed in anticipation and slowly, with a breathless and unhurried dignity, the vast theatre of the estuary opened before their eyes.

Napier sat cross-legged on the ground, his back resting against the wrecked fragment of the boat, and watched the dawn come up. He was cramped with cold, his clothes had set on to his body and the skin of his face was stiff and lifeless, but as the sun rose, molten red behind the pale ashes of the morning mist, he felt a surge of intense pleasure – a sort of numbed ecstasy.

With the rising of the sun came hope.

The ordeal was over, they were going to survive; it could only be a question of time now before they were rescued.

He had been awake all through the night, unable to relax long enough to sleep. Occasionally his head had dropped and he'd dozed fitfully for a few minutes. The rest of the time he'd sat and studied the distant shoreline, trying to estimate their position in the estuary. At first it had been meaningless, a confusion of winking lights, but as time passed he'd begun to make sense of them. The largest cluster of lights on the southern shore lay just to the west. These he had calculated must belong to Trouville, those further along to Deauville. Beyond this was scattered a sequence of smaller towns. On his extreme left was a lone flashing light; this he knew came from the beacon on the Cap de la Roque above Tancarville. From that he had been able to pinpoint Honfleur closer in and now clearly recognisable from its single lighthouse.

Rubbing his hands into his eyes, Napier looked about himself. Albert was sulking on the far side of the raft. Throughout the night he had been muttering and grumbling to himself, occasionally clearing his throat to spit at his feet. Napier had gathered from these complaints that he was nursing an appalling hangover.

Breaking from his lethargy he clambered to his feet and stretched himself, his joints cracking like dry twigs at the unexpected movement. He plunged his hands into his pockets and walked over to where Spooner stood on the water's edge gazing out to sea.

The island was growing smaller by the minute.

Twice in the night they had been forced to pull the raft further up the shore. It had been Spooner who first detected the tide coming in. He'd been marking the level of the water with pebbles and had suddenly shouted out in the darkness when it began to turn.

The green-grey strip of land was now half the size it had been when they first landed.

'How much longer do you think we have?' he asked.

Spooner shrugged. 'An hour, maybe less,' he replied, turning back from the sea.

Napier looked at him in astonishment. He had aged thirty years. The salt had crusted over his face, catching in the lines of the skin, turning his hair prematurely grey.

'What are you grinning at?' Spooner inquired.

'It's your face,' he said. 'It's gone white.'

'Speak for yourself, John,' he replied with a shy smile. 'You look as though you've been salted away for the winter.'

There was a sudden yell from Albert. He had jumped to his feet and was waving his arms excitedly.

They ran over to where he was dancing on the shore and stared out across the estuary.

A little shoal of shrimping boats had emerged from the mist about a mile away. They could make out the wedge-shaped hulls with their upright deck cabins, the masts and raised nets and the triangular sails they carried on their sterns.

192

Napier felt hope coursing through him, hot and intoxicating. Immediately they were all jumping and shouting, galvanised into action.

The boats lay quite still.

'Do you think they can see us?' Spooner panted after five minutes of frantic activity.

'Fishermen have pretty good eyes.'

'Couldn't we catch their attention in some way?'

'I can't think how,' Napier replied, 'short of putting a message in that whisky bottle and throwing it at them.'

Albert grabbed at his chest. Fumbling in the pocket of his denim smock he drew out a cigarette lighter and held it up in triumph.

'Perfect. But is it still working?'

The lighter was one of the old paraffin-wick models. Albert snapped open the cap and thumbed the wheel. There was a faint sound of scratching steel but no spark.

'The flint's wet,' Spooner said.

Albert agreed. Carefully he removed it from the head of the lighter. The flint was no larger than a broken section of lead from a pencil, minute in his thick fingers. He rubbed it on his sleeve while Napier cradled his hands beneath to catch it should it fall.

Replacing the flint Albert tried again.

There was a dry rasping and the wheel spat out a spark. On the third attempt the wick caught and fluttered into life. Albert gave a growl of satisfaction.

Holding the lighter above his head he was about to attempt a signal when Spooner caught his arm.

'Look!' he gasped, pointing back behind them.

They turned to see a single fishing boat not half a mile away.

'Have they seen us?' Spooner asked, running back along the shore, his overcoat flapping wildly.

'I think they have . . .'

The boat was swinging round in their direction, the hull listing to one side, its wake carving a long black line across the glassy water. A cloud of smoke belched from the exhaust stack and it began to pick up speed.

'Yes!' he cried excitedly. 'They're coming.'

Twenty yards off-shore the fishing boat slowed to a halt, the water creaming around its stern, and then approached the sandbank with painstaking caution, nosing its way forwards through the water until the keel nudged into the bottom.

It was a large sea-going vessel, solid and reliable, its hull dark green with white registration letters stencilled on the bow. To Napier it was the most beautiful sight he could imagine at that moment.

They waded out through the sea and scrambled up the high wooden sides. Lean arms reached down, catching hold of them, hauling them over on to the deck.

As soon as they had tumbled onboard, the engines were thrown into reverse and the boat slipped free of the land.

The three of them sat on the hatch cover. Mugs of hot coffee arrived. One of the crewmen opened a locker and drew out some thick fishermen's sweaters for them to put on, while the rest stood in a circle around them. Lean, sun-tanned figures, grotesque in rubber overalls. They listened to their story in silence, looking them over with the superstitious awe that sailors reserve for survivors of a shipwreck.

Leaving Albert to fill in the details, Napier walked to the stern and looked back at the sandbank. It had practically gone now, the tide was licking over the grey spit of land that had been their home for the night and already it was almost invisible against the water.

Going across to the wheel-house he knocked on the door.

The captain nodded as he came in. A pipe was clamped between his teeth and the smoke filled the little cabin with a pungent sweetness.

'You were lucky, monsieur,' he said when Napier had explained how it was they came to be out there on the estuary. 'Those sandbanks come and go as they please. Sometimes they are here for a day or more, sometimes for no more than a few minutes.'

'What brings them up?'

The captain shrugged. He was a small man with bright brown eyes that were constantly moving. His face was tanned and wrinkled, the skin of his throat loose across the thick cords of his neck. 'Who knows?' he said. 'The wind, the current maybe. They're dangerous little beggars, that I can tell you. It's all right when you see them, but more often than not they lie just below the surface.' He removed his pipe and jabbed the curved stem out of the window. 'There's one over there, for example.'

194

Napier looked where he pointed but could see nothing but the calm mirror of the sea.

'How do you know it's there?'

The captain's eyes twinkled and stretching out one finger he tapped the side of his nose. 'After forty years you get to smell them,' he said.

Napier could believe it. Opening the cabin door he turned to go. 'Oh, there was something I meant to ask you,' he said. 'Do you have a chart of the estuary?'

The captain nodded towards a locker. 'You'll find one in there.'

A few minutes later Napier stepped down on to the deck and thanking the captain he walked up into the bows.

Through the exhaustion and the cold that still ached in his limbs he felt a glow of satisfaction.

It hadn't been for nothing. The long night on the sandbank had served its purpose.

He could now prove that *The Estuary Pilgrim* was a fake.

Chapter Fourteen

The waitress brought coffee and hot rolls. Napier ate them hungrily, breaking open the crusts in his hands and spreading butter on the soft white insides.

He had no money but the woman had waved this aside. 'You can pay me when the time comes.'

She stood above him now and watched him eating with approval. She was a large, comfortable woman, in an apron and print dress. 'Good, eh?' she said.

Napier nodded and smiled up at her.

Waddling over to the counter she returned with a glass of Calvados.

'Drink this,' she said. 'Bread is good for the body but the soul needs something stronger.'

Napier thanked her and sipped at the spirit.

He had washed himself as best he could, rubbing the salt from his face and combing back his hair with his fingers. He was still wearing the heavy oiled jersey the fishermen had loaned him and for the first time in hours he was beginning to feel warm and comfortable.

The clock on St Léonard chimed out six-thirty.

Through the open door of the café Napier could see across the quayside to where a trawler was swinging plastic crates ashore. Fish and crushed ice were spilling over the cobbles while the seagulls swooped and hovered on outstretched wings, squabbling loudly for position.

He noticed old Madeleine at that moment. Small and round as a hedgehog, she was hobbling down the quayside. There was a basket over her arm and she was pushing a bicycle along with the other hand. She paused by the trawler and began searching through the slippery crates of fish, occasionally picking one out and testing it against her nose, calling down to the men onboard, cackling at their replies.

Slowly the sun crept up over the rooftops, melting the slate-stone buildings and the aluminium masts of the yachts into quicksilver.

Napier waited until nine before leaving the café. Walking around the harbour he made his way up to the Boudin Museum.

'Jacqui Fontenay?' said the lady in the ticket office. 'I don't think she's in this morning.' She went to check. 'No, I'm afraid she's working at home today.'

Napier ran up to the gallery, checked two of the paintings and then, returning to the door, asked if he could have Jacqui's address.

'Well, I'm not sure,' the woman said, looking at his dishevelled appearance, 'we're not supposed to give away personal information of that sort.'

Napier assured her that this was an emergency.

She hesitated, uncertain, and then ran her finger down a list by the phone. 'Nine, Rue des Petites Boucheries,' she said. 'It's on the other side of the harbour.'

He found it without difficulty. It was a small square just off the Quai St Étienne. The buildings were half timbered and hung out over the street like piles of badly stacked books. Jacqui's apartment was set above a small gallery selling postcards and silver jewellery.

Napier pressed the bell and waited.

Standing by the wall beside him was a disused pump. The plunger had been removed and a geranium planted in its place, the petals bright red against the dusky brown of the house.

The door was opened by Pacquetta.

'Yes?' she asked, barring the entrance with her presence.

'Have I got the right house?' Napier asked. 'I was looking for Jacqui Fontenay.'

'She's having breakfast.'

'I see . . .'

At that moment Jacqui's voice came down the stairs. 'Who is it, Kettie?' she asked, leaning down over the banisters. Catching sight of Napier standing in the doorway she gave a start and her hand jumped to her throat in surprise.

'Oh,' she said in a small voice, 'it's you.'

She ran down into the hall and came to the door in her

197

bare stockinged feet. Without heels she looked smaller and more vulnerable than before.

'I'm sorry to disturb you,' said Napier.

'It's all right,' she replied quickly, looking at his heavy jersey and untidy hair in astonishment. Her curiosity got the better of her. 'What have you been doing to yourself?'

Napier brushed the question aside and taking a deep breath he asked, 'Do you have a few minutes to spare? There's something I want you to see.'

'Now?'

He nodded. 'It can't wait.'

Jacqui looked at him speculatively. 'Do I have time to go and put some shoes on?'

A smile flashed into his eyes. 'If you're quick.'

She turned and ran back up to her apartment. A few moments later there was a clatter of heels on the wooden stairs and she reappeared pulling on a long blue overcoat.

Pacquetta began to protest but Jacqui silenced her with a glance and followed him out into the street.

Without another word Napier set off. He seemed excited, intent, and was walking rapidly.

Jacqui tied the belt of her coat and hurried after him. 'Where are you taking me?' she asked as they reached the quayside.

'Down to the harbour.'

'But why . . .?'

'I'll show you when we get there.'

He crossed the narrow bridge above the lock-gates and headed out along the western jetty. The trees that lined the waterfront were blazing in the morning sunshine, their leaves drifting down around him as he strode along ahead of her.

'Wait!' she cried, running to keep up. 'What am I supposed to be looking at?'

'The lighthouse,' he called back over his shoulder.

'What of it?'

'It's wrong.'

'Wrong? I don't understand. What do you mean – oh, would you please slow down for a moment.'

At the end of the jetty he paused and turned around, his eyes bright as berries.

'How much do you know about navigation?'

Jacqui shook her head. 'Nothing,' she said hurriedly. His

excitement was infectious, she could feel it mounting in her. 'I know it's all about buoys and charts and things.'

Napier pointed out across the channel of water to where the lighthouse stood at the mouth of the harbour.

'That's the lighthouse that appears in the background of *The Estuary Pilgrim*,' he said, looking round at her for confirmation.

Jacqui nodded quickly.

'And in the painting you'll find it has a red light on it.'

'Well it does have a red light.'

'Exactly,' he replied. 'But it should be white.'

His voice had dropped as he spoke and instinctively she found herself doing the same.

'Why should it?' she whispered.

Napier pointed back across the town to where the stump of a tower stood in the public gardens, its upper parts just visible above the trees.

'Because in those days there were two lighthouses in Honfleur, one on either side of the harbour.'

Jacqui looked at the tower, struggling to follow his meaning. 'But why should that make a difference?' she asked.

'According to a fisherman I was talking to this morning, that one was the larger of the two,' Napier told her. 'It carried a flashing red light to mark the southern tip of the estuary. Whereas this one, which appears in the painting, is a beacon to identify the approach to the harbour. The two had to be distinguished apart . . .'

'And so it had a white light,' she breathed in understanding.

Napier nodded. 'Then, at the turn of the century, the other silted up and had to be abandoned. Only one was now left and consequently it inherited the red light.'

Jacqui gazed at him in amazement.

'Whoever forged *The Estuary Pilgrim* didn't know this. He painted the colours just as they are now.'

Jacqui walked to the tip of the jetty and stared from one to the other. 'Are you sure about this?' she asked.

'Yes, I checked in the museum. The same lighthouse appears in the background of two or three paintings and in each case it has a white light.'

She came and stood in front of him. Napier leaned against the railing and looked down at his feet. Now that he had said his piece he seemed suddenly shy. 'Is that enough?' he asked.

'Enough what?' she queried.

'Evidence.' He looked up at her through the tangled fringe of his hair. 'You told me not to come back to you until I had evidence that *The Estuary Pilgrim* was a fake.'

Jacqui studied him thoughtfully and then very slowly she smiled. The collar of her coat was turned up and held close to her face. Her lips were covered and so Napier wasn't aware of the smile until it was shining in her eyes, the grey crystals warming as though touched by the sunlight.

'Yes,' she said gently. 'I think it's enough.' Reaching forwards she plucked his sleeve. 'Now I think we should go back inside before you frighten the seagulls with this jersey of yours.'

They walked back along the jetty, keeping in step with each other as they talked.

Napier told her of the night they had spent on the estuary, of how the tug had trampled them down in the darkness and how they'd drifted on the raft and been washed ashore on the sandbank.

As she listened Jacqui's eyes grew round with horror.

Pacquetta spotted the look of concern on her face the moment they came back into the apartment. She studied the two of them closely, sensing a change in their attitudes. There was an intimacy, she noticed, which hadn't been there before. For some reason the barrier between them had been lowered. They were standing closer together and their voices were quiet and attentive.

Immediately her manner became brusque. 'You've let your coffee go cold,' she scolded.

'Then I'll just have to make some more,' Jacqui replied, whisking the pot off the table.

Pacquetta followed her into the kitchen. 'You can't bring that man back here,' she hissed as soon as they were alone.

'Why ever not?' Jacqui asked, measuring out ground coffee with a spoon.

'It's only ten in the morning.'

'So what?'

'It's not proper.'

'Oh don't be so stuffy, Kettie,' she laughed.

'And besides, he's filthy dirty.'

'Of course he is,' Jacqui told her, pouring water into the pot. 'He's been out on a sandbank all night.'

This effectively silenced Pacquetta.

'You go off and forget all about it,' Jacqui ordered, and putting her hands on Pacquetta's shoulders she propelled her to the front door.

Napier noticed them talking heatedly together in the passage. He sensed that he was the subject of their argument and turned his attention elsewhere, glancing around at the apartment. It was neat and feminine, decorated in soft, summer colours that sparkled in the morning sunshine.

After a few moments he saw Jacqui bend down and kiss the old woman on her iron-grey hair before hustling her away downstairs.

'Who's that?' he asked as she came back in.

'Pacquetta? She was my nanny when I was a child.'

'Strange name.'

'Yes,' Jacqui said lightly, 'she was born on Easter Day and so they named her after it.' She closed the door and looked at Napier thoughtfully. Standing there by the window in his absurd baggy jersey he looked tired and drawn, his eyes dark in his pale face.

'Have you had anything to eat?' she asked.

'I had some rolls in a café.'

'That's not enough,' she replied firmly.

Napier nodded, feeling the hunger leap in his stomach at the mention of food. 'As a matter of fact I'm starving.'

Going next door Jacqui returned with a bathrobe and a thick white towel in her arms. 'Take a shower,' she ordered, handing them to him, 'and I'll make you some breakfast in the meantime.'

Ten minutes later, when he came out of the bathroom, he found her busy frying onions in butter.

'Ah, that's better,' she said, glancing up from the oven with a smile, 'you look almost human again.' Breaking eggs into a bowl she whisked them together, adding a pinch of herbs and ground pepper. She poured the eggs into the pan where they clucked and hissed with the heat and the warm fragrance of their cooking filled the kitchen. As soon as they had scrambled she piled them on to a slice of buttered toast and carried the plate through into the living room.

'English breakfast,' she announced, taking a seat beside him and pouring out two cups of coffee.

The eggs were sweet and delicious and Napier ate them

eagerly. All the while Jacqui sat and watched, plying him with more questions.

'So if *The Estuary Pilgrim* is a fake what happened to the original?' she wanted to know.

Napier shrugged. 'I suppose it must have been blown up on that road above Criquetot, just as the books say.' He saw the flash of disappointment in her eyes and added, 'That is unless it's still sealed up in a canister somewhere nearby, as you suggested.'

As soon as Napier had finished eating Jacqui jumped up and began to clear the table. He tried to help her but she prevented him.

'Go and sit down,' she ordered. 'I'll just put these in the kitchen.'

Napier did as he was told and crossing the room he settled himself on the sofa.

He listened to the clink of crockery from next door and the rustle of Jacqui's skirt as she moved about the kitchen. He couldn't see her but the little domestic sounds made him suddenly acutely aware of her presence and the knowledge that she was there close to him filled him with a deep and mysterious contentment.

'Who's responsible for the fake, do you think?' she called out.

'I don't know,' Napier replied, gazing up at the ceiling, his mind drifting back to the desolate expanse of the estuary. 'That's what we have to discover.'

The sunlight gilded his vision. The room was warm and cosy. He felt his eyelids dropping. Jacqui was saying something but he didn't catch the words.

Her voice was coming from a great distance.

When she came through a moment later she found him sleeping.

Napier woke up with a start.

Opening his eyes he looked around the room, momentarily lost. Recollection flooded back to him and he sat up, apologising for dropping off like that but Jacqui hushed him quiet.

'It was a good thing to do,' she said gently, 'you were worn out when you arrived here.' Getting up from the table where she'd been writing letters she went over to him. 'How are you feeling now?'

202

'Much better,' he replied, stretching his arms. 'What's the time?'

'It's midday.' She paused and then added lightly, 'I have to go over to Étretat this afternoon and pick up a picture. I was wondering whether you'd like to come with me?'

Napier's eyes lit up at the suggestion.

'I thought maybe we could have lunch together.'

Dressing in his salt-caked clothes, Napier went back to the hotel to change while Jacqui put together a last-minute picnic. She was feeling pleased with herself. There had been no particular hurry for the picture, it wasn't needed by the museum for another two weeks but Napier wasn't to know this.

When they met on the quayside half an hour later he was looking fresh and tidy once more, dressed in his neat English way and carrying a little bouquet in his hand. 'I brought this for you,' he said, holding it out to her bashfully.

Buried in the cocoon of ribbon and coloured paper was a bright green bunch of parsley.

'You left some with me last time we met.'

Jacqui was enchanted. 'Oh,' she cried with pleasure, 'doesn't it look sweet all wrapped up like that.'

'The shop thought I'd got the word wrong and kept trying to sell me roses instead,' Napier told her.

'I'm so glad you didn't let them,' she said, touching the bouquet to her nose. 'I must put it in water before we leave.'

Further along the quayside a crowd had gathered. As they were passing by it parted and the juggler, in his red and yellow clothes and flat shoes, stepped out in front of them. He bowed and rolled his hat down into his hand.

'Good day, Dr Napier,' he said, looking from one to the other with his sharp black eyes. 'I hear you were out swimming last night.'

The audience gave a little laugh in anticipation but the juggler said no more. Stepping back with a second sweeping bow, he returned to his act.

'How did he know your name?' Jacqui asked as they reached the car.

Napier shrugged. 'He must have picked it up from one of the fishermen, I suppose.'

★ ★ ★

203

Crossing the Seine at the Tancarville Bridge they drove around to Étretat.

The sea was still and sparkling in the autumn sunshine when they arrived, the great cliffs hazy in the warm air. They walked along the front together, watching the bathers splashing about in the waves that lisped up the shingle beach.

'Look,' Jacqui cried, pointing towards the rocks, 'the tide's going out, we can get through to the next bay.'

Napier looked where she indicated but couldn't see what she was referring to.

'Have you never been through there?' she asked.

He shook his head.

'Then I must show you.' Quickly she took off her shoes and put them in the basket he was carrying and then reaching up under her skirt she slipped off her stockings. Jumping down on to the beach she ran to the edge of the shingle and made her way across the slippery stones exposed by the tide, skipping from one to the next with her arms held out on either side like a child imitating an aeroplane. From time to time she turned back to Napier, watching him, laughing at his clumsy attempts to keep up with her.

She was flirting outrageously, she told herself; if Pacquetta could see her now she'd be horrified. But it didn't matter. She was feeling happy and shameless.

'It's so lovely here,' she called to him.

The cliffs seemed to rear up above them as they approached, growing larger and more majestic until they blotted out the sun entirely.

Jacqui led the way to a cave in the rock face. 'It goes right through to the other side,' she told him. 'You must crouch down low or you'll bang your head in the dark.' She scuttled through ahead of him. The tunnel twisted and turned for fifty yards and then suddenly burst out into the sunshine.

Jacqui saw the surprise on Napier's face as he emerged from the darkness and looked at the bay that lay stretched out before them, the sea enamel blue, the cliffs white and crumbling as a new loaf of bread.

'There,' she cried proudly, 'isn't this the perfect place for a picnic?'

They ate their lunch on a large rock above the sea. Jacqui had brought pâté and cheese, mushrooms à la grecque and crab salad in little cardboard packages. They drank Chablis from wine glasses that she'd carefully wrapped in napkins – 'Because it always tastes so horrid in paper cups' – and they kept the bottle cool in the meantime by lowering it down the rock into the water on a length of string which Napier had discovered on the beach.

They weren't alone in the bay. One or two people had found their way through the tunnel, but they were both too absorbed in each other to notice the instrusion.

Napier discovered that beneath her sophisticated, professional knowledge Jacqui had a charming and entirely romantic view of art. 'Sometimes, when I'm in the fields above Honfleur,' she told him, 'I imagine I can still hear the artists talking. It's the same here. Whenever I'm in this bay I can picture Monet at work, with Maupassant behind him watching him painting.' And then she blushed crimson, embarrassed by the confession. 'Do you think that's silly?'

Napier shook his head. 'When I was at Oxford I would never go back to a place where I'd been happy in case it damaged the memory. It's much the same thing.'

'Yes it is,' she agreed seriously. The sun and wine were making her drowsy and stretching herself out on the warm rock she gazed up at the sky. 'How did you become interested in art?' she asked.

'It was beaten into me.'

Jacqui looked up in surprise. She'd heard stories of English schools where little boys were flogged for the slightest misbehaviour. 'You were beaten if you didn't learn about art?'

'Not quite,' he said with a grin. 'I was actually beaten for being out of bounds after dark. There was a Sotheby's catalogue on the headmaster's desk. I pushed it down the back of my trousers while he wasn't looking and didn't take it out again until I was back in my room. There was a picture on the cover – the *The Canal St Martin* by Sisley – all bent round to the shape of my backside.'

'And that was the first picture to interest you?'

He nodded, laughing at the memory. 'Even now, when I look at that painting in Paris I see it all crumpled up.'

Jacqui stirred herself, for some reason she found the story strangely arousing. Rolling over on to her side she looked at Napier. He wasn't good-looking in any conventional sense and yet he was extraordinarily attractive. She wondered why

205

she hadn't noticed it before. She liked the firm line of his nose and forehead, the way his eyes smiled when he talked. There was a strength to him, an assurance, but held in reserve. Napier made no open display of masculinity.

He was tossing stones into the sea, catching the waves as they turned and flopped on to the beach. Jacqui watched the material of his shirt tightening across his shoulders each time he drew back his arm and as she looked she felt her nipples grow firm and press against her shirt front. She lay back, savouring the sensation, storing it away in her mind to be examined later when she was alone.

In the distance women stood ankle deep in the water, minute silhouettes against the expanse of flat sea, their skirts rucked up around their hips as they searched for oysters and hermit crabs.

Jumping down they walked along the water's edge, their feet leaving pale bruises on the wet sand. Jacqui told him of her first visit to the Orangerie in Paris, the sight of Monet's waterlily paintings on the walls and how she had been given Napier's book as a present afterwards.

'I thought you hadn't read anything by me.'

'I just said that on the spur of the moment,' she confessed, pleased to have the lie off her conscience. 'I was so cross with you that day, Jean.'

She used the French equivalent for his name. He liked that, it was more personal.

'I didn't want you to be young,' she explained. 'I'd always imagined you as a nice old man with a white beard and twinkling eyes.'

The idea of Napier as an elderly academic made them both suddenly laugh. At that moment a wave rushed up over their feet, pounding them with tiny pebbles. Jacqui gave a little squeak of surprise at the tingling sensation and grasped hold of her ankles. The locket slipped from her shirt and dangled from her neck.

'What's that?' Napier asked.

She straightened up, hesitated for a moment and then lifting the chain over her head she handed it to him.

Napier studied the two tiny portraits inside.

'People say I look like my father,' she said, a touch of defiance in her voice as though willing him to agree.

'He's much darker than you.'

'Yes,' she agreed, 'the whole family is. My brother's hair is almost black.'

'You have a brother?'

'I have two,' she said, wriggling her toes down into the sand. 'Both much older than me.' She grinned up at him mischievously. 'I think I was a mistake.'

The afternoon was almost spent, already sky and water were glowing in anticipation of the sunset.

When they reached the cave they found the tide had risen, the channels of water between the rocks now deeper and wider. Cautiously they picked their way across the surface. At one pool Jacqui paused, stepped forward, hesitated, lost her balance and darted out her arm for support. Napier took her hand and held it and they walked on again, their fingers meshed together, both suddenly self-conscious at the touch.

The evening had drawn in by the time they arrived back in Honfleur.

'I must go and change,' she told him in the hallway of her apartment, 'I'm meant to be going out in a few minutes.'

'When will I see you again?'

She scribbled a number on a piece of paper and gave it to him. 'Give me a call.'

'Tomorrow?'

'If you like.' She paused and looked up at him, 'Or you could ring me later tonight if you prefer. I'll be back by eleven.' Reaching up she kissed him quickly and ran upstairs. A thought struck her and she turned around, the sun still glowing on her cheeks and hair.

'Jean?'

Napier glanced around.

'I've just realised something.'

'What's that?'

'We forgot to pick up that picture.'

Chapter Fifteen

'And that's about all I can tell you, Inspector.'

Chaumière stared across the office, shoulders hunched, hair unruly from the constant furrowing of his fingers.

'So if there's nothing more you need of me . . .'

Giving a jerk of his head, Chaumière roused himself, breaking through the shell of his thoughts.

'No – not at all.'

'I'll be off then.'

Chaumière followed Napier to the door, offering his hand in parting. 'It was good of you to call by.' He paused as though a new thought had struck him and added, 'But should there be any further developments, we'd be interested to hear of them.'

'Of course . . .'

'Straight away, Dr Napier, not a day later if you don't mind. We like to be kept informed.'

Napier smiled and assured him that he'd be the first to hear if anything happened to him.

After he had left Chaumière turned and pondered. Hands thrust in his pockets, counting small change through his fingers in time with his thoughts.

Napier had given him a clear account of their night on the estuary. His manner had been dry, almost laconic as he related the circumstances, describing their reasons for visiting Le Havre, the delay while they searched for Albert, the collision with a tugboat and their survival on a sandbank throughout the night.

He turned to the sergeant. 'What did you make of it?'

'Is he to be believed?'

Chaumière nodded. 'Oh, it happened all right. I've talked with the crew of the boat that picked them up. The three of them were there, stranded on some split of ground at the mouth of the estuary, with a raft no bigger than a bathtub.

An hour longer and they'd have been swept away on the morning tide.'

The sergeant blew out his cheeks. 'Damnest thing I ever heard.'

Whether it had been an accident was another matter. There had been a slight fog that night, he'd checked with the harbour master. The tug's navigation lights could well have been obscured in the darkness, only appearing to be switched off. And then, on Napier's own admission, the captain of their boat had been stone-drunk and scarcely responsible for his actions.

But all this was, to an extent, academic. What puzzled Chaumière was the connection. Napier was convinced there was a direct link between this incident on the estuary and the death of Charles Barnabas. He'd been adamant on that point. 'Ever since he was drowned I've been dogged by trouble,' he'd explained. 'Back in London I was warned off the case by a couple of bullies, then I find I'm being followed about the streets of Honfleur and now somebody tries to drown us. It's too much of a coincidence, Inspector, there has to be a connection.'

If he was right they were going to have to rethink the entire situation, start all over again.

The sergeant was watching him speculatively.

'Are we going to look into it?'

Chaumière threw himself down in his chair. Taking the coins from his pocket he scattered them on to the desk-top, arranging them into patterns. His own investigations into Barnabas's death had drawn a blank. He'd reconstructed the man's movements here in France, interviewed those who'd come in contact with him, checked his background with Scotland Yard. But he had found nothing. No motive, no positive reason why anyone should want to see him killed.

Chaumière nudged the coins into a circle and then swept them back into his pocket. There might be something in what Napier had said. At least it wouldn't do any harm to check.

'What we are going to do,' he said eventually, 'is take rather more interest in Dr Napier while he's with us.'

Spooner sounded interested but not convinced.

'You believed her, did you?' he asked.

'I think so,' replied Napier. 'Nadine Lebas knows that her husband has nothing to do with faking the painting. It's just an instinct, she has no proof but she's convinced of it nonetheless.'

'Feminine intuition you mean?'

'Something like that. Showing me the wreck of *The Estuary Pilgrim* was her way of describing what she feels but can't explain.'

'Did you tell Chaumière this?'

'He didn't ask.'

They walked across to the garden seat and sat down. The morning dew glistened on the ground, the long grass bowed by the weight of moisture. Spooner crossed one leg over the other and stared at the polish on his toe-cap.

'How was she able to recognise you?'

'We met briefly at the National Gallery last summer,' Napier told him. 'Margot Latchman introduced us.' At the mention of Margot's name he felt a memory stir in the depths of his mind. He paused and looked across at the hotel. Tentatively he tried again, touching the fragile image, gently grasping hold of it. He could see her before him: lavender dress and auburn hair, her eyes hooded and slightly seductive. Was it at the National? No, she was sitting down; he could hear her voice, low and husky. She was turning as she talked.

Suddenly he had it.

'My God,' he breathed. 'Enrique.'

Spooner looked at him sharply.

'That's where I saw him last,' Napier said excitedly, and as he spoke the memory opened before him, like the lights coming up on a stage set. 'It was with Margot Latchman. We were having lunch together in Green's. She was telling me that appearances could be deceptive and to prove her theory she pointed to a man sitting at another table. It was Enrique.'

'Are you sure it was him?'

'Absolutely. I can see him now. He was at a table in the corner of the room, there was a dark-haired girl with him and he was smoking a cigar.'

Spooner was immediately alert. He began to speak but Napier cut him off.

'She told me that he was involved in some mischief – arms dealing I think it was – but that nothing had ever been proved.'

They looked at each other in amazement.

'And he's the man who does business with Ashford,' Napier continued.

'But if nothing's been proved . . .'

'It doesn't matter, the connection is there. It must be worth following up.'

Spooner's eyes twinkled. Sitting back he allowed himself a small and secretive smile, like a man who's remembered a mildly amusing anecdote during a particularly dull board meeting.

'I may be able to help you,' he said. 'Wait here a second.' Getting to his feet he went into the hotel, returning a few minutes later with a file in his hand. 'Fortunately I had removed this from my briefcase,' he said as he handed it to Napier, 'otherwise it'd be at the bottom of the estuary by now.'

The file contained a detailed biography of Ashford's life.

Napier read through it with growing interest. Listed there in chronological order were all his company holdings, business enterprises and financial assets; the entire empire he had built up over the years.

'This is extraordinary,' Napier murmured as he skimmed down the pages. 'I'd no idea he had his finger in so many pies.'

'It's considerable,' Spooner agreed dryly.

'Look at this,' Napier said, pointing to one entry in the file. 'He's been in jail.'

Spooner nodded in satisfaction. 'A phase of his life he rarely mentions. Ashford served a three-year sentence in the States for fraud in the early sixties. It was there that he met Enrique de la Pena, and it's presumably then that they forged some sort of business alliance.' He leaned across and ran his finger down the page. 'You'll notice that Ashford opened his first art gallery shortly afterwards. It was in the Rue Lafayette, Paris. It must have done well enough for itself because a year later he opened a second, rather grander establishment, in the Faubourg St Honoré.'

'Coming up in the world.'

'Exactly.' Spooner took the file back and began thumbing through, indicating relevant passages. 'Let me give you a précis of Rupert Ashford's career. By the late sixties he had set up a chain of galleries across Europe. All of them were successful and prestigious with a well-established clientele. With the profits he was able to buy that château of his and began living in the style of a pre-Revolution aristocrat. At much the same time as he settled in France he had moved in on the American market with a gallery in San Francisco, another in Washington and two in New York.

Napier listened in silence, while thoughts and questions fizzed up in his mind like fireworks.

'The success of Ashford's galleries depended on considerable capital backing,' Spooner continued, getting into his stride now. 'He had a little money of his own by now but the greater part came from outside investors. Quite who these were remained obscure. Many of them preferred to remain anonymous. Film stars, oil millionaires, philanthropists, even members of the English Royal Family were rumoured to be behind Ashford's empire, all of whom, for reasons of notoriety and publicity, didn't want their names broadcasted.'

'That's quite common in the art world,' Napier pointed out.

'Of course it is,' Spooner agreed gravely. 'Only in this case none of them existed. An investigation last year revealed that Ashford had no sponsors discreetly hiding themselves from the glare of publicity. At least he had none of any significance. The enormous bulk of capital that he's been drawing on for the last few years really is anonymous and it comes from elsewhere.'

'Enrique?'

Spooner nodded. 'I would have thought so.'

'With money he's harvested from arms dealing.'

'Amongst other things. As you said, nothing has ever been pinned on him but he's almost certainly involved in arms, narcotics, prostitution – nothing's too good for him.'

'While Ashford launders the profits through his art galleries.'

'That's the way it looks from this end. Mind you this is only speculation at present.'

Napier gazed at him for a moment and then leaning across poked him on the shirt front with one finger.

'How do you know all this, Spooner?'

'Ah, well that's rather complicated.'

'Out with it.'

Getting to his feet, Spooner straightened his waistcoat and looked down at the ground. 'I haven't been entirely honest with you I'm afraid, John.'

'So I'm beginning to realise.'

'Nothing I've told you is untrue,' he added hurriedly. 'It's just that I haven't given you the entire story.' He rearranged the gravel with the tip of his toe. 'For some time now we've been interested in Rupert Ashford.'

'We?'

'Wallace-Jones,' he replied, 'the firm I work for. I didn't deceive you there, we really are accountancy consultants.'

'I thought you said you were loss-adjusters?'

'We are in a sense.'

'You mean you work for the Government rather than Lloyds,' Napier replied bluntly.

Spooner blushed at the accuracy of this conclusion and nodded. 'The City of London Fraud Squad, to be precise. Although on this occasion we were alerted to the problem by the Inland Revenue.' He waved a hand to one side. 'Rupert Ashford is still a British citizen, you see. We've been working on his case for almost two years now. It's not easy, his business affairs are like a rabbit warren. To make matters worse he has a number of quite legitimate dealings with Enrique, which is why he can speak of the association so openly.'

'But what has all this got to do with *The Estuary Pilgrim*?'

'By the beginning of this year our investigations had gone stale. We had discovered a few interesting facts about Ashford but no more. Then this painting appeared. We noticed that it had been lost at exactly the same moment as Ashford had been in Honfleur and reappeared not far from where he now lived. Added to this its resurrection had been prophesied by his own ward, Jacqui Fontenay. The coincidence seemed too good to miss. If it did turn out to be a fake, and we could pin the blame on to Ashford, it could be just the sort of lucky break we were looking for.'

'But why bring me in on it?'

Again Spooner smiled, now unmistakably pleased with himself. 'We needed someone who understood pictures but with no preconceived ideas to look into the case.'

Napier shook his head in disbelief.

'We were all prejudiced, you see, no longer able to judge

213

the situation objectively. And you were already involved in the painting.'

'So you shot me a story about tracking a notorious forger.'

'We wanted to see if you would discover a connection between Ashford and the painting of your own accord.'

'Which I have . . .'

'I'd never doubted you would.'

Through the blur of thoughts that flashed through Napier's mind one hit the surface. 'So if you've been waiting for me to come up with an answer, what have you been doing in the Archives for the last few days?'

Spooner appeared to be mildly embarrassed by the question. 'I've been examining some of the mediaeval manuscripts they have in there,' he confessed in a small voice. 'It's really the most remarkable collection.'

Sitting back on the bench Napier gazed up at him. 'You really are the most extraordinary man I ever met,' he said.

Spooner averted his eyes at the compliment.

'So what happens now?' Napier asked.

'I imagine we continue our investigations, collect our evidence together and then take it to the police.'

'Not the police!' Jacqui cried.

'But Ashford must be involved in some way.'

'He can't be,' she replied desperately. 'It wouldn't help him to fake the picture.' She shook her head and looked down at the table.

Napier had been describing the conversation he'd had with Spooner that morning, and the conclusions they'd drawn from it. He'd spoken gently, without any aggression but the words had filled her with a black despair that flooded into her mind, rising with the sudden, ungoverned force of panic. She didn't want to believe what Napier was saying but at the same time she knew he was right. Rupert was somehow involved with *The Estuary Pilgrim*. She didn't know how or why this was so, only that he was undoubtedly at the root of the whole business. 'There'd be no reason for him to do it,' she added miserably.

'I don't pretend to understand what's going on,' Napier told her, 'but the dates and places do all seem to fit. Ashford was in Honfleur at exactly the same moment as the painting vanished.'

'But he was being held by the Germans.'

'Yes,' he agreed, 'but in the very building where the picture was hanging.'

Jacqui gave a resigned nod. 'And then it reappeared just after I'd written that wretched article. I wish to God I'd never started on it now.'

'There was nothing wrong with what you wrote,' he calmed her, 'only in the use it was put to later.'

'Rupert kept asking me about how the article was coming along,' Jacqui said bitterly. 'I was so pleased; it was the first time he'd shown any interest in my work. He advised me not to publish my discoveries. The evidence was rather thin, he told me. Who was going to pay attention to the reminiscences of an old man, even if he was a Resistance fighter?'

Reaching across the table, Napier took her hand in his, and she responded quickly, holding it tightly.

He had waited until they had finished lunch before raising the subject of Ashford. He hadn't been certain how Jacqui was going to react. He had expected her to disagree, even resist, but he hadn't been prepared for the violence of her outburst. When he'd suggested going to the police, she had recoiled back from him and her eyes had clouded over with an expression that was neither anger nor surprise but more like terror.

He could feel her trembling now, as though some powerful current was running through her body. 'You're very loyal to him,' he said, looking across at her.

She shook her head again.

'Although I can't see that he has done anything to deserve it.'

'It's not that,' she mumbled.

'But you're fond of him.'

'I'm not!' she said throwing back her head, golden hair spilling across her shoulders, speaking with a sudden passionate energy, unable to contain the truth any longer. 'I'm not loyal, not fond, not any of those things people imagine . . .'

'But—'

'I hate him!'

Snatching back her hands she buried them in her hair, covering her ears as though trying to prevent herself from hearing the words that had escaped her lips.

Napier paused, momentarily taken aback by the ferocity of this confession.

'It's true,' she said after a few moments. 'I hate the way he's always touching me and stroking me. I hate the way he treats me as though I was some . . . creature.' Her voice was quieter now, more controlled. Looking up at Napier she smiled sadly and ran her hand across his. 'Oh Jean, it's a terrible thing to say . . .'

'Not if—'

'It is,' she said urgently, 'but I just can't help it. I've tried to be affectionate, to do what he wants, as he expects of me but it's no good. Rupert fills me with a sort of revulsion. I can't bear to be near him, to feel him.'

'Then why don't you let us go to the police?' Napier asked softly.

She gazed at him with wide, imploring eyes and shook her head. 'You mustn't,' she whispered.

'But why not?'

For a moment she considered trying to explain, to describe the black, whirling fear that darkened her mind but she fought back the desire. It was hopeless.

'I can't explain,' she said quietly.

'He seems to have mesmerised her.'

Eugenie gave a nod. 'That doesn't surprise me in the least.'

'It's as though he had some hold over her,' Napier continued, 'and yet I can't think what it can be.'

'Ashford likes to control people,' she replied, 'it flatters his sense of power.'

Walking down the front steps of the hotel they strolled across the gravel drive together. Eugenie had slipped her arm through his with the quick, trusting gesture of a child and was now listening intently to what he said.

'At first I thought it must be money,' Napier explained. 'I even wondered whether she was his mistress.'

She gave a little snort at this.

'But I discovered quick enough that this wasn't the answer. Far from accepting money from him she goes out of her way to refuse it. She's bought her own apartment and drives a car that she's paid for with her earnings from the museum. Whatever it is that Ashford uses to hold on to her is far less tangible than money.'

'He can be very subtle,' Eugenie told him. 'Ashford has a talent for manipulation that approaches genius.'

'At lunch today, Jacqui told me she hated him.'

She smiled and drew in her breath in a little sigh.

'What I can't understand is what he wants of her. Why has he gone to such elaborate lengths to assert himself over her?'

Eugenie paused and looked up at him with her round, olive-black eyes. 'The girl is one of his possessions,' she replied. Her voice was quick and assured as though the answer to the question was obvious. 'Ashford is obsessed with possession.' she told him. 'It's a malignancy that dominates his mind. Anything that is beautiful or rare fascinates him. He has to own it. The Fontenay girl is part of his collection, as much as one of his paintings or some rare orchid. She's a status symbol for him. He'd like to keep her locked up in that house of his like a precious object to bring out on occasion to impress his guests.' She turned and moved on again. 'If she has any sense she'll get away from him before he hurts her.'

'Would he do that?'

'Of course,' she replied. 'If she ever tried to cross him he'd destroy her, just as he destroyed this house.'

217

Chapter Sixteen

It was a suspicion, nothing more.

Jacqui considered it as she drove out to the château, turning the possibilities over in her mind, and with her thoughts came the first stirrings of apprehension. She hadn't said anything to Napier as she wasn't sure whether he'd have thought it relevant.

To tell the truth she wasn't sure herself.

Parking the car she ran up the graceful steps of the château and went inside. Louis heard her arrive and came into the hall to meet her, appearing from the direction of the kitchens and standing framed in the doorway.

'Is Rupert at home?' she asked, pausing on the staircase.

For a moment he stared at her, silent and inscrutable, then shaking his head he said, 'No, mademoiselle, he has gone into Trouville. I don't expect him back until this evening.'

Jacqui thanked him and carried on upstairs.

Going to the gallery she closed the door and looked about herself. The shutters had been partially shut and the long room was dark and still, the shadowed floor pierced with fine splinters of daylight.

She waited until she was satisfied that Louis had returned to the kitchens before crossing over to the wall of the gallery. Carefully she searched down its length until she found one panel in particular. It was decorated with garlands of flowers on a ground of misted grey. In the angle of the lower corner, where the painted panel met the wainscot, was a scroll-work of ormolu, beautifully inlaid into the wood.

Kneeling down she examined it closely.

There was nothing out of the ordinary about the design and for a moment Jacqui thought she must have been mistaken. Reaching out her hand she ran it across the surface, following the intricate gold pattern. In the centre of one scroll her finger touched a tiny protruding pin.

It appeared to be a catch of some sort.

Putting her fingernail to the pin she moved it to one side. It slipped round a few degrees and a shutter opened, like the protective cover on the end of a telescope, revealing a small round hole in the wall.

This is what had caught her attention.

It must have been left open that weekend. She'd noticed it when she was picking up her locket which Ashford had thrown across the floor, although she had been so pre-occupied at the time that the observation hadn't registered consciously. It was only later that it had thrust its way back into her mind, like a fresh young shoot pushing its way into the light.

Getting to her feet she checked the rest of the panel. One edge was hinged, the craftsmanship was so good that this was only apparent at very close range and might never have been visible at all had she not known what she was searching for.

Standing back Jacqui looked up at the wall. It was not a solid surface she realised. The little aperture hidden in the lower corner was the key-hole to a door.

The whole panel could be opened.

She moved along to the next. It was identical to the first. With a tremor of excitement she discovered that the entire expanse of panelling was hinged in this way. The gallery wall was hollow.

Jacqui felt a sudden warm rush of guilt at the discovery. Quite by chance she had stumbled on one of Rupert's secrets, found what he had gone to great lengths to disguise.

Slipping out of the gallery she ran up to her room and changed her clothes. As she came downstairs she met Louis in the hallway.

'I'm going out riding,' she told him.

He was looking at her strangely.

Jacqui was about to say more, to make some excuse for her presence in the gallery, but she held it back. She had never felt obliged to explain herself to Louis in the past. It would be quite unnatural for her to do so now.

With a little bow he opened the front door and his eyes followed her outside.

Going over to the stables Jacqui led Bastian, a large bay gelding, out into the yard. She saddled him quickly and swinging herself on to his back she rode him up into the woods above the château.

It was a day of autumnal stillness. There had been rain earlier that afternoon and the trees dripped on her head and shoulders. A faint mist clouded the ground, lifting the sweet scents of damp earth and decaying leaves to her as she cantered past.

Following a track, she rode for over a mile through the woods, the unspoken communion between horse and rider helping to calm and order her thoughts. By the time she came out on to the open ground above the estuary she had reached a decision.

The prospect scared her but it was unavoidable.

Turning the horse's head she galloped him back down the hillside and returned to the stables.

Back in the château she went directly upstairs to the gallery. Laying her hat and riding crop on a side table she pressed the bell and waited for Louis to arrive, her heart hammering against her chest.

The room was still in darkness. Opening two of the windows Jacqui pushed the shutters apart, letting the daylight flood across the walls.

'You rang for me, mademoiselle?' Louis asked from the doorway. His expression was wary, uncertain. It was unlike her to summon him in this way.

'Yes Louis,' she replied. Her voice was shaking and she had to fight to keep it sounding casual. 'I'd like the key to these panels please.'

Louis stood quite still. 'I'm sorry,' he said after a moment, 'I don't understand what it is you are asking.'

'It's quite simple,' she replied archly, 'I want you to open these doors for me.'

'But do you— '

'Of course I know what's in them,' she cut in, anticipating his question, holding the advantage.

Louis looked at her steadily. 'In that case I'm sure you also know that only Monsieur Rupert has the key to the locks.'

'He told me you keep another,' Jacqui returned. It was a guess but it seemed to hit the mark nonetheless. Louis glared at her sullenly. She could see the indecision on his face and sensed the struggle taking place beneath. Tilting back her head she met his gaze with her fierce grey eyes, defying him to refuse her.

For a moment they confronted each other and then quite suddenly Louis gave in. 'Very well, mademoiselle,' he said with stony politeness, 'if that is what you wish.'

He left the room, closing the doors behind him.

Jacqui let out her breath in a rush. Walking a few paces down the floor she crossed her arms and shivered in the sudden release of tension. Her heart was still beating uncomfortably and for the first time she felt truly frightened by what she had undertaken.

Louis was back within the minute. In his hand was a long silver key. Without saying a word he crossed over to the central panel and crouched down.

'Give it to me,' Jacqui ordered from the open window, 'I'll do it for myself.'

Louis paused. He was performing mechanically now, accepting orders without question, shifting the responsibility for his actions on to her in so doing. Straightening his back he turned and faced her.

Jacqui stood her ground, hands on hips, legs set apart, forcing him to come right over to her.

'Thank you, Louis,' she said as he handed her the key. 'That will be all for now.'

His face betrayed no emotion.

As soon as he had withdrawn Jacqui hurried across to the panelled walls. Selecting one at random she knelt down and lifting the little gilt shutter she inserted the key. The lock opened without a sound. She pulled back on the head, using the key as a handle to open the door, but it merely slipped out of the lock. There was no tooth on the shaft to hold it in the mechanism.

Jacqui stood up and looked the panel over carefully.

There had to be another catch somewhere. She ran her hands over the decorated paintwork but it was smooth and quite without blemish. She felt her way round the edge, searching for some sort of purchase, but found nothing. In exasperation she hit the woodwork with the palm of her hand. There was a soft click and the panel sprang open with a little inward sigh of suction.

The solution was simple, it was held on a pressure-release catch.

221

Jacqui swung the panel back. It reached to the ceiling and was surprisingly heavy.

Inside was a single picture. It hung in a shallow compartment, not two feet deep and lined with claret-red silk.

She recognised the painting immediately.

As the door opened the light had fallen across a large gilt-framed canvas. It was a scene of wild, fighting figures on a stone bridge. Horses were rearing, standards fluttered and the air was full of fear and shouting. Over their heads the sky was ablaze with fiery red clouds above a setting sun.

It was the *Battle of the Amazons* by Delacroix.

Jacqui had never seen the painting before but she knew it intimately from the photo in the museum. It was part of the von Eichendorff collection, one of the pictures that had been hanging in the General's apartment in Honfleur.

Stepping back from the opened door she stared at the picture in horror.

The shock of the discovery had knocked the breath from her lungs but at the same time she realised that she was not surprised. Deep in the centre of her being she had guessed this, known what it was she would find in these secret vaults.

Closing the door she moved to the next panel, unlocking it in the same way. Here there were four smaller paintings, bright sun-drenched views of the Mediterranean by Bonnard.

As she reached out to close the door a hand caught her by the wrist.

She spun around.

It was Ashford.

His face was close to hers, almost touching. He was gripping her tightly.

Jacqui felt fear and guilt collide into panic. Where had he come from? He wasn't supposed to be here. She gave a cry and pulled away, frantically trying to break free of his grasp, but he held her relentlessly. For a brief instant they struggled, their bodies pressed together in a slow, involuntary dance. And then, without warning, he released her.

'You stupid, irresponsible little bitch,' he hissed, and drawing back he slapped her in the face with the back of his hand.

The blow was hard and vicious.

Jacqui staggered backwards, threw out her arms to keep her

222

balance and fell heavily, banging her elbow on the floor.

Ashford moved with the speed of a striking cobra.

Picking up the riding crop that lay on a side table he stepped over her as she was scrambling to her feet, and raising it above his head he struck her across the back. She gave a little whimper at the sudden pain and fell down, twisting away from him. Ashford caught her by the hair, pulling her over on to her face, and began systematically to beat her, the crop hissing and cracking in his hand. The strokes were calculated and well aimed, cutting her deliberately across the shoulders and the back of her neck.

Jacqui was given no chance to escape.

Throwing her arms about her head to protect her face she squirmed at his feet, while the crop whipped through the thin material of her shirt. She cried out as each blow landed, struggling to get away from the terrible stinging strokes. Lashing out her foot she tried to kick him but her hair was in her eyes and she was blinded by the pain and violence of the moment and couldn't find the target.

On the sixth stroke Ashford paused, the crop raised in his hand. The madness left him like the passing of a summer storm. Dropping his arm he let her go.

Jacqui rolled over on the floor and looked up at him. Her eyes were brimmed full of pain and shock which receded to be replaced immediately by anger: a white, diamond-hard fury.

Springing to her feet she confronted him.

'Where did you get those paintings from?' she shouted.

Ashford gave no answer. Strolling over to the open window he looked down at the gardens spread out beneath him in the mellow afternoon light.

'Where did you get them?' Jacqui repeated, following him across the floor.

Ashford turned suddenly from the window. For a moment she thought he was going to hit her again and jumped back out of range but he simply smiled at her.

'I take it that your friend Dr Napier has discovered that *The Estuary Pilgrim* is a fake?'

Jacqui was not going to be deflected in this way. Dropping her voice she said, 'I insist you tell me where those paintings came from, Rupert.'

'You insist?' he echoed, with a note of sarcasm. 'And who are you to insist anything? You force your way in here, prying into secrets that don't concern you and now you expect to be given answers and explanations. I've already given you all you deserve.' He turned and looked down at the view again. 'But since you ask, those pictures are mine. They belong to me.'

'How can that be?' Jacqui replied quickly.

'I earned them.'

Jacqui nursed her smarting arms and looked at him with incomprehension. What did he mean by that?

'I earned those paintings,' Ashford continued softly, 'by risking my own neck.'

'I don't understand,' she said with a shake of her head.

Ashford's face was pale and drawn and he considered her thoughtfully. 'Then let me explain,' he said. 'Since you now know part of the story, it is only right that you hear the rest.

'In the spring of 1944 I was here in Normandy. The invasion was coming and the war was nearly over.'

Strolling over to the gallery wall Ashford studied the four Bonnards with interest. 'These pictures, that you've so ingeniously managed to uncover, belonged to General von Eichendorff in those days. As you know, he'd looted them from numerous private collections in France.

'I knew practically nothing about paintings at the time but I'd seen how the Germans treasured them and appreciated that they must be intrinsically valuable, like gold or precious stones. I decided therefore to take the General's collection from him.'

He had Jacqui's full attention now. As he spoke she felt anger melting away, dissolving into a strange, horrified fascination.

'It wasn't too hard,' Ashford continued. 'Von Eichendorff was a good soldier and an intelligent man in many ways but it wasn't difficult to outwit him. The only problem was contriving some sort of meeting. I arranged to have a set of false identity papers made. They were a competent forgery, good enough to pass in a casual examination but not likely to go undetected for long. These I carried with me in Honfleur until, after three days, they were spotted and I was arrested.'

Jacqui listened with growing dismay as he described how he was taken to a house in the Rue du Puits and tortured by the Gestapo, how he'd been taken before a firing squad and pretended to break down at the last minute.

'I had to convince them, you see. My plan was only going to work if the Gestapo were certain I had valuable information on offer.' Ashford seemed to be enjoying himself now. His voice had sunk to a murmur and he gazed across the room as he told Jacqui how he had persuaded his guards to take him before von Eichendorff. In a few words he outlined the proposition he'd put to the General.

'I offered to hide his paintings until the war was over and then sell them back to him. Von Eichendorff was a rich man, like most of the German high-command he had been salting money away in a Swiss bank since the war began. He didn't like the idea, of course, but he could see the logic behind it. He knew the war was lost and he should grab hold of everything he could. But still it took him four days to come to a decision. Four long days while I sat rotting in a cell waiting for his answer.' He paused and brooded for a moment, the memory bright in his mind. 'Finally he summoned me. It was late at night. He was alone in his private apartment. The arrangement we came to at that meeting was simple. He would have his paintings sealed into metal containers and buried in five separate places in the hills behind Honfleur. This job was given to his adjutant; I wasn't to be told where he'd hidden them until the war was over.

'In the meantime a set of identical containers were made and filled with rolls of bare canvas, primed and smeared with oil paint, so that after a fire the charred remains would resemble those of a burnt masterpiece. These were loaded on to a convoy and shipped back across France by road.

'I was then allowed to escape.

'The General created a diversion by starting a fire in the building where I was being held and in the commotion that followed I was able to get away. As soon as I was free, I contacted the Maquis, told them that the convoy was carrying vital components of some new secret weapon and left them to deal with it.'

Jacqui glanced quickly round at the gallery walls. She'd followed what he said, understood what he had planned. But the pieces didn't fit, there was an inconsistency. 'But you didn't send the pictures to him. They're still here.'

'Ah, well I hadn't been entirely honest with the General,' Ashford replied with a gleam of satisfaction. 'We had a forger working for us in the Resistance. He made passports, identity papers, anything else we needed at the time. The documents I was carrying on the day of my arrest weren't his handiwork, of course, they were far too crude. This man was an artist, a true craftsman.

'After the war the General contacted me through the central post office in Geneva, as we had agreed, giving me the first of the burial sites. I dug the paintings up and had them copied. My forger did an astonishing job, even I couldn't recognise the original from its double. But then I'm forgetting, you've seen his work, haven't you?'

Ashford held up his hand, staunching her unspoken question. 'Don't worry, he's no longer alive. The poor man died in Nantes about five years ago. Sadly, like all great forgers, he'll never be awarded the fame he deserves.'

'So the paintings you sent to von Eichendorff were fakes?' Jacqui was appalled.

'Yes,' Ashford replied and with sudden conviction he added, 'It was right that I should have the originals. They belonged to me.'

'How can you say that?' she cried.

'Von Eichendorff never paid for those pictures, whatever he might have said at the time. He had given nothing for them and he got nothing back in return. It was justice. But I had earned them; in three days of torture from the Gestapo, in sitting waiting for his decision, not certain whether I would ever live to see the outside of that cell again, I had earned the right to take those paintings.'

Ashford paused. Reaching up he dug his fingers into his face and plucked the glass eye from its socket.

Jacqui gave a little inwards gasp and fell back, sickened by the sight. The eye had come out with a soft, damp plop, as though pulled from mud. The fine membrane of the lid had fallen inwards and the empty, gaping cavity now stared at her.

'I bought those paintings,' Ashford spat at her. 'And this was the price I paid.'

Jacqui held her hands to her face, as though trying to blinker the sight. She knew he was wrong. Everything he said was warped, distorted to justify his actions, but his self-assurance, the force of his conviction were overwhelming and as he spoke she felt a terrible primaeval fear invading her. She couldn't resist this man, he was too strong for her. She wished

226

Jean was here, he'd know how to handle him. The thought gave her renewed courage and thrusting out her chin she looked straight into his deformed face.

'Why did you put that fake in Criquetot?' she demanded.

Ashford turned and his single eye looked at her in surprise. 'Isn't that obvious?' he asked. 'It was to stop this witch-hunt you've started. You could have been right. Maybe one of those canisters had survived the ambush. I couldn't risk the consequences of it being found out.'

'But why didn't you put the real painting on that building site?' she asked. 'If *The Estuary Pilgrim* had been genuine when it was discovered there would never have been any witch-hunt.'

Ashford shook his head.

'With all these paintings in your possession couldn't you have let one go?' she demanded.

The question seemed to amuse him. 'No,' he replied, 'that's the irony of it. I couldn't.'

Picking up the key that Jacqui had dropped he went over to the panels and began to open them one by one. Gradually the serene gallery was transformed as painting after painting was revealed in its hiding place, each one rich and sensuous and glowing with light.

When he had finished Ashford turned and indicating the ranks of framed canvases he said, 'I didn't put the real painting in Criquetot, my dear, simply because I don't have it.'

Jacqui looked at him in amazement. He must have it. *The Estuary Pilgrim* was the central painting of the collection, the most important, the most desirable of them all.

'I've never had it. When I unearthed the General's collection after the war I found every painting just as he described, with the exception of one. *The Estuary Pilgrim* was missing.'

'Then where is it?'

'Who can tell?' A suggestion of sarcasm curled the edge of his voice. 'I imagine someone stole it.'

'Does it still exist?'

'Possibly.' Ashford stared away into the distance. 'But if it does I can't imagine where it can be.'

Jacqui looked across at the wall of paintings.

'The fake, as you choose to call it, was made from photographs,' Ashford continued. 'Although in its own way it was

227

a masterpiece. Even the alterations in the underpainting were meticulously reproduced so that it could stand up to X-ray treatment. As it happened I never had to send it to the General. He died in 1947 and the painting remained with me.'

'Why are you telling me all this?' Jacqui asked suddenly.

The ghost of a smile touched his lips. 'I want you to understand, my dear. I need you to know what I did. Because now you are going to help me.'

Jacqui bristled. 'Help you?' she shouted. 'After what you've done? Never!'

'I tricked one man out of some paintings he never owned in the first place. Where's the crime in that?'

'It's not the General you've tricked,' she spat back at him, 'it's everyone else – your friends, the people who live around here. They admire you, look to you for advice. To them you're a hero of the Resistance, a man to respect.'

Ashford brushed it aside. 'I'm not concerned with their fantasies,' he replied shortly. 'They like to talk of patriots and war heroes; it covers their own sense of inadequacy. But if that's what they want why should I shatter their illusions?'

His words cut Jacqui to the quick. 'Because it's a lie,' she replied hotly.

Ashford turned on her. 'And who are you to moralise?' he asked softly. 'You live in your safe, protected world where nothing dangerous is permitted. All you have to worry about is when you are next going to have your hair done, where your boyfriend is taking you that evening, which dress you should be wearing, whether you should open your legs to him.'

He was angry now and his voice grew silky as he spoke.

'What do you know of those years, you silly spoiled little fool? There were no comfortable rules then, the whole world was in chaos. Only the strong survived. The victims were those who hadn't the guts or the initiative to take what they wanted in life.'

Again Jacqui felt the compelling force of his personality bearing down on her but taking her courage in her hands she resisted. Her voice was firm, her eyes smouldering with anger. 'You can say what you like, Rupert, it makes no difference. I'm not going to help you.'

'I'm afraid you have no option, my dear.'

'You can't make me . . .'

'Oh but I can.'

'If you try to force me I'll go to the police,' she flashed at him.

Walking over to the paintings Ashford looked at them for a moment with affected interest.

'The police?' he repeated thoughtfully, as though the idea was new to him. 'No, you'd never do that, my dear.'

Jacqui glared back defiantly, holding the threat before her.

Ashford turned. The smile was there once more. 'No, my dear, you would never go to the police,' he said, his voice sinking to a whisper. 'Not knowing who I am – what I am to you.'

He saw her falter at his words.

'It just wouldn't be right, would it, my dear?'

For a moment longer Jacqui held his gaze and then slowly her resistance crumbled. The fire died down in her eyes, her shoulders sagged and she hung her head.

Ashford watched this transformation and his lean face blazed in triumph. Drawing her close he reached out and taking her chin in his hand he lifted her head, looking down into frightened eyes.

'You are not going to the police, my dear,' he told her. 'In fact quite the reverse. You will return to Honfleur as though nothing had happened this afternoon.'

Jacqui gazed up into his face, her shoulders were smarting painfully and the bleak despair chilled her once more.

'Yes Rupert,' she said meekly.

'Does Dr Napier know you are here?'

'Yes,' she lied with the last flicker of defiance.

'Good,' he purred. 'Then the next time you see him you'll tell him that you found some pictures while you were in the gallery – nothing of any great interest but worth looking at nonetheless. You'll then suggest that he sees them for himself and bring him here to the château.' He stroked her hair with his hand. 'Is that understood, my dear?'

'Yes Rupert.'

Louis closed each panel in turn. The radiance of painted canvases was contained, locked away in the dark once more, and the gallery regained its former restrained elegance.

Ashford stood by the window, staring out at the gardens,

229

watching the evening light steal across the sculptured lawns. He was holding a cigarette in his fingertips, drawing in his thoughts with the smoke.

'She tricked you, Louis,' he said after a few minutes.

Louis stood and faced him, accepting the criticism humbly. 'I wasn't to know,' he said steadily. 'She was so very sure of what she was asking. I naturally assumed that— '

'Never assume anything with women,' Ashford cut in. 'They will deceive you whenever they have the chance. Deception is second nature to them.' He turned back to the window. 'There is very little time left, we must finish this business now.'

'Mademoiselle Jacqui has returned to Honfleur?'

'Why do you ask?'

Louis shrugged. 'After what she has seen – after what you have done to her – do you think it wise to let her go?'

'Of course.' Ashford's confidence was in his voice, in the turn of his head as he dismissed the remark.

'But you said yourself that— '

'She will do as I have instructed her,' Ashford interrupted. He knew this to be true. It was the role for which he had groomed her over the years, the part he had carefully coached her to assume. There could be no mistake, no question of doubt. She may not want to obey him but then she had no option.

'The silly girl is a victim of her own conscience.'

'The man's a monster,' Pacquetta cried. Pulling back the collar of Jacqui's shirt she examined the angry red weals on her neck and shoulders.

Jacqui had tried to hide from her. Returning home she had gone straight to her bedroom to change but Pacquetta, sensing that something was wrong, had followed her.

'How did you get these?' she demanded, propelling Jacqui across the room and sitting her down on the bed.

'We had an argument.'

'Argument?' Pacquetta said darkly. 'I'll give him argument. Just let him lay a finger on you again.' Pacquetta's anger was indiscriminate. Whenever she was upset she vented her indignation on whoever was closest. In the circumstances it was usually Jacqui who took the brunt of it.

'He should be locked away,' she announced, and marching

into the bathroom she came back with a tube of cream clasped in her solid red hand. 'Take your shirt off, my girl.'

Jacqui was still wearing her riding clothes. Unbuttoning her shirt she eased it off and dropped it on the floor. Her back was raw, the skin tight and stiff as though badly sunburnt.

'And the rest,' Pacquetta ordered, taking the cap off the tube and squeezing cream out on to her fingers.

Jacqui did as she was told, unclasping her bra and letting it slip from her shoulders. Holding her breasts in her hands she leaned forwards submissively and allowed Pacquetta to rub the ointment into the raised marks of the crop.

'Why did you let him do it to you?' she demanded.

'I didn't let him – ouch!'

'What's the matter.'

'That hurts.'

'It wouldn't do if you held still and stopped yelping,' Pacquetta said illogically, working the cream into her skin. After a few minutes it began to soothe the pain. Jacqui felt her back grow supple once more, the stinging receded. She rested her head on her knees. There was neither anger nor shock any longer, her mind was a void, a cold grey mist that blotted out all emotion.

'Kettie?' she said after a moment's reflection.

Pacquetta didn't pause in her work but gave a grunt to indicate that she was listening.

'Do you think I look like Papa?'

'You have his temper at times, my love,' she replied standing back, satisfied that the job was done. Picking up the discarded clothes she went back into the bathroom.

'But do I look like him?' Jacqui insisted.

Pacquetta paused in the doorway and turned. 'Of course you don't, my love. You're fair haired – he was as dark as a gipsy.'

Chapter Seventeen

It was twelve-thirty. Ponderously the bells tolled out the half-hour, scattering the pigeons from the belfry. Down below the square was bright and bustling with activity at the stalls of the Saturday morning market.

Napier sat down at a table outside the Restaurant Sainte Catherine. The waitress came out, unclipping the pen from the cleavage of her cardigan, smiling in recognition, plump and contented in her movements. He ordered a bottle of Côtes-du-Rhône and leaned back against the restaurant wall.

The breeze stirred the awning above him, rippling along the fringe like waves running down a breakwater. Small clouds tumbled overhead, brushing quick shadows across the slate roofs of the town, and the stone wall was warm against his back.

Jacqui arrived a few minutes later.

Napier saw her coming across the square, walking between the bare bones of the market stalls, between the crowded tables and sparrows that hopped on the ground, the golden mane of her hair shining out against the dark overcoat.

She didn't wave. He was faintly disappointed, she normally did when she first caught sight of him, but she seemed pleased to see him nevertheless and kissed him warmly on both checks.

'I thought it would be pleasant to be out here,' Napier told her, sitting down and pouring her some wine. 'It seemed a shame to be indoors in this weather.'

'Yes,' she agreed shortly.

They ordered lunch. Jacqui spent a long time deliberating what she was going to have. Again Napier was surprised. It was quite unlike her to take so long, usually she knew exactly what she wanted. Finally, when the waitress had returned for a third time, she ordered a salad.

'I'm not really very hungry,' she said in explanation.

As they ate Napier told her of his morning, talking lightly, trying to break the spell that had been cast over her. Jacqui listened attentively but without any great enthusiasm, toying with her fork as he spoke.

'Are you feeling all right, *chérie*?' he asked suddenly, breaking off in mid-sentence.

'Yes,' she replied with a quick shake of her head. 'I'm just a little tired, I didn't sleep very well last night.' She smiled bravely, trying to match his mood. Her eyes were unnaturally bright, he noticed, and she was looking across the table at him intently. It was as though she was willing him to read her thoughts, to see what was troubling her without having to speak of it herself.

As soon as lunch was over she stood up to go. 'I should be getting back to the museum now,' she said.

'It can wait,' Napier replied calmly. Taking her by the arm he led her away from the restaurant and down the little flight of steps that ran in the shadow of the cathedral. She didn't try to resist, if anything she seemed pleased that he was making the decisions for her and pressed close to him as they walked.

The harbour was noisy and cheerful when they arrived, the cafés spilling colour and gaiety across the quaysides.

Leaving the crowds they walked out along the pier, past the piles of cordage and drying nets. At the far end was a large cast-iron capstan, a relic of the days when the Channel steamers moored in Honfleur. Napier paused and catching Jacqui round the waist he lifted her up, sitting her on to its smooth, rounded cap.

'Now,' he said, placing his hands on either side of her so that she was trapped between his arms, 'what's the matter?'

'There's nothing the matter—' she began, feigning surprise, but Napier cut her short.

'You must tell me,' he said quietly. 'I can't help you unless you tell me what's on your mind.'

Jacqui sat and looked down at him, her hands in her lap, ankles crossed. Her eyes were round and trusting. She hesitated for a moment longer and then slipping off her overcoat she unbuttoned her sleeve. Pulling it back she showed him her bare arm.

The strokes of the riding crop were still clearly visible. The virulent red weals had died away to pale blue–black

233

bruises but the violence of the attack spoke for itself.

Napier took her forearm in his hand and ran his fingers along the line of one bruise. Jacqui could sense the sudden rise of anger in the delicacy of his touch, the stillness of his expression as he examined the whip-lashes.

It was good; she wanted him to be angry for her.

'Did Rupert do this to you?' Napier knew the answer but still asked the question.

She nodded.

'But why?'

'Because I found von Eichendorff's pictures.'

Napier looked up into her face and the tiny flecks of amber that seeded his walnut-brown eyes lent his gaze a strange and luminous intensity at that moment.

'Where in God's name did you find them?' he asked.

She told him, describing the hidden doors in the gallery, the tiny key-holes and the pictures she'd found inside. At first she spoke slowly but gradually as the story unfolded she became caught up in it once more and the words poured out of her.

Napier stroked her arm as he listened.

'And Rupert caught you looking at them, did he?'

'Yes,' she said, her eyes growing fearful at the memory. 'He just went wild, Jean, like an animal. For a moment I thought he was going to beat me to death.' She gave a little sob and fumbled in her bag for a handkerchief.

'My poor love,' he murmured, slipping his arms around her waist. 'It must have been very frightening for you.'

He waited while she dabbed at her nose.

'I'm not meant to be telling you this,' she said after a moment.

'Oh?' He drew back so that his hands were resting on her hips. 'And what are you supposed to be telling me, *chérie*?'

She tucked the handkerchief back into her bag, composing herself.

'Rupert wants me to take you over to the château,' she explained in a small, unsteady voice. 'He told me to say that there were some pictures for you to see.'

Ashford must be very sure of himself, Napier observed, confident of the power he held over her.

Jacqui had pressed her fingers to her temples, her hair was tumbling about her face.

'Oh Jean!' she burst out. 'I've been so confused. I was

awake all last night trying to decide what to do. Rupert told me I had to take you over to see him, but if I do I think he's going to do something terrible to you.'

'They why do you obey him?'

She made a small, helpless gesture, indicating their present conversation. 'I haven't obeyed him,' she said, 'that's the point.'

'But why does he expect you to?'

Jacqui gave no answer.

'What is it, *chérie*?' he asked softly, gathering her hands into his.

She tossed her head. 'Please don't ask me that.'

The alarmed expression that Napier had first seen when he suggested reporting Ashford to the police had flooded back into her eyes.

'I must know,' he told her.

She looked down at him, fear and trust mingled together, both struggling for supremacy. Still she made no reply but Napier could sense that she was wavering. Now she wanted to tell him.

He pressed harder, his voice low and insistent. 'What is this power of authority that Rupert has over you?'

Her eyes were pleading with him.

'Tell me.'

'Isn't it obvious?' she whispered, suddenly giving in. 'Rupert's my father.'

Napier held her hands cupped in his. 'Did he tell you that?' he asked carefully.

'Not in so many words.'

'Then what makes you so certain?'

'Just look at me,' she flashed with sudden passion. 'You only have to look at me to realise he's my father.'

Napier was incredulous. 'Why?' he asked. 'Because you have blonde hair and your parents were both dark?'

She nodded.

'It's not much to go on.'

Jacqui gazed at him for a moment and then away to the harbour. 'Maybe not,' she replied sadly, 'but there are all sorts of other indications. Rupert's never even met my brothers, for example. When my parents died he showed no interest in them at all – only in me.'

'But that doesn't prove anything.'

She reached out and ran the back of her fingers down his cheek. 'I know, Jean,' she said, 'but it doesn't change the situation either. Rupert's my father. He's practically told me so himself.'

'In which case he's lying,' Napier replied.

Jacqui opened her mouth to protest but he stilled her with his hand.

'How old are you?'

'Twenty-six.'

He gave a quick nod. 'That's what I thought. And when was your last birthday?'

'Two months ago,' she replied in a puzzled voice. 'What's that got to do with anything?'

'A great deal,' he said with a smile. 'Because on the day that you were born Rupert Ashford had just completed the first two years of a jail sentence.'

'How do you know this?' she faltered.

It had been chance, a calculation that he had made out of curiosity one day. 'It's in Spooner's notes,' he explained. 'Rupert served three years in a State prison in Florida. You were about eight months old when he was released.'

Jacqui stared at him in disbelief.

'Don't you see,' Napier said earnestly. 'He's been black-mailing you over the years. You conceived this wild idea that Rupert was your father, it was your invention not his, but he's capitalised on it ever since. I'm certain he never said anything openly, just dropped the occasional remark, made supercilious expressions whenever your mother's name was mentioned and God knows what else, but it's very effective. I know, he tried it on me the other day.'

'On you?' she said indignantly. 'When?'

'During that cocktail party of his, just before he showed me his pictures. It was very subtle, he just sowed the seed of an idea in my mind and left it at that. Of course I fell for it completely. Had I not seen Spooner's notes I'd still be believing him.'

Jacqui's eyes had darkened. 'But why has he done this?' she demanded.

'To hold on to you,' Napier replied. 'It was his way of keeping you in his power. By suggesting he was your father he gave himself complete control of you.'

Jacqui stared at him for a moment and then jumping down from where she was sitting she walked to the end of the pier. Napier made no attempt to follow but leaned back against the capstan and watched her. For almost five minutes Jacqui stood there, gazing out to sea, deep in thought, her aristocratic features silhouetted against the sparkling water, while the breeze lifted and spread the heavy cape of her hair.

Abruptly she turned and strode back towards him.

Her face was radiant. She smiled and reaching out her hands to him said, 'Come, *chéri.*'

'Would you like something to drink?' she called out from the kitchen.

'Some brandy, if you have it.'

'Yes.' She opened a cupboard and took out a bottle. There was a little left at the bottom. '*Merde,*' she said with a click of her tongue. 'Maybe you can't. Kettie's been using it in the cooking again.'

'It's not important.'

'No,' she said, 'I think there's just enough for two.' Putting the bottle on the coffee tray she carried it through into the living room.

Napier was sitting sprawled on the sofa, his arms stretched out along the back. He jumped up as she came in and took the tray from her, slipping it down on the table.

'Help yourself, *chéri.*' Kneeling down Jacqui began searching through a stack of compact discs. 'I'm not entirely certain how this thing works,' she said, selecting one and feeding it into the player. 'I only bought it the other day. It was very extravagant but it has such dear little records.' She pressed a switch and sat back on her heels, waiting expectantly.

It was the overture to *Tristan und Isolde.* The music opened quietly, approaching from a distance, delicate and hesitant, growing richer until it filled the room. Jacqui made no movement as she listened but lifted her face to the ceiling, eyes closed, as though she were looking up into the sun.

She had been slightly apprehensive when they had arrived back at her apartment. 'I shouldn't really be taking the afternoon off like this,' she'd said to him.

'Give the museum a ring.'

'What shall I say?'

'Tell them that you're entertaining an important client

237

and are not to be disturbed under any circumstance.'

Jacqui had giggled and gone next door to make the call.

'All right?' he'd asked when she returned.

She'd nodded. 'I talked to Chantal. She couldn't have been more glad that I wasn't coming back this afternoon. I was being such a bitch this morning.'

The music came to an end, the climax breaking in great waves and then suddenly withdrawing, a summer storm rolling past. As it died away Jacqui relaxed and falling back she stretched herself cat-like across the floor.

'I love Wagner,' she purred. Turning her head she looked up at Napier with a mischievous smile on her lips. 'Do you think that's very unladylike?'

Napier laughed and leaving the sofa he came and sat beside her, setting his glass by her far shoulder. Jacqui lay on her back and gazed up at him, her hair fanned out in a golden halo about her head. Her neck was long and slender, breasts firm beneath the taut material of her shirt.

A shaft of sunlight fell across her at that moment and with a little contented noise she closed her eyes, her lashes dark against her cheek. A single lock of hair had fallen across her face and hovered on her breath. Reaching out, Napier stroked it to one side.

Jacqui stirred slightly, as if stretching in the warmth, and her face lifted towards him.

The invitation was offered timidly and discreetly.

Napier stooped over her. Their faces were close together. He paused, hardly daring to break the sanctity of the moment, and then kissed her gently on the lips.

Jacqui held perfectly still, as though she hadn't noticed him approach. It was only as he lifted his head once more that she opened liquid eyes and, looking at him, whispered, 'I didn't mean to hide from you just now, Jean.'

He smiled and gave a small shake, dismissing the remark.

'I won't do it again,' she promised, and reaching out she slipped her arms around his shoulders, drawing herself up to him. Her lips tasted sweet and warm, her perfume filled his head. The nervous girl who'd sat opposite him at lunch was transformed. She was eager and generous, pressing her body into his.

As the afternoon slipped by they sat together on the floor of her apartment, exchanging thoughts and memories and contented confessions, touching each other with their words. Their voices low and reassuring. Exploring and discovering, expressing their desire through small signs and caresses.

It was only as evening drew in and the sunlight had crept high on the walls that Jacqui returned to the question of the paintings. Stroking Napier with an outstretched arm, she asked, 'What do you think became of *The Estuary Pilgrim*?

Napier smiled. He had been carefully avoiding the subject, not wanting to break the gentle pattern of their conversation. 'Are you sure it's not hidden in the château?'

Jacqui watched her fingers furrowing through his dark hair and nodded. 'Rupert wasn't lying,' she said. 'I could tell. It was quite the reverse, if anything he seemed to be revelling in the truth.'

Napier rolled on to his back and gazed up at the ceiling. 'It's odd,' he said. 'The painting can't have been discovered after the war or all the others buried along with it would have gone also. Added to which I'm sure we would have heard by now if someone had dug it up.'

'Do you think the General could have buried it separately, kept it for himself?' Jacqui asked, lifting herself on to her elbow and looking down at him.

'I doubt it. He might have wanted to but it just wouldn't have been practical. He'd have known that.' He settled his hands behind his head. 'No, I think it must have been stolen sometime after the paintings had left his room but before they were buried.'

'But who can have done it?' she asked. 'The whole operation was carried out in secrecy. The only people who could possibly have known about it were von Eichendorff, Ashford and . . .' Jacqui paused and her eyes stretched wide as she realised what she was about to say.

'And Schwartz,' Napier finished for her. He sat up, resting on straight arms. 'Didn't you say that Schwartz was there at the meetings between Ashford and the General?'

'Yes,' she cried excitedly, holding up her hands, the fingers splayed, words coming in a rush, 'and it was Schwartz who was given the task of actually burying the pictures. Rubert said so yesterday.'

They stared at each other in silence, thoughts racing ahead, absorbing the implication of the words that had been uttered.

'Could Schwartz have stolen *The Estuary Pilgrim*?' Jacqui breathed, her eyes shining with speculation.

'Certainly. And no one would have been any the wiser at the time.'

'But what would he have done with it?'

'I've no idea,' Napier replied, 'and I imagine no one else does either. He died a few days after the pictures were buried.' He scrambled to his feet, drawing Jacqui up with him.

'Where are we going?' she asked, seeing the excitement that had come into his eyes.

'Schwartz is buried here in Honfleur,' he explained hurriedly. 'He was shot for desertion about a week after *The Estuary Pilgrim* was lost.'

'You think the two are connected?'

'Don't you?' He picked up his jacket and began pulling it on. 'Where is the local cemetery?'

'There are two.'

'How can we find out which one he's in?'

'In the Hôtel de Ville. They keep a record of all the burials.' She glanced down at her watch. 'It will still be open if we're quick.'

Napier was already halfway down the stairs. Grabbing her coat Jacqui ran after him, skirts billowing about her legs, high-heels clattering on the wooden boards. Out into the narrow street and on to the quayside where the evening crowds were filling the cafés.

It was five twenty-five when they arrived. The registry office was closing for the evening.

'We're trying to find a grave,' Jacqui explained to the clerk who was locking the door.

'You'll have to come back tomorrow,' he replied formally, 'it's after office hours.'

'Is it?' she inquired solicitously, concerned for the smooth running of his department. 'But maybe you could make an exception? This wouldn't take a moment and it's so important.'

The clerk blinked at her. His adam's apple lifted up out of his loose-fitting collar, bobbed twice and dropped back again as he considered the impropriety of the request.

Jacqui encouraged him with a dazzling smile that spoke of gratitude beyond words.

'Very well,' he said, unlocking the door once more and throwing it open. 'If it really is quick.'

'You are kind,' Jacqui purred as she followed him into the office. Institutional beige walls, posters warning against burglars and the dangers of rabies. Iron-framed chairs, gritty floor and no smoking signs with a crossed-out cigarette.

The clerk marched back behind the office counter, lifting the flap and closing it again behind him, reasserting his status. He was a thin man with a stringy neck and large ears and an expression of perpetual indignation on his face, as though life had proved to be an insult.

'Now,' he said, 'what name is it you are wanting?'

'Schwartz. Dietrich Schwartz.'

He fetched a large ledger and arranged it on the counter. Taking a ruler he ran it down the relevant pages, rapidly assimilating the entries in the calculator of his mind. 'There's no one of that name in St Léonard's cemetery,' he announced, snapping the ledger shut and returning it to its place. He brought out a second, covering the cemetery of Ste Catherine, but Schwartz wasn't in that either.

'You're sure you have the name right?' he challenged Jacqui.

'Yes, quite sure.'

'This burial took place in 1944,' Napier told him. 'Perhaps your records aren't accurate for the war years.'

The suggestion was a heresy. 'These registers are amended regularly,' the clerk reprimanded, 'no inaccuracy could pass undetected.' He paused and considered, his sense of bureaucratic pride now piqued. 'Do you know in which month the funeral was held?'

'It was in late May of 1944.'

'In that case we should be able to track it down,' he replied. 'The cemeteries are all cross-referenced chronologically.'

'That's very clever of you,' Jacqui said admiringly, shooting Napier a glance out of the corner of her eye as the clerk retired to find the volume in question.

'Here we are,' he announced in triumph. 'Dietrich Schwartz, German National, buried on the 25th May 1944.' He permitted himself a brief smile of self-congratulation.

'Where is the grave?' Jacqui asked.

'In the private cemetery of Notre-Dame de Grâce,' he told her, closing the register, his voice assuming a note of

241

authority. 'That would explain why it wasn't in the other volumes.'

They thanked the clerk warmly, left him double-locking the door and returned to the evening sunlight of the harbour.

'I didn't know there was a cemetery in Notre-Dame,' Napier said as they walked down the quayside.

'Neither did I,' Jacqui admitted. 'Do you want to go and look for it?'

'I would have thought so.'

She looked around at the waterside restaurants wistfully. 'We couldn't have dinner first, I suppose? I'm starving.'

Napier laughed and pausing in the Place Hamelin he bought her a *pâtisserie*. She ate it as they made their way up the hillside above Honfleur. The street was steep and crooked. Shutters hung open, posters for exhibitions were pasted on glass panes behind mediaeval iron bars. Occasional snatches of conversation reached out to them and the rich smells of evening cooking drifted from open windows as they passed.

Jacqui finished her *pâtisserie*, neatly licking each finger in turn.

The events of the day had come so quickly that she hadn't fully grasped their significance. She needed time to evaluate and arrange them in her mind. All she knew was that she was happy, unreasonably and intoxicatingly happy.

She was as eager as Napier to discover Schwartz's grave but above all she wanted moments such as these to last. There had been times in the last few weeks when she had cursed the day that *The Estuary Pilgrim* had been found but they were no longer important.

It was the painting that had brought Jean into her life, she reasoned, and that was all that mattered now.

She stole a glance at him. Napier must have been thinking along the same lines for he smiled, as though reading her mind. Without speaking they slipped their arms around each other and continued on their way, falling into step, each helping the other up the steep hill.

Notre-Dame de Grâce stood in a grove of beech trees, high above the estuary. It was a mariner's chapel, built as a place of worship, a spy-point and a familiar landmark, visible from miles out at sea. It was squat and tough, with thick walls, a low belfry and a blue-slate porch that covered the door like a toadstool.

Inside it was dark and still. Dank oak, empty pews, votive plaques on the walls. A few candles guttered in the stale air. Jacqui and Napier walked up the stone-flagged aisle, their footsteps disturbing the empty silence.

Instinctively Jacqui crossed herself as she looked around. 'It's spooky in here.'

Hanging from the beams above their heads were rows of little wooden ships, models of brigs, fishing smacks, paddle steamers and frigates, that sailors had carved over the centuries and given to the chapel to bring luck. They were dusty and blackened with age and reminded her of the stuffed reptiles that can sometimes be found dangling from the ceiling of junk shops.

There was a sound from the direction of the altar. The vestry door opened and the curé appeared, busily zipping himself into a leather jacket. Jacqui stopped him as he hurried past.

'We were looking for the cemetery,' she explained.

He paused in the aisle and looked at them through thick glasses.

'You do have a cemetery?'

He nodded and pointed towards the door. 'It's round the back of the chapel.' He considered them for a moment and then turning and hurrying on he added, 'Come, I'll show you.'

Outside the leaves were dripping from the trees, falling soft as snow-flakes on each other, muffling the gravel path as they followed him to the rear of the building.

The cemetery was joined to the chapel and almost hidden behind the arm of one transept. Clanking open the latched gate the curé led the way inside. The enclosed space was small and intimate, a place for reflection and privacy, surrounded on three sides by a high flint-stone wall.

A garden seat, green and moist with lichen, was set at the end of a short pathway and the graves were laid out symmetrically on either side. Grey slabs, artificial flowers, portrait photos in ornate frames. Obelisks and chain walls and mourning angels with wings folded over their heads. The grass between was unmown and licked over the headstones, breaking the hard geometry of their arrangement. The walls sheltered it from the breeze and pleasant smells of moss and pollen hovered in the motionless air.

Jacqui and Napier walked down the short avenue, their voices lowered, reading inscriptions, quotations and snatches of text from the bible, looking at faded pictures of forgotten relatives, while the curé remained at the gateway, standing sentry, watching from a distance.

They found Schwartz's grave in the shadow of a yew tree. It was simple and unpretentious, just a name and a date cut on to a block of smooth granite. The roots had burrowed beneath the headstone, lifting it and tilting it to one side.

Perched on the ground in front was a jam jar, grimy from the rain, containing a handful of wildflowers. They had been picked from the grass nearby and arranged without art, dandelions and daisies and round rabbit-eared leaves. One or two of the heads had grown heavy and flopped down over the rim.

Napier turned to the gate where the curé waited. 'How did a German soldier come to be buried here?' he asked.

Taking the prompt the curé walked over to them and looked down at the grave. His hands were thrust into the front pockets of his jacket and clasped together, swelling and pointing the curve of his belly, the knuckles showing through the taut leather. 'Can't say,' he replied, 'it was before my time here.' He gave a shrug. 'Strange things happened during the war.'

Napier gave a grunt of understanding.

'You're not the first to have noticed it,' he added. 'It was vandalised some years ago.'

'That doesn't surprise me.'

'German, you see. The people here have long memories.'

'But not all of them unpleasant memories by the look of it.' Napier nodded towards the little jam jar. 'You don't happen to know who put those flowers there I suppose?'

The curé looked up at him with damp, myopic eyes, the lenses of his spectacles magnifying his pupils so that they filled the frame like oysters in their shells.

'Children,' he replied flatly. 'I often catch them playing with the graves.'

He was a man without curiosity, content with a solution, any solution, provided it closed the subject. With a nod of his head and a word of apology he excused himself and left the cemetery, scraping the gate shut after him.

'Jean?'

Napier turned. Jacqui had moved away while he was talking to the curé and now stood further up the pathway, tall and handsome in her long overcoat, her hair swelling out over her upturned collar. She was studying a row of graves.

'Look at these,' she said as he joined her. 'They're all members of Eugenie's family.'

The Delaroche ancestors were clustered together, large architectural tombstones, set apart from the others, remote even in death. Some of the inscriptions dated back to the 18th century, Napier observed, the lettering soft and eroded with age, hard to make out in the crumbling stone. Husbands with lengthy Christian names to signify aristocratic breeding, the death of the wife reported beneath and the children after that. Brief obituaries, terse descriptions of a lifetime.

'You don't think Eugenie had anything to do with Schwartz being buried in this cemetery?' Jacqui asked, glancing back to where the little headstone was set beneath the yew tree.

'Could be. It would certainly explain how he was allowed in here,' Napier agreed, and as he spoke the image of Eugenie standing on the steps of her house came to him. He saw the slight smile as she told him she had lied, that she remembered Schwartz. 'But it can't have amounted to much,' he added, 'she told me he was nothing – a little postman was what she called him.'

Leaving the cemetery they walked back along the ridge of the hillside above Honfleur, both quiet, still touched with the slight melancholy of the graveyard. By the entrance to a private house they paused and sat on a bench, thighs pressed together, heads close, sharing the warmth of their bodies. Beneath them the town slipped away, a rockfall of slate roofs, stacked chimneys, television aerials and half-timbered frames. Casement windows and yellowed stucco façades glowed like glass beads in the dying evening light.

Jacqui lifted her head from Napier's shoulder. 'Why did you say you weren't surprised?' she asked, pulling a remark of his back into her mind. 'When the curé told you that the grave had been vandalised you said you weren't surprised.'

Napier stirred and shifted round on the bench. 'Ashford knows that Schwartz stole *The Estuary Pilgrim*,' he explained. 'He would have worked it out, just as we did. He's bound to have wondered whether the painting wasn't buried in that grave. Ashford never actually saw Schwartz killed, there was nothing to prove he was down there. The General might have tricked him in some way.'

'So he dug up the coffin to see if *The Estuary Pilgrim* was locked away in it?'

'I imagine so.'

Jacqui studied Napier's profile thoughtfully. Had Rupert done it himself, she wondered, or employed another to do the dirty work? Almost certainly himself. He would never have entrusted the job to a minion. It was a gruesome picture. Ashford scrabbling in the earth, searching for his possession, burrowing into the damp night soil for the great painting that was his right, his legacy, the reward that he had paid for in pain and mutilation.

She gave a shudder and jumped to her feet, dismissing these morbid thoughts. Taking Napier by the hands she pulled him up too. 'It's getting cold, *chéri*,' she said, 'let's go back now.'

They made their way down to the town, following the steep zig-zag of the path, legs braced against the sharp incline, occasionally breaking into a run, losing control, catching at the branches on either side of the narrow track to slow them again. Into the Rue du Puits, past the ancient well head and on to the Place Ste Catherine. They had a drink by the harbour and then dined at the Tilbury, finding a table by the window, sharing an *assiette de fruits de mer* together. Oysters, clams and mica black winkles piled on seaweed and crushed ice, crabs with crouched, robotic legs and malignant eyes. Jacqui, neat and meticulous, cracking open the shells, scraping every morsel of white meat from the crevices before starting. 'You can tell so much about people from the way they eat crabs,' she explained when Napier commented on it. 'Some are lazy and don't work at all the difficult little bits, some are messy, others eat while they go along – it's the way they think.'

They finished a bottle of Muscadet and ordered another. The talk was light and drowsy, dipping, hovering on dragonfly wings, touching and flitting from topic to topic. Jacqui was radiant, vivacious, and Napier followed her wherever she led the conversation but in the lulls, the moments of quiet, he found his mind drifting back to the graveyard above the estuary. He saw the crooked headstone, the little jam jar and the drooping flowers set in the grass. That night, after they had kissed good night in the shadowed doorway of Jacqui's apartment, hugged tightly, whispered small personal things to each other, he lay on his bed and stared up at the ceiling. The image of Eugenie returned to him, standing there on the front steps of her house. Another came to him, thrusting unexpectedly into his mind. The quayside in the early morning, the trawlers swinging fish on to the shore.

The two linked, fused together, became an idea. Napier brushed it aside; it was wildly improbable. He studied the plaster landscape of the ceiling, re-examining the possibility, turning it around in his head.

Was it so improbable? Maybe not. The facts all fitted.

Reaching out he took his travelling clock from the side table, directed the hands to half past six and set the alarm.

There was no harm in checking. The curé might be right. Strange things did happen during the war.

On second thoughts he set the hands at six in the morning, placed the clock back on the table and switched off the light.

There was a log fire burning in the grating. Orange tongues of light licked up over the bookshelves, gleaming on polished veneers, leather spines and gold fittings. The carpet silenced Luc Gabot's movements, deadened the sounds of his existence in this opulent room.

The man rested in his chair before him. Grey suit, silk cravat, cold and confident in his manner. A green director's lamp on the desk splashed light on to an arrogant face.

He sat staring without speaking.

Luc tore his attention off the man and looked around the room, quickly and furtively, his eyes flicking uneasily in his head like a caged animal. He didn't like this room, didn't like this huge house. There was power here, an intangible faceless power that Luc didn't understand. It had no shape, it belonged to another world. Luc understood the quick, immediate power of guns and knives, the violence, the blood, the sense of release and exhilaration that followed. It was visible, lasting, exciting, but this was strange and suffocating. There was no escape here, no way out.

Luc glanced back at the man at the desk. He sat very still, watching with pale eyes. There was contempt in those eyes, no measure of respect, only disdain for what he saw. Bastard.

Don't let him get the better of you. Show him you're not concerned.

Luc pulled out a packet of cigarettes, thumbed one up, touched it to his lips. The gesture was casual, experienced. He was his own master, not to be trifled with.

Ashford's voice slashed him. 'Put them away, Luc. You can smoke after you leave, not in here.'

Cold, commanding, a voice of authority. A bastard. Luc did as he was told, pushing the packet back into his pocket with ill grace.

Ashford considered him and then turned to the desk, speaking without bothering to look up.

'I want you to do something for me, Luc.' It was an order put like a request, politeness from a man who can't be disobeyed.

'What sort of thing?' Luc asked in the silence that followed.

'I want you to watch someone for me, keep me informed of his movements.'

It would be the Englishman. A second meeting, a chance to get even. Pleasure trickled down into Luc's belly, hot and molten as lust. It would be good, he wouldn't fail this time. He knew what to do, what he wanted. He'd been thinking about it, planning this meeting.

Ashford turned, the cold eyes struck him once more. 'You think I'm referring to John Napier?'

Luc's tongue flicked out and licked thin lips.

'You'd like that, wouldn't you, Luc?' The contempt was still there but it carried a smile with it now. Ashford leaned forwards. 'He made a fool of you, didn't he, Luc?'

Luc made no answer.

'Made you look small, treated you roughly, and now you want your revenge.'

Ashford's gaze bored into him.

'Good,' he said softly, settling back in his chair. 'Revenge is good. Hold that desire Luc, don't lose it. I can use it later, but not now. This is not the moment to settle old scores. I have someone else to watch John Napier at present.'

Luc's eyes darted.

'It's not Napier you'll follow. He knows you too well I'm afraid, Luc. He'd recognise you.' Ashford spoke slowly and caressingly, as though coaxing a small child. 'It's his friend

I want you to watch. He's called Spooner, Edward Spooner. Do you know the man I'm referring to?'

Luc nodded.

'Good. No mistakes this time, Luc. There must be no slips, no bungling.'

'I'd rather follow the other,' Luc said stubbornly, fixed in his intention.

Ashford smiled. 'Later, Luc,' he murmured. 'I'll give you your chance when the time comes.'

Chapter Eighteen

The alarm broke into Napier's dream, tugging at his mind, pulling him up from his sleep.

He rolled over in bed, warm and soporific, and reached out, taking the clock in his hand, his fingers fumbling with the controls. He found the catch and switched the alarm off. The insistent trilling bell fell silent. He set the clock on his chest and looked at the luminous dial. Six in the morning. At first incomprehension and then recollection flooded back to him.

With an effort he clambered out of bed.

Through the open shutters a cold dawn was breaking, washing the room with a dull grey light. He pulled on corduroy trousers and a heavy guernsey, his movements becoming quicker as the warmth seeped out of his body. He shaved himself in front of the mirror, brushed his hair from his eyes, tugged on his jacket and left the room, closing the door softly after him. Down into the hallway, past the deserted reception desk and out on to the balcony. Hands plunged in pockets, his breath pluming out before him, Napier crossed the drive and walked up the road. Apple trees ghostly in the orchards, birds beginning to sing. A car swished by, searching ahead with orange headlights.

Notre-Dame de Grâce waited in the half-light, crouched in the shadow of the trees, the roof and blunt belfry of the chapel just silhouetted against the morning sky.

Napier lifted the latch on the cemetery gate. He'd wondered whether it would be locked, as the municipal graveyards were, but it swung back with a small complaining creak of bracket hinges.

Inside the cemetery was silent, breathless, preserving the stillness of night. Headstones shone white, the long grass was bowed and crystalline with dew, the yew trees smudging into the darkness of the walls.

He made his way over to Schwartz's grave. It was undisturbed, the single tooth of the headstone crooked, the wildflowers limp and exhausted from their long vigil.

Stepping off the gravel path Napier picked his way amongst the ranks of standing tombs. He spent some time searching for the position he wanted, the correct angle, finding it in a flat slab of blue-black marble, engraved with the name Jean-Jacques Duclos. From here he had a clear view of both the cemetery gate and the yew tree that rose above Schwartz's grave. It would serve his purpose. He sat down, resting his back against the sculpted chalice that graced one end. The cold of the marble crept up through the seat of his trousers, his shoes were damp from the long grass. Drawing up his knees he hugged his legs and waited.

He was feeling less sure of his reasoning now. The certainty that had come to him in the warmth of his bed had evaporated, the improbability returned. Blowing on his hands, he rubbed the numbness from his arms. He should have brought something with him to fight off the cold, some coffee maybe, or brandy.

Time crawled by. The light clarified, details emerged from the darkness, taking on shape and personality.

Napier stretched his stiff limbs and looked up at the sky. A hint of warmth now, the first stains of colour in the greyness. His mind drifted back to the night on the estuary and the feeling of ecstasy as he'd watched the dawn come up.

A noise.

Napier froze.

It was the latch of the gate.

The cold, the stiffness of waiting were forgotten. He watched it swing open, the slight creak of the hinges loud in the silence of the cemetery. Through the entrance came a figure, short and humped, wheeling a pushbike in one hand.

Napier couldn't make out the features but the lowered head, the rounded hedgehog body were unmistakable. He knew her from the hotel, had nodded to her each morning, paused to say a few words in passing. It was the simple one, Eugenie's maid.

Old Madeleine.

With a clatter she hefted the bicycle against the wall.

Turning round she stumped up the pathway, her boots crunching gravel, small snuffles and mumbles of exertion issuing from her lips as she walked.

Napier crouched low, wrapping himself in the shadow of the stone chalice.

At Schwartz's grave Madeleine paused, a hand on her chin, the other clasping the elbow, surveying it with pleasure. Her plot of land, her possession. Stooping down she brushed leaves off the grass and picked up the jam jar. Taking out the flowers she inspected them closely, appreciated that they were spent and threw them aside impatiently. Going over to the nearby bank she began rummaging amongst the long grass for more.

Napier lifted his head from the shelter of the shadows and watched her in wonder. It was as he expected. The childlike bunch of flowers, the Delaroche graves nearby, the sight of Madeleine on the quayside in the early hours of the morning had led him to this conclusion. Napier had guessed it was the old woman who visited the cemetery at dawn. He'd fitted the pieces together as he lay in bed the night before, but still as he watched this ritual he felt a sudden chill. He was an intruder, treading on sacred ground.

The old woman turned. Napier shrank back into the shelter of the shadows. Fresh flowers had been found and plucked from the ground. Madeleine fitted them into the jam jar, patting them into place, and set them before the headstone, standing back to admire the effect. Hands on hips now, back straightened. She was speaking, words too soft to be coherent, her face contented, thoughts focused as she gazed down at the grave.

Who was she talking to? Napier wondered. Was it to Schwartz? To the memory of a lover who had died forty years ago?

For they had been lovers, Madeleine and Schwartz. He was sure of it. Why else would she put flowers on the grave of a German soldier, a little postman, who'd died when she was still a girl? Besides, Eugenie had almost confessed as much to him on that first day. Standing there on the steps she had said that she knew nothing about Schwartz – except that he had the strangest taste in women.

Eugenie had known Dietrich Schwartz, remembered him when others were forgotten because he had come to her house for a different reason It was not to discover the pleasures she arranged in the upstairs rooms, not to join in with his fellow officers, laughing and swaggering, but to see a retarded Norman girl, to pay court to a maid. And the memory of that love still burned, in a simple mind where the past and present were never separated, where time had left no mark, a memory rekindled each morning in this ceremony of wildflowers.

An ancient love, a single precious possession.

With a grunt of satisfaction Madeleine turned from the grave, trundled back to her bicycle and left the cemetery, banging the gate closed after her. There was a rasp of gravel as she set off towards the harbour to buy fish for the breakfast table, to call out and squabble and handle the day's catch, her voice mixing with the crying of the seagulls.

Ashford set his cigarette on the rim of the ashtray. Drawing the telephone across the desk towards him he lifted the receiver and dialled with his forefinger. He didn't need to check the number, he had it in his head.

The line warbled softly as it rang. Ashford touched his cigarette to his lips, drawing in a feather of smoke, and waited in his study. A clean white light fell through parted curtains, dust particles hovered in the shaft. The porcelain clock ticked on the mantelpiece, a precise mechanism in a delicate setting.

Jacqui's voice came on the line, eager and hopeful. 'Hello?'

'Good morning, my dear.'

He could sense the girl stiffen, recoiling at the sound of his voice. Whoever it was she'd been expecting had been dashed from her mind.

'How are you this morning?'

Jacqui was collected now, formal and correct. 'I'm all right thank you, Rupert.'

'I rang you at the museum yesterday but your secretary told me she hadn't seen you since lunchtime.'

'No,' she admitted. 'I took the afternoon off.'

'I see. And did you meet Dr Napier during that time, my dear?'

Again Jacqui paused before answering. 'Yes Rupert,' she said quietly, 'I was with him.'

Of course you were, you silly creature, rushing out to lunch

253

at twelve-thirty, taking the rest of the day off without a word of explanation, flushed and irresponsible with love. Ashford took another morsel of smoke from the filter tip. 'And did you find time to invite Dr Napier over to the château?'

'No Rupert.'

'But I specifically asked you to.'

'If you wish to see him you must talk to him yourself. I'm not carrying messages for you.'

Ashford's eyes narrowed. How very annoying, the girl was becoming wayward, unpredictable in her behaviour. He was losing his grip on her. She needed to be goaded again, pressed back into service.

'You know how important this is, my dear.'

Jacqui made no response and the silence between them hummed in the telephone wires.

'Do you not remember?' Ashford inquired softly. 'The last time you were here I explained it all to you. I thought you understood what it is I want of you.' He let the meaning of his words sink in, take hold of her. 'On that occasion I thought I had also made it clear why you must do this small thing for me— '

There was a neat metallic click and the line went dead. Ashford removed the receiver from his ear and stared at it in surprise.

Jacqui had hung up on him.

The little bitch had put the phone down while he was talking. He twisted round in his chair, legs crossed, weight on his elbow, one hand held over his deformed eye.

Damn her! She was cheating him, betraying his trust in her. But how could that be? He had given her a task, a single simple mission, and she had failed him. It was impossible, he found it hard to believe. After all the care he had taken, the time he had wasted on her.

Ashford stared across the polished floor. Louis was right. He should never have let her go, that was the truth of it. Once she had found the pictures he should have held her, gagged her. She knew too much, prying into the past, searching out the secrets of his house. Nevertheless, it was not too late. He still had the advantage, that was some-thing, but he must act, and act swiftly if he was to keep it.

Taking two quick, disinterested puffs at the cigarette

Ashford stubbed the butt out in the ashtray and prodded the bell on the desk beside him.

Louis was there in the doorway.

'Jacqui,' he said over his shoulder, 'bring her to me. Pick her up, have her brought to the château.'

Louis accepted the order without comment.

Ashford paused and considered, gazing across the room. 'On second thoughts bring the others too.' It would be risky, they'd need to cover their tracks, but it was necessary. There was no alternative. He glanced up, the movement quick and predatory. 'Make it discreet, Louis. No fuss, no difficulties.'

'It'll take time.'

Ashford shook his head. 'We don't have time, Louis. I need them out of Honfleur today, before they talk, before they think of going to the police.'

They hadn't so far. Ashford had contacts in the police, they would have informed him had Napier been talking. But the danger was there, very close now, very real. He must take them, hold all three of them at the château, where they could do no damage. He could decide what to do with them later, once he had regained control. All he needed was time to think, to breathe. The solution could come later.

Louis was still standing in the doorway.

'That's all, Louis.'

He turned to go, moving slowly, hesitating after he'd been dismissed. 'May I ask you something, monsieur?'

Ashford swung round, his pale gaze falling on him.

Louis averted his eyes, looking down at his feet, searching for words. A man who spoke little, who knew how to take orders, trying to express the thoughts in his mind.

'What is it, Louis?'

'The girl,' he said carefully. 'May I ask what you intend to do with her?'

Ashford sat quite still, as though sensing the air for danger. 'Is that any concern of yours?'

A small shrug from Louis's shoulders. 'She has meant you no harm, monsieur . . . she simply found what you hid from her. It was not her fault.'

Ashford's voice cut him, quick and sharp. 'Are you criticising me, Louis?'

He shook his head. 'No monsieur, of course not. It's just that I wouldn't like to see her . . . hurt again.'

Ashford looked up, his face cold and drawn. 'Bring her to me, Louis,' he said in the silence that settled in the room. 'Don't ask why, simply do as I tell you.'

Spooner was having breakfast in the hotel dining room. Neat and fastidious in his table manners, the lozenge of his napkin symmetrical on his lap. Dipping his knife into apricot jam, leaving no crumbs as he broke his croissant, he ate in silence. A folded newspaper lay on the table beside him, the crossword puzzle untouched, articles as yet unread.

He looked up as Napier joined him. 'You weren't in your room just now,' he reproved.

'No, I went for a walk.'

'I knocked on your door but you'd already gone.'

Napier poured himself a cup of coffee and drank it thoughtfully, holding the bowl in both hands, his elbows planted before him. The dining room was large and almost empty. A little draught of conversation reached them from the nearby tables, voices held low and confidential, privacy maintained in invisible boundaries. It wasn't the place to tell Spooner of his morning in the cemetery. He waited until they had finished breakfast and moved out into the garden at the rear of the house, through the French windows still misted with condensation, before bringing up the subject.

'Do you still have that Iron Cross?' he asked Spooner as they crossed the lawn, their footprints dark on the damp grass.

'You mean that medal they found on Barnabas's body? Certainly. Why do you ask?'

'Just an idea.'

Spooner glanced at him, speculation bright in his eyes but keeping his questions to himself. 'I'll go and fetch it,' he said, hurrying back into the hotel.

Napier followed him, waiting in the corridor outside his room.

'Why the sudden interest in this?' Spooner asked as he emerged.

Napier took the Iron Cross and examined it once again, feeling the weight in his palm, the blunt edges of its corners. It was the talisman, the last tangible link with Dietrich Schwartz. It had to be relevant.

'I'll show you,' he said, closing his hand around the medal and heading off along the passage. Across the landing, splashed with morning light, down the broad flight of stairs with its gilt banisters and threadbare carpet.

Madeleine was in the hallway beneath them, sweeping up the leaves that had blown across the marble floor. She paused as Napier approached, leaning on the broom handle as though it were a pike. There was no anticipation on her face, the flat features were washed clean of expression, the deep-water eyes innocent and childlike.

Napier paused before her. Reaching out his arm he showed her the Iron Cross, opening his fingers like petals about the medal. 'Do you know this, Madeleine?' he asked gently.

The dark blue gaze broke away from his and lowered, absorbing this new curiosity. But there was no interest. She looked at the Iron Cross blankly, eyes unblinking, mind undisturbed.

Napier waited but there was no reaction. He was wrong. There wasn't a connection to be made here. The medal found on Barnabas's body was just a coincidence. And yet it didn't seem possible. Carefully he turned it around in his hand, showing the old woman the reverse side.

For some moments Madeleine stared at the name engraved on the rear face and then slowly and cautiously she reached out one hand. A hand that was hard skinned and wrinkled, a strong hand with short pointed fingers, the hand of a burrowing mole. The fingers closed about the Iron Cross, taking it from Napier, lifting it reverently from his palm. Drawing it up to her face she examined the lettering with a little murmur of interest.

'Do you recognise it, Madeleine?' Napier inquired.

The eyes turned to him, the skin crinkling at the corners, lids squeezing into a smile. Her fingertips ran over the engraved name, touching it, following its meaning.

'Dietrich,' she whispered. The word was a sigh, a memory stirring in its sleep.

Had she read the name or just recognised it, Napier wondered. 'You knew him, didn't you, Madeleine,' he pressed, taking back the medal. He was treading gently now, uncertain of where his questions would lead, coaxing her forwards.

She nodded. Again the face was radiant, the skin tucking and crumpling into wrinkles, lips parting on ancient teeth. Turning about she marched over to the wall and propped her brush against the plaster, encouraging it to stay there with a grunt. She returned and tugging at Napier's sleeve she stumped away across the hall.

'Come,' she ordered.

With a glance at Spooner, who stood a few yards behind, Napier followed on behind the old woman.

Down the badly lit passage, Madeleine moving slowly on arthritic hips, walking in round black shoes that laced up, glancing back over her shoulder from time to time to see that they were still with her. Into the kitchen where breakfast was being washed: plates and cups clattering into the soapsuds; two maids at the sink, loading the racks above them with the clean crockery, not bothering to look around as they passed; a scrubbed table on one side and a cast-iron range as black as coal on the other.

Madeleine didn't pause to observe these details but crossing the floor she led the way down a flight of stone steps, throwing open a door at the far end.

It was her bedroom, a clean white-washed room, vaulted like a wine cellar. They were below ground level now, the single sash-window looking out on to a brick wall, the drive-way just visible above their heads.

Napier paused in the doorway, Spooner close behind him, but Madeleine beckoned them in.

The room was as plain as a hermit's cell. The floor un-carpeted and resonant. A brass bedstead with polished knobs and quilted eiderdown stood against the far wall, a wooden crucifix hanging above. Nearby a heavy oak wardrobe and a print of Raphael's *Ste Catherine*, the colours rinsed out by years of exposure to the sunlight.

Madeleine had gone over to the table by her bed and taken up a photograph that stood propped in a silver frame. Bringing it over to Napier she held it up to him, standing close, inclining the picture backwards so that she could see it at the same time.

It showed a group of German officers, all smiling in welcome, immaculate in their formal dress uniforms. Some sort of official occasion by the look of it. On the right hand side was a short man. An imposing figure with clipped hair, sharp intelligent eyes and crow's feet etched into a perma-nently tanned face.

General Field Marshall Erwin Rommel.

Without the leather coat, without the peaked hat and desert goggles but unmistakable nevertheless.

He was shaking hands with a junior officer, a younger man with spectacles and a receding hairline who was bowing as he was introduced, polite and obsequious, overwhelmed by the enormity of his honour.

Madeleine pointed to a signature that had been scrawled beneath.

'Dietrich,' she announced proudly, stabbing her finger between the officer and the name, explaining the connection.

Napier nodded his understanding, appreciating as he did so the value this picture must have had to a junior adjutant. To have been caught by the photographer at the very moment he shook hands with Rommel – the Desert Fox, the people's hero. What a memory. What a story to have to tell your grandchildren.

But what held Napier's attention was not Dietrich Schwartz or the smiling officers with their ribbons and insignias but the far wall of the room. For there above their heads, caught in the flash of the camera, was a painting. Large and magnificent in its carved frame, instantly recognisable. The painting that had brought them to France, that had occupied their thoughts ever since.

The Estuary Pilgrim.

Napier wasn't able to see more. At that moment Madeleine pulled the photograph away and turning the frame around she gazed at it herself.

'Dietrich,' she repeated to herself.

Napier reached towards her. 'May I see?'

She looked up at him. Seeing his outstretched hand she snatched the picture away, clasping it to her bosom, her expression startled.

'I won't take it,' he promised.

She shook her head.

'I'd just like to look at it again.'

Suddenly the eyes were flashing in anger. 'No!' she cried, backing away, screeching out the words. 'It's mine, do you hear? Mine. It belongs to me!'

Napier paused, astonished by the ferocity of this outburst, dropping his hand to his side. His gesture had touched a raw nerve, some hidden phobia in the old woman. Madeleine stood

259

before him, crouching low, clutching her precious souvenir, wild and frightened like a cornered animal.

'I'm not going to take it,' Napier repeated calmly. On impulse he reached into his pocket and drew out the Iron Cross. He held it out to her.

An offering, a fair exchange.

Madeleine glared at it for a moment, sensing the bait, undecided how to react. Gradually, as she studied the little medal, her fear lifted, the curiosity returned. She hesitated, making up her mind, relenting. Timidly she approached him, the little clawlike hand extending.

Napier made no move, letting her come close enough to take the medal from his opened palm. She smiled as she grasped it, a child accepting a sweet. Meekly she handed him the photograph in return and retreated back across the floor, sitting down on her bed to examine the new acquisition.

Now that he had it close, Napier observed that it was not a photograph that he held in his hands but a cutting from a magazine. Beneath the printed picture was a caption, written in French.

'General Rommel talks with fellow officers on a one-day tour of inspection of coastal defences.'

It was dated, Honfleur, May 18th 1944.

Two days after the convoy was destroyed. A picture of von Eichendorff's suite taken two days after the convoy was ambushed and it showed *The Estuary Pilgrim* still hanging on the wall.

It was proof. Positive proof that the painting was never lost, that it was not destroyed at Criquetot. You didn't need to be an art historian to appreciate the implication. You didn't need to know anything about periods or styles of painting to understand its meaning.

At once Napier's mind was back in the wine bar behind the National Gallery. Shadowed, smoky, jostling with anonymous figures. Barnabas was before him, his face white and complacent, the raspberry lips still wet with wine as he spoke of the information he'd discovered.

Could this be it? Could this be the evidence Barnabas had promised to bring him, that he had set off into the night to find?

A voice behind him, sharp and imperious, breaking into his thoughts, jolting him back into the present.

260

'How did you get in here?'

Napier and Spooner jumped at the sound, turning quickly in the little cell, both guilty as schoolboys.

Eugenie stood in the doorway. Wary, poised and black as a raven. The dark eyes swept around the room, taking in the scene, coming to rest on Napier, staring at him intently.

Madeleine had scarcely bothered to look up at her arrival but stayed where she was, turning the medal around in her hands, crooning and muttering to herself at the discovery.

Without another word Eugenie crossed the floor and sat down beside her, protective and reassuring, stroking the steel-grey hair.

'How do you know this?' she asked, glancing up at Napier.

'I saw her putting flowers on Schwartz's grave,' he replied simply. 'I guessed they must have been lovers.'

Again the dark eyes studied him, searching into his mind, and then she gave a quick shake of her head. 'Not lovers,' she said. 'They were in love with each other. It's different.'

Spooner opened his mouth to speak but no words came and he stood rooted to the ground gaping at Eugenie.

'They were both innocents in their own way. Neither of them had any experience of love. It was a new discovery.'

Madeleine had turned now and was listening to Eugenie, aware that she was being talked about.

'It's less surprising than it may seem,' she added when Madeleine's attention had wandered again, 'she was a good-looking girl in those days. And there was no malice in her, you see. She had no grudge against the Germans, they were just men who came to the house in the evenings.' She smiled sadly.

Getting to her feet Eugenie went over to Napier. 'May I have it now?' she asked. He handed her the photograph and she studied it thoughtfully for a moment. 'Dietrich gave this picture to her shortly before he was killed. It had appeared in some local newspaper that week, a piece of propaganda. He was very proud of it, brought it round one night, signed it for her on the kitchen table. It was to remind her what an important man he was, he said, to show her what influential friends he'd made while he was in France.'

Dietrich Schwartz writing his name on a magazine cutting, signing it like a film star to impress his girlfriend.

Eugenie set the frame back on the bedside table.

'Madeleine has kept it ever since,' she added. 'It's very important to her.'

Napier's voice was quiet. 'So important that when Barnabas tried to take it from her she killed him?'

The question hung in the air.

Eugenie adjusted the picture frame, correcting its balance on the table, turning slowly to face him.

There was fear in the dark eyes now.

'You know this?' she asked.

Napier gave no answer.

'But how?'

He had seen it. Seen it in Madeleine's terror, in the hunted, desperate expression on her face, in the explosion of fury when he tried to take the picture from her.

Eugenie made a sudden quick gesture, tossing aside her guilt as though it were a used rag.

'It was no loss,' she said bitterly. 'He was a despicable man, forever prodding and grasping, poking his nose where it didn't belong. He deserved to die.'

Spooner was listening, pale and shocked, trying to take stock of the scene before him, to grasp what it was he was hearing. Madeleine perched on the brass bed nearby, her legs dangling off the floor.

'How did he find the photo in the first place?' Napier asked.

Eugenie jerked her head to where Madeleine was sitting. 'It was that medal,' she said. 'He'd discovered it in some junk shop in London, brought it with him. Madeleine came across it while she was making the beds. She saw the name on the back.'

Napier could imagine her as she snuffled about the room. The Iron Cross lying there on the table. Madeleine surprised and excited by the discovery, taking Barnabas by the arm, leading him down into her room, with its white-washed walls and clattering floorboards, to show him her precious picture in its cheap pressed frame.

'He didn't seem interested at the time,' Eugenie continued, 'just looked at it and left. I told him to stay away in future, not to bother her again.'

'But he came back.'

She nodded, her voice dropping into the memory. 'Later that summer. He attempted to buy the picture from her, offered her money, but of course she wouldn't part with it. So he broke into the room one night and tried to steal it. Madeleine was in the kitchen peeling potatoes for the following day . . . She heard the sound of him coming . . . Went to see what it was . . .'

Barnabas had returned, greedy and determined, dropping down from the driveway, prising open the sash-window. The room dark and strange as he picked his way across the floor, his hands reaching out for the bedside table.

Madeleine had heard the sound, come down into the room to check. The electric light breaking into the darkness.

Barnabas caught in the sudden glare. Leaning forwards, bending over the table as he fumbled with the picture frame.

The blaze of anger, the wild, blind fury. Madeleine with the knife still in her hands. Plunging it down, driving the blade into his back.

'It was very quick,' Eugenie told him. 'He was dead by the time I arrived.' Instinctively she looked down at the floor where Barnabas had fallen, as though the body still lay there, curled into the foetal position of death.

'But he was found in the harbour,' Napier said, collecting the events together in his mind.

Eugenie gave a shrug, lifting her hands in a gesture of despair and dropping them once more. 'That was Albert,' she said. 'I told him to take the body, to wrap it up and dump it in the estuary, to let the current take it out to sea. Like the fool that he is, he miscalculated the tide.' She spat out her contempt. 'The body drifted back inshore, right into the harbour.'

Spooner was incredulous. 'You attempted to dispose of the body?'

'Yes of course,' Eugenie replied. Her voice was dry now, the expression weary. With her hands thrust into her pockets she turned, confronting Spooner. 'Would you not have done the same?' she inquired softly. 'Madeleine remembers nothing of this, I doubt whether she even realises what it is we're talking about. There is no guilt in her mind.'

They glanced across to where the old woman sat, gazing back at them with her deep mediterranean eyes.

'If she has committed a crime she doesn't know it. The whole affair has been forgotten.' Eugenie turned to Napier. 'And still can be, unless . . .'

She paused, leaving the sentence unfinished.

Napier looked around the little room, at the sash-window where Barnabas had broken in, at the framed picture on the bedside table, at Madeleine with the medal in her hands, and then back to Eugenie who stood waiting for his decision.

'I'm not a policeman,' he said quietly. 'I can't see that this is any business of mine.'

Louis stared into the distance.

He had made the phone calls, issued his instructions. The wheels were in motion now. It was only a matter of time before Jacqui and John Napier and the other were picked up and brought over to the château.

Safe, out of circulation, no longer able to make a nuisance of themselves.

That was what Ashford wanted and that was what he, Louis, had arranged as he always had in the past. Only now it was different. He was no longer sure, no longer certain that he had done the right thing.

Sitting with his elbows set on parted knees, his hands locked together, he gazed into the future.

Ashford was losing control, beginning to turn on his own kind.

Louis hadn't seen him take the whip to Jacqui but he had been within earshot. He'd heard the pain and the terror in her voice as she cried out, seen the shock in her eyes as she ran down the stairs.

It was strange, as the girl had strode out of the house, head held high, fighting back the tears that brimmed in her eyes, he'd stepped forward and politely opened the front door for her.

Stupid really, a pointless gesture, but what else could he do? It was not his place to interfere, not his job to have opinions. He did as he was told. Took his orders and asked no questions.

But the sight of Jacqui brushing past him, running out of the house, still haunted Louis.

She had been loyal to Ashford in her own way. Always there at the weekends to entertain his guests, always smiling and gracious, never complaining or asking anything in return.

And that was how he repaid her.

Louis twisted his hands together, the knuckles showing white through the skin.

Was a similar fate in store for him? he wondered. He had served Ashford faithfully over twenty years, smoothing the way, covering his tracks, organising and arranging his affairs.

How was that to be repaid?

'I must go back to London.'

'What immediately?'

Spooner nodded, straightening his cuffs as he stood up. 'Unfortunately there's no reason to delay any longer.'

Now that the circumstances surrounding the death of Charles Barnabas had been explained, the crime solved in its own way, his investigation was complete. He had the information that he needed, that he had set out to France to find.

'I thought you were going to the police.'

'Oh, I am,' Spooner assured him, 'but not here in France. When I mentioned the police it wasn't the local gendarmerie that I was referring to. In fact quite the reverse, the less they get to hear about this affair the better. They'll only want to ask questions, start interfering, and that would be a disaster at this stage. It's essential that Ashford isn't alerted. Any suggestion of an official inquiry and he'll give us the slip. No, this must be done properly, through the correct channels, and that I fear means returning to London as soon as possible.'

Spooner felt a gleam of satisfaction. He was quite prepared, all that remained was to add the conclusions to his report, ready to present to the agency on the following morning, but that could be done on the journey back. There would be plenty of time on the ferry. It was a long crossing over to Southampton.

'I'd better go and start making my arrangements,' he said to Napier as they emerged from Eugenie's study into the passageway.

They had spent over an hour talking together in the little shuttered room with its yellowish, beehive light, discussing the events of the last few days, evaluating and testing the facts they had discovered. It was a debriefing, Spooner told himself, the final assessment of their work.

At the reception desk in the front hall he put a call through to Le Havre and booked himself a place on the afternoon ferry.

'The next boat leaves at four-thirty,' he said, stepping out on to the balcony where Napier leaned against the railing. 'That gives me plenty of time to collect my things together.' He paused, setting his plans for the day, estimating the timing. 'How long does it.take to drive around to Le Havre?'

'You should give it an hour.'

Add another thirty minutes to pick up the ticket, pass through Customs and find his way on board. Call it an hour and a half. 'I'll order a taxi to be here at three.'

Napier glanced at him. 'You don't need to do that,' he said quickly. 'Jacqui is coming here in a few minutes. We can drive you round to the docks in her car.'

Spooner beamed at the offer. That was far more satisfactory.

'We can have lunch together before you go.'

'In that case I'll go and start my packing.' He hesitated in the doorway, looking back at Napier. 'I suppose there's no chance of you coming back to England too, is there?'

He smiled. 'Not at present.'

It was the girl of course, he'd want to be with her. Spooner nodded his understanding. Actually it would be useful to have him over here, to help co-ordinate events this side of the Channel.

'I'll ring you tomorrow,' he said. 'Once I've had time to set the ball rolling.'

'What time of the day?'

'Around two-thirty,' he replied. 'And John . . .'

Napier glanced up at him.

'You won't attempt anything yourself will you? Not until you've heard from me.'

'Nothing,' he promised.

Hurrying upstairs, Spooner began to pack. He worked quickly and methodically, clearing the wardrobe, taking the neatly stacked shirts from the chest of drawers. In a matter of minutes the bedroom was empty, stripped clear of his possessions.

Spooner plumped down the lid of the suitcase, fastened the strap, and putting it into the passage he turned, looking back over his shoulder. The room was clean and bare, anonymous once more, just as it had been the day he arrived. Only now it seemed different. The brass bedstead, the striped wallpaper and enamel wash basin were familiar, more friendly than they had been. Even the painting of Eugenie was less offensive. He had grown accustomed to it.

For a moment Spooner stood there, running his eyes around the walls, taking in the details that had been commonplace up until now, committing each one to his memory. Then softly he closed the door and locked it behind him.

Chapter Nineteen

'I think he was sad to go,' Jacqui said.

Napier nodded. It was true, Spooner had been quite silent on the way over to Le Havre, gazing out of the window, staring at the dull grey water of the estuary.

They'd arrived at the docks in good time only to discover that the ferry was delayed. It had been a rough crossing that morning and the ship had been late coming in. Spooner had insisted that they didn't wait for him. He was suddenly distant and preoccupied, collecting his tickets, tutting at the delay, covering his shyness with a brusque efficiency. Darting out his arm he'd shaken hands with Napier, avoiding his eye as he murmured a few words in parting, blushed crimson when Jacqui had reached forward, enveloping him in golden hair, and kissed him on both cheeks. Turning on his heel, with a hasty reminder to Napier that he would call the next day, he'd marched away, a suitcase in one hand and a bundle of papers in the other. A short, nondescript man in a grey suit, dwarfed by the cranes and derricks and dreary concrete buildings of Le Havre.

'He reminded me of a little boy being sent away from home for the first time,' Jacqui added as the car bounced into Honfleur. 'He made me feel quite mean.'

'He nearly had a heart attack when you kissed him.'

She shot him her quick, mischievous smile. 'It was good for him,' she said, parking the car on the quayside, its headlights overlooking the water. 'Besides, he's really very sweet.'

They went indoors to pick up a coat and then walked around the harbour, Jacqui clasping Napier's arm, dragging him back to look into shop windows. Up the Rue de Dauphin into the square where the market was still in full swing. Brightly striped stalls clustered about the cathedral, noise and activity filling the open space.

Threading through the crowd they paused to have a drink

in the Restaurant Sainte Catherine, going inside, the door giving a ting as it opened, packing themselves into a table by the window.

'We could buy some supper in the marketplace and have it at home tonight,' Jacqui suggested when they were ready to leave.

'If you like.'

'There's a Renoir film on television . . .' Her voice trailed away. She had stiffened, straightening in her seat, concentrating on the bustling square outside.

Napier was counting coins on to the table. 'What's the matter?' he asked, glancing up.

'That man.'

He twisted around, following the direction of her gaze.

'I know him,' she said. 'He works for Rupert.'

'Which one?'

'In the denim jacket. Standing by the entrance to the café.'

Napier could see him now. A short figure with black hair and bowed legs, a little spider of a man. He was leaning against the metal frame of a stall, watching the world go by, his attention occasionally lapping up against the window where they sat.

'Are you sure?'

Jacqui nodded, eyes round and startled. 'Absolutely. His name is Willi. He was over at the château earlier this summer. I can remember him clearly. He was hanging around the stables one day when I came back from riding, kept making loud remarks to the others.'

Napier could picture the scene. A temporary hand of Ashford's catching sight of Jacqui, the boss's daughter, a forbidden fruit. Trying to catch her attention with suggestive remarks, asserting himself in front of his friends.

'Could be coincidence,' he said turning back to her. 'He has to live somewhere.'

'No, he's watching us.'

'Well we'll soon find out,' Napier said as he squeezed himself out from behind the table.

They went outside. Willi browsed at the stall, not catching their eye as they passed him. Strolling away from the café they worked their way back into the market square, losing themselves in the crowd.

Rich smells on either side. Women barging and jostling, baskets bristling with loaves. Voices calling out to passing customers, drumming up trade.

'Is he still with us?' Napier asked, stopping in front of a stall, looking it over. Stacked cheeses, ripe and pungent. Round boxes of flimsy wood, straw clinging to white rind.

Jacqui craned round, looking back across his shoulder.

'Make it casual,' he murmured, picking up a cheese, touching it to his nose. 'Don't let him realise you've noticed.'

Her eyes lost interest, swept listlessly across the square and then returned to Napier.

'Hard to tell at present,' she said under her breath, joining in the inspection of the Brie in his hand. 'He hasn't made a move yet.'

Napier stole a glance to where Willi still stood, lounging against the stall.

A voice beside him, very close: 'Monsieur?'

He jumped at the sound, looked up to see the proprietor confronting him, hands spread on the counter, eyebrows raised, face expectant.

'Just looking, thank you,' he said pleasantly, putting the Brie back in place, sauntering on to the next stall.

Cold meat, pâté in earthenware pots, tripe in white plastic containers. Slices of ham falling off the cutter, plumped down on to scales, wrapped into coarse paper. Money passing into an outstretched hand.

Jacqui hissed in his ear, 'Yes, *chéri*. He's following us.'

They moved on down the market, quicker now, threading between late shoppers. Willi's eyes behind them, burning into their backs.

Not too fast, Napier told himself, keep it natural. Don't give the game away.

'Still with us?'

A flick of the tawny hair. 'Yes – definitely.'

It was Ashford, he was drawing in the net. It was not surprising, he couldn't let them go free, not knowing what they did. It would be too great a risk for him. But it didn't matter, Napier told himself as they hurried along. Ashford was too late, he'd missed his chance. By now Spooner would be on board the ferry, out of the country. In a few hours he'd be back in London, setting the system in motion. The trap would be sprung.

270

In the meantime all they had to do was keep out of the way, not get themselves involved.

He pushed through into the next row. 'We must try to lose him,' he said to Jacqui. Fighting through jostling figures, past laden stalls. Vegetables still black and grubby, fresh from the soil. Second-hand clothing on hangers. Salami and smoked bacon and rabbits dangling on strings. Jacqui behind him, high-heels tapping on the cobbles, her hand reaching out, feeling its way into his.

'I think there are two of them,' she cried.

'Two?'

'He keeps signalling to someone.'

It must be that little weasel Luc Gabot, back again, eager to have his revenge. Napier searched the crowd for the slicked black hair, the pale moon of Luc's face, the lazy hooded eyes.

'Can you see the other?'

'No.'

Past the old belfry tower, their breath coming harder now, pouring out into the evening air. Pausing at the Hôtellerie Lechat, undecided, looking for the route to take.

There must be a way to escape. It had to be possible, in this crowd it should be easy. But how?

Jacqui suddenly tugged at his arm, taking the initiative, her mood quickening. 'The church.'

'But it only has one entrance.'

'There's another.'

She headed back across the square, leading the way, past the sweet scent of roasting chestnuts, past a stall selling doughnuts and toffees to the children, into the wooden porch of Ste Catherine's. Pushing open the door, slender hands on the heavy iron ring, drawing Napier in after her.

The latch clicked shut behind them, the rough, noisy gaiety of the market was closed out.

The silence of the vast interior engulfed them.

Hearts hammering, breath loud in their ears, they walked up the nave of the church. Between dusty chairs laid out in rows, beneath the mediaeval timbers of the twin ceilings, the bilges of the building, cut and shaped by the shipbuilders of Honfleur centuries before. Carved saints on every side, white plaques set into the walls, the evening light glowing in leaded windows.

271

The place was almost empty. A few figures sat staring at the altar, faces set, minds dulled, one huddled down into a prayer. In the side aisle a woman was lighting a thin candle, setting it amongst its fellows that had already burned low in the twilight.

No one looked round at the couple who had burst into the reverent stillness. The man who searched about himself, slim and neatly dressed, taking in his surroundings with quick movements of the head. The girl, tall and sleek with polished blonde hair, who clung close to him, looking back at the entrance with huge eyes. No one bothered to notice the door open for a second time, admitting two men who stood framed in the doorway, their eyes scouring the gloom.

'Is it them?' Napier asked, pausing in the nave to look up into the cavern of vaulting.

Jacqui nodded.

He let his gaze flow round the wooden beams, over sculpted gargoyles and ornamental corbels, down on to the organ loft with its cabinet of tightly stacked pipes. He could see the two of them now, out of the side of his eye.

It wasn't Luc Gabot, someone quite different, tall and angular with a scruffy beard and balding head. Willi stood beside him, alert and wary, looking straight up the body of the cathedral, fixing his prey, holding them in his sights.

What were their orders? Napier wondered. What were they intending? He couldn't believe they were going to try anything here, not in public, not with witnesses to testify afterwards. But they had some intention, this wasn't just a routine surveillance. The two men were moving away from the door, Willi snapping directions with his finger, sending his companion up the aisle, herding them away from the entrance.

Napier glanced at Jacqui.

'This way,' she breathed, urging him forwards.

On up the nave of the cathedral, their footsteps loud and hollow in the silence. The altar before them, ornate with tarnished gilding, guarded by wrought-iron railings, separated from the rest of the church. Sacred ground, forbidden territory.

'There's a door,' Jacqui murmured, as she crossed herself, 'just to the left of us.'

Napier brushed his eyes around, a tourist admiring the

architecture. He caught a glimpse of the door, set in the angle of the choir stall, close to the wall.

'It's a vestry, there's a way out on the other side.'

'Are you sure?'

'Yes, I used to go to confirmation classes in there.'

Strolling away from the altar they stood against the wall. Napier with his hands behind his back, peering up into the roof beams. Jacqui beside him, pointing out a small detail.

The doorknob was in Napier's hands, he grasped hold, turning it gently in his palm. There was a sudden loud creak as the catch slipped back. Jacqui's eyes met his. At the same time he felt the door give, opening from the wall. A ribbon of draught struck him on the back of his neck.

Pushing it wide, he slipped Jacqui through, ducked his head beneath the lintel and followed after her.

Two steps down into a small, dark room. A narrow corridor with a sloping roof. Roughly stacked chairs against the wall, cassocks heaped on to pegs. Old air in their nostrils, clinging to their bodies like a contagion.

The door slammed shut behind him. Napier heard a cry from the far side, imagined Willi's surprise, his anger as he saw them vanish from his sight, pictured the sudden spurt of acceleration as he realised that he had been tricked.

There was no key in the lock. Shit! His hand fumbled up the woodwork, found a bolt, thrust it across. That would do, the door was sealed, the escape route cut off.

Jacqui was pulling at his arm, her smile triumphant, eyes flashing in the half-light. Scampering across the floor she found the outer door, scrabbled with the latch and threw it open.

A sudden gasp of fresh air and they were outside, back in the open once more. Pigeons scattering from the ground as they ran out into the evening light. The crowds, the noise were around them again. Only a row of iron railings separated them from the back of the market stalls.

There was a gate further along. Napier rattled open the catch but it was chained. No time to look for an alternative. Putting his hand between the spikes he vaulted over, coat tails flying, knocking a pile of boxes aside as he landed. Jacqui was ready for him, waiting on tiptoes. Her hands locked around his neck as Napier caught her around the waist and swung her high into the air. Kicking up her ankles she cleared the railings, her hair tumbling down into his eyes.

They thrust past a stall of wet fish, shuddering the table, scattering mussels and crushed ice and imitation parsley. Back into the thoroughfare, the proprietor calling after them, telling them to stop, asking to know what their game was.

Down the flight of steps below the apse of the church. Into the Rue des Logettes, a sea of faces all around them. Running down the street past open shop doors and racks of postcards, past tourists who paused to look at restaurant menus and women returning with their shopping. Jacqui beside him, her hair streaming out.

Had they done it? Had they managed to give them the slip? Napier turned as he ran, looking back over his shoulder.

Willi was there, standing at the top of the steps, crouched ready to move, scanning the crowd. But he was looking in the wrong direction, bounding down into the street, heading away up the Rue de la Bavole.

He's lost the scent, taken off after the wrong couple.

They reached the corner of the street and turned into the harbour. It was safer here, no longer visible from the square. They slowed their pace, cheeks flushed, pulses racing.

'Have we lost them?' Jacqui panted.

'I think so.'

Evening had filled the waterside cafés, the lights were coming on, inking in the buildings above. A band was playing to the tables, cheerful bouncy music, and there on the far shore was the juggler, going through his act.

It was calm, reassuringly unchanged.

'Where do we go from here?' Jacqui asked.

'Somewhere, anywhere, provided it's out of Honfleur.' Grasping her by the hand, Napier headed off down the quayside towards the car, 'And the sooner we get there the better.'

Jacqui followed him, suddenly drawing back with a little wail of despair. 'But I don't have the keys, chéri!'

He turned about. She was scrabbling through her bag in desperation. Oh Christ, she must have them.

'No,' she cried.

'Where are they?'

'Back in the apartment. I left them on the table.'

Napier glanced around the harbour, checking the approaches. How long before Willi discovered his mistake

274

and retraced his tracks? How long before he found them again?

'We must pick them up,' he said. 'It's the only way.'

Ashford waited.

Standing with his hands folded behind his back, his head erect, he waited in his study. The clock on the mantelpiece ticked in the silence, the spring uncoiling, the rachet catching the cog wheels in precise, regulated movements, cutting the passing time into minutes, into seconds.

There was a knock on the door. Louis came into the room, a bucket of coal in his hand. Kneeling on the carpet he began to lay the fire, arranging splinters of wood over crumpled paper, stacking lumps of coal above.

Ashford's impatience broke surface.

'Any news?'

'Not so far, monsieur.'

'What's taking them so long?'

'I can't say, monsieur.'

'I thought you said Willi had found them?'

'I imagine that he is waiting for the right moment to make his move,' Louis replied, standing up to leave.

Ashford studied him coldly.

'I'm holding you responsible in this matter, Louis,' he said quietly. 'Don't fail me.'

Jacqui let them into her apartment, shut the street door behind her and clattered up the wooden stairs.

The keys to her car lay on the table. She pounced on them with a little cry of satisfaction, digging them deep into her coat pocket.

'We should leave a note for Kettie,' she said, searching for a scrap of paper, 'she'll only worry otherwise.'

She had every reason to do so. 'What are you going to say?' Napier asked from the doorway.

'Something vague, just to set her mind at rest,' she replied and then, with a quick, flashing smile, 'Not that it'll make much difference, she's bound to jump to the wrong conclusion.' Picking up a pencil she went across to the window to give herself better light.

She froze.

'What is it?'

275

Jacqui sprang back from the window. 'It's them,' she hissed. 'They're down there, in the street.'

'Did they see you?'

'I'm not sure – I think so.'

Napier moved over to the wall, holding to the shadows. Cautiously he approached the little casement window and peeped down into the street from the safety of the curtain.

Willi was directly below, standing against the far wall, scanning the upper windows. So close that Napier could make out the dark skin, the hollow cheeks and sharp features.

The other, the bearded individual, was by the front door, trying the handle. It was self-locking, that was something. They wouldn't want to break it down, the noise might alert the neighbours, bring the police.

It gave them a little time.

'Is there another way out of here?'

Jacqui shook her head, a quick gesture, charged with adrenalin. Her eyes held his, searching for a solution.

The door-bell broke the silence.

Napier held quite still, listening, expecting at any moment to hear the sound of an apartment door opening, feet crossing the landing. Someone going down to answer the call, to see who was there.

But there was nothing. Jacqui touched him in the dark, nudging close. The scent of her hair filled his head. He put his arm around her shoulders and felt her give a shiver beneath her coat, sensing the sudden cold fear that had seized her.

Again the bell rang, a long insistent demand. Still no response. They waited in the twilight, their eyes searching, ears straining for the slightest sound.

The minutes dripped by. Hearts beat hard in the stillness.

Napier moved the curtains a fraction. Willi had turned, uncertain now, moving away up the street.

'I don't think he saw you.'

Jacqui relaxed, letting out her breath with a rush. 'Thank God there was no one else in the building.'

Sneaking across the floor, keeping clear of the window, Napier picked up the phone. It was dead.

'In the meantime they've cut us off.'

'What can we do?'

'Are you absolutely certain there is no other way out of here?'

276

Jacqui's face lit up, suddenly animated. 'Yes,' she remembered. 'There's a window at the back, in my bedroom.'

'Can you get out of it?'

She nodded, beckoning him next door. 'I often climb out on to the roof in the summer to sunbathe.'

Napier followed her. Into a neat, feminine room with a crisp white counterpane on the bed and a fluffy rug beneath. A large mirror, jars and little bottles on the dressing table, clustered thick as crocuses.

Jacqui was reaching up, fumbling with the catch of a rear window. It opened upwards with a screech of complaint.

She turned, pleased with herself.

Through it Napier caught a glimpse of slate roofs, lead flashing and tottering chimney stacks.

'Where does it lead?'

'I've no idea,' she said lightly, 'but it must go somewhere.' Grasping hold of a chair she ejected the teddy bear that occupied it on to the bed, and set it beneath the window.

'You go first.'

Clambering up, Napier wriggled his shoulders through the narrow aperture and spilled over the ledge. Landing on a hard gritty surface between two steeply sloping roofs. Jacqui followed, reaching out her hand for help, tumbling down beside him, her shoes tucked in her pockets.

Getting to his feet, Napier scrambled up the hip of the roof, grasping at the base of a television aerial for support. A breeze struck him, fanning his face, ruffling at his hair. Reaching back he hauled Jacqui up beside him.

'All right, *chérie*?'

She nodded quickly. Her eyes were shining, skin glowing in the fresh air. The fear that had gripped her a moment before had passed, dispelled by the new activity. She placed her hand on his shoulder, steadying herself.

'Although I'm hardly dressed for the occasion,' she added with a quick smile.

Balancing precariously, arms outstretched, they made their way forwards, Napier leading her across the wasted landscape of slate roofs. In the distance the estuary flashed silver in the evening light. Clouds stacking up the sky, plump and soft as folded blankets. The clean, fresh smell of rain in the air.

Forget the bloody weather, he told himself, concentrate on getting out of here.

Over a low parapet, holding on to the guttering. A glimpse through a skylight into a room below: wash-basin, bare boards, unclean sheets on a bed. Down the other side, Jacqui slithered into him, catching at his waist. Two slates dislodged and tinkled down the roof, smashing like dinner plates far below.

A fire escape took them down into a small yard. It was a crude iron ladder, pitted and weakened with rust, that came to an end some height up the wall. Napier went first, taking his weight on his hands as he reached the last rung, swinging free and dropping to the ground. Straightening up he reached above his head.

Jacqui had hesitated, clinging to the safety of the ladder.

'Jump!' he told her.

'It's too high, *chéri.*'

'I'll catch you.'

'I can't.' She let go as she spoke, taking him by surprise, arriving in a confusion of legs and parachuting skirts. They rolled over on the ground, dislodging a stack of timber that clattered about their ears. A flower pot toppled over and burst with a hollow report, scattering its earth.

Indoors a dog began to bark.

Jacqui concerned, struggling off him: 'Did I hurt you?'

'Nothing permanent.'

The yard was narrow, an untidy space caught between two buildings. A small wooden door let them out into the street. Lifting the bolt, Napier shuffled it open and peered round cautiously.

Jacqui close behind him asked, 'Where are we, Jean?'

'In the Rue de Ville, by the salt houses.'

The street was almost deserted. A few pedestrians trotted by, talking amongst themselves, taking no notice of the couple who had stepped out of the door in the wall.

They took a long circuitous route to the harbour, approaching from the Place Thiers. Following the avenue of trees, through leaves that whisked and billowed about their feet, pausing as they reached the end. From the shelter of a tree-trunk they had a clear view of the waterfront.

Willi had emerged on to the quayside and was now staring up at the rooftops, sensing the escape. Quick and jerky in his movements, he was issuing orders to his companion, venting his frustration in violent gesticulations.

'What do they want of us, Jean?'

'I'm not entirely sure,' Napier replied, 'but I don't think we should hang around to find out.'

He looked across the harbour to where the yellow Citroën waited patiently on the further shore. It seemed so close, so easy to reach, just a short stroll away from where they were standing.

Slipping out of the shelter of the trees they began to walk towards it, joining in with a group of young people, blending into the scene.

Legs aching as they sauntered along, begging to break free, to run this last short distance.

A quick glance back.

Willi had turned now, he was looking across the harbour in their direction.

Dammit. They should have planned this, changed their clothes, altered their appearance when they had the chance. Jacqui needed a scarf, something to cover her hair. It was like a beacon in the crowd.

But Willi hadn't spotted them, he was distracted, gazing down at the water.

Nearly there now. Don't rush it, just keep ambling along as though you had nothing better to do.

The crowd in front parted. A figure had stepped out, bowing low.

'Good evening, Dr Napier.'

They both started at the name.

The juggler stood before them. Red breeches, flat black shoes, smiling with his sharp white teeth. There was a breathless hush of expectation. The faces all around were watching, waiting for him to perform.

'Are you going somewhere?' he inquired.

They ignored him, kept on walking towards the car.

His voice followed, mocking them, chiding in its tone. 'I imagine you'll be needing these.'

They spun around at his words. The juggler stood poised, the smile enticing and confident, his arm held out towards them.

Dangling from his finger were the keys to the car.

Jacqui clasped at her pockets, horrified. She took a pace back towards the juggler.

'Please,' she said, 'give them to me.'

279

He shied away.

'It's really very important.'

He relented. Stretching forward he offered them to her. His hand shut and opened again. The fingers were splayed wide, the palm was empty.

The keys had vanished.

A murmur of appreciation from the crowd. This was fun, this was good sport.

'For God's sake!' Jacqui cried in frustration.

On the far shore Willi was watching . . . registering what he saw . . . beginning to move.

'Give them to me!' ˙

Stepping close the juggler reached into her coat, drawing the keys from her collar. A burst of clapping from the crowd. Jacqui snatched at the bundle of keys but he flicked them away again with an effortless skill born of long practice.

Willi was running now . . . calling to his companion.

There was no more time. Jumping forwards Napier took the juggler by his collar, grasping the feather-light body, throwing him back against the harbour wall. It took the man by surprise, his legs lifted and flapped the air like a broken doll as he slammed into the stone.

A gasp from the audience, voices raised. 'Steady there . . . No need to lose your temper . . .'

Napier had him by the throat. The juggler hissing, his eyes fierce and malignant.

' . . . fellow can't take a joke.'

The keys flew from the juggler's hand, clattering across the cobbles. 'Take them,' he spat into Napier's face.

Jacqui scuttled across the quay, snatched them up. Without pausing she ran on to the car.

Tossing the man aside, Napier followed her, breaking out of the crowd who were clamouring, threatening to hold him.

'You drive,' she shouted as he reached her, throwing the bundle of keys across the roof.

The engine fired first time. The little car roared into life. Swinging it around, Napier crashed into first gear and headed down the quay. Figures scattering before the bonnet, surprised faces on either side.

'Where's Willi?'

'Behind . . . running after us.'

He swung the car round the harbour, the tyres chattering angrily on the cobbles. Jacqui had thrown herself around in the seat and was peering out through the rear window.

'Still with us?'

'Yes . . . no,' she corrected, 'he's slowing down . . . I think he's giving up.'

Reaching the smooth tarmac of the road the car began to pick up speed. In the frame of the mirror Napier caught a glimpse of Willi standing on the quay behind them, bent over double with his hands on his knees, heaving out deep breaths.

Jacqui gave a sudden cry of warning. 'Look out!'

A van, coming straight at them.

Napier swerved across on to the right hand side of the road. Jacqui looked at him with wide eyes.

'Sorry – force of habit.'

With the accelerator flat down on the floor they drove out of Honfleur. Jacqui keeping watch out of the back.

'Do you think they could have a car?' she asked as they cleared the outskirts of town.

'Possibly.'

'Because there's one behind us.'

Napier adjusted the mirror. It was a red BMW, coming up fast, closing the distance effortlessly. There was no way they could outstrip it, they hadn't the power. Jacqui's Citroen was already at full stretch, the engine whining under the bonnet.

'Is it them?' he called out.

'I can't tell.'

It was no time to find out. With a shout of warning, Napier wrenched on the steering wheel, grasping at the handbrake as he did so. The car spun round in the road, tyres squealing on the tarmac. Jacqui hurled herself to one side, clutching at the dashboard as the car heeled over, righted itself again and dived off into a side road.

The road wound up the hill, twisting between hedges and private houses. Napier nursed the engine, shifting rapidly through the gears, getting the maximum from the little car.

'Any sign of them following?'

Jacqui shook her head, turning to the front again. 'I think it was just a coincidence.'

281

They reached the crest of the hill, the car moving more easily now. Trees loomed up on either side, darkening the road, the occasional snatched view of the estuary beyond, the distant lights of Le Havre glimmering on the water. Napier's attention was fixed on the rear view mirror, watching the stretch of road behind as he ducked and turned the car through the lanes, covering his tracks.

'Where are we going, *chéri*?' Jacqui asked as they skimmed through a small village and dived out into the countryside on the far side.

Napier looked at her in the shadows. 'I haven't the faintest idea,' he replied, laughing at the confession. It was absurd, his whole attention had been focused on escape, getting away from Willi and his companion. He hadn't given a thought to where they might be heading.

He checked the mirror again. The road was clear, there was no sign that they were being followed.

'In here,' Jacqui cried suddenly, pointing to the left.

Napier acted automatically, swinging the car off the road where she directed. Through high gates of exposed flint and wrought-iron, the tyres crunching into well-raked gravel. It was a private driveway of some sort, bordered by rhododendrons and sculptured flower beds. He braked, slowing to a more becoming pace.

'Where on earth are we?'

'In a hotel.'

'How do you know?'

Jacqui was surprised by the question. 'Because it said so above the gate, *chérie*. The Hôtel de la Grande Forêt.'

'Good God,' said Napier as they came round the corner, 'it looks like a sanatorium.'

The drive swept up to a massive façade. The Hôtel de la Grande Forêt stood silhouetted against the evening sky, its roof fretted into fairy tale turrets and dormer windows.

'A sanatorium for those suffering from a surfeit of cash by the look of it,' he added. Parking the car he switched off the engine and the silence settled around them.

Jacqui looked out of the window, a little uncertain now. 'I thought it seemed like a good idea.'

'It was,' Napier replied, kissing her quickly to chase away the doubt. 'You go inside and see if they can take us. I'll try to get this car out of sight.'

282

She smiled, reassured, and collecting her bag she ran up to the steps into the porch.

Leaving the Citroën, which was quietly clicking and creaking as the engine cooled, Napier walked around the hotel, noting the clipped box hedges, formal gardens and manicured lawns that slipped away into the darkness.

The whole establishment breathed an air of respectability, of well-maintained protocol. This was a retreat, a place of rest where business-men could recover from their nervous breakdowns, actresses escape the demands of their public and politicians conduct discreet affairs with their press secretaries. Where residents dropped hundred-franc notes into the wishing well and waiters accepted tips by credit card.

It was perfect, Napier thought to himself as he strolled back across the gravel. Willi could never follow them here. Sudden acts of premeditated violence wouldn't be permitted in a hotel such as this. The management wouldn't allow it.

The front doors opened. Napier turned, expecting to see Jacqui returning, but instead two porters emerged, formal in white shirts and striped waistcoats. Between them, and a good head shorter in height, was a rotund figure in a black suit. He came skipping down the steps towards Napier, moving sideways in the manner of a tap-dancer, hands held high, jowls wobbling in greeting.

'Good evening, monsieur, and welcome to the Hôtel de la Grande Forêt. I am the manager.' He offered Napier a damp hand to shake. 'The Comtesse has signed in, she is waiting for you indoors.'

'Is she just?' he replied evenly.

'So if you could be so good as to show us your car these gentlemen will bring in your luggage.'

How embarrassing, Napier observed to himself, and how very tactless of the Comtesse not to admit that they had none. Going across to the Citroën he opened the boot. It contained a spare wheel and an emergency triangle, the only movable object he could see was Jacqui's raincoat neatly folded on the back seat. Taking it out Napier passed it to the nearest of the porters.

A gleam of interest flickered awake in the manager's eyes.

'The rest of the Comtesse's luggage will be arriving shortly,' Napier told him gravely.

With a snap of his fingers the manager dismissed the

283

two porters. He had grasped the situation. A beautiful young lady, well bred and expensively dressed but slightly flustered. Arriving without any sort of booking in a ridiculous little car, clearly not her own – and without any luggage. No, it didn't take much to appreciate the arrangement.

'Of course, monsieur,' he simpered, assessing Napier through small eyes. And what of this young man? Fluent in French but evidently foreign. Well-tailored clothes, an air of confidence about him – almost certainly English.

There was the faintest suggestion of a smile on Napier's lips. 'I was wondering whether I could move the car?' he murmured. 'Put it somewhere less conspicuous.'

The manager paused to consider the request.

'You understand my problem?'

He flicked one hand aside. Of course he understood. Monsieur would be wanting to remain anonymous, to disguise the Comtesse's presence at the hotel. From her father was it . . . or the husband maybe? He couldn't recall whether she'd been wearing a ring when she signed the register, how very remiss of him, he really must check at the next opportunity.

'I would be most grateful . . .'

Naturally monsieur would be grateful, and no doubt generous. A large tip would be in order, a token of gratitude willingly given and meekly accepted. What a pleasant prospect, how very satisfactory – it called for another quick bow.

Dropping his voice the manager confided, 'There are garages round in the stable block for the convenience of residents.'

What a revolting little man, thought Napier as he backed the car across the drive. But still, it suited their purpose. If the hotel manager wanted to believe that he had run off with a French aristocrat's wife it saved him from coming up with some alternative, and no doubt less plausible, excuse.

Shutting the garage door he went indoors, checking that the car was no longer visible from the driveway. He found Jacqui in the drawing room, flicking through a magazine, reviewing her new surroundings with evident satisfaction.

'Ah Jean, there you are,' she purred as he came in. 'Have you managed to hide the car?'

'You mean did I park the Comtesse's limousine?'

She blushed, suddenly coy. 'Oh . . . you heard?'

'It happened to slip out in conversation.'

'I had to call myself that.'

'Of course you did . . .'

'It's true,' she insisted, all righteous indignation now. 'We would never have got in here otherwise. The manager told me they only accepted guests who had booked. He said the hotel never allowed casual custom from the road. I could have smacked him.'

'But you managed to get your way?'

She gave a little giggle. 'I told him my family had been coming here for years and that none of them had ever been expected to book before.'

'Whose name did you use?'

'An old gentleman who occasionally lends pictures to the museum.'

'And when he heard the title the manager suddenly remembered he'd had a cancellation?'

'Exactly, he's such a snob. I expect he'll be looking it up right now.' She paused, glancing round at Napier with serious eyes. 'I'm afraid the rooms they've given us are rather different, Jean. They only had one good one. Yours is on the top floor; it's just a little matchbox.'

'Ideal for storing your spare luggage.'

'I couldn't see the prices,' she added, taking him by the arm, 'but I think it must be very expensive here.'

'I'm sure they accept luncheon vouchers.'

She whispered, 'Are we going to stay?'

'Do you want to?'

Jacqui's eyelids dropped for an instant and her smile when she looked up at him was voluptuous.

'Lost them!' Ashford shouted. 'How in God's name can you have lost them?'

Willi stood in the centre of the study floor, scowling down at the carpet.

'Answer me!'

Willi gave a shrug. He didn't need this, didn't have to take this crap from anyone. 'They saw us coming.'

'How can that be?' Ashford was incredulous, his voice dropping as he put the question.

'The girl – she recognised me. I'm sure of it.'

'But she's never seen you before.'

Again the shrug, the refusal to acknowledge guilt. 'She's seen me.'

'When?'

The question was sharp, fired at point blank range. Ashford was standing close now, watching his every moment.

'Earlier this summer,' Willi snapped. 'She was riding that horse of hers, all grand and haughty, flaunting herself in front of us.'

'Did you speak to her?'

'Not really – might have said a few words.'

'Did she speak to you?'

'Not her, stuck up little cow.' Willi spat out his contempt. 'Wouldn't even look at us. That's why I didn't think it mattered.'

Ashford turned away in disgust. 'Get out of here, Willi. Go down to the kitchens, stay there until I need you.'

After the man had left he stood at the window, staring out into the darkness.

Jacqui was getting away from him, slipping through his fingers. He should never have let her go, never have trusted her in the first place. That was his mistake.

It was his own fault. He'd allowed himself to be captivated by her, seduced by her grace, her classical beauty. What a fool. Jacqui was no different from the others. Under that cool exterior, that elegant façade she was a slut like all the rest of her sex.

But he'd find her. Sooner or later she had to creep out of hiding and he'd catch her, bring her to heel. He didn't care what happened to John Napier, that was irrelevent at present, it was Jacqui that occupied him. She must be made to pay for her part in this, made to suffer . . .

Ashford caught a movement out of the corner of his eye.

He turned quickly.

Louis was standing in the doorway, arms folded. The cold, inscrutable eyes were staring at him, boring into him, reading the thoughts in his mind.

'There's no one in here under seventy,' Jacqui whispered under her breath.

Napier looked around the hotel dining room with its white-aproned waiters, its aspidistras and bold overhead lighting, at the tasselled menus, the turtle-backed meat salver, the trays of

286

hors-d'oeuvres and desserts. 'You probably need that number of years to amass enough money to pay the bill.'

Jacqui giggled, leaning forwards across the table, eyes shining. She had spent some time in the ladies room before dinner, repairing the damage caused by their frantic escape from Honfleur. Carefully brushing the stains off her skirt, combing the knots and tangles from her hair so that it now shone in the light of the chandeliers.

The head waiter drew alongside their table, handsome in his tails, a white waistcoat stretched tight across his belly. 'Is everything to your satisfaction?'

'Yes, thank you – it was excellent.'

They had dined on fillet steak, carved into plump slices, and Jacqui had insisted they follow this with crêpe suzette. 'It's disastrous for the figure,' she told him, 'but we must have the flames, it makes this into a proper occasion.'

The head waiter bowed at the compliment, inclining forwards into the position of a ship's figure-head. 'And would you like coffee at the table, Comtesse, or through in the drawing room?'

'Neither thank you,' Jacqui replied, dismissing him with her dazzling smile.

Napier was surprised. 'Wouldn't you like something to drink?'

'Yes chéri, but not here.' She was conspiratorial. Reaching out she took Napier's hand in hers, drawing him out of the room with the eyes of every waiter following in their wake.

In the hallway they met the manager, bobbing and pirouetting, reversing back as he bade them good night. Carrying on up the staircase, Jacqui led the way along the passage to her room.

'Do you think he knows I'm bringing you in here?' she asked as she searched for her key.

'It would destroy his faith in humanity if you didn't.'

Closing the door behind her, she switched on low lights that glowed in saffron-coloured shades and hurried across the floor.

Neatly hidden by the wardrobe was a small fridge. Kneeling down Jacqui opened the door and drew out a half-bottle of champagne. She turned about, brandishing this trophy above her head.

'Good thinking,' said Napier, throwing himself down on the bed, 'how did you know about that?'

'I found it earlier this evening.' She came back with two glasses and kicking off her shoes she sprawled down on her stomach beside him, holding them up in readiness.

Napier stripped off the wire cage and thumbed out the cork, it ricocheted across the ceiling, leaving the muzzle of the bottle smouldering with blue gases.

Jacqui touched her glass to her lips, watching him over the rim. 'I love champagne,' she breathed, lying back on the pillows. 'Why is it that everything I like is so expensive?'

'It's to stop you from having too much, *chérie*, and making yourself sick.'

'You sound like Kettie.' She nuzzled close to him, feeling the warmth of his body.

Napier slipped his arm around her. 'All we need is a little smoked salmon in that fridge of yours and we could survive a siege.'

'We could,' she agreed, 'except as soon as this is finished you are going back to your room, aren't you, Jean?'

'You're referring to the little matchbox?'

'On the top floor.'

'Of course,' he promised. 'I have the key in my pocket.'

She rolled over on to her back, golden hair spilling out on the cover, looking up at him.

'Do you?'

'They gave it to me at the desk.'

'Did they, Jean?'

'It's strange,' he murmured, drawing his hand down the front of her shirt, parting first the top button and then the next. 'It fits your door as well as mine.'

Jacqui moved very slightly. 'Really?' Her smile was seductive now, irresistible.

'It also has your number on it.'

She watched his hands through her lashes. 'And is that what has given you permission to start undressing me, Dr Napier?'

'Probably.' He parted the silk of her shirt, lowering his head into the cleavage.

'You weren't supposed to know,' she said softly. 'The hotel only had one room free . . .' Napier kissed the softness between her breasts, his lips touching just above the little pink bow in the centre of her bra. 'I had to take it,' she faltered, ' . . . but I didn't want you to think . . .' Her voice trembled and fell away. She tried to speak but the words failed her. Diving her fingers into his hair she drew him up to her lips. Holding him hard against her, her tongue touching his, exploring the sweet taste of his mouth.

Quite suddenly she drew back her head. Napier's eyes questioned hers, he made as if to speak but she pressed her forefinger to his lips, compelling him to silence. Slipping off the bed she glided over to the door and switched off the lights. Crossing to the window she drew back the curtains and unfastening the shutters she pushed them apart.

It was a clear night and the estuary shone in the reflection of the sky, bathing the room in a silver-blue brilliance.

Jacqui turned, looking back to where Napier lay, his eyes bright in the moonlight. Loosening the zip at her waist, she stepped out of her skirt and dropped it over the back of the bed. For a moment she stood above him, her body framed against the window, and then slipping back on to the bed she knelt over him, straddling him with her legs.

His hands reached up inside her opened shirt, holding her around the waist, drawing her down. She kissed him on the eyes, the chin, the throat, her fingers searching on to his bare skin, stroking his chest. He felt hard and strong beneath her hand and the rich, warm musk of his body filled her nostrils.

Rapidly they undressed each other. Jacqui pushing the jacket from his shoulders, tugging at the knot of his tie, opening the buttons beneath with hasty fingers. Napier reaching upwards, his arms caught in the straitjacket of his shirt sleeves, kissing her firm breasts, feeling the hard acorns of her nipples between his lips.

With a little moan of contentment, Jacqui stretched herself back on the bed, shifting slightly to allow him to remove her underclothes, flimsy white garments that he dropped on to the floor. She felt beautiful and desirable, closing her eyes as she lay before him, proud of her nakedness, wanting him to admire her.

His hands moved over her body, warm and gentle, stroking her breasts, flowing down on to the hollow curve of her stomach, brushing over the dark pelt of hair below. With slow caressing movements he drew his palms along the creamy

289

flesh inside her thigh. Shyly Jacqui raised her knees to him, parting her legs in invitation, pressing her hips into him, crowing with pleasure at the delicious sensation of his fingers.

'Inside me, Jean,' she whispered with sudden urgency. 'I need you inside me.'

Her arms were around him, her lips hot on his flesh. Reaching downwards she fumbled with his belt, Jean helping, half cursing, half laughing as he struggled free.

Falling back Jacqui pulled him down between her thighs, encouraging him with small crooning words, directing the frantic energy of his passion, guiding him into the warm darkness of her body.

She cried out as he entered her, feeling the strength of his body against hers, his weight crushing on to her, gasping at the wave of desire that surged up within her.

She began to move with him, locking him in her arms, urging him on. Her voice was hoarse in her throat, her head thrashing the pillow, the words losing coherence until only his name was left and she heard herself crying it over and again into the night.

All the love, the tenderness she felt for him concentrated into this one moment, uniting into a single burning passion that threatened to overwhelm her, to destroy her completely. She felt herself lifted, as if by some massive force, reaching the limit of her endurance, fighting to hold on. 'No Jean . . . please, stop, I can't . . .' Desperate now, gripping him between her legs, losing control.

And then the release. The sudden wild shriek of pleasure as she gave in to him, falling back on the bed, shuddering as she came, and in the quick spasms of her body she felt him burst within her.

They lay quite still, listening to their breath slowing and growing calm, feeling the cool of the night on their bodies. Jacqui with her arms around him, holding his head in the cradle of her neck, stroking his hair.

'Did I make you happy, *chéri*?' she whispered.

Gently he withdrew and knelt back on the bed. Rolling her over he stroked the smooth, boyish back, praising her with small kisses across the shoulders and neck and down the long ridge of her spine.

★ ★ ★

The Sealink ferry ploughed forwards into the night.

Spooner made his way down the companionway, holding on to the railing, bracing himself against the sluggish pitch of the hull.

The main lounge was crowded with sleeping figures who sprawled across the reclining seats, surrounded by canvas holdalls, discarded anoraks and empty beer cans. The stale smell of cigarette smoke hung in the air and the deck trembled and juddered with the thrust of the screws.

Pushing open the swing doors Spooner walked along the passage, past plate-glass windows streaked with spray. In the duty free shop he collected a wire basket and bought himself a bottle of Calvados, paying with a credit card. He very rarely drank spirits but he thought he'd make an exception to the rule, this was by way of a souvenir, something to remind him of his days in Normandy.

The girl at the till slipped the bottle into a bright yellow carrier bag and he took it up on to the deck. It was quite deserted out there and suddenly cold in the wind. Turning up his collar he leaned against the railing and peered down at the sea creaming away from the ship's side. He had been standing in this same position when they left port, looking out across the estuary to where the single lighthouse of Honfleur winked at him in the darkness.

He thought of John Napier and of Jacqui, wondering where they were at that moment, what they were doing with themselves. He didn't notice the door open behind him or the figure who brushed by him, pausing by his shoulder to ask if he had a light.

Spooner turned at the sound of the voice.

As he did so an expression of astonishment came over his face. It was not the question that had surprised him, or the man's sudden movement as he stepped in close.

It was the agony of the knife sticking into his belly.

The blade had come from below, angling upwards into his stomach, piercing his waistcoat just between the second and third button.

Slowly Spooner reached down to touch it but as he did so his limbs trembled, his body began to jerk, as though he had touched an electric current.

He looked up, uncomprehending, into the eyes of Luc

291

Gabot. They were very close to him, fierce eyes burning with the savage light of conquest, intoxicated by the violence of the kill.

Spooner tried to speak but choked. His mouth fell open and a worm of blood crawled out of the corner of his mouth. A second thrust of the knife threw him back against the railing.

The yellow carrier bag dropped from his hand and smashed on the steel deck and he toppled back into the darkness.

Chapter Twenty

Napier stirred, lifting himself from the heavy drugging of sleep. At first there was just a sense of well-being, a glow of pleasure, it was only gradually that the feeling began to clarify, to take on shape and definition, and the memory of the previous night returned to him. Rolling over he reached out across the sheet, but the other side of the bed was empty. He was alone. Pulling himself up on his elbows he looked across the room, now bright in the morning light.

Jacqui was standing on the balcony, leaning against the wrought-iron railing, admiring the view. Hearing him wake she turned and stepped back through the window. She was wearing his shirt, loose and ill-fitting about her slim figure, the upper buttons undone, the collar parted so wide that it scarcely caught on her shoulders.

She hesitated as she crossed the room, momentarily unsure of herself. Napier held out his arms towards her and she came into them, slipping on to the bed beside him, snuggling her head into his neck.

'How are you this morning, my darling?' she whispered.

Pressing his face into warm hair, he kissed her behind the ear, and for a few minutes they lay together unconscious of anything beyond the embrace of their arms.

There was a knock at the door.

Napier lifted his head, questioning Jacqui with a quick glance.

'It's breakfast,' she said, swinging her feet on to the ground. 'I rang reception while you were asleep.'

'What an industrious little ant you are.'

Wrapping herself in a heavy white bathrobe, Jacqui opened the door, collecting the tray with a murmur of thanks. Her expression as she turned back with it was of outraged dignity.

'He winked at me,' she gasped. 'The little squit. He asked

me if I had slept well and then gave me a great wink – and he can't have been more than seventeen.'

'Did you tell him to go and count his spots?'

'I should have.' She set the tray down on the bed and tossing aside the bathrobe she knelt beside it. There was coffee in a tall glass percolator, croissants and jam. A single rose, pale yellow to match the decoration of the room, was arranged in the centre.

Jacqui poured the coffee, leaning forwards so that the shirt fell away from her shoulders and Napier caught a brief glimpse of the small pointed breasts beneath. He felt himself stir at the sight.

'Lie still, *chéri*, you're upsetting the tray.'

He apologised meekly and took the cup she passed to him.

For a few minutes they busied themselves with breakfast. When she was finished Jacqui sat back on her heels, brushing crumbs from her lap.

'What do we do today, Jean?' she inquired.

Napier sat up in bed, hugging his knees in his arms as he considered. 'I must get back into Honfleur this morning.'

'But they'll be watching the hotel, *chéri*.'

'I know, but Spooner is going to ring at two-thirty, I must be there to take the call.'

'Will I come too?'

He looked up at her, hair tumbling down over bare shoulders, eyes wide with concern. 'No, my love, you must stay here.'

'That's not right, Jean!'

'It's more sensible.'

She shook her head in protest. 'I must be with you.'

He took her hands, kissing the tips of her fingers. 'I'll be back,' he promised, 'just as soon as I've heard from Spooner.'

'But I don't want to be left behind.'

'It's quite safe, my love, they'll never manage to find you here.'

'Hello . . . Marcel?'

'Speaking . . .'

'This is Rupert . . . Rupert Ashford.'

The voice at the far end of the phone relaxed, a note of suavity returned now that the caller had been identified. 'Rupert, how very good to hear from you.'

'And you, Marcel.'

Marcel Lamartine was a producer at the local radio station. A man in his mid-fifties with bristly grey hair and bad skin, who dressed sloppily in baggy jumpers and carried a perpetual cigar in his mouth. Ashford couldn't claim to know Marcel well but he had invited him over to the château on more than one occasion. He'd found that it often paid to cultivate the media. There were times when they could be useful.

'What can I do for you, Rupert?'

'I was wondering if you could help me out with a minor problem?'

'What's on your mind?'

Ashford touched the first cigarette of the morning to his lips, licked in smoke, and smiled into the receiver. 'Just a small domestic crisis, Marcel, nothing too serious. My chef had a tiff with his wife last night, ran off into the night.'

'I'm sorry . . .'

'It's no matter except unfortunately he took Jacqui's car as he went – that ridiculous little Citroën she drives. I'm sure you've seen it when you were last round here.'

'So you'd like us to put something out over the air?'

'If you could,' Ashford murmured, 'I'd be most grateful. I don't want to bother the police with the affair but it would set my mind at rest to have the car returned. Jacqui will be so upset if it's lost . . .'

'It's no problem.'

'Naturally I'll be offering a reward for the recovery.'

'That always helps.'

'If I were to give you the registration number . . .?'

Napier parked the Citroën a mile outside Honfleur.

Halting in a wooded stretch of the road he reversed up a small farm track until the car was hidden from sight. Locking the doors he walked back to the road, approaching the town on foot.

He found the silence disturbing. After the cheerful chattering of the car engine it was strangely quiet, the only sound was the crunching of his shoes on the gritty surface of the road. It filled him with a faint sense of apprehension, he felt exposed out here and vulnerable.

Climbing up the bank he ducked under a fence into an orchard. The ground was spongy from the recent rain, the grass nibbled short by the cows who stood domino black-and-white beneath the apple trees. Napier moved quickly, keeping close to the cover. Scrambling through a gap in the hedge he emerged into the road three hundred yards above the hotel.

He paused to consider his strategy. There was no chance of going in through the front gates, it was too easy for Ashford to have the entrance watched. He didn't actually think this was likely but it wasn't worth taking the risk either. If he was to get into the hotel unnoticed he needed to come from the other side, from the direction of the garden.

Crossing the road he dived down from a footpath that took him out on to the open face of the hill. The town was spread out below him, blue-misted and vague in the afternoon light. Following the narrow thread of the chalk path, brushing through small saplings that caught at his clothing, he made his way round to the outer wall of the hotel.

It was eight feet tall on this side, a forbidding barrier, eroded and slumped with age. Set in the brickwork towards one corner was a garden door. Napier tried the handle but it hadn't been opened for years, the woodwork was warped, the hinges rusted solid. He abandoned it and moved further along, searching for an alternative way in. The stump of a tree-trunk gave him the solution. Clambering on to it, he threw his arms over the top of the wall and pulled himself up, locking his elbows in place. He found a foothold in the brick and wriggling into a more comfortable position he peered down into the gardens.

The hotel lay before him, serene and peaceful, its routine passing undisturbed. Napier could detect slight movements in the dining room where lunch was still in progress. Out in the driveway a couple were unloading luggage from a car and the sound of their voices drifted over to him. He looked out towards the entrance but there was no sign of Willi or his bearded friend.

For fifteen minutes he waited, checking the windows of the out-buildings, the parked cars and the distant undergrowth. When he was satisfied that it was safe, that the coast was clear, he kicked his legs over the wall and dropped down into the garden. Casually he strolled across the lawn, entering through the high French windows at the back of the house.

He met Eugenie in the passageway.

'Where the hell have you been?' she cried, her eyes dark and fierce with relief at seeing him. 'We've all been worried sick.' Taking him by the arm she drew him into her study, closing the door behind her.

'They were here looking for you.'

'How long ago?'

'Last night, two of them, and then again this morning. I told them you weren't here but they wouldn't believe me. They started searching the place, there was nothing I could do to stop them. In the end I threatened to call the police.'

Crossing the floor Eugenie closed the shutters and returning to her desk she switched on a glass-shaded lamp. The room slipped back into its shadowy atmosphere in which scents and sounds were more vivid than visual appearances.

'Where were you last night?'

He told her of their escape from Honfleur, of the rapid drive through the lanes and the chance discovery of the Hôtel de la Grande Forêt. At the mention of this name Eugenie's eyebrows raised, her professional instincts were touched.

'That was an expensive accident,' she remarked dryly.

'Hopefully we won't be there too long.'

'And the girl is still back at the hotel?'

Eugenie could be trusted with the information. 'She'll ring the police if I'm not back within the hour.'

In the glow of the lamp Eugenie regarded him seriously. 'You are going to get him, aren't you, John?'

'Who Ashford? I imagine so.'

'That's good.' For a moment the hatred was there again, the consuming passion. It was like a lust burning in her eyes. 'Do you have enough evidence?'

He nodded. 'All we need now is the means to bring him in.'

'The means,' she murmured, dropping her lashes. 'That's all it's ever needed – and that's what we've never had.'

'Spooner is about to ring me with instructions. That's why I'm here now.'

Her manner relaxed. Opening the walnut cabinet she drew out the bottle of brandy, poured two glasses and handed one to Napier. 'Have you had anything to eat?'

'Not since breakfast.'

'I could fetch you something from the dining room.'

'It's not important.' He glanced at his watch. It was two-forty, Spooner should have called by now.

Eugenie noticed the gesture. 'He's probably been held up.'
It was true, the ferry had been delayed. Spooner would
have been later back to London than he expected but still
it was unlike him to be unpunctual.
'He's usually meticulous about timing.'
They waited for another fifteen minutes, draining their
glasses and recharging them again before Eugenie said, 'Why
don't you ring him yourself?'
'I would, except I don't have the number of his office
with me and I imagine it's not listed in the directory.'
'I have it,' she replied. Flitting out of the room, she
returned a moment later with Spooner's business card. 'He
gave me this before he left.'
Napier dialled London, listening to the staccato clicking
of the relays as he was connected to the number.
A crisp voice answered the phone. 'Wallace-Jones, can
I help you?'
In a few words Napier explained his business and asked
to be put through to Spooner's office.
'I'm afraid he hasn't returned from France yet, Dr Napier.'
'But he left yesterday afternoon.'
There was a pause, the voice warmed slightly, becoming
confidential. 'We were expecting him this morning, he'd
rung to say he'd be in first thing, but he hasn't put in an
appearance yet.'
Napier felt the wings of anxiety flutter awake in his stom-
ach. Thanking the man he hung up.
Eugenie read his frown. 'Bad news?'
'Spooner hasn't arrived back in London.'
'Do you think something could have happened to him?'
It was possible, but what? he wondered. Spooner couldn't
have missed the ferry. They had practically seen him go on
board.
'I think I should drive over to Le Havre,' he told her.
'Find out what's going on.'
Picking up the phone he put a call through to the Hôtel
de la Grande Forêt. Jacqui wasn't in her room but he left a
message at the reception desk to say that he would be back
around five.
'Where's your car?' Eugenie asked as he drained his glass.
'Parked in the woods behind the town.'
She leaned back against the desk, arms folded, gazing

at him with her bright, satyr eyes. In the light of the desk lamp she appeared no more than twenty at that moment. The years had left no patina, no visible blemish on her skin. She was ageless and enigmatic.

Napier paused. He was eager to be away but there was something he needed to know. It was something that had been nagging at his mind for the last few days, something that made him turn in the doorway.

'Eugenie?'

Her smile had already anticipated the question.

'Yes John?'

'Do you have *The Estuary Pilgrim?*'

In the silence of slippered feet she moved across the room until she stood before him.

'Why should you think such a thing?'

Because it was the only answer he had. Because every way he looked at the riddle of the past he was drawn back to the same conclusion. She had to have the painting.

He explained his reasoning more carefully.

'I believe Schwartz stole *The Estuary Pilgrim.* His orders were to bury it along with the others in the hills above Honfleur. But he didn't, he kept it for himself.'

'And so?'

'He would have needed somewhere to hide it, somewhere where it would be safe until the war was over.'

'And you think he brought it here?'

'To give to Madeleine.'

For some moments Eugenie stared at him and then with a little shrug she stepped away. 'Yes,' she said lightly. 'Dietrich brought that painting here one night. It was in a great steel canister in the back of his car,' she laughed dryly. 'He had worked himself up into a terrible state. I don't think he really knew what he was doing. He wanted Madeleine to hide the picture for him, store it away in the cellars. It was to be their insurance, their nest egg after the war.' Again she paused, her voice dropping as she drew on the well of her memory. 'Not that it did him any good, they murdered him the next day.'

'Murdered? I thought he was shot for deserting.'

She gave a thin, humourless smile. 'Desert? He would never have deserted, never have thought of such a thing. No, Dietrich was shot because he knew where those damned paintings had been hidden.'

It figured. Schwartz had known too much for his own good. His execution would have been part of Ashford's plan, a way of ensuring complete secrecy. It was his own fault. Schwartz should have seen it coming, should have guessed that once the pictures were hidden he was disposable. But that type never did, that was the tragedy. Schwartz had carried out his orders, done as he was told, and never questioned the motives. For that he'd died. Poor little sod.

'So what became of *The Estuary Pilgrim*?'

Eugenie shook her head. 'I've no idea. Dietrich took it away with him that night and I never saw it again.'

It wasn't true – she knew where it was. Napier could sense it in her expression, in the look of triumph that lit her eyes.

'You're lying,' he said quietly.

'Yes,' she replied, 'I'm lying.'

Turning away from him, Eugenie plunged her hands into her pockets. 'You're a clever man, John Napier. You've come into our lives, turned over memories, discovered secrets that have been buried for years. But not this one. *The Estuary Pilgrim* is lost. It belongs to the past and that's where it will remain.'

'There's a message for you, mademoiselle,' the receptionist called as Jacqui came in from the garden.

She paused and took the note he held out to her. It was from Jean.

'When did he call?'

'About ten minutes ago.'

She felt a little stab of disappointment as she read it through. He'd been due back about now, she had been sitting in the garden waiting for him, expecting to see the yellow Citroën sweep round the drive at any moment.

Now he wouldn't be back until five. She glanced down at her watch, that gave her another hour and a half to kill.

In a passageway beyond the main hall there was a row of boutiques. Jewellery arranged on black velvet trays, expensive gifts, cashmere jerseys and silk ties.

Jacqui inspected the curved glass windows. The worst of being locked up in this hotel was that she had no change of clothing, nothing clean and pretty to wear. She had considered ringing Paquetta to ask her to send some clothes over

300

by taxi but it seemed risky. Rupert could easily have her apartment watched and that would be just the sort of slip he'd be waiting for. There might on the other hand be a dress here she could buy for the evening, something to surprise Jean when he returned.

She stepped inside the tiny boutique.

The assistant appeared from a back room, lacquered hair and high-arched brows painted on powdered skin. Her expression was expectant, acquisitive, the spider responding to the trembling of her web.

'May I be of help . . .?'

Jacqui told her that she was just looking and with the faintest whiff of a smile the woman retired.

There wasn't much choice, the boutique was too small to hold more than a handful of dresses. Jacqui searched along the rack. Slipping one down she turned and held it against herself, hips thrust forwards as she reviewed the effect in the mirror. It hung a little lower below the knee than she liked but it was of a delicate grey silk that matched her eyes. She checked the price tag, it was marked at just under four thousand francs. Hurriedly she put it back in place. It would have looked smart on her, the cut was good and the design was elegant, but four thousand francs. *Merde.*

She moved further along the rack. The assistant was standing beside her again, rather too close for comfort now. Jacqui stepped aside.

'Please don't move, mademoiselle.'

A male voice, clipped and authoritative.

Jacqui spun around.

It was not the assistant beside her but Willi.

Her heart leapt into her throat. She heard herself give a cry of surprise.

Willi spoke. 'You will come with us mademoiselle . . .' Over his shoulder the assistant was staring at her white-faced. 'I have a gun in my pocket, if you try to run I have instructions to shoot you.' He beckoned towards the entrance.

Jacqui didn't hear what he had said but she understood the gesture and sensed the presence of the gun in the way in which Willi's right hand was held in his pocket.

Meekly she stepped out of the boutique. The Beard was there, lounging against the wall, covering her escape. He

301

straightened as she appeared, falling in beside her as they headed down the broad passage.

Jacqui could feel herself trembling. There was a sickness in her stomach, sending small aching pains down the inside of her thighs, weakening her legs as she walked. It was shock more than fear. Willi shouldn't be here, shouldn't have been able to find her. The hotel had been safe.

Across the hall, her heels silent in the thick pile of the carpet, a few heads turning to watch them.

The manager was busy at the reception desk. He looked away as they passed, averting his eyes, studying the hotel register – such an unpleasant incident, really most unsavoury. The sooner it was over the better.

This was the culprit, Jacqui realised. She could read the guilt in his affected disinterest, in his frown of concentration as she was hurried away. Despicable man. But how had he done it? What was it that had connected them with Rupert?

The blue Rolls was parked in the drive, its roof down, the cream leather seats mellow in the afternoon light.

Running down the steps, the Beard opened the rear door for her. Jacqui's instinct was to thank him, but this was not good manners just a precaution. Grasping her arm he thrust her into the car, ramming in behind, sitting with his body pressed hard against hers.

Willi took the wheel, swinging the car up the drive and out into the road without pausing to check for passing traffic. He drove rapidly along the narrow country lane. Down into a small village, the powerful engine growling as it picked up speed on the far side.

Jacqui could feel the slip-stream plucking at her collar, the wind lifting and spreading her hair. The rear window was down, her arm lay along the door. She looked at the open countryside, at the grass verge racing by. If they were to stop, even slow down for a moment, she could jump free. It would be easy to vault out of the car.

The bearded man was close beside her, his legs crossed, shoulders towards her as though engaged in an intimate conversation. His body smelt of sweat and garlic. Jacqui turned and stared at him, letting the disgust show on her face. He moved slightly, shifting round on the seat.

They had reached the coastal road, the estuary was spread out below them, its water bronzed with the anticipation of evening. Through Villerville – the street almost empty, the town lulled with Sunday indolence. Up on to the high ground once more, the Rolls breasting the slope without effort.

In front of them was a road works, a generator parked by the curb, red cones reducing the road to a single lane. The temporary traffic lights showed red. Willi chose to ignore the command but a lorry was approaching from the far side, he had no option.

The Rolls began to slow.

Jacqui looked away, showing no interest in the delay. The ground fell away towards the estuary on one side of the road, on the other was a tree-covered hillside. They were down to walking pace now. Under cover of the seat she slipped off her shoes in readiness. Her heart-beat quickening in anticipation.

The lorry was approaching, winking its lights in appreciation. Jacqui rested her weight on her arm, moved it back a few inches on the door, searching for the centre of gravity. The palm of her hand was damp on the smooth paintwork.

Willi was changing gear, the engine just idling over. The Beard was looking away, the car was almost at a stand-still.

Cold fingers of anticipation gripped her, twisting in her belly, this was the chance.

The lights had turned amber.

It had to be now.

Her nerve failed her, she changed her mind. But it was too late. Charged with adrenalin her body had already reacted, the muscles responding of their own accord. To her own astonishment, she felt herself bounding up, kicking free of the soft leather seat.

The Beard countered in the same instant.

With a cry of alarm he swung round, hurling himself on to her. One hand caught her around the ankle, jerking her back.

Jacqui twisted in his grasp, struggling in desperation, half in and half out of the car, lashing out at him with her other foot.

She felt it strike into the pulp of flesh.

The Beard let go of her with a stifled curse and clutched at his nose. The force of the kick threw Jacqui back, toppling her over the side. She hit the road, rolling over with a yelp of pain as it grazed her shoulder.

The Rolls had stopped, the doors had opened. The two men were spilling out.

Scrambling to her feet she began to run for the trees, bare feet on the gritty road, legs stretching. Not looking round, concentrating on the grass verge, on getting away from these bastards.

Willi's voice behind her, shouting at her, ordering her to stop.

Jacqui running, waiting for the shot, the crack of the revolver as he fired at her fleeing figure. Picturing the velocity of the bullet, the force of its impact as it crashed into her spine, tearing through her body, throwing her down into the kerb.

Off the road on to the bank. Leaping over a ditch, the ground suddenly soft beneath her feet. Bushes ahead of her and thick undergrowth. Brambles scratching at her legs, catching her skirt as she ran.

The Beard was close behind her, she could hear his feet pounding on the ground, the grunting of his breath as he followed. Suddenly she was back to her childhood, to games of tag on the lawn, her brothers chasing her, the shrill cries of excitement as they caught her. But they had been gentle as they rolled her down on the ground. These men were hard and cruel and the thought gave her the strength to run, the will to keep on going.

Over the roots of a tree, branches whipping at her face, her heart racing, blood thundering in her ears.

She glanced back over her shoulder. The Beard was falling behind, he was heavier than her and less fit.

A surge of hope, she was winning, getting away.

Out in the open again, sprinting across flat ground. In front of her was the road.

'Oh God! She'd been running alongside it. The Rolls had shadowed her all the way. It was there, parked in the road. Willi was jumping out, coming towards her, yelling to the other.

With a cry of despair she changed direction, driving her feet into the soft earth as she turned back, heading for the tree covered hill. Scrambling up the slope, her feet slipping in the soft soil, clawing at tufts of grass with her hands.

Willi behind her, fresh and energetic, scuttling up with

304

quick insect movements. He was close now, she could hear the snarling of his breath as he closed the distance between them.

She grasped at a branch, pulling herself over the trunk, sobbing for breath, looking back over her shoulder.

Willi was on her.

His hand reached out, catching her around the calf. She kicked herself free, rolling over, crying with exhaustion. His other arm locked around her waist, his face was against hers, his breath in her nostrils.

'Got you, you bitch!'

With a wail of frustration Jacqui fell across him, tumbling back down the hillside in a landslide of loose earth and leaves.

Willie landed heavily on her chest, knocking the wind from her lungs. He grabbed her by the collar, tearing open her shirt.

She screamed, flailing at him with her fists. He struck her across the face with the flat of his hand.

'Don't mark her!'

It was the Beard clambering up behind, his face smeared with blood, throwing himself on Willi, tearing him off.

'I'll kill the bitch . . .'

'You do and we're all for it . . .'

They faced each other for a moment, both panting heavily, and then with bad grace Willi shook himself free of the other and stood up. Grabbing Jacqui by the hair he pulled her to her feet, thrusting her down the hillside ahead of him.

'Get back into the car.'

'What was the name again, sir?'

'Spooner, Edward Spooner.'

The port official tapped plastic keys, feeding information into the company computer, scanning the screen from beneath the peak of his cap.

Napier glanced around the small dockside office as he waited for a response. Through the window he could see the Channel ferry manoeuvring itself against the quayside, its thick mooring ropes snaking down on to the ground, the white walls of the ship blotting out the view.

'Here we are, sir.'

Napier jerked his attention back to the desk.

'Mr E. Spooner, he was booked on the sixteen-thirty ferry yesterday afternoon.'

'And did he go on board?'

'The ticket was accepted at emigration.'

'But do you know whether he disembarked at the other end?'

The question puzzled the officer. 'I don't quite follow you, sir.'

Napier didn't want to raise the man's suspicions any more than he had to. 'He hasn't arrived in London yet,' he explained cautiously. 'I just want to be certain he left the ship this morning.'

The officer sucked on his teeth. 'You'd have to check with British Immigration, sir. We don't have that information at this end of the line.' He consulted a list by his desk. 'I can give you their number if it's any help.'

Napier noted it down. 'Could I ring from here?'

'The office won't be open at present.'

He glanced down at his watch. It was only four-forty.

'It's Sunday, sir.'

Napier grunted his understanding. Thanking the officer for his help he walked out across the quayside to where the Citroën was parked.

Wrenching on the steering wheel, Luc Gabot pulled out of his lane, overtaking the dark red Fiat. A car was coming in the other direction, flashing its lights in protest. He jerked his arm at the driver, mouthing him a silent obscenity. Sodding traffic, sanctimonious pricks out for a spin with the wife and kids.

The road ahead was clear, Luc changed gear, accelerating hard. The traffic lights at the far end were changing, he jumped them as they reached red, turning right into Commercial Dock.

He was guessing now, taking the autoroute out of Le Havre, past apartment blocks and high-rise buildings, weaving through the Sunday traffic. Diving down the underpass, neon lights strobing overhead. Thumping his hand on the wheel to vent his frustration. Paris two hundred-and-five kilometres, Rouen eighty-three. Out into the evening light again, billboards for Marlborough cigarettes, yoghurt and Ricard on either side. The town beginning to thin out, oil refineries straggling the road, orange street lamps spitting by.

Then he saw it. Half a mile ahead of him was the yellow Citroën. A spurt of adrenalin, a growl of satisfaction in his throat. He had been right. It was John Napier, heading back to Honfleur just as he'd anticipated he would.

Drawing out into the fast lane Luc overtook two more cars and then dropped back into place again, reducing his speed to match the other, keeping the Citroën in sight without crowding it.

Luc relaxed, the racing of his pulse calmed.

He had him now.

It had been easy following Spooner on to the Channel ferry. He had shadowed him all the way to the docks, watched as he said goodbye to Napier and that classy blonde and made his way on board. The two hour delay in sailing had given him enough time to return to his digs, pick up his passport and follow on behind. He had no doubt that this was the right move. His orders had been to watch Spooner, to prevent him from going to the police or from trying to leave Honfleur. Luc had done as he was told. He'd been paid good money to carry out instructions.

But finding Napier at the docks when he returned was just luck. He had hardly been able to believe his eyes. As he was walking down the gangway he had seen Napier coming out of an office, strolling across the tarmac towards his car.

What an opportunity, what an incredible stroke of good fortune.

Luc's only fear had been that he would lose him in the traffic. It had taken him almost fifteen minutes to clear Customs and Passport Control and pick up his car. By then Napier had vanished into the town. Luc had made a decision, taken a guess that he'd be heading for Honfleur and he was right. The Citroën was there just a few hundred yards in front of him.

He slowed, falling back in the traffic as they approached the Tancarville Bridge. He didn't want to be too close to Napier in the queue for the toll gate.

Chapter Twenty-One

Ashford was waiting for them in the gallery.

His manner was calm and relaxed, only the rapid tapping of the cigarette to his lips betrayed his impatience. Behind him a log fire was burning in the grate, the flames translucent as water in the evening sunshine.

At the sound of footsteps on the stairs he turned, tall and gaunt in his pale grey suit, a silk cravat wrapped around his neck. He watched as Jacqui was brought into the room. Willi and his scruffy associate on either side, Louis behind them, pausing in the doorway, remaining in the background.

Jacqui strode across the floor towards him, her eyes blazing. Willi tried to hold her but she snatched her arm away from him. She was not allowing herself to be led before Rupert like some captive. Her shoulder ached from the fall on the road and her feet were cut and painful but she was damned if she was going to let anyone know it and walked ahead of them with her firm, purposeful stride.

Willi had made no more mistakes on the way over. The roof of the car had been raised and the doors locked. He had ordered the other to drive while he sat over Jacqui, his hand twisted into her hair, holding her head down, pressing her face into the seat, so that she could hardly breathe let alone escape.

She paused before Ashford, angry and defiant, her hands planted on her hips. He noticed that the upper buttons had been torn from her shirt and the collar hung open, her legs and arms were scratched and the thick mane of her hair was tangled.

He turned his attention to Willi. 'How does she come to be in this state?'

'She tried to run.'

The suggestion of a smile trickled across Ashford's lips. 'Did you, my dear, how very heroic.'

She stared at him in silence, concentrating her hatred into her eyes, directing it at him.

'But then no one has ever denied you have spirit.'

'We had to hold her,' Willi complained.

Ashford nodded. Slowly he walked around Jacqui, studying her critically. The sight of her disarray seemed to annoy him, his expression soured.

'You look a disgrace,' he murmured.

At this Jacqui's temper flared. The shock of her capture, the fear that had gripped her as she was thrown back into the car ignited into fury, breaking through the stillness of her silence.

'How dare you do this to me,' she hissed. 'Why am I here Rupert . . . What do you want of me?'

'You have only yourself to blame, my dear,' Ashford replied quietly. 'If you had done as I asked none of this would have been necessary.'

'I'm not your slave . . .'

His expression was offended.

'You behave as though you own me, as though I was put here for your convenience.'

A flicker of irritation crossed Ashford's face. He turned away, cutting short her outburst.

'We're wasting time.' Touching the cigarette to his lips he collected himself, redirecting his thoughts.

'I wish to know where Dr Napier has gone.'

Jacqui hesitated. There was a spark of hope in the question. Jean was free, they hadn't managed to catch him yet. He'd be coming. When he found her gone from the hotel he'd follow. All she had to do was delay, to play for time.

'I've no idea where he is,' she replied curtly. 'He didn't tell me.'

Ashford turned, reading her mind. 'Don't think for a moment that he will escape, my dear. It is simply a matter of time before he returns to that hotel of yours.' A hint of sarcasm at the mention of this. 'I simply wish to know where he has been in the meantime.'

'I'm not going to tell you anything, Rupert.'

'You will answer me, my dear.'

Her eyebrows arched at the tone of his voice. She lowered her head, studying her feet in silence.

'Don't get sulky with me, girl!'

Stepping forward Ashford seized her by the chin, jerking her head up to his.

Jacqui's eyes flashed at the touch. Lifting her shoulders she spat into his face. It was unpremeditated, an instinctive reaction, the physical extension of her hatred. Normally she would have been revolted by such an animal act but now it delighted her and she glanced up at him in triumph.

Ashford had recoiled with a cry of disgust. Twitching the handkerchief from his upper pocket he wiped it across his eyes and lips.

'You little slut.' He was white and shaking, incensed by her attack, but he mastered the emotion, bringing himself under control.

'But I suppose I shouldn't expect better from you, my dear,' he reminded himself, tucking the handkerchief back in place. His expression had grown thoughtful, deliberate. Without taking his eyes off Jacqui he reached out his hand to one side, the palm upward, spreading his fingers.

Willi understood the gesture, it was a command, a mute instruction, a surgeon requesting the scalpel. Drawing out his knife he placed it in Ashford's waiting hand.

'Hold her,' he whispered.

Jacqui's back arched, breasts thrust forwards as Willi caught her by the wrists, twisting her arms up behind her back.

'Now, my dear, you will tell me where he has gone.'

She shook her head.

There was a click and the thin, silver tongue of the knife flicked out at Ashford's touch.

'If you hurt me I'll scream,' she warned him. 'I'll say the first things that come to mind but none of them will be the truth.'

'Is that so?' he inquired softly.

Reaching forwards he laid the knife on her brow, the tip of the blade resting between her eyes.

She tensed at the touch, pulling back her head. He wouldn't cut her, she was sure of it, not in cold blood. It's a bluff, she told herself. He wants to see you crumple, to see you humiliated, begging for mercy.

Well damn him!

Gently Ashford ran the knife across her face, resting its weight on her skin, running the blade down over her nose on to her mouth, parting her lower lip as it passed.

He seemed fascinated by the sight. His face was drawn, his eyes damp and red-rimmed. One alert, watching the passage of the knife, the other slack and dull, the lid hanging loose.

Jacqui held perfectly still as the blade glided over her. She could feel the tickle of its point on her flesh as it tracked down the curve of her chin and slipped underneath, coming to rest on the crest of her throat.

Here Ashford held it still. Then, with an imperceptible movement of the hand, he increased the pressure, digging the knife into her flesh.

She felt her skin indent and prick open, the minute tingle of warmth as a bead of blood ran down her neck.

And then the knife was withdrawn.

Jacqui ran her tongue across dry lips. She swallowed, trembling involuntarily in the release of tension.

Ashford's voice was reasonable. 'No, my dear, I don't intend to hurt you. That would be a crude solution – Willi's method, not mine. And besides I don't believe it would work. Pain would only encourage you to resist, to make another of those heroic gestures of yours. I've no doubt that you would see yourself as some sort of martyr.'

He was speaking softly now, without listening to his words, while all the time his attention wandered across her face, watching her, judging her reaction.

Suddenly he reached up, slipping the blade into her hair. She gave a cry, jerking her head away. But it was done. With a quick twitch of the wrist Ashford had cut off a lock of her hair.

He held it up to her, noting the surprise, the look of horror that had come into the girl's eyes.

'You didn't like that, did you, my dear?' he asked softly.

A slow, lazy smile crept across his face. It was triumphant, exalted. He had the key now, the means to make her talk.

'Oh no,' she whispered, reading his thoughts, 'not that, please not that.'

He drew close again. 'You're proud of your beauty, aren't you?' he inquired. 'You like to have men admiring you, setting you up on a pedestal. It satisfies your vanity, makes you feel superior.'

He spoke deliberately, his tongue caressing the words. 'You expect them to fawn over you, to take you out, to treat you like some goddess.'

311

He dropped the golden lock, watching it float down to the floor. 'But what if you were to lose all this fine hair?'

Jacqui gave a little moan. She'd seen pictures of collaborators shaved by the Resistance in the war. Pathetic deformed creatures, human victims. White skulls hanging heavy and ungainly, vulnerable as china, fragile as egg shells. The image filled her with a sudden unreasonable terror.

'Not that,' she pleaded. 'Oh God, please, not that.'

'What would you look like then?' he wondered.

It was only hair, she told herself, it would grow again, return to normal, but the nightmare image of those plucked heads, that cold shaved skin had possessed her. Throwing herself to one side, she struggled to break free but Willi gripped her tightly, twisting her arm upwards until she cried out.

Reaching forwards, Ashford ran his hand into the thick golden mane, lifting it in his fingers.

'You wouldn't be so fascinating, would you, my dear? There'd be no one to admire you, no one to pander to you any more.'

'Not my hair!' she screamed in panic. 'Please don't touch my hair.'

'You'd be ugly and deformed.'

Kicking back her legs, Jacqui fell to her knees, choking, panting for breath.

'Let her go.'

Willi released her arms and she fell forwards on to the polished floor, confused and bewildered, surprised at the discovery of her own weakness.

Ashford stood above, looking down at the sobbing figure prostrated before him and then turning on his heel he walked away.

A mile outside Honfleur Napier drew into the kerb. Jumping out of the car he crossed the road into a café, pushing open the plate-glass door with its advertisments for Stella-Artois, Gauloise and ice cream.

The *patron* was leaning against the counter talking to two locals. He nodded to Napier as he came in, shifted down the bar towards him, wiping a cloth along the plastic top as he came.

Napier ordered coffee and taking it over to a table by the window he drank it thoughtfully.

Something had happened to Spooner, he was sure of it. There was no other explanation left. Spooner would have made contact by now if he had been delayed, rung his office, left a message of some sort. But if he hadn't managed to reach London the situation was changed, the odds were suddenly stacked against them.

For ten minutes Napier sat turning the problem over in his mind, considering the options open to him and then going back to the counter he asked the *patron* if he could use the phone.

Luc sat waiting in his car. He had parked two hundred yards further up the road, adjusting the side mirror so that he could watch the entrance to the café.

He saw Napier come out and saunter across to his car. Sliding down in his seat Luc hid himself from sight. When the yellow Citroën had passed he pulled himself up again and started the engine. Cautiously he followed, holding the Citroën at the limit of his vision, just keeping in contact.

Napier drove back into Honfleur at a steady speed, winding round into the harbour, beneath high timbered buildings and complaining seagulls, crossing the lock gates. Up into the market square, nudging through the pedestrians in the road, parking at the foot of the church.

Luc stayed in the safety of his car, watching through the windscreen, trying to calculate Napier's movements.

It was curious, he didn't appear to be in any hurry. Strolling across the cobbled square, hands in his pockets, Napier paused by the stump of the belfry and looked about himself. It was growing dark now and his slim figure was just a shadow against the ancient masonry. Satisfied that he wasn't arousing interest Napier opened the door of the belfry and stepped inside.

Luc gave him five minutes before he made a move.

Reaching down across the passenger seat he lifted the rubber mat on the floor. Secreted in a neatly cut cavity was a tool-kit bundled into black plastic. He unrolled it on his lap. From the pocket designed to hold the wheel-jack he slipped out a Walther PPK, hefted the gun in his hand, feeling the comfortable weight, the snug fit of the stock in his palm. From the next he removed the stub of a silencer, clicked it to the muzzle, screwing it down into place. He tucked the gun into his waistband, well back in the shelter of his jacket and returned the tool-kit to its hiding place.

Leaving the car he approached the belfry casually.

The door was ajar but Luc wasn't falling for that trick again. Walking round to the side wall he found a small window set behind ragged iron bars. The glass was dense and thick with dirt but through it Luc could make out the gloomy interior of the belfry.

Napier wasn't waiting for him, in fact quite the reverse. He was over against the wall, crouched on the ground examining something in his hands. Quite what it was that held his attention Luc couldn't see.

Returning to the front Luc eased himself through the entrance without touching the door. The hinges would creak, give the game away. At first he couldn't see Napier, the place was used as some sort of store room, the walls stacked with steel frames and rolled up awnings, the bare bones of the market stalls.

Easing himself forwards, his feet silent on the earth floor, Luc moved into the centre of the room. Napier was there before him, still crouched on the ground, his head turned away, unaware and defenceless.

Luc stepped forwards. The fierce lust of the kill was on him, the fire in his stomach, in his loins. He could feel himself stirring with the excitement, pressing hard against the zip of his jeans. He liked this moment best of all, the sensation of power, the anticipation of the conquest.

His hand had been on the butt of his gun but he removed it again. Napier hadn't heard him approach, he could draw in closer. Feeling into the pocket of his jacket Luc drew out his knife. He held his palm over the tip, muffling the click of the blade extending.

With a quick pounce forwards he struck.

Napier turned at the last moment. It was strange, he wasn't looking at Luc but behind. But it made no difference, he was too late to escape.

Luc jerked the knife into him, already anticipating the effect, the comical expression of surprise in Napier's eyes as the blade slipped into him.

But the knife didn't move. His arm was held rigid.

With a cry of rage Luc felt himself pinned from behind.

314

There was a grip on his wrists, on his throat, he was wrenched backwards, falling away from Napier.

Twisting around he caught sight of the blue serge, the silver epaulettes of the gendarmerie. Bastards! He'd been tricked, led into a trap. In desperation he struggled, his breath whimpering in his throat.

With a quick heave the two policemen threw him up against the wall, pinning him face forwards. His right hand was smacked against the stonework, the knife dropping from his fingers, tinkling away into the shadows. Luc freed one arm, lashing backwards but his fist didn't make contact.

'Steady there,' came a voice in his ear, 'there's a good fellow.'

Luc felt his legs kicked apart on the ground, his hands extending on the rough surface of the walls. A hand ran up his inner leg, quick and efficient, smoothing round his waist, finding the gun.

The policeman drew it out, tossing it across the floor.

'Naughty,' he said conversationally. 'Very naughty. Thinking of doing a little target practice were we, or was it the rats you were after?'

Luc swore back at him, hard bitter words that distorted his mouth into ugliness as he spat them out, but the policeman remained unruffled. The practised hands stroked through Luc's clothing, pulling out his wallet, his passport, the stub of the ferry ticket, throwing them down with the gun.

Napier had straightened up, slightly shaky from the proximity of the attack, and watched in cold fascination as the two policemen frisked their captive.

Jesus, they'd left it to the last minute, waited until Gabot had practically been breathing in his ear before stepping in to seize him. It was not an experience he wished to repeat.

He looked down at the passport lying on the packed earth, the gun and knife nearby, and he felt a weariness, a terrible sense of loss.

Poor Spooner, he wouldn't have stood a chance.

It was the merest luck that he had spotted Luc himself. It was just after the Tancarville Bridge. He'd taken a wrong turn, headed towards Rouen by mistake and been forced to make a detour across country. At first it had surprised him to see another car taking the same route, then it raised a hackle of suspicion, but it wasn't until he stopped at the

315

café to check that he had been sure that it was Luc Gabot driving.

The door opened and Chief Inspector Chaumière stumped into the room, raincoat swept back, hands dug into baggy trouser pockets. He looked Luc up and down, touched the gun with his foot, and turned towards Napier. His face was granite, the expression tired and disgruntled, that of a man taken away from his wife and family on a Sunday night.

Napier began to speak, to offer a more detailed explanation than he'd given on the phone, but Chaumière held up his hands, staunching the words. 'Later,' he said quietly. 'Tell me later, Dr Napier. I don't want to know about it now.' He beckoned Napier towards the door. They went out into the darkened square. Two police cars were parked before the belfry door, their blue lights flicking round the high buildings.

Chaumière turned to Napier.

'Rupert Ashford,' he said. 'Do you know the way to his house?'

Napier nodded, his heart leaping into his mouth as he grasped the implicaton of his question.

'Yes . . . but why?'

Chaumière nodded towards the nearest police car. 'Get in.'

'What's happened, for God's sake?'

'I'll explain on the way over.'

Chapter Twenty-Two

Jacqui rolled over on the bed. Twisting around, forcing her arms about her body, she tried to reach down to the knot that bound her wrists. The rope bit into her skin, the joints of her shoulders strained and ached with the effort but it was hopeless. Willi had tied them skilfully, lashing each arm separately before securing them together and strapping them on to the brass bedpost.

Falling back with a sob of frustration Jacqui leaned against the wall, breathing heavily. She eased her hips around on the mattress, the springs of the bed screeching with the movement. Tied in this way she could neither sit nor lie with any degree of comfort but hung forwards, dangling from her arms, the muscles of her back and neck burning with the pain.

'Don't fight it,' Willi had said as he stood back to admire his handiwork. 'It's not that bad. Who knows, in time you might even get to enjoy it.'

She'd held perfectly still as he spoke, resting her cheek against the wallpaper, ignoring him. As soon as he'd gone, locking the door behind him, she'd thrown herself against the ropes, fretting and struggling, trying to slip her hands out of the knots but the effort had been wasted. It was a professional job, there was no chance of escape.

She was high in the roof of the château. The floor of the attic room was small, hardly large enough to contain the bed, and the wall opposite leaned inwards, cramping the space. An oval, boar's-eye window threw a pale phosphorescence on the darkened ceiling. In the twilight she could make out the silhouette of a wardrobe and wash stand but there was no indication that the place was occupied, no sign of life, nothing personal to relieve the gaunt features of the room.

Her fingers were growing numb, she balled them into a fist, trying to stimulate the circulation. Struggling up on to her knees she leaned forwards, lifting her arms behind her back. Carefully she felt the knots that held her to the bed-post, exploring them with her fingertips. Dropping her head on to the mattress she peered up, watching her hands as they fumbled with the rope, trying to direct them, to instruct them in their work. But the knots were too tight and too dense to untie, she hadn't the strength in her fingers alone, if only she could use her teeth she might be able to pick them loose.

Her wrists looked so close, so easy to reach.

Digging her head down into the mattress she curled herself round, a puppy straining at the leash, and tried once more, snuffling and grunting with the exertion.

There was a sound outside in the passage.

Quickly she righted herself, wriggling back against the wall. Rupert had given her an hour before he returned for his answer. It had been his last words as he left the gallery. 'Think it over, my dear,' he'd said. 'Consider the alternatives in the meantime. When I return I'm sure you'll find a way of giving me the information I need.'

A rasp of the key in the lock and the door swung open.

It was Louis.

Jacqui shrank back from him, the horror of what was about to take place returning to her, the image of the knife in her hair rushing back into her mind. 'Make no mistake, my dear,' Rupert had continued, 'we will do whatever is necessary to gain that information. It is simply a matter of deciding how hard you wish to be on yourself.'

For a moment Louis stood in the doorway, short and powerful, his figure dark against the dull light of the passage, and then closing the door behind him he walked over to the bed.

He made no sound as he approached. Jacqui drew back, bunching up her legs to lash out at him. Seeing her tensed ready to strike Louis gave a quick shake of his head and touched his fingers to his lips. Jacqui hesitated, uncertain of his motives.

Kneeling down beside the bed Louis began to untie the ropes around her wrists, untwisting the knots in strong, capable hands.

'Get out of the house,' he told her as the ropes came free. 'Stay out there, hide in the darkness until it is safe.'

Jacqui, struggling round on the bed, nursing chafed wrists,

was startled as much as relieved by his words. She had always thought of Louis as Rupert's man, an extension of his power, the instrument of his will. It had never occurred to her that he might act of his own accord. She had misjudged him and the realisation of the error shocked her. But it was not the time for such thoughts, Louis was taking a terrible risk in helping her.

'You mustn't do this,' she whispered urgently. 'Rupert will never forgive you.'

The hollow eyes, the blank unresponsive expression on Louis's face told her that he knew this to be true.

'I have rung the police,' he explained quietly. 'They will be here in a few minutes. You must keep out of harm's way until they arrive.'

Taking her hands he rubbed them in his until the feeling returned and then standing up he helped her to her feet.

'But what about Willi?'

'He's gone. They've both been sent back to that hotel where you stayed last night.'

Cautiously Louis opened the door, checking the way was clear. Looking back he nodded down at her feet. She understood his meaning and slipping off her shoes she followed him along the passage without a sound.

Down an attic staircase, the silence hanging heavy as ground-mist, the creaking of the steps loud in their ears. Louis moving ahead, quick and sure in his directions, feeling his way through the twilight. Jacqui close behind, keeping near to his protection, touching him for reassurance. Into the long corridor on the first floor, the waxed boards cool beneath her feet, past closed doors and blackened drapes, the space unnatural, the scale strangely magnified in the dark.

The hallway beneath them, a deep pool ghostly in the moonlight. Louis paused on the staircase, turning back to her. He pointed across the floor to where a crack of light showed beneath the study door.

Taking her by the arm he led the way across the floor.

'Don't look back,' he breathed into her ear. 'As soon as you're outside run for the trees.'

Soundlessly they ran towards the door. Jacqui could see the carved steps, the expanse of gravel and sheltering trees beyond the drive. It was no distance to run, it wouldn't be difficult. Her teeth flashed in a smile of excitement, the fierce

319

joy of escape was on her, she turned to speak to Louis, to make some sign of thanks, but he had already stepped ahead of her, reaching out to open the door.

He touched the handle and the hall lights crashed on.

Jacqui gave a cry of fright as the chandeliers blazed up, exposing them, broadcasting their escape. She swung round towards the study door but it was still closed.

Ashford was above them.

He stood at the head of the stairs looking down, seeing their collusion, appreciating their treachery as they tried to slip away.

Louis standing square as a bulldog in the hallway, his eyes cold and stubborn, the girl behind, holding on to his arm. Both frozen by the sudden shock of the light.

'Bring her back, Louis.'

Jacqui stared up at him in awe. Rupert held himself erect as he issued the command. One hand was folded behind his back.

The other carried a gun.

She had no idea what make or type it was, she knew nothing about such things. All she could see was that it was small and black, an evil instrument protruding from his hand with the stub of a barrel no longer than her thumb.

They had walked into a trap, Rupert had been waiting for them, letting her reach the door unchecked, allowing her to think she was free before switching on the lights and reasserting himself, jerking her back on the leash.

'Do as I say.'

Louis shook his head. 'No, monsieur.'

Jacqui tried to step forwards but Louis held out his arm, holding her against the door. Slowly he made his confession, voicing the extent of his betrayal, the words stumbling out of him.

'She must be allowed to go . . . It has gone too far . . .'

'Don't be a fool, Louis.'

'I've called the police . . . They will be arriving shortly.'

Ashford stared down in silence but Louis held the gaze.

'It's finished, monsieur.'

As he spoke, Louis turned to Jacqui, taking her by the shoulders, pushing her roughly towards the door.

'Get out,' he ordered.

Ashford's voice piercing in the stillness. 'Stay where you are.'

'Do as he says, Louis.' It was Jacqui who pleaded with him but Louis had already reached down to the handle. He was opening the door, thrusting her into the night.

'Get out!'

His voice was lost in the explosion of the gun. The bullet struck him between the shoulder blades as he was turning, covering her escape, the impact simultaneous with the blast of the muzzle, the two sounds coming as one. The shock throwing him forwards into Jacqui's arms, a violent embrace, his body suddenly heavy as the strength left him.

Jacqui staggered, the weight pulling her down on to her knees, pinning her to the ground.

She didn't look up at Ashford, didn't see him raising the gun once more, for Louis was lying on her lap, his eyes open. He was trying to speak but his teeth were clenched. There was a great strain in his body, a twisting pain that arched his back, pricking out the veins on his forehead. She ran her hand across his face, stroking him, calming him. Her hair tumbled about his head and her throat found small mewing sounds, those of a mother cradling a child, to soothe him. And then it was over, Louis's muscles relaxing in a sudden release, the breath rushing out of his lungs, his shoulders falling back.

Jacqui wrapped his head into her arms, covering it, hiding the sightless eyes in the softness of her breasts.

Lifting her face to the staircase she gazed up at Ashford, at the muzzle of the gun as it levelled on her.

'But what did he say exactly?'

'Not much,' replied Chaumière, bracing himself against the roll of the police car as they swung round a corner. 'He said that Mademoiselle Fontenay was being held at the château against her will and that he feared for her safety.'

Napier gave a grunt of exasperation. How in God's name had Ashford found her? There must be a thousand hotels around Honfleur, what had led him to theirs?'

'The caller didn't give his name, I suppose?'

Chaumière shook his head. 'He only said a few words, gave his information and hung up. Hardly the communicative type.'

It was Louis. It had to be. There was no one else who

could have made the call. But why had he done it? Louis
who never spoke unless he had to, who carried out his orders
without comment. Louis the loyal henchman, always there
in the background, silent and inscrutable, ready to carry out
Ashford's instructions. What had made him turn?

Napier's mind was racing with speculation. Leaning forwards, hands spread on the back of the car seat, he gave
the driver hasty directions, exorcising his impatience in the
urgency of his commands.

'How much further?' Chaumière asked, catching something
of his apprehension.

'About a mile.'

The car lifted over the crest of the hill, its headlights
bleaching the colour from the road, from the grass verge
in front, bobbing as the suspension took the weight once
more. Down into the dark tunnel of trees, the distant lights
of Trouville pin-pricking through the branches. Bursting out
again, the estuary before them, the horizon stained with the
last embers of the day. Napier craning forwards, searching
through the twilight, pointing towards the entrance to the
château.

'In there!' he cried. 'On the left, through those gates.'

The gun held steady.

Jacqui could see the short snout of its barrel pointing
towards her. She knew its intention, understood what was
to come and her eyes were calm with the knowledge.

In the silence of the hall she heard the two sharp clicks
as the hammer was drawn back.

Carefully she laid Louis down on the floor and straightening up she stood before Ashford, unaware of the blood
on her arms and on her skirt, of her tangled mane of hair
golden in the light. The smell of cordite was in her nostrils,
the report of the gun still loud in her ears.

In the distance a siren was wailing.

Jacqui looked up at Ashford, waiting for the roar of the
gun, the impact of the bullet on her body. But he had
hesitated. The thin insistent wail of the siren had touched
him, broken into his concentration. Lifting his head from
the sights he listened to it, identifying the sound, sensing its
destination.

The muzzle of the gun wavered in his hand.

The sirens grew louder.

Jacqui half-turned, there were cars approaching up the drive behind her. Flashing blue lights broke in through the high windows, playing on the ceiling.

The police. Louis had said he'd called the police.

A rush of hope, the will to escape surging up in her again. She swung back at Ashford but he had lost interest in her. His attention had wandered, it was on the cars outside, on the flashing blue lights that flickered like methane flames in the darkness. They seemed to have captivated him, to have entranced him.

Seizing the moment Jacqui turned and ran out of the opened doorway, the hope thawing the fear from her limbs. Down the stone steps, stumbling in her haste. A car was parked below, others were flooding up the driveway. Lights were licking round the building, doors opening, voices calling to her. Figures spilling out on to the gravel, running in towards her, spearing out through the glare of the headlights.

Jean was there ahead of them, his face white with concern, catching her in his arms.

She was laughing and crying at the same time. There was no weight to her body, her legs were giving way. She felt herself slipping, falling down on to the gravel.

Uniformed figures crowded around her but she didn't care. Pressing her face into Jean's neck she held him, feeling the warmth of his body against hers, hearing his voice in her ear.

'It's all right, my love. It's all right . . . you're safe now.'

Ashford stood at the head of the stairs and looked down through the high windows.

He saw the headlights streaming up the driveway, heard the doors opening, watched the uniformed figures as they closed in, surrounding the building.

Outside in the darkness he could hear the voices of the policemen, the guttural orders of their commander.

Slowly he raised his arm, the revolver was still in his hand. He placed it on the carved banister. He didn't need that any more. The ache in his eye was growing worse. His face felt puffed and bruised from the beating it had taken. In the distance the bells of Ste Catherine's were tolling.

It was six in the morning.

Ashford was standing at the window of his cell once more, looking down into the grey yard, watching the corporal forming his men up into line. He could see their hard weatherbeaten faces, the green-grey uniforms. The clatter of their weapons was loud in the confined space.

Ashford looked up at the ceiling where the blue lights were flickering.

They'd be coming to get him now. The jackboots would drum on the wooden floorboards, the cell door would burst open. He'd be dragged out into the yard.

The rifles were raised, he could see the insignias on the helmets, the raised hand of the corporal.

It was finished.

Louis had said that to him. Ashford looked across to where his body lay in the doorway, the arms spread, the white shirt blackened with blood.

The girl had gone.

That was good, he wanted to be alone now.

Turning around, Ashford walked back into the gallery. He closed the doors behind him and locked them. The flashing lights, the raised voices were shut out.

The silence of the gallery welcomed him.

Loosening the cravat around his neck, Ashford drew out the long silver key and began to unlock the wall panels. Swinging back the doors, revealing each painting in turn.

The light in the gallery was low, scarcely illuminating the canvases, but Ashford saw them bathed in morning sunshine. They were hanging on the wall of the General's apartment, the light sparkling off the harbour, playing across the gilt frames, the glowing colours.

When every door was opened he walked across to the fireplace. Reaching into the flames he caught hold of one log and dragged it out. Those above cascaded down into the hearth in a livid storm of sparks. Ashford carried the burning log into the centre of the floor and dropped it on the polished boards. The mirror-smooth waxing blackened and scorched with the heat.

Crossing over to the furthest of the opened panels, Ashford lifted down a painting. It was a view of the estuary by Boudin: the hillside of Honfleur to one side, the Hospice lighthouse in the distance, fishing smacks running out to sea – a painting of sun-washed skies and spring breezes, a painting of a better world.

He threw it down on to the burning log.

As first it smothered the flames, the cool blues of sea and open sky drowning the heat. Then the canvas blackened, a small hole appeared in the upper corner, the fire eating greedily across the surface of the picture, and it was gone, the paint blistering, the sunlight disappearing into ashes.

Taking another Ashford dropped it over the burning frame of the little Boudin, then the next, working quicker now, not bothering to look at the pictures in his hands, not watching the fire that engulfed them, no longer caring.

Crouching low, Napier approached the château.

Behind him was Chaumière, black as a bat in his flapping raincoat, bent double as he scuttled across the drive. He was carrying a gun. Napier had seen him take it from one of the policemen, slip it into his pocket before they left.

Napier hadn't given a reason for coming forward and Chaumière hadn't questioned him. He knew the layout of the house, he knew Ashford.

That was reason enough.

Reaching the wall, Napier paused, touching the cool stone in the darkness. Chaumière bundled in beside, breathing hard into the night air.

In front of them were the steps of the château. The door was open and the lights of the hallway poured out on to the carved stonework.

Turning his head he looked to where the cars were parked, the headlights blinding the windows, covering their advance.

Napier had only the vaguest image of the events that had taken place in the château during the last few hours. Jacqui had tried to explain them to him but it had been nothing more than scraps, disjointed sentences that had flowed out of her without sense or sequence.

Napier's relief at finding her alive, seeing her hurtling down the steps of the château towards him, had flashed to shock as he saw the blood on her skirt and arms and the wild expression in her eyes as she ran. She had collapsed as he caught her, her knees buckling beneath her, but she wasn't hurt, just frightened and bewildered. Picking her up he had carried her back to the shelter of a police car, perching her on the bonnet.

He'd felt her shivering in the cold and taking off his jacket he'd wrapped it around her shoulders, warming her hands in his, while she leaned against him gabbling out snatches of explanation. Telling him of Ashford firing a gun, of Louis setting her free, how she'd jumped from a car, of the ropes that had held her.

Napier couldn't follow what she was saying but he'd listened without interrupting, happy to hear her voice, to see her face, pale in the flashing lights, her hair spilling out over the collar of his jacket.

There would be time later to fill in the gaps, to bring it all together. Time for the fear to pass, for the wound to heal.

Once this was over.

Napier moved forwards along the wall of the château, keeping his head down below the level of the windows. Up the stone steps, the lights splashing over his shoulders as he ran. Pressing himself against the door-frame, inching his way forwards.

Chaumière beside him, taking the gun from his pocket, pulling back the head, checking the chamber was loaded. Nodding his head in readiness.

Dropping to a crouch Napier looked round the door.

The hall was empty.

Louis was sprawled across the entrance before him, his arms spread, eyes wide, staring up at the ceiling. There was no expression, the blunt features of his face were wiped clean of emotion.

He lay on the floor still and alone, strangely incongruous in the splendour of the deserted hall.

Chaumière dropped the raised gun and stepped inside, glancing about himself. Turning back to the driveway he beckoned with his arm. A handful of uniformed police broke through the lights and covered the distance between, clattering up the steps behind them, filling the entrance.

Quickly they combed the lower floor, bursting open the doors of the study and dining room, searching the rooms in practised, ritualised movements.

'The gallery,' Napier breathed.

Chaumière nodded.

Running up the stairs they paused on the landing, backs flat against the wall. Below them two policemen covered the twin

326

doors, both kneeling on the ground, their arms extended, left hand clamped on right wrist.

Ashford's revolver lay on the banister. Chaumière picked it up with a grunt of interest, showing it to Napier.

'I don't think we need the precautions any longer.'

'I shouldn't be too sure.' Napier touched the door handle and sprang back in surprise.

'What's the matter.'

'It's hot.'

Cautiously he put his palm against the wooden surface, feeling the glow of warmth, noticing the paintwork softening, blistering before the heat. A fine blade of smoke was dribbling under the door.

'My God, the room's on fire.'

'Kick it open,' Chaumière ordered.

'It'll fan the flames.'

Taking a pace back Chaumière stamped his foot against the doors, the blow landing just beneath the handles. He tried again, shouting over the banister to the men below, summoning help, instructing others to call the fire brigade.

Napier joined him, throwing his weight against the lock, feeling the doors beginning to sag and weaken. On the fourth attempt they gave way, bursting inwards with a loud crash of splintering wood.

There was a gasp of suction, dragging at their clothes and hair. A searing heat belched out at them.

The long gallery was a tunnel of fire.

Hungry flames licked round the wall and ceiling, twisting and swirling, drawing back at the sudden intake of air, gathering strength from the oxygen, pouring forwards again, the dragon tongues reaching out to engulf them.

The sharp rifle crack as a window shattered and fell inwards, a deep throating roar of fire running uncontrolled, fingering, feeling and consuming, destroying everything in its path.

The furnace heat scorched their clothing, singeing their hair. Suffocating fumes filled their lungs, smothering them, forcing them back on to the landing.

Napier had only had a brief glimpse of the burning gallery before he had leapt aside, throwing his arms up before his eyes.

In that instant he had a clear view of the inferno: the

blazing outlines of opened panel doors, the fire streaming up the painted surfaces, the ornate ceiling beginning to crash inwards. A pile of pictures in the centre of the floor, the charred bones of the stretchers black in the belly of the fire. Priceless canvases peeling and curling like burning leaves, flames reaching out, rolling up and over like the fantastic carvings on a Chinese pagoda.

It might have been his imagination, a trick of the light, or some chance configuration of the flames, but in that split second, as he gazed into the ruins of the gallery, he was sure that he saw the dark outline of a man. A pillar of fire, standing above the pyre.

Above his head he held a painting.

He was throwing it down on the fire, losing balance, toppling after it. Pitching himself forwards into the burning core.

Chapter Twenty-Three

'So what became of *The Estuary Pilgrim*?'

'It's anyone's guess.'

'You've no theory of your own?'

'Eugenie told me that Schwartz had the painting on the night before he died, that he drove away taking it with him.'

Charles Picard took a sip of white wine and stared out across the dusty court. Napier sat opposite. Jacqui beside him, leaning back, her face turned up to the late autumn sun, listening to the two men talking with eyes half closed in the warmth. Her arm lay on the back of Napier's chair, the tips of her fingers making secret movements across his back.

Picard said, 'So it could be anywhere.'

'Presumably.'

'Still buried in the ground or hidden away in some cellar.'

'Or it could have been destroyed.'

'That's always a possibility.'

They had spent the morning in Picard's office alongside the Faubourg St Honoré. Here, gathered around the desk overlooking the courtyard with its armed guards, its anonymous façade, its fluttering tricolour, they had told him all they knew. How Ashford had conspired with von Eichendorff to hide the paintings, how he later had them faked and kept the originals for himself. Of his alliance with Enrique de la Pena and the financial systems they had set up between themselves. They'd described Ashford's attempts to silence them, the death of Louis and Jacqui's escape from the château.

Picard had heard them out patiently, asking the occasional question, prompting them to continue. But it was only after they had walked up the dark Rue de Rivoli, past the hotel entrances and shop windows, past the dark shadow of the Louvre to a restaurant in the Palais Royal, only now as lunch was drawing to a close and the sunlight was bright on the white damask that he asked what had become of *The Estuary Pilgrim*.

'So you have no private thoughts of your own?'

Napier smiled in the crow's feet of his eyes. 'If I do I'll probably keep them to myself.'

'You know the fake is going to the Musée d'Orsay?'

'So I heard.'

'They're going to hang it there until such time as the original is discovered.' Picard gave a little shrug. 'It's only a fake but that's better than nothing.'

Napier nodded. And no doubt the public would flock to see it, there would be postcards on sale and articles in the press. The huge painting would be a sensation in its own way. But it wasn't the original. That was lost. The real painting belonged to the past, just as Eugenie had said.

It would never be discovered.

Jacqui stirred, drawing her legs beneath herself, standing up with a smile.

'Will you excuse me a moment?'

Picard leapt to his feet, watching her as she went into the dark interior of the restaurant, tall and chic in her smart suit with a full skirt over polished black boots.

His manner was confidential as they sat down again.

'Is she all right?'

'She's been much better recently.'

'It must have been a terrible ordeal for her.'

'She'll put it behind her,' Napier replied. He didn't tell Picard of the nightmares, didn't tell him of the nights she had woken sweating and shaking, her eyes panic-stricken as she relived the last moments in Ashford's house, didn't tell him how they had lain in the dark talking it through, going back over each detail, smoothing the image back into her memory until she had grown calm once more and fallen asleep.

'You know she stands to be a very rich young lady?'

Napier glanced across at him.

'As Rupert Ashford's only legal heir.'

'But isn't his money forfeit in some way?'

'There'll be an inquest inevitably and I'm sure there'll be heavy duties to pay but much of his empire was legitimate.'

Whether she'd accept it was another matter. Only that

330

morning Jacqui had said that she wanted nothing to do with Ashford. 'I'm free of him now, Jean, finally and completely. I wouldn't mind if I never heard his name mentioned again.'

Picard had jumped to his feet.

'We were just talking about you,' he said to Jacqui as she returned.

She smiled, pleased by the attention.

'Something complimentary I hope?'

'Naturally,' he replied with his quick, nervous laugh and turning to Napier he held out his hand. 'And now I must leave you both. Unfortunately there are other affairs I must attend to this afternoon.' His voice became confidential. 'I have talked to the waiter, the bill is taken care of, so if there is anything else you want . . .'

A flourish completed the sentence.

When he had gone Jacqui sat down opposite Napier, taking his hand in hers.

'Did he mean that, do you think?'

'I'm sure, it's the taxpayers's money.'

'And do you think they could rise to a bottle of champagne?'

'It'll sent you to sleep, chérie.'

Her eyes were bright in the sunlight. 'That would be nice, Jean. We could walk along the river, have a siesta on one of the benches.'

'You're just a tramp at heart.'

'And we could watch the fishermen.'

'I thought you had an important appointment with the shops this afternoon?'

'They'll wait,' she told him, turning around to catch the waiter's attention.

It was almost four by the time they left the table.

Linking their arms around each other, hips pressed close together, they walked across the court of the Palais Royal, through the milling of the afternoon crowds, through the sparrows that spun and shivered in the dust, the fountain that fanned its spray through the still air.

As they passed beneath an archway, in the shadow of stone by the Comédie Française, Jacqui turned to him.

'Jean?'

He paused.

'Do you think they'll ever discover the original painting?'

Napier shook his head.

331

'What makes you so sure?'

'Because it was lost many years ago.'

She looked at him, serious as a small child. 'But you told Picard that you hadn't any idea where it was, *chéri*.'

'I did,' he admitted, 'but it wasn't entirely true. That picture was destroyed just after the war. It will never replace the fake in the Musée D'Orsay.'

'Why did you not say so?'

'Because it would make no difference, my love. What was done then cannot be undone. The picture is gone and nothing that we say now can bring it back again. Best to let it be forgotten.'

'But how do you know this thing, Jean?'

Napier made no reply to her question but walked out into the friendly bustle of the street. The yellow Citroën was parked in the kerb nearby. Opening the boot he drew out a large flat package.

Jacqui watched as he took a penknife from his pocket and cut the string, stripping away the brown paper wrapping.

He held it up for her to see.

It was the nude painting that had hung in Spooner's room.

'Eugenie gave this to me this morning,' he told her, 'just before we left the hotel.'

'She wanted you to have that?'

Eugenie lay stretched on the studio bed, abandoned as a cat in the sun, black eyes and rouged lips smiling up at them.

'Don't you like it?'

'It looks like a blancmange.'

Napier propped the painting on the bonnet of the car.

'This was just one of several pictures that Eugenie had done of herself. There must have been twenty or thirty of them originally, all looking much the same as this.'

Eugenie's smile was triumphant as she gazed from the painting.

'Over the years she sold the others to Ashford. But for some reason she kept this last one back, hung it on the wall as some sort of souvenir. Then when she heard of Ashford's death she gave it to me.'

As he was speaking Napier ran the knife over one corner of the canvas, gently scraping at the surface.

The paint came away, dry as plaster.

Behind them the cars hooted and jostled in the street, the bonnet of the Citroën was warm in the sun. Jacqui leaned over his shoulder, watching him working on the picture.

And then she saw it.

Through the sugared pinks, the pale peppermints and oranges of bare flesh, a patch of green paint had appeared.

She knew it, recognised it instinctively.

It was a deep viridian green.

The colour of water. The colour of translucent reflections, of sunlight on the harbour at Honfleur.

A fragment of the painting known as *The Estuary Pilgrim*.